Prometheus h... was kindling it.

The Greeks were not children. The legend of Prometheus was not a child's explanation for man's possession of fire. It said rather that fire was what would make men akin to the gods, and like unto the gods themselves. It would bring them above the beasts. It might take them, in the eruptions of flaming engines, to the stars.

And the Greeks were wary, for this might be pride in man, and carry in it the seeds of their downfall. Prometheus had expiated his crime, chained to a rock in Scythia, but while he screamed in the sun, the ships, in their thousands, carrying coals of fire, set forth from the rocky inlets to colonize a world.

Man will get to the stars, had cried Herjellsen. He will put his flags, and his children, beyond the perimeter of Orion; he will make his camps on the shores of Ursa and build cities in the archipelagoes of Antares and Andromeda.

But first, Herjellsen knew, man must go back to his primitive origins, the days of the great hunters, and rectify a mistake in his genetic heritage.

TIME SLAVE

John Norman

DAW BOOKS, INC.
DONALD A. WOLLHEIM, PUBLISHER

1301 Avenue of the Americas
New York, N. Y.   10019

FIRST PRINTING, NOVEMBER 1975

4 5 6 7 8 9

PRINTED IN U.S.A.

◇ 1 ◇

Herjellsen's device was deceptively simple.

Had he not been insane, had he not been an isolate, lonely, scorned, maddened, dissociated and crazed, the uniqueness, the simplicity of it, would doubtless not have occurred to him.

It was irrational.

It was as irrational as existence, that there should be such. The void was rational, space, emptiness. That there should be anything, gods or particles, that was the madness.

That there should be anything, that was the madness.

Dr. B. Hamilton, mathematician, Ph.D. California Institute of Technology, looked up, fingering the pencil.

It seemed startling, wondrous, that it should be.

As wondrous as suns and stars, the passage of light, and the slow turnings in the night of luminous galaxies.

Who could have predicted that there should be being? From what discursive statements of initial conditions and laws should such a prediction follow? And in the nothingness what entities might serve as values for those individual constants, and as values for those variables, for in the void there was nothing.

. From nothing can come nothing.

Dr. Hamilton lit a cigarette, and drew on it, angrily, defensively.

But smoke cannot screen thoughts from themselves.

It did not appear to be a truth of logic, a matter of the meanings of words, or even of the possibilities of thought, that nothing could come from nothing.

Surely one could imagine nothing, and then something. It was imaginable, and whatever is imaginable is logically possible, conceptually possible.

Yet in some sense it did seem true, so true, that from nothing could come nothing.

It made no sense to call it a necessary truth, for its nega-

5

tion was semantically consistent, conceptually possible, and
yet it seemed, somehow a strong truth, a likely truth.

Astronomers had speculated that, even now, matter grew,
forming in the blackness.

Dr. Hamilton studied the smoke. It drifted upward toward
the fluorescent tubes, lit from the compound's generator.

If it could come into being, there seemed little reason to
suppose it might not be doing so still.

But it did not seem likely.

The quantity of matter-energy in the universe remains
constant.

This was an article of faith, of a transient science in a
provisional epoch.

But it might be true.

But if it were true then matter, or its forms, or energy,
or its forms, of which particles and smoke might be illus-
trations, and music and worlds, then the substance—whatever it might be—was eternal, coeval with space. There
was nowhere for it to come from, nowhere for it to go.

Dr. Hamilton crushed the cigarette out.

Who was to say what was, ultimately, rational or irrational, for these are anthropomorphic predicates, indexed to the
brain of an evolving primate, only within the last few thousand years discovering itself in the midst of mysteries.

The lights in the bleak room dimmed and then again
waxed bright and soft.

Gunther, with William, Herjellsen supervising, was busy
in the hut.

There was not a great deal of power needed for the apparatus. The compound generator produced ample power.

Hamilton speculated, smiling. Electric power, from a gaso-
line-driven engine, no more than five hundred volts, was
ample to the needs of the crazed Herjellsen.

Hamilton did not care for Hegel. Yet the thought, that of
Hegel, was difficult to dismiss. We are where the world has
opened its eyes.

We were the first animal, to our knowledge, to wonder,
to seek to learn, the first to seek not only love and food,
but truth.

Men had found truths, in their millions, in its pebbles
and grains, but he had not yet found its mountains.

Herjellsen had looked in a different direction. If he had
not, he would not have seen what he had.

Herjellsen was mad, but he had seen it, where others
had not.

It had come to him in the night, in his cell in Borga. He had screamed and laughed, demented in the cell, tearing the blankets, biting at his own flesh, shrieking with joy.

Hamilton recalled that Kekulé's hypothesis, of the ring theory of the benzene molecule, had come to him in sleep, in a dream, frought with twisting snakes, before his own hearth. Three-quarters of organic chemistry, some thought, derived, directly or indirectly, from Kekulé's hypothesis. Herjellsen's had come to him in a madman's cell. There is no rational procedure for the discovery of hypotheses. There are no machines to produce them. They come as gifts, and sometimes to the mad, to the diseased and crazed, as to Herjellsen. But the procedures for testing hypotheses, be they real hypotheses, if they are genuine hypotheses of science, are public, accessible. The objectivity of science lies not in its genesis, but in its warrants for validity, its procedures for examination and testing, for experiment and confirmation, for, to the extent possible, proof and demonstration. Hamilton was terrified, yet exalted.

It was possible that the Herjellsen conjecture was true.

The preliminary tests had been affirmative.

Again the fluorescent tubing dimmed and then again resumed its normal degree of illumination.

The artifact lay not more than a yard from Hamilton's hand.

It was rounded, chipped, roughly polished; it weighed 2.1 kilograms. Anthropologists would have referred to it as a tool. It was a weapon.

That there was something, that was the madness.

Who was to say what was natural and what was not? That there was something was undeniable.

Its nature had not yet been ascertained.

Hamilton arose, pushing back the chair.

A remark of Julian Huxley was difficult to dismiss from the mind.

The universe may not only be queerer than we suppose, but it may be queerer than we can suppose.

Hamilton smiled.

Laughter is the shield. Humor is the buckler against madness, against the mystery, against the immensity. Humanity had little else with which it might protect itself in the forest. It had its brains, its hands, a bit of fury, a loneliness for love, and its laughter. And that laughter, like the gravitational field of a pencil on a desk, miniscule and yet profound, might be heard to the ends of space.

We are smaller than stars but the magnitude of our laughter has not yet been measured.

All that we know rests upon a slender data base, our first-person experiences, and nothing else. Each of us in this sense is alone, in his cage of sensation, limited to his own perceptions. And each of us, a perception to the other, builds his view of the world.

Hamilton was lonely.

How do we explain the succession, the continuity of our experiences. We postulate an external world of such-and-such a type. In various times and places we would have entertained postulations quite different from those which are now taken to define the truth, and beyond their perimeters we define madness.

Herjellsen had ventured beyond the perimeters of the given speculations, the customary postulations, those postulations that define not only what answers may be given but what questions may be asked.

Particles and forces, gods and demons, fields, purposes, collisions, all had served, and some still served, to make sense out of the chaos of sensation, that which must be reconciled and accounted for, our experiences.

Science is not a set of answers, Herjellsen had once told Hamilton; it is a methodology.

We learn from Egyptian star charts that the positions of the fixed stars have changed in the past five thousand years.

They change position slowly.

So, too, with the dogmatisms of science; what seemed eternal truth when the Parthenon was fresh seems now but a mood of cognition, a moment of advance, a footstep on a path whose destination is not yet understood.

Perhaps a thousand years from now, Hamilton thought, we will see that our current truths, too, were not the eternal verities we took them for, but rather another step on the same journey, leading perhaps toward a truth we do not now understand and may forever fail to comprehend. We must not despise ourselves, Herjellsen had cried, even though we shall pass, and shall be superseded in our turn, for we are a moment in a grand journey, one that began in the caves and must someday, if we do not slay ourselves, take us to the stars.

I have an appointment, he had laughed, with Arcturus, and with infinities beyond.

But Herjellsen was dying.

He was mad.

Hamilton went to the door of the room, and looked out into the Rhodesian night.

The work of Herjellsen had nothing to do with the stars. Why should he insist that it did? He was mad.

Hamilton looked back at the artifact on the table. It weighed 2.1 kilograms. Anthropologists would have termed it a tool. It was a weapon.

Herjellsen's work did not have to do with the stars.

What is on the other side of our sensations? Is it truly atoms and the void, or is it an alternative reality?

We may only postulate, and test.

Hamilton could hear the generator now. A black servant was crossing the compound, a box on his shoulder.

There were only two blacks in the compound. The moon seemed bright over the high, wire fence.

Hamilton stepped out on the porch. It would not be wise to stay outdoors too long. It was late in summer.

Hamilton looked at the moon. Then, Hamilton looked at the stars.

There was a reality. It was only that its nature had not yet been ascertained.

It was, Hamilton supposed, a reality beyond contingency or necessity, as we might understand such things. Such predicates were unintelligible in their application to what most profoundly existed. Hamilton thought of Schopenhauer's *Wille*, never satisfied, violent, craving, inexhaustible, relentless, merciless, demanding, greedful, incessant, savage; of Nietzsche's *Macht;* of the atoms of Lucretius; of the god of Spinoza, one with the terribleness and sublimity of nature. The reality, conjectured Hamilton, is more profound than gods and men. If there be gods, they, too, are its offspring, as much as stones, and twigs and men, as much as the spaniel and the mosasaur, as much as the pain of love, the smile of a child, the gases of Betelgeuse, the tooth of the shark and the chisel of Michelangelo. It is a reality which may have spawned us, in a moment of bemusement, if only to set us its riddle, to watch us sniff about, and scratch and dig, to try to find truths which it has perhaps, in its irony, not constructed us to understand; the reality, perhaps, once fathering us, has forgotten us, leaving us to one side as a neglected toy, no longer of interest, or perhaps, a sterner father, has abandoned us that we may learn how to grow by ourselves, and be lifted only should we rise upon our own feet; seek me in the godship, it might say; I am waiting for you; but to Hamilton it seemed that the reality, whatever might be its nature, was clearly beyond morality; it was as innocent of morality as the stones of the moon, as the typhus bacillus, as the teeth of the Bengal tiger. The world was built on greed, and on killing, and hunger. To the reality doubtless the barracuda, in its way, was as perfect as the saint. The reality did not choose between them. They were both its children. Hamilton shuddered. The reality was sublime; before it even worship was an affront, a blasphemy. It wanted nothing of men. It needed nothing. It was sufficient unto itself.

But its nature? What was its nature?

Herjellsen did not know, but he had learned that its nature was not as men now thought.

Herjellsen had discovered a small thing. A clue, not well understood.

He did not know, truly, what he was doing.

But he would do it.

I do not understand this, he had said, but I see how I can use it, and I will! I will use it!

Man will go to the stars, Herjellsen had cried.

But what had the stars to do with Herjellsen's work?

Hamilton recalled the artifact lying in the bleak room. It had little to do with the stars.

At best, it lay at the beginning of an infinity.

Yet, like zero, a nothingness, it, like each instant, both initiated and terminated an infinity.

The artifact, like each moment, was an end and a beginning, a pivot between complementary, divergent eternities.

The Romans saw this, in their sternness, their solemnity and sadness, and pride, and called it a god, and called it Janus.

I see two ways, said Herjellsen. I am Janus.

Herjellsen is mad, had laughed Gunther. Hamilton did not doubt that.

But the Herjellsen conjecture? What if it were true?

Heraclitus has seen it, had laughed Herjellsen. Hamilton's thoughts drifted to the ancient Ionian, the poet and philosopher. I had rather discover one cause, had written Heraclitus, than become the King of Persia. He had taught all is fire. A man cannot step twice into the same river.

I believe all is pea soup, had said William. And I have often stepped twice into the same river. I stepped twice into the Thames, and once fell into it while punting.

Hamilton smiled. William made the compound bearable.

TIME SLAVE   11

Hamilton, too, had speculated if all might not be pea soup. It seemed a plausible guess.

Herjellsen had not been offended. That all is transience, flux—fire—is only part of the teachings of Heraclitus, he had told William. And then Herjellsen had quoted the Greek, that swift, liquid tongue sounding strange in the careful, northern accents of Herjellsen—the way up and the way down are the same.

I never doubted it, had admitted William.

Herjellsen had smiled at Hamilton, lifting a fork. And the beginning, he had said, is the end, and the end is the beginning. That is what Heraclitus had seen.

I do not understand, had said Hamilton.

Time does not pass, said Herjellsen. No. It is we who pass.

Hamilton had not responded. Herjellsen, in his late fifties, bald, small eyed, the eyes seeming large behind the thick, ovoid lenses of his wire-rimmed glasses, had peered at Hamilton. Herjellsen was a large man, but short, a broad, short man, with large hands. His head was rounded and unusually large, set on a heavy neck. Yet he seemed gentle. There was usually a sheen of sweat on his forehead and cheeks, and almost always when he spoke. Herjellsen seemed to speak easily, but he was uncomfortable in doing so. He was free only when lost with his own thoughts. He seemed to fear even Hamilton. His speech, with its Finnish accent, was precise and fluent. He rarely, even in English, made a grammatical error or hesitated in his expression, or wavered in the selection of a word or gesture. His mind worked apparently with such rapidity that he spoke as though he had spoken these thoughts before. Hamilton wondered if he had.

What if the Herjellsen conjecture were true?

Hamilton put aside the thought. The conjecture could not be true.

In a sense, though, Hamilton was willing to suppose that he had. He had conceived of them, and examined them, and then rephrased them and organized them, in the lapse of time perhaps of a syllable's utterance, and then, as though they might have been carefully written, he spoke them. Herjellsen seemed a gentle man. It was difficult to believe that he was criminally insane, that he had, in his time, in the course of strange robberies, killed four men.

In the cell at Borga could it have been the truth that he had seen?

But Herjellsen, whatever the flaws of his being, was a scientist. He well knew that self-evidence was a psychological variable, differing idiosyncratically from individual to individual, from culture to culture. Hamilton knew of men to whom it was self-evident that a piece of string forming a closed figure, in any shape, would inclose the same area. Standing on the porch Hamilton quickly lit another cigarette, and watched the lights in the window of the experimental shack. The lights in the small, rectangular, metal-roofed, stuccoed building waxed and waned with the humming whine of the generator. Such obvious falsities could be taken as self-evident by some men, at least for a time, and yet their patent falsity could be in a moment demonstrated empirically. And there had been men who had believed that motion was impossible, for nonbeing could not exist and thus, motion requiring place, or emptiness, or nonbeing, could not exist. To such men the self-evident had withstood the contradictions of their own eyes. Experience must yield to reason; fact to illusion. But Herjellsen was a scientist. He distrusted the light of reason, the flash of intuition, and more sternly in his own case than in that of others. There can be no genuine hypothesis without test. A truth must have its disconfirmation conditions.

The test sequence had begun.

The lights grew brighter in the experimental shack, and then dimmed.

What had come to him like wine, like the gift of a drunken god, the bequest and gratuity of a laughing Dionysus, inexplicably to a criminal in a madman's cell in Borga, was now being subjected to test in a small shack in an isolated compound in the dry lands of Rhodesia, some two hundred and fifty miles southwest of Salisbury.

Hamilton thought of fire burning in the thieving hand of Prometheus.

The first test sequences had been fruitless. Herjellsen had sought perhaps a hundred tests to subject his conjecture to experiment, and each had failed; the conjecture had neither, to a rational degree, been confirmed nor disconfirmed; data had been unclear; results were irrelevant or indecisive; new procedures had been sought; and then, after months of work, found; it was only then that Gunther and William, and Hamilton, had been brought to the compound.

Hamilton regretted having come. The retainer had been impossible to resist, and Hamilton, in the tense job market, had been without position. The position was to last four weeks. Already Hamilton had been at the compound more than two months. The supply truck no longer came. Herjellsen himself, in his British Land Rover, to which he kept the keys, made overland journeys to Salisbury and back, taking Gunther and William with him. Hamilton was not permitted to accompany them. Hamilton had received traveling expenses from California and an initial fee of four hundred British pounds. But Hamilton had received nothing further. Hamilton wanted to return to the United States.

"We need you," had said Herjellsen. "You may not leave now."

"I will tell you who Herjellsen is," had said Gunther, speaking to Hamilton privately. He showed Hamilton, too, the clippings, the police bills.

Hamilton was not permitted outside the compound. The blacks saw that Hamilton remained in the compound.

"Do your work, Doctor Hamilton," had said Herjellsen. "We need you." Sweat had broken out on his broad forehead. His hands had opened and closed.

"I will walk you to the shed," had said Gunther.

"No," Hamilton had said. "I will go alone." Hamilton feared Gunther. Hamilton did not care for Gunther's eyes. They frightened Hamilton.

Hamilton threw away the cigarette, onto the dry dust of the compound.

The high wire fence about the compound was said to protect the compound from animals. It was electrified. Hamilton was not permitted beyond the fence.

Prometheus had stolen fire. Herjellsen was kindling it.

The Greeks were not children. The legend of Prometheus was not a child's explanation for man's possession of fire. It said rather that fire was what would make men akin to the gods, and like unto the gods themselves. It would bring them above the beasts. It might take them, in the eruptions of flaming engines, to the stars.

And the Greeks were wary, for this might be pride in men, and carry in it the seeds of their downfall. Prometheus had expiated his crime, chained to a rock in Scythia, his body prey to the avenging eagle of Zeus, but while he screamed in the sun, beneath the beak and talons, the ships, in their thousands, carrying coals of fire, set forth from the rocky inlets, to colonize a world.

Man will go to the stars, had cried Herjellsen. He will put his flags, and his children, beyond the perimeter of Orion; he will make his camps on the shores of Ursa and build cities in the archipelagoes of Antares and Andromeda.

Hamilton wondered if Prometheus might have regretted his decision.

Herjellsen sometimes spoke of Prometheus.

"Did he regret his decision?" had asked Hamilton of Herjellsen, amused, for Herjellsen seemed to take such tales seriously.

"I do not regret what I have done," had said Herjellsen.

Hamilton had not pressed the matter further. Nothing more had been said at the meal.

Herjellsen was mad.

He was also a dying man. He had angina pectoris, and was subject to attacks of increasing severity. He drove himself cruelly, foolishly, mercilessly.

The generator whined to a halt.

The lights in the experimental shack went out.

Hamilton was startled.

The four light bulbs, set on poles about the compound, had been extinguished, and the dust of the compound was no longer the bleak, bright reflecting surface that it had been, hot, hard and yellow, but now, in the light of the African moon was white and cold.

The door to the shack opened. One of the blacks, a lantern swinging in his hand, went to the door. William slipped from the door, swiftly.

He passed Hamilton. "I must get my bag," he said.

"What is wrong?" asked Hamilton, frightened.

"It's the old man," he said.

Hamilton tensed.

William had gone to the hut he shared with Gunther. In a moment he emerged, carrying his bag.

William was a physician. He had practiced in London. He was also a gifted mathematician. Many of the equation resolution procedures which Hamilton had programmed into Herjellsen's analyzer, a modified 1180 device, had been provided by William. A condition of Hamilton's employment had been, oddly, a medical examination in William's London office. "The employer," had said William, indicating the man Hamilton was later to learn was Herjellsen, "requires excellent health in those working in his service." Hamilton had understood that the employer's facility was in Rhodesia, in an out of the way area, and that medical facilities would not be readily available. Hamilton had been surprised to learn, later, that William was a member of the staff at the compound. He had arrived, returning to the compound, the day before Hamilton. Gunther, and Herjellsen, and the blacks, had been waiting. His quarters were well stocked with supplies. He himself, Hamilton was aware, was a competent, respected physician. Medical facilities, it seemed, were quite adequate. Perhaps, Hamilton had speculated, the employer is a hypochondriac, with a phobia concerning infections, or some such affliction. But Herjellsen, Hamilton had learned, was not a hypochondriac. Indeed, he was an actually ill man, a desperately ill man who took too little care of his own body.

Hamilton moved as though to leave the porch. "Do not come to the shack," said William sharply. It was unlike William to speak sharply.

"Oh," said Hamilton. "Very well." Hamilton had never been allowed in the experimental shack.

William disappeared in the door of the shack. It closed behind him. Hamilton could see the light of the black's lantern through the white-painted window.

It had been Hamilton's health in which Herjellsen had been critically interested. Not his own. "You are in superb condition," had said William in his London office. "The employer will be pleased."

The work that Hamilton had performed in the compound Hamilton had discovered could have been performed by Herjellsen himself, or Gunther. Hamilton had done a great deal of work, but it was not work which only Hamilton, of those on the staff, could have performed. The services of Hamilton, it seemed, were not, strictly, required.

"It frees us for other work," Herjellsen had said, "and, too, should one of us be unable to function, another will be able to take his place."

"Skill redundancy," had added Gunther, "is policy with Herjellsen."

"I expect to be able to function," had smiled Hamilton.

"I am confident," had said Gunther, "you will fulfill all our expectations."

Herjellsen, then, with Continental gallantry, had lifted his glass of wine to Hamilton. Hamilton had looked down at the table.

But the services of Hamilton, Hamilton had come to discover, more and more, day by day, were truly not needed. Two nights ago Hamilton had, deliberately, slipped an error into the print outs. Herjellsen, in less than fifteen minutes, had discovered it.

"This was careless of you, Doctor Hamilton," he had said, "—and obvious."

Herjellsen himself had corrected the program and completed the run.

"I wish to leave your employment," Hamilton had told Herjellsen that evening.

"You are needed," had said Herjellsen.

"I am not needed," had said Hamilton.

"You are mistaken," had said Herjellsen.

Now Hamilton stood on the porch of the computer building and looked to the experimental shack. "For what am I needed?" had demanded Hamilton. Herjellsen had said only, "You are needed," and then left. The experimental shack was dark, save for the light of the black's lantern, like a flickering pool within the white-painted window. Hamilton wondered if Herjellsen were dead.

After that night, that of the computer error, Hamilton had done little work, but much reading. Herjellsen provided books. Among them were an English translation of Diogenes Laertius, the Ancilla of Pre-Socratic Fragments, translated by Freeman, from Diel's original translations, Kirk's book on Heraclitus, Plutarch's *Lives*, the autobiography of Benvenuto Cellini, FitzGerald's second translation of the Rubáiyát of Omar Khayyám; Harrison's *Prolegomena to the Study of Greek Religion;* in German, Nietzsche's *Also Sprach Zarathustra;* Whitman's *Leaves of Grass;* and the *Meditations of Marcus Aurelius.*

"You are needed," Herjellsen had said.

Frightened, Hamilton looked at the fence which encircled the compound.

Hamilton was not permitted beyond the fence.

The fence was to protect the occupants of the compound from the predations of wild animals.

"It is dangerous beyond the fence," Herjellsen had told Hamilton, and given his orders. Hamilton was not permitted by the blacks beyond the fence.

There were no animals dangerous to men in the vicinity that Hamilton knew of.

She wondered why the blacks were armed.

Hamilton was not permitted beyond the fence.

"No," had said the black with the rifle at the gate, when Hamilton, testing Herjellsen's order, had attempted to leave the compound. The black had not been rough. Hamilton was simply not permitted to leave.

It was not necessary for the black to threaten, or resort to his rifle.

Hamilton had looked up at the ebon face.

Frustrated, furious, Hamilton had turned about and returned to the computer building.

. That night, at supper, Herjellsen had admonished Hamilton.

"My dear Doctor Hamilton," had said Herjellsen, "you must not leave the compound. I had thought that was clearly understood."

"I wanted to take a walk," had said Hamilton icily.

"It is dangerous outside the compound," said Herjellsen.

"Very well," had said Hamilton.

Hamilton stood on the porch of the computer building. No one had emerged from the experimental shack since William had entered.

"You are needed," Herjellsen had told Hamilton.

Hamilton looked at the high wire fence, slim strands of strung wire, lit in the white light of the great moon.

For what am I needed, wondered Hamilton.

The moon glinted on the wire.

There was a sound at the shed.

One black emerged, and then, between him and William, staggering, Herjellsen.

The two men supported Herjellsen, and made their way across the compound, toward Herjellsen's small sleeping shack.

"We can move you on a cot," said William, supporting the short, older man.

"I can walk," said Herjellsen, pushing him away. Then, too, he pushed away the black. Another black, he with the lantern, stood behind them.

Herjellsen stood unsteadily on the dust of the compound, hunched over with pain. His face was tight, ashen.

"Do not help me," he warned them.

William and the two blacks, one with a lantern, stood to one side.

Herjellsen saw Hamilton. He straightened up. "Good evening, my dear Doctor Hamilton," he said.

"Good evening, Professor Herjellsen," whispered Hamilton.

"Yes," said Herjellsen, looking about. "It is a good evening."

Gunther was still in the shack. Hamilton had not seen him come out.

"I think I shall go to my quarters," said Herjellsen. "I am weary."

William put out his hand.

"I need no help," said Herjellsen, sharply.

William glanced at Hamilton.

Herjellsen wished to show no weakness before Hamilton.

"Good-night, Doctor Hamilton," said Herjellsen.

"Good-night, Professor Herjellsen," said Hamilton.

A voice within the shed suddenly cried, "Bring the lantern!" Hamilton was startled. It was Gunther's voice. She had never heard such a cry from him.

Herjellsen did not move, but stood on the dust of the compound. He did not turn to the shed.

The black with the lantern rushed to the shed.

Hamilton waited on the porch.

Herjellsen stood quietly in the compound. William looked to the shed. He seemed frightened..

Gunther's figure emerged from the shed. He was a tall man, large, broad-shouldered, blond haired, muscular, blue eyed. He was a strong man, hard, lithe, swift. He had much stamina. He enjoyed hunting, and was a superb hunter, skilled, tireless, merciless, efficient. Next to Herjellsen, whom Hamilton regarded as mad, Gunther was rated by Hamilton as the most intelligent in the compound. Gunther's mind was brilliant. It could be, at times, as sharp and keen as surgeon's steel, and like that steel, cold and hard; and at times, when he pleased, it could be as sardonic as acid; or, when he wished, as swift and stinging as a quirt in the hands of a horseman. Hamilton feared him. In his presence Hamilton felt uneasy, and small and weak. Before Gunther, Hamilton felt clumsy, and found it difficult to speak. What Hamilton felt, not understanding it, in the presence of Gunther, was the presence of a superior, dominant animal. Gunther was clearly stronger and more intelligent than Hamilton. "He is a bit overawing," had joked William. Hamilton resented Gunther. Hamilton hated him. William, too, resented him. It was a bond between them, their dislike for Gunther. It was not simply that Gunther was a splendid organism, but that he made no attempt to conceal his superiority. He seemed little motivated by the conventions whereby superior animals sheath their claws and conceal their teeth. Gunther was a lion among men, a blond lion. His eyes made Hamilton angry, and afraid. He looked at Hamilton with such casual, unquestioned superiority, as though Hamilton might have been a servant, and, too, he looked at Hamilton in another way, sometimes grinning, that frightened Hamilton. He seemed so sure of himself, so strong.

"What is it?" asked William of Gunther, who stood, dazed,

as Hamilton had never seen him, in the door of the experimental shack.

Hamilton was frightened.

Never had Gunther seemed so shaken. His tall, muscular frame trembled in the doorway.

Then he spoke. "The cage," he said, "—the cage is gone!"

Herjellsen, Hamilton thought, seemed to smile, and then he began to walk slowly to his sleeping quarters.

William and the black who had attended Herjellsen waited for Gunther, who walked slowly towards them.

Gunther looked at William. "The cage is gone," he said.

"Impossible!" cried William. William ran to the shed.

"I don't understand, Gunther," said Hamilton. "What cage?"

Gunther did not answer Hamilton but turned to face the shed.

In a moment William, followed by the black with the lantern, who understood no more than Hamilton, emerged from the shack.

William's face was white. "It's gone," he said.

"Gunther!" said Hamilton.

But Gunther had turned away and was walking slowly toward the hut he shared with William.

"William!" cried Hamilton.

"Yes?" said William, looking at Hamilton on the porch.

"What cage is gone?" begged Hamilton.

"The one we were using in the experiment," said William, slowly, blankly.

"What does it mean?" begged Hamilton.

"It means, I think," said William, smiling thinly, "that the Herjellsen conjecture is true."

Hamilton stood silently on the porch.

"Good-night, Brenda," said William.

"Good-night, William," said Brenda Hamilton.

◊ 2 ◊

"Splendid!" cried Hamilton, delightedly.

She worked at the side of the men in the experimental shack.

In the past days she had felt herself a full member of the team, welcomed and respected. She was one with them. Herjellsen was gentle, perceptive, directive. William was helpful, amusing. Even Gunther was bearable, and seemed now, for the first time, to see her as a human being. He had even, once, called her "Brenda."

The interior of the translation cubicle, seen through the heavy, clear, plastic walls, was beginning to glow, pulsating with a diffused, photic energy; this phenomenon, Herjellsen had explained, was a concomitant of the transference phenomenon, not a manifestation of the phenomenon *per se;* it was related to the phenomenon derivatively, not directly; it was like the waves that are displaced by the passage of an invisible ship, not the ship but the sign of its passage; yet the photic phenomenon, like turbulence in a medium, in water or an atmosphere, signaled the presence of the force Herjellsen had called P.

Gunther's eyes blazed, looking into the cubicle.

William touched Hamilton's arm. "Do not be afraid now," he whispered.

"I'm not!" cried Hamilton, happily. "It's beginning, is it not?"

She looked to Herjellsen.

Herjellsen sat to one side, in a straight wooden chair, before a wooden table. To one side was the amplifying mechanism, wires running to it from the generator, and from the mechanism to the steel hood mounted on the table. Two cables, in a loop, passed from the hood to the cubicle and back, as though a self-reinforcing cycle might be established.

Under the hood Herjellsen's head was down. His fists were clenched.

Suddenly, for no reason she understood, Brenda Hamilton was apprehensive.

Gunther and William were intent.

There is only one reality, had said Herjellsen, in its infinite modes and attributes.

"Spinoza thought something like that," had remarked William earlier.

"Spinoza did not understand," said Herjellsen. "It is neither God nor Nature. It is deeper than nature, and too deep and terrible to be God."

"What is it?" had asked William.

"The reality," had said Herjellsen.

"I do not understand," had said William.

"The reality—and the power," had said Herjellsen.

Hamilton shivered.

"And nature, and gods," had said Herjellsen, "and spiders and stars are but its forms, the lion and the child, flowers and galaxies, perceptions, modes, diversities, transiencies, all!"

William had been silent. It was not wise to argue with Herjellsen at certain times, in certain moods. He was at most times eminently rational, pleasant, but when the mood was upon him, the frenzy of the conjecture, one did not speak with him.

"And," Herjellsen had cried, "the reality—the power—is as much and wholly present in a blade of grass, in the petal of a flower, as in the furnace of Betelgeuse!" He had looked wildly at William, who had not met his eyes. "And that means," had cried Herjellsen, "that here—in my hand—in my head—as much as anywhere, as full and perfect, lies the power. We, each of us, are the reality, the power."

"I'm sorry," had said William. "I'm sorry."

"There are continuities!" had wept Herjellsen. "Continuities!" His voice had trembled. "You know of continuities between heat and light and sound, and between the particles of an apple and those of a stone, and between the fluid cell in an algae in the pristine sea and the brain of an Alexander, a Beethoven, an Einstein!"

"The relevance is obscure," had said William, hesitantly.

"Time and space are modes of intuition," had whispered Herjellsen. "Do they exist in their own right?"

"Yes," had said William.

"How do you know?" asked Herjellsen.

"I perceive them," said William.

"You have begged the question," said Herjellsen.

"I do not know what space and time are in their own right," said William.

"Do they pertain to things in themselves?" demanded Herjellsen.

"I do not know," grumbled William. "Perhaps they do."

"Yes," said Herjellsen, "perhaps they do—but perhaps they do not."

Gunther had not spoken during this interchange, but had listened. He did not generally discuss this sort of thing with Herjellsen. He respected Herjellsen. Herjellsen was perhaps the only man whom Gunther respected.

"All that you know," said Herjellsen, "is a succession of perceptions—indeed, you find even yourself, in so far as you dare to search—a perception and perceptions among others."

"Perception requires a physical body—a brain," snapped William. William was normally polite. This time he was not.

"And what is your evidence of a physical body—a physical brain?" inquired Herjellsen.

William was silent.

"Perceptions," said Herjellsen.

William refused to speak.

"A slender ribbon of perceptions flowing among mysteries," said Herjellsen, wearily. "All that we know are these conscious scraps, these sparks in darkness, and, to be sure, we fling out our speculations from them, reaching out, like hands to touch something real. From these scraps, these tiny pieces of paper, we try to construct a world, a time and a place, a map, a home in which we may feel secure. We build for ourselves, on these bits of sand, a world in which we claim to live."

"We must do so!" said William.

"To be sure," said Herjellsen. "That is not at issue."

Herjellsen looked at William intently. "You know, as a rational man, from studies in logic and mathematics, that any given conclusion follows from an infinite diversity of sets of premises, even sets incompatible with one another."

"Yes," said William.

"And, too," pressed Herjellsen, "every event, accordingly, is subject to an infinite variety of explanations."

"Theoretically," grumbled William.

"Do you not see the consequence of these truths?" asked Herjellsen. "The world we construct, extrapolating beyond the stream of our data, to explain our ideas, our perceptions, is but one logical possibility among infinite alternatives."

William looked away. His face was white.

"I am simply saying," smiled Herjellsen, "let us not be dogmatic."

William looked at him.

"You see, my dear William, all I am asking you to recognize is that we may not live in the world—within the reality—you think we do."

"But we may!" blurted William.

"Yes," granted Herjellsen, "we may—and we may not."

"Our view of the world," said Gunther, speaking for the first time, "has given us science."

"You argue," said Herjellsen, "from the utility of science to the truth of its world picture."

"Yes," said Gunther.

"Ultimately," said Herjellsen, "the utility of science reduces to its capacity to reconcile, harmonize and predict perceptions. Theoretically, an infinite number of intellectual constructions would be equally efficacious in this regard. Suppose, for example, that we have a thousand sciences, each with its different world picture, each with its own theoretical entities, one making use of atoms, one not, and so on, would we then have a thousand truths, each incompatible with the other?"

"No," said Gunther, "there would be only one truth."

"But a thousand utilities?"

"Yes," said Gunther.

"What then," said Herjellsen, "of utility as a guide to truth?"

"It is still," said William, "the best we have."

"Yes," said Herjellsen, "I think that is true." He smiled at William. "Only I do not find your 'science' too useful. There are many things I find of interest which it does not explain."

"You refer, perhaps," said William, "to reputed psychic phenomena, extrasensory perception, psychokinesis, and such?"

Herjellsen shrugged, neither admitting anything nor disagreeing with William.

"Such phenomena do not exist," said William.

"Perhaps not," said Herjellsen, "but it is interesting to note that, even did they exist, science as it is presently constituted could not explain them."

"So?" asked William.

"So we must be wary," said Herjellsen, "that we do not take as our criterion for existence what science can explain. At one time science could not explain the functioning of a magnet, at another time the falling of a stone, the digestion of food, the circulation of the blood."

"That is different," said William.

"Surely it is an obvious fallacy to argue from the inexplicability of a phenomenon to its lack of existence."

"Not always," said William.

"Explain to me," said Herjellsen, "the fact of consciousness, the fact that when I wish to move my hand, my hand moves."

William said nothing.

"Of these things," said Herjellsen, "I am more certain than I am of the existence of the world, and your science cannot explain them."

"Do you demean science?" asked William.

"I only require it," said Herjellsen, "to be adequate to the whole of experience." Then he looked at William. "I am confident," he said, "that whatever may be the nature of the reality it cannot be as our science maintains it to be."

"Why not?" asked William.

"Because of the radical discontinuity of mind and matter," said Herjellsen.

"I do not understand," said William.

"I am confident," said Herjellsen, "that the same power that causes water to flow moves in the dreams of a sleeping lion, that causes fire to burn and worlds to turn guides the equations of Descartes, the stick of Archimedes, drawing its circles in the sand, that causes a seed to germinate and a flower to open its petals to the sun moves in your mind and mine."

"Perhaps," said William.

"The reality and the power is one," said Herjellsen.

"What do you propose to do about it?" asked William.

"The power is in me," said Herjellsen, "as much as in any seed, in any leaf, in any tree, in any world."

"But what are you going to do?" asked William.

"I am going to touch the reality," said Herjellsen.

William was silent. Then he said, "And with what tool are you going to do this?"

"With the only tool I have," said Herjellsen, "with that which is most akin to it, most unexpected, most alien to science's accustomed modalities."

"And what tool is that?" asked William, skeptically.

"My mind," said Herjellsen. "My mind."

Hamilton could not take her eyes from the cubicle.

It was some seven feet in height, and some seven feet in length and breadth.

The walls were of clear, heavy plastic. Access to the cubicle was by way of a small, sliding panel, some eighteen inches in width, some four feet in height. It was closed now.

It seemed very primitive, somehow. But Hamilton understood its primitiveness as one might have understood the primitiveness of the first steam engine. It was simple, and crude, and yet the wonder of it was what was herein, per hypothesis, harnessed. It would have been simpler, more reassuring, could one have seen a wheel turn, a valve lift and fall, but there was little to note within save an odd play of light, a photic anomaly, now at the fringes of the cubicle, now like beads of bright water at its edges, pulsating, corruscating, then in small threads darting across the heavy plastic to join other threads, other ripples of light across the cubicle. These beads, and leapings, and threads increased. But the light was not the phenomenon, but its accompaniment. It was no more than the footprint of a summoned force, an impression, not the force, marking its passage. It was a crushed leaf, a snapped branch in its path, that was all, not the beast, not the power, but the sign, the sign of the beast, the power, the force which Herjellsen called P.

P was present.

In the cubicle was P.

Hamilton was terrified. She was a little girl crying in the night.

"Do not be afraid," said William. He was tense.

"It is tomorrow!" cried Hamilton suddenly.

"No," said Gunther. "No. It is like the light. It will pass. It is a subsidiary effect, meaningless."

Hamilton shuddered. William held her arm.

"It is tomorrow," said Hamilton. "I know it is tomorrow."

"It is a disordering of your sense," said William. "Part of your mind senses the presence of P."

"It is today, too," wept Hamilton.

"Do not be frightened," said William. "This is similar to a temporary drug-induced schizophrenia. It is irrelevant to the experiment, the substance of the work."

William's eyes were closed. He smiled. "I now have the

consciousness of an afternoon, when I was six, in London, on a holiday. It is real."

"It is a memory," whispered Hamilton.

"No," said William. "It is not like a memory. It is real, and it is now."

"It cannot exist at the same time as now," whispered Hamilton. "This is a different time."

"Two times exist now," said William. "Each is real. Both are real."

"No," said Hamilton.

Hamilton shook her head. Herjellsen sat silent, his head beneath the steel hood, his heavy fists clenched. He was leaning forward, tense in the wooden chair. His shoulders were hunched. The toes of his heavy shoes pressed at the boards of the floor, the black, rubber heels lifted. His body, powerful, muscular, squat, seemed then like a rock, but a rock that might contain a bomb, a cart of granite that might explode. His large head was bent, his eyes closed. He was alone under the steel hood, with the coils and receptors, with the darkness, with the tension, the straining of that large, unusual, maddened brain.

Hamilton knew that the brain emitted waves. These could be empirically verified.

They were real.

"The reality and the power is one," Herjellsen had claimed.

"Why then," had asked William, "do you not think you might touch the reality with electricity, or magnetism, or even the blow of your fist?"

"They are crudely intraphenomenal," had said Herjellsen. "They are relative to the perceptual mode."

"I do not understand," had said William.

"They are the furniture of the room," had said Herjellsen. "They are not the key to the door."

But the waves of the brain were crudely physical.

But, Hamilton recalled, Herjellsen had cried out that the simplistic dichotomy between the physical and the mental was an intellectual convenience, not corresponding to what must be the case. "The dichotomy is false," had said Herjellsen. "If it were true, the mind could not move the body or the body affect the mind. If it were true, then I could not move my hand when I wish. If it were true, I could not feel pain when my body was injured."

"What then is true?" had asked William.

"A more useful distinction, though itself ultimately dubious," had said Herjellsen, "is that between the phenom-

enal and the nonphenomenal, that between the categories
and sensibilities of experience and that which exceeds such
categories and sensibilities, that which is other than they."

"Which is?" asked William.

"The reality," had said Herjellsen, "and the power."

"The distinction, you said," commented William, "was
ultimately dubious."

"I think so," had responded Herjellsen, "because the
phenomenal is itself a mode of the reality; it is a way in
which the reality sees itself, a perspective, perhaps one of
an infinite number in which the reality chooses to reveal
itself. Thus, I see no complete and categorical distinction
between ourselves and the reality. Indeed, the distinction itself seems relativized to our modes of consciousness. In the
reality itself such a distinction would be, one supposes,
meaningless."

William had shaken his head.

"Oh, we are quite real!" had laughed Herjellsen. "We are
as real as anything that is real; it is only that there are
other manifestations, other truths, other dimensions, that are
quite as real as ours."

"How do you know?" demanded William.

"I do not," said Herjellsen. "But it seems to be likely.
It seems implausible, does it not, that our handful of categories, our tiny, evolving package of sensibilities, our tiny
phenomenal island of awareness, emerging from sensed, but
uncharted seas, should be unique." Herjellsen had then leaned
back. "Rich as we are, I suspect," he had said, "we are
only one penny in the riches of reality."

"What is the reality in itself?" demanded William.

"We are one thing, I suspect," had said Herjellsen, "that
the reality is in itself—but what other things the reality
may be in itself I do not know."

"Is the reality to be distinguished," had asked Gunther,
"from the totality of its diverse phenomenal representations
or manifestations?"

"I think so," whispered Herjellsen. "I think that it is in
itself these manifestations, but that it is, in itself, too, more."

"This seems contradictory," said William.

"I do not think so," said Herjellsen. "Representations or
manifestations are not like shells or costumes in which something else hides; they are a way in which reality, in itself,
truly, has its being; they are not other than the reality but
a way in which it is; but, too, it seems probable that reality's
riches, in their unmanifested profundity, exceed phenomenal

expressions. It is not that the phenomena are not reality, but that there are realities beyond phenomena. Reality contains, I suspect, depths and inexpressibilities beyond those of any set of phenomenal configurations."

"This is hard to understand," said William.

"The words 'in itself' are hard to understand, perhaps unintelligible," said Herjellsen. "Perhaps they are misleading. Let us forget them. Let us think what might be meant, not trouble ourselves with a particular semantic formulation. I am saying that there is no adequate distinction, in this matter, between real and unreal. All that exists is equally real. All that I wish to say is that there is a reality—doubtless identical with all that exists—but that this reality far exceeds our perspectives upon it, or those of other perspectives. It is, perhaps, infinitely profound and inexhaustible. There is more to it than we see. It is not that it is not as we see it, but that it is also other than we see it. And perhaps, if we held other perspectives, we would see that it was also other than we conceived it."

"Granted these things, supposing them intelligible," said William, "is it not your belief that in extraphenomenal reality, reality as it is apart from our particular, or some particular, mode of experience, time and space do not exist?"

"Certainly not as we conceive of them," said Herjellsen. "Time and space, as we conceive of them, are irrational. It seems irrational both that space should be infinite, that it should have no end, and irrational, too, that it should at some boundary terminate, for what would be on the other side?"

"What of an expanding, finite space?" asked William. Hamilton's mind had swept to a speculative conjecture common in astrophysics.

"Irrational," said Herjellsen. "What is it expanding into?"

William looked angry.

"What if it were closed and static?" asked William.

"What would lie outside its sphere?" asked Herjellsen.

"That question would be answered 'nothing,'" said William.

"Yes," said Herjellsen, "but scarcely answered rationally." He smiled. "A sphere requires place," he said.

"What of the Moebius strip?" demanded William.

"It, too, requires place," smiled Herjellsen.

"I suppose there are difficulties," admitted William.

"Too," said Herjellsen, "consider time—it is irrational both to suppose that it had a beginning and that it had no beginning—each hypothesis affronts the intellect, challenges sanity itself."

"So, then," said William, "space and time are irrational?"

"Space and time, as we conceive of them," said Herjellsen, "make little sense."

"So what should we think?"

"We should think at least," said Herjellsen, "that they may not be as we conceive of them." He smiled. "They are relative, in my conjecture," said Herjellsen, "to our mode of perception—I think it quite unlikely that they characterize, or characterize in the same way, the reality as it is apart from our sensibility. It may be that what we experience as space and time is, apart from our experience of it, quite unlike space and time."

"This sort of thing," volunteered Gunther, "is quite common in science, though seldom extended to space and time. The distinction between the sensibility-dependent and the sensibility-independent property is germane. Sound, for example, considered as physicalistic atmospheric concussions is quite unlike the auditory phenomenon of listening, say, to a symphony. The reality is like blows; the auditory phenomenon is music. Similarly with other properties. Consider color, as the physicalistic property of a surface, selectively absorbing and reflecting waves of light. This is quite different from the painting one sees or the blue sky. The world of physics is one of particles and motions, of invisible motions, silent, unlit, dark, hurried. But our world of experience, the human world, is bright with sound, with feeling, taste and touch, with odors, with light and color. Our sensors dip into alien spectra. Our brain is a transducer that transforms physical energies into a human experience, one congruent with the world of the physicist, and yet quite different from it."

"You are familiar, are you not," asked Herjellsen of William, "with the distinction between the sensibility-dependent property and the sensibility-independent property?"

"Any educated man is," said William. "That distinction dates from the time of Galileo."

"From the time of Leucippus and Democritus," corrected Herjellsen.

"Very well," said William.

"It is then my belief," said Herjellsen, "that time and space, as we conceive them, are sensibility-dependent, a mode of our sensibility, a condition for experience, given

whatever we may be. That we experience the reality spatially
and temporally does not imply that the reality apart from
our experience is as we conceive it to be. That we experience a bright yellow does not imply that in the physicist's
reality such a yellow, apart from our experience, exists.
That we experience a symphony of Beethoven does not imply that in the physicist's reality such music, apart from our
experience, exists as we experience it. Rather it would be only
a pounding on the skin. For the lobster, for the sponge, for
the spider, it presumably would not exist, not as music.
Similarly, of course, for them there might be beauties and
rhythms that would be lost on us, we lacking the appropriate
sensors, the appropriate sensibility."

"Space and time are unreal?" asked William.

"As phenomenal reality, relative to our mode of perception," said Herjellsen, patiently, "they are quite real."

"Is that all?"

"Perhaps," said William, "they are a mode of perceiving
something which is doubtless quite real, or, perhaps they
are themselves perceptions of something—or things—which
are quite real."

"Perhaps," said William, "they are modes of perceiving
space and time, or, if perceptions, perceptions of space and
time."

"Does the music of Beethoven, the color of bright yellow,
exist in nature as you hear it, as you see it?"

"No," said William.

"Why then do you fear to extend the distinction of sensibility-dependent and sensibility-independent property to
space and time?" asked Herjellsen.

"I am afraid," said William, "because then I would be
lost."

"Yes," said Herjellsen, "you would then be alone—without your maps. Your very world would totter."

"Why do you suspect that space and time are not of the
reality itself, or are different in that reality?"

"Space and time, as we conceive of them," said Herjellsen,
"are irrational. Thus, I conjecture they are not as we conceive of them."

William said nothing.

"It is interesting," said Herjellsen, "men who conceive
placidly of irrationalities are accounted sane. I who question them am accounted insane. I wonder who is truly sane
and who truly insane."

Brenda Hamilton fought the terror. She shook her head. She looked into the cubicle.

It had begun with a soft glow of light, vibrating, filling the interior of the cubicle with a fog of crystals, and then it had seemed to slip to the floor of the cubicle, like beads, like molecules forming chains of light, first keeping to the margins of the cubicle, then, strand by strand, darting across the plastic floor, until now the entire floor of the cubicle seemed laced with light, and then, tendril by tendril, it began to climb the walls of the cubicle. Now the floor of the cubicle was covered, it seemed inches thick, with a matting of light strands, and more light, like illuminated vines began to grow about the interior of the cubicle.

But it was not the light that frightened Hamilton. It was turnings and terror in her mind.

William seemed calm. He had had the experience before. He was patient.

"There are two times now," he said, "that are present."

"One is a memory," whispered Hamilton.

"No," said William. "Both are quite real. It is like a mountain and a lake. They are times, but they co-exist."

"That is not possible," said Hamilton.

"It is like the parts of a picture. They are different parts but they are all now. There are two times, and they are now."

"No," said Hamilton.

She shook her head in terror. She recalled Herjellsen saying that time, as we think of it, did not exist in the reality.

"It is like a sphere," said William. "It is like a transparent sphere. I see two points on one surface, each opposite the other. They are related to one another. Each is different and yet they are the same, and they are both now."

"Is it truly that way?" asked Hamilton.

William looked at her blankly. "No," he said, "that is only a poem, a poem."

Hamilton shuddered. She sought a concept, a root to grasp, a branch to seize, even a poem that might try to speak what could not be spoken.

"No metaphors from the phenomenal realm are adequate or clarifying," Herjellsen had insisted. "It is its own reality, not ours. We cannot understand it in the modes of our perception. It is another reality."

Hamilton shuddered. There were no charts, no diagrams, no

schemas, no pictures. Nothing would be adequate. It was
not our reality. It was another reality.

William smiled. "It is gone now," he said. "Are you all
right?"

"Yes," said Hamilton.

"Frightening, the disordering of the time sense," he
said.

Brenda smiled. William, light, pleasant, cool, witty, sharp,
sophisticated, was again his self. His attention was now
drawn to the cubicle, watching the phenomenon of the light.
Now the cubicle was almost filled with the interwoven ten-
drils of brightness, like beaded strands of brightness. Hamilton looked at William. "Pretty good trick, what?" he asked
Hamilton, not looking at her, referring to the light.

Brenda wanted to cry out with joy. Suddenly William, in
his casual manner, had made the world real again for her.

It was William's mathematics which Herjellsen utilized.
William, a physician, but gifted amateur mathematician, had,
utilizing analogies from the mathematics of polydimensional
spaces, developed, as a fictive sport, a *jeux d'esprit* of ideas,
a calculus for polydimensional temporalities. He had pub-
lished this privately. The slim volume had come to the
attention of Herjellsen; an omnivorous reader. What had
been a form of fictive play for William, an engaging pastime,
a lighthearted diversion, had given Herjellsen the language,
the equations, for his conjecture. Men before Herjellsen had
doubted the sensibility-independent nature of space and
time, notably and most famously the tiny, hunchbacked, brilliant Prussian, Immanuel Kant, but Kant had not had at his
disposal the mathematics of polydimensional temporalities,
and Kant had been rational in a way that Herjellsen was not.
Herjellsen brought to the problem the conviction that the
mind might have the capacity to touch the reality. Kant
had been of the Enlightenment. Mind, for Kant, had been essentially an organ of rationalities, conscious, reflective,
clear, logical, Euclidean, a sunny, felicitous instrumental
mechanism, common in all men, incorporating the canons of
reason, a suitable device whereby man might, within his
limitations, know the true, solve problems and advance in
social progress. Kant was unfamiliar with the storms of the
mind, the turbulences unleashed in the Nineteenth Century,
the intellectual and technological explosions, and horrors, of
the Twentieth. Kant was before the teachings of Freud, the
investigations of the darknesses of the mind, the first organized probings into psychic phenomena, the first organized

attempts to understand what might be the nature, and the powers, some perhaps untapped, and the reaches, of this mysterious, evolutionary oddity, the mind of the human being. Herjellsen, a crazed Finn, was the first man to bring together, in a madman's brain, the conjecture, the mathematics, and the suspicion that the reality could be touched, that the key could be found, and that it lay in the mind.

The translation cubicle was now aflame with light.

Hamilton, and William, watched it with awe.

Hamilton, glancing about, cried out. Herjellsen had not moved, but there was blood on the back of his neck, beads of blood. His collar was stained. His fists were clenched. He seemed oblivious of the world, of anything, save for one thing, the thought he held in his brain.

Hamilton looked at Gunther. He had not spoken. His eyes were closed.

The cubicle was exploding with light.

"Kill it!" cried Gunther. "Kill it! Kill it!"

Hamilton cried out with fear. William put his arm about her.

"Do not be frightened," said William. "It is the disordering of the time sense. In a moment he will be perfectly all right. It is only his reaction."

"It's coming!" cried Gunther. "Give me the rifle, you fool!"

Hamilton looked at him, frightened.

"It's dead," laughed Gunther. "It's dead." He looked at Hamilton. "I killed it," he said.

"Yes, Gunther," she whispered.

Gunther smiled, and shook his head.

"Do you hear it?" asked Hamilton. She knew it was not an actual sound. But it began to scream in her head, a high-pitched, whistling note. It began to grow louder and louder. The light seemed now ready to shatter the heavy plastic of the cubicle. Hamilton could no longer look at it. She pulled away from William, shielded her eyes. The whistling note was intolerably loud. She shut her eyes against the pain of the light and, though she knew the sound was from within her brain, covered her ears with her hands. Then it seemed her brain would burst with the note, and then it was suddenly still, absolutely still.

She opened her eyes, lowered her hands.

"Look," said William.

The light was gone from the cubicle. It now seemed heavy, silent, very empty.

"There is nothing," she whispered.

"No," said William, "you are mistaken."

"What do you mean?" she whispered.

"P is now present," said William. "It is in the cubicle. The cubicle is now open."

Hamilton looked at the cubicle, the heavy, sliding plastic panel. The cubicle was closed.

"It is closed," said Hamilton.

"No," said William. "The cubicle is open."

Hamilton looked into the cubicle. It seemed very quiet now, absolutely still. The energies of P, asserted to be present, she knew, would not be, if they existed, in the visible or tactual spectrum. They could not be heard. They could not be seen. They could not be tasted, or smelled or touched.

"Such energies cannot exist," she had once said to Herjellsen.

"Gravitation," had said Herjellsen, "too, cannot be heard, nor can it be seen, or touched, or smelled or tasted, and yet it commands the motions of material bodies; it balances universes, plays with planets and guides meteors; does it not exist?"

"Of course," had said Hamilton. "We know it does. We can see its effects."

"And so, too," had said Herjellsen, "can one see the effects of P."

Hamilton stared into the cubicle.

"It's closed," she whispered. "It's closed."

"No," said William. "The cubicle is now open."

Hamilton regarded the cubicle. It was three hundred and forty-three cubic feet in content, seven feet in height, width and depth, but, if William were correct, it was unfathomed in depth in another dimension. Hamilton wondered how deep was it? It was closed to three dimensions. She could see that. But, if William, and Gunther, and Herjellsen were correct, it was open to another.

"It's there!" cried William. "It's there!"

Hamilton screamed.

In the center of the cubicle, on the floor, was a small, heavy-wire cage, about a foot wide, a foot high and two feet in length. There was straw in the bottom of the cage, and a pan of water. Hamilton saw it was a trap, that had been sprung shut. It must have been baited. Inside, peering out through the cage wire, its eyes bright, was a large rodent.

Hamilton slipped to the floor, unconscious.

◈ 3 ◈

Gunther turned the Land Rover abruptly from the graveled road onto the plain.

Hamilton, pleased, sat between Gunther and William. It was the first time she had been permitted out of the compound since her arrival.

She, too, was now excited about Herjellsen's work. The identification had not yet been made on the animal in the cage.

When she had learned that Gunther and William were to take the Land Rover and seek another animal, a live specimen, wild, for the third series of experiments, she had begged Herjellsen to be permitted to accompany them.

"Of course, Doctor Hamilton," Herjellsen had readily agreed.

Hamilton had been frightened that he would refuse. She had been incredibly relieved, elated, at the readiness with which he had acceded to her request.

How marvelous it was to be outside the compound, away from the high, wire fence, the small, plain, severe buildings, of stucco and tin, the watching eyes of the armed blacks.

The Land Rover churned dust from the plain, in a stream of debris cast into the air behind it.

Gunther, his eyes narrowed, drove swiftly, too swiftly for the terrain.

Hamilton did not mind. It gave her a sense of release. She sensed the air pressed aside by the passage of the vehicle, sensed the dirt, spitting away, beneath the tread of the heavy sand tires.

On the graveled road, which passed not more than a half mile from the compound, which lay concealed from the road, the three of them had talked. William, as always, was affable. Gunther, as he usually was, was tight-lipped, taciturn. Neither man wore a hat. A bag of water was slung to the right-hand door handle.

35

Hamilton had been permitted to come with the men. Herjellsen had willingly acceded to her request. She was fully fledged now, a member of the team.

The computer runs she had conducted on Herjellsen's modified 1180, from data furnished by William, she had not completely understood, but she knew that they were integral to the development of the experimental sequence.

On the road, away from the compound, the men had spoken more openly with her about Herjellsen's work, particularly William. Gunther, too, had commented from time to time. And when addressed, he responded to her questions, carefully, exactly. Hamilton leaned back. She was pleased. She was out of the compound. She could speak with the men alone, with Herjellsen not present. They seemed more communicative outside of the compound. Within the compound, they were less willing to speak freely. Though Herjellsen himself was commonly pleasant, and congenial, he tended, without meaning to, to dominate any group of which he was a member. When he was present, there was always the waiting to hear what he would say. It was not only Herjellsen's ponderousness, his erudition, his brilliance which tended to cause him to loom among his colleagues, but also the imponderables of age and experience; he was in his late fifties; and, too, that he was their head, the leader, the determiner of action, the employer. Perhaps most simply there was the fact that he was Herjellsen, short, incisive, powerful, dominating. To him even Gunther, like a young, powerful liegeman, deferred. It was pleasant then for the hour, or afternoon, to be beyond the wire of the compound. Gunther, Hamilton and William were young. They were more of an age, were more commonly equal, and had more in common with one another than any of them might have had with Herjellsen. It was pleasant to be apart from him, his experience, his weightiness, the innocent oppressiveness of his maturity, his dominance. The three of them were young, and were now alone together, Herjellsen left behind. And, too, though she did not perhaps fully realize it, it was pleasant for another reason, for Hamilton, to be with the younger men. She sat between them, one with them, talking, with closeness. She felt very pleased to be with them, male colleagues. She did not fully understand her feelings. Perhaps it was simply the relief of being out of the compound, beyond the wire. She looked at Gunther. Suddenly he looked at her, too. Startled, she looked forward again, out the jolting, dusty, insect-stained windshield. His attention was again on his driving. If William were not present, and Gunther began to make love to her, she felt she would be unable to resist him. Gunther would not ask her if he might make love to her; he would simply begin. And she knew she would be unable to resist him. She fantasized his hands opening her shirt, unhooking her brassiere, freeing her slacks from her body, his hands then at her thighs, lifting her legs, putting her on her back across the front seat of the rover, half stripped. She knew she would be unable to resist him.

But she put such thoughts from her mind. She was a colleague, not a woman.

"I still suspect Herjellsen is a charlatan," said William.

"It is possible," said Gunther.

"Yet—the artifact," said William. "It seems genuine."

William referred to the piece of stone, spoken of by them as the Herjellsen artifact.

It was commonly kept in the computer building. Hamilton had seen it many times.

The artifact was rounded, chipped, roughly polished; it weighed 2.1 kilograms. Anthropologists would have referred to it as a tool. It was a weapon.

The artifact was the most surprising result of the first series of experiments. There had been many abortive experiments, many failures, many disappointments, in the first series. But in the first series, bit by bit, rudimentary translation techniques, relevant to testing the Herjellsen conjecture, had been conceived, developed and refined. The first object to appear in the translation cubicle, two months before Hamilton had been employed, was a piece of broken branch, seared and splintered as though torn from its tree by claws of fire. It had appeared in the cubicle blasted and smoking. The radiocarbon dating on the branch, conducted by Gunther, indicated the branch, though of an unknown wood, was contemporary. This was as it should have been. The branch had been living, had been torn from a living tree. Other results, in the beginning, were similar, though the objects collected were generally simple stones, sometimes pebbles, or chips. Most appeared stained, some half fused and glazed. Toward the end of the first series Herjellsen had, with the aid of William and Gunther, considerably refined his techniques. One of the major difficulties to be surmounted in the practical application of the Herjellsen conjecture was the coordination of diverse terms in appropriate binary combinations; many such combinations yielded nothing; one had destroyed a generator; Herjellsen spoke often of interphenomenal translation, namely, the translation of an object from one phenomenal dimension to another; speaking phenomenally, one might have said from one time and place to another; two pairs of values were stipulated, those of the translation cubicle in a compound in Rhodesia and a given time, sidereal scale, for its longitude at the moment of projected translation; the other two values, the crucial binary combinations, coordinated with the space and time of the cubicle, presented fantastic difficulties; the mind of Herjellsen was like the hand of a blind man reaching out in a dark room of incredible dimension; generally it would close on nothing; but then, once, suddenly, blasted and smoking on the floor of the cubicle had lain a branch, torn as though by fire from a tree; the hand had closed on something; this was the first successful set of coordinates; Herjellsen, with William, had studied them intensely, noting parameters and matrices, resemblances and divergencies. They had been computerized and examined from more than two hundred aspects. They were repeated, but this time yielded nothing.

"Of course," had cried Herjellsen, "we are fools! It is phenomenal time we are translating! It is like reaching out twice to touch a moving object and expecting to touch it a second time in the same place one did at first! The equations must be adjusted, relativized!" But this did not prove simple. Primarily it was discovered that the spatial coordinate as well as the temporal coordinate alters. It was as though the blind man were trying to touch two moving spheres, each different, and touch each at precisely the same place that he had touched them before. Yet Herjellsen and William worked, and the 1180 was modified, programmed, remodified, and reprogrammed again and again. Gradually, a pattern, though one of fantastic complexity, began to emerge. The second collection, a piece of seared shale, occurred a month after the branch. From that time on collections became more frequent, more predictable. Herjellsen could not tell to what time or place his coordinates corresponded, only that they were successful in generating collections. It was as though he printed a number, possibly meaningless, on a card, and then mailed it. If there was an answer it had been an address, somewhere; if there were no answer, then he did not know if it had been an address or not; it had perhaps been nothing; it had perhaps been an address that had not responded; he did not know.

Toward the end of the first series of experiments notable

results had been achieved. Collections had become statistically predictable. In one experiment a fragment of rock had been obtained; in the subsequent experiment its matching counterpart; this had indicated a refinement of considerable delicacy, the complexity of which would not have been possible without the modified 1180 device; the calculations, by hand, might have consumed years. It was as though the blind man were finally learning to touch the two spheres, in precisely the same places, on subsequent attempts. He did not know what places he touched, but he knew that whatever places they might be he could touch them at least twice. While William, aided by Herjellsen, fought to refine the mathematics of the Herjellsen conjecture, Gunther, partially working under the instruction of Herjellsen, partially improvising relays and circuitry, gave his attention to the sophistication of the amplifying mechanism. Specimens had been collected generally in a shattered, or seared condition, almost as though torn through atmospheres and exploded from one dimension into another. For reasons that were not clear to William and Gunther at the time, these effects were not found acceptable by Herjellsen. Coils to the translation cubicle were multiplied. Significantly, generator power was reduced; the distributions and focuses of power, as it turned out, were more significant than its amount. Most significant of all, of course, was the strange mind of Herjellsen. Though abetted and sharpened by the equations of William, though reinforced by the genius and electronics of Gunther, it was that mind, and that mind alone, that could reach out, that had the power to reach out and touch, for an agonizing moment, the reality. It is not known how we can move our hand, and yet we understand that it can be done, and do it; it is not clear whether Herjellsen was perhaps a mutant, or that he, of all men to his time, alone intuited his power, and understood what might be done; it is not known, so to speak, whether Herjellsen discovered a hand that other men do not possess, an instrument, a power, or that he was the first to discover what all men might, though it lie forever dormant, possess. The infant, weeping, alone, wished the bright toy, and lo, a hand, to his astonishment and pleasure, his own, reached forth, and drew it to him. He had learned to will, and grasp. He would never forget this. He would never understand it, but neither would he forget it. It was his now, this power.

"We will succeed!" had cried Herjellsen.

Late in the first series of experiments the success had come.

There had appeared on the floor of the translation cubicle, in a bit of water, fresh and cold, a handful of ice moss. Herjellsen had entered the cubicle, and, on his knees, had lifted it in his hands. It was delicate and cold. Each fiber was intact, and perfect. Herjellsen had wept. William and Gunther had not understood his emotion.

He had looked at them, from within the cubicle, the ice moss cupped gently in his hands. "We will succeed," he had wept. "We shall succeed."

Herjellsen's interests, for no reason that was clear to either William or Gunther, were narrow. Only certain categories of equations were utilized by him, and within these categories there was investigation in fantastic depth and subtlety. It was as though Herjellsen were seeking some particular reality, some destination, some special address in the vastnesses and wastes and mysteries of the reality.

It was with a startled, and eerie feeling, that they had heard his shriek of pleasure in the experimental shack.

In the cubicle had lain the Herjellsen artifact, the rounded, chipped, roughly polished stone; it weighed 2.1 kilograms. It was a tool, a weapon.

"Gentlemen," had said Herjellsen, "the first series of experiments is herewith concluded."

"I still suspect Herjellsen is a charlatan," said William.

"It is possible," said Gunther.

"Yet—the artifact," said William. "It seems genuine."

Hamilton had seen the artifact many times. It was commonly kept in the computer building.

"You believe," asked Hamilton of William, "that there is some trick involved in all this?"

"That certainly seems plausible," said William, looking out the window of the Land Rover. The glass was rolled down. His face was dusty, particularly the right side. There was dust, too, on his sunglasses.

"It takes years to make such an object," said Hamilton, archly. "Herjellsen couldn't have made it, could he?"

"It does not take years to make such an object," said Gunther. "Flint is a soft stone. It can be worked swiftly. Such an ax could be chipped by a skilled craftsman in forty minutes, and polished in an hour."

"How would you know?" asked William.

"It is simply a matter of the physics of the stone," said Gunther. "The physics of the stone makes the answer clear."

"I had always thought it would take a long time," said Hamilton.

"You are incorrect," said Gunther.

"Oh," said Hamilton.

"If such a stone can be worked quickly," said William, "and I shall take your word for that, then it seems quite likely that the Herjellsen artifact was manufactured by our dear colleague, the amiable professor himself."

"I do not regard that as likely," said Gunther.

"You realize what you are saying," said William, slowly.

"Precisely," said Gunther.

"It could have been stolen," suggested Hamilton.

"The stone is fresh," said Gunther. "It bears no signs of age."

"What better evidence that it is a fake?" asked William.

"What better evidence that it is genuine?" asked Gunther.

Hamilton shivered.

"If the Herjellsen conjecture is correct," said Gunther, "the stone should be as it is, fresh, clean, newly worked."

"That is true," said William.

"Herjellsen, did he not," asked Hamilton, "once steal such a stone." She said nothing more. Gunther, when speaking to her of Herjellsen, had told her this among other things. Hamilton did not mention that it had been stolen from a museum in Denmark. A guard had been killed in the theft.

"He stole it to study it," said Gunther.

"Why should he wish to do that?" asked William.

"I do not know," said Gunther. "Perhaps he wished to conduct tests. Perhaps he wished only to know it thoroughly, so that he might recognize such an artifact again."

Hamilton stared out the dusty windshield. They were now in trackless bush country. Gunther because of the terrain had slowed the vehicle. He occasionally shifted gears, the machine lurching up slopes or pulling out of sand pits. A pack of bush pigs, grunting and snuffling, scattered into the brush. The country was hot, dusty, desolate. In the back of the Rover Gunther had two rifles.

"Why would he wish to recognize such an artifact again?" asked William.

"I do not know," said Gunther. "But I suspect, that for some reason, it is important to him."

"He speaks often of the stars," said Hamilton.

"What has a piece of shaped stone, the head of a primitive ax, to do with the stars?" asked Gunther.

"I'm sure I do not know," laughed Hamilton.

He looked at her, angrily.

Hamilton was silent.

"Do you truly believe," asked Gunther of William, "that the Herjellsen artifact is not genuine?"

"It is a fake," said William. "All of this is a matter of tricks, a magician's illusions."

"Do you truly believe that?" asked Gunther.

"Of course," said William. "I am not mad."

"Why do you remain in the compound? Why do you continue to work with Herjellsen?" asked Gunther.

"Oh," smiled William, "the pay is remarkably good, you know, free trip to the bush and all that, not bad for humoring the old fellow."

Gunther said nothing. He drove on, picking his way among clumps of brush. It was toward noon. The three of them were sweating. Dust, churned up by the Land Rover, like a screen of dust, drifted behind the vehicle. They did not speak for some time.

"I do not believe the Herjellsen artifact is genuine," said William, slowly. "It is impossible that it should be genuine."

Gunther laughed. "I see now," he said, "why you stay in the bush."

"Yes," said William, looking out the window. "What if it should be genuine?" He turned to look at Gunther. His lips were tight, thin, pale. "What, Gunther," he asked, "if it should be genuine?"

Gunther laughed. "My dear William," he said, "that is the difference between us! I hope eagerly that it is genuine! You, on the other hand, just as eagerly hope that it is not!"

"I do not know what I hope," said William. "Sometimes I, too, hope that it is genuine. At other times I am terrified lest it be genuine."

Gunther laughed.

"If it should be genuine," said William, slowly, "do you realize its meaning?"

"I think so," said Gunther. "I think I do."

"I think I do, too," said Hamilton.

"Be silent," said Gunther. Hamilton flushed.

"Please, Gunther," snapped William. "Be civil at least."

"She is an ignorant woman," said Gunther.

"I have a Ph.D. from the California Institute of Technology," said Hamilton angrily. "I have a doctorate in mathematics."

"You are an ignorant girl. Be quiet," said Gunther.

"I am a colleague," said Hamilton.

"You understand nothing," said Gunther.

Hamilton looked at him angrily.

"You were a fool to come to the bush," said Gunther.

"You can't speak to me like that!" cried Hamilton.

"Quiet, little fool," said Gunther.

"I'm needed!" said Hamilton.

"Yes, little fool," said Gunther. "You are needed. That is true."

"There!" cried William. "Look there!"

Gunther, in the instant that William had spoken, had seen. In the same instant he had cut the engine to the Land Rover and stepped on the brakes.

"Excellent," said Gunther. "I had not hoped to have such luck."

"What are you looking for?" asked Hamilton.

"An animal for the second series of experiments," said William, "preferably a large animal, between one hundred and one hundred and fifty pounds in weight."

"What do you see?" asked Hamilton, peering through the dusty, insect-stained windshield.

"There, in that tree, some ten feet from the ground," whispered William, pointing, "on that branch."

Hamilton looked closely. "It's a calf," she said. "A native calf. But it can't be. It's on the branch. And it's dead. How could it be on the branch?"

"Look more closely," said William.

Hamilton looked more closely. Across the body of the dead calf, half lost in the sunlight and shadows, sleepy, gorged, peering at them, was a leopard.

"Superb," said Gunther.

"They pull their kills into the branches of trees, to keep them from scavengers," said William. "They are incredibly powerful, lithe brutes, extremely dangerous."

Hamilton gasped. She had never before sensed the sinuous power, its deceptive strength, the teeth, the jaws, the resilient incredible sinews of the leopard, perhaps the most agile and dangerous of the predators.

The beast lay across the body of the calf, watching them.

"You go there," said Gunther to William. "Do not approach it. I shall circle to the back, and come within range. It will smell you, and see you, but it is not likely to attack you. If it seems to sense me, attract its attention. It will not wish to abandon its kill. If all goes well I shall have a clean shot."

"What if it darts into the brush?" asked William.

"Then," said Gunther, "we will have lost it." He smiled. "I have no intention of following it into the brush."

"Are you going to kill it?" asked Hamilton.

"You take the hunting rifle," said Gunther to William. It was a medium-caliber, bolt-action piece, with a five-shot box magazine, with telescopic sight, of German design.

"Yes," said William. He looked relieved.

"I'll take the tranquilizer rifle," said Gunther. It was a powerful, compressed-air gun, custom-made, of British manufacture, designed for the discharge of anesthetic darts.

William looked at Hamilton. "Herjellsen wants the bloody animal alive," he said.

Gunther handed William five bullets. He himself, from the glove compartment of the Rover, removed four plastic-packaged darts. He broke two open. Both men wore side weapons, William, a revolver, Gunther, an automatic, a Luger, 9 mm., the classical 08 model.

Gunther looked at the leopard in the tree.

"Be careful," said Hamilton to the men.

Gunther looked at Hamilton, and then he drew the keys out of the ignition, and slipped them in his pocket.

"Why did you do that?" asked Hamilton.

Gunther did not answer her. Then, to Hamilton's astonishment, Gunther drew forth from a leather pouch at his belt a pair of steel handcuffs.

"Give me your left wrist," he said to Hamilton.

Hamilton felt her left wrist taken in the strong hand of Gunther. She could not believe her eyes, nor her feelings. As though it might be happening to someone else, she saw, and felt, the steel of one of the cuffs close about her left wrist, snugly, and lock. In an instant the other cuff was locked about the steering wheel. She was handcuffed to the steering wheel.

"What are you doing!" she demanded.

William and Gunther were getting out of the car.

Hamilton jerked against the handcuff locked on her wrist. She was perfectly secured.

"Release me!" she cried. "Let me go!"

She looked at them, wildly.

"I'll scream!" she cried. "I'll scream!"

William smiled at her, the inanity of her threat. Hamilton flushed.

Gunther was serious. He glanced to the large cat in the tree, some one hundred and fifty yards away. He did not want the cat disturbed, the hunt interfered with. He glanced at William, and nodded. William, too, nodded.

"Release me," whispered Hamilton.

William climbed back into the seat beside her, and then, quickly, to her consternation, put his left hand over her mouth, and held her right hand with his. She could utter only muffled noises. Her eyes were wild over his hand. Gunther was now reaching toward her, he had something in his hand. She felt her shirt on her right side pulled out of her slacks, and shoved up, exposing her right side, over and a bit forward of the hip.

She tried to shake her head no.

Then she felt Gunther's hand and the needle, slap and press forcibly against her flesh. She felt the needle thrust better than a half inch into her body, and the hand of Gunther holding it into her, patiently, waiting for it to take effect. She felt dizzy. Everything began to go black. She tried to shake her head, no, again. And then she lost consciousness. She had been tranquilized.

◆ **4** ◆

Dr. Brenda Hamilton awakened in her own quarters. She stared at the ceiling. The half light of late afternoon, golden, hazy, filtering, dimly illuminated the room.

The white-washed interior seemed golden and dim. She looked at the arched roof, its beams, the corrugated tin. It was hot, terribly hot. She seldom spent time in her quarters before sundown.

She was vaguely aware that she lay on her mattress, on her iron cot, and that there were no sheets beneath her.

She recalled, suddenly, her trip with Gunther and William, the heat, the dust, the seeing of the leopard, her being handcuffed, tranquilized.

She was angry. They could not treat her in this fashion. Herjellsen must hear of this!

She tried to rise, but fell back, fighting the lethargy of the drug.

Again she stared at the ceiling, at the hot tin above her. She closed her eyes. It was difficult to keep them open. It was so warm.

She opened her eyes again.

The room seemed familiar, and yet somehow it was different. She moved one foot against the other, dimly aware that her shoes, her stockings, had been removed.

Suddenly she sat up in bed. The room was indeed different, it was almost empty.

She looked about herself, alarmed. She swung her legs quickly over the side of the bed. Startled, she realized she was clothed differently than she had been.

Her dresser, her trunk, her suitcases, her books, were gone. The table had been removed. The only furniture remaining in the room was three cane chairs, and her iron cot.

A mirror was in the room, which had not been there before. She saw herself. She wore a brief cotton dress, thin, white and sleeveless. It was not hers. It came well up her thighs, revealing her legs. She noted in the mirror that her legs were trim. She was terrified. The tiny dress was not belted. It was all she wore, absolutely.

She leaped to her feet and ran to the door of the almost empty, bleak room. The knob had been removed. She dug at the crack of the door with her fingernails. It was closed. She sensed, too, with an empty feeling, it must be secured, on the outside. She turned about, terrified, breathing heavily, her back pressed against the door. She looked across the room to the window. She moaned. She ran to the window and thrust aside the light curtain. Her two fists grasped the bars which had been placed there.

She turned about again, regarding the room. It was bare, except for the three cane chairs, the iron cot with its mattress, no bedding.

She felt the planking of the floor beneath her bare feet. She looked across the room to the mirror, which had not been in the room before. It its reflection she saw, clad in a brief, sleeveless garment of white cotton, a slender, trim-legged, very attractive, dark-haired woman. She was a young woman, not yet twenty-five years of age. Her eyes were deep, dark, extremely intelligent, very frightened. She had long straight dark hair, now loose, unpinned and unconfined, falling behind her head. She knew the woman was Brenda

Hamilton, and yet the reflection frightened her. It was not Brenda Hamilton as she had been accustomed to seeing her. No longer did she wear the severe white laboratory coat; no longer was her hair rolled in a tight bun behind her head. The young woman in the reflection seemed very female, her body in the brief garment fraught with a startling, unexpected, astonishing sexuality.

Suddenly, to a sinking feeling in her stomach, she realized that her body had been washed, and her hair combed. The dust of the Rhodesian bush was no longer upon her.

She looked at her figure, her breasts lovely, sweet, revealed in the cotton. She wanted her brassiere. But she did not have it.

She threw her head to one side. She fled from the window to the closet, throwing open its door. It, too, was empty. There was nothing within, not even a hanger.

There was no hanger; such might serve, she supposed, as a tool. Her shoes were gone, with their laces, and, too, her stockings. The bedding from her cot, was missing. Her brief cotton dress lacked even a belt.

She returned to the center of the room, near the cot. Over it, dangling on a short cord, some four inches long, from a beam, was a light bulb. Its shade was missing. The bulb was off.

Numbly she went to the wall switch and turned the bulb on. It lit. Then, moaning, she turned it off again.

She went then again to the center of the room, and looked slowly about, at the white-washed plaster, the bleakness, and then up at the hot tin overhead, then down to the thin, striped mattress on the iron cot.

Then suddenly she ran to the door and pounded on it, weeping. "William!" she cried. "Gunther! Professor Herjellsen! Professor Herjellsen!"

There was no answer from the compound.

She screamed, and pounded on the door, and wept. She ran to the barred window, which bars had been placed there in her absence with William and Gunther. She seized the bars in her small fists and screamed between them. "William!" she screamed. "Gunther! Professor Herjellsen! Professor Herjellsen!" Then she screamed out again. "Help! Please, help! Someone! Help me! Please help me!"

But there was again no answer from the compound.

Dr. Brenda Hamilton, shaking, walked unsteadily to the iron cot.

Her mind reeled.

"You understand nothing," Gunther had told her. "You were a fool to come to the bush," Gunther had told her.

"I'm needed!" had cried Hamilton.

"Yes, little fool," had said Gunther. "You are needed. That is true."

Hamilton was bewildered.

She sank to the floor beside the cot. She put her head to the boards, and wept.

"Here is a brush, cosmetics and such," said William, placing a small cardboard shoe box on the floor of Brenda Hamilton's quarters.

Brenda Hamilton stood across the room from him, facing him. She wore still the brief white garment, that of thin cotton, sleeveless.

He sat on one of the cane chairs. It was ten P.M. Mosquito netting had been stapled across the window. The room was lit from the single light bulb, dangling on its short cord from the beam.

A tray, with food, brought earlier by William, lay on Brenda Hamilton's cot. It was not touched.

"Eat your food," said William.

"I'm not hungry," she said.

He shrugged.

"I want my clothing, William," she said.

"It is interesting," said William. "In all your belongings, there was not one dress."

"I do not wear dresses," she said.

"You are an attractive woman," said William. "Why not?"

"Dresses are hobbling devices," she said. "They are a garment that men have made for women, to set them apart and, in effect, to keep them prisoner."

"You do not appear much hobbled," observed William.

Brenda Hamilton flushed.

"I feel exposed," she said. "Another function of the dress," she said, "is to make the female feel exposed, to make her more aware of her sexuality."

"Perhaps," said William.

"Give me my own clothing," begged Brenda Hamilton.

"You are quite lovely as you are," said William.

"Do not use that diminishing, trivializing word of me," snapped Hamilton. "It is as objectionable as 'pretty'."

William smiled. "But Brenda," he said, "you are quite pretty."

"Please, William," begged Hamilton.

She looked in the mirror. It was true what William had said. She was, to her fury, very lovely, very pretty.

"Actually," said William, "you are rather more than lovely, and certainly far more than pretty."

"Please, William," begged Hamilton.

"You are beautiful, quite beautiful, Brenda," said William.

"Call me Doctor Hamilton," said Hamilton.

"Very well," agreed William. He looked at her, appreciatively, scrutinizing her casually, to her rage, from her trim ankles to her proud head. "You are indeed far more than pretty, Doctor Hamilton," said William. "You are beautiful, quite beautiful, Doctor Hamilton," said William.

Hamilton turned away, stifling a sob.

"Be careful, Doctor Hamilton," cautioned William. "That is almost a female response."

She spun to face him. "I am a female!" she cried.

"Obviously," said William.

"Why am I being treated like this?" demanded Brenda Hamilton.

"Like what?" asked William.

"Why has that mirror been placed in the room?" she demanded. "Why am I dressed like this?"

"It seems strange, does it not," asked William, "that you, an attractive female, should object to being clothed as an attractive female?"

"I do not wish to be so clothed!" she cried.

"Are you ashamed of your body?" asked William.

"No!" she cried.

"Of course, you are," smiled William. "But look at yourself in the mirror. You should not be ashamed of your body, but proud of it. You are extremely beautiful."

"I am being displayed," she wept.

"True," said William.

"I do not wish to be displayed," she said.

"You are not simply being displayed for our pleasure," said William.

She looked at him.

"You are being displayed also for your own instruction, that you may be fully aware of what a beauty you are."

She looked at the mirror. "It is so—so different from a man's body," she said.

"Precisely," said William. "It is extremely different, its softness, its vulnerability, its beauty."

"So different," she whispered.

"And you, too, my dear Doctor Hamilton, are quite different."

"No!" she snapped.

William laughed.

"Being a female is a role," cried Hamilton. "Only a role!"

"Tell that to a sociologist," said William, "not to a physician, or a man of the world, one experienced in life."

Hamilton turned on him in rage.

"The body and the mind," said William, "is a unity. Do you really think that with a body like yours you might have any sort of mind, one, say, like mine or Gunther's? Do you not think there might not be, associated with such a body, an indigenous sensibility, indigenous talents, emotions, brilliancies? Do you really think that the mind is only an accident, unrelated to the entire evolved organism?"

"I have a doctorate in mathematics," said Hamilton, lamely, defensively.

"And we both speak English," said William. "I speak of deeper things."

"Being feminine," said Hamilton, "is only a role."

"And doubtless," said William, "being a leopard is only a role, one played by something which is really not a leopard at all."

"You are hateful," said Brenda Hamilton.

"I do not mean to be, Doctor Hamilton," said William. "But I must remind you that what you seem to think so significant, a cultural veneer, is a recent acquisition to the human animal, an overlay, a bit of tissue paper masking deeper realities." William looked down. "I suppose," he said, "we do not know, truly, what a man is, or a woman."

"We can condition a man to be feminine, and a woman to be masculine," said Brenda Hamilton. "It is a simple matter of positive and negative reinforcement."

"We can also stunt trees and dwarf animals, and drive dogs insane," said William. "We can also bind the feet of Chinese women, crippling them. We can administer contradictory conditioning programs and drive men, and women, insane with anxieties and guilts, culturally momentous, and yet, physiologically considered, meaningless, irrelevant to the biology being distorted."

Brenda Hamilton looked down.

"You are afraid to be a woman," said William. "Indeed, perhaps you do not know how. You are ignorant. You are frightened. Accordingly, it is natural for you to be distressed, hostile, confused, and to seize what theories or pseudotheories you can to protect yourself from what you most fear—your femaleness."

"I see now," said Doctor Hamilton, icily, "why I have been dressed as I am, why there is this mirror in my room."

"We wish you," said William, "to learn your womanhood, to recognize it—to face it."

"I hate you," she said.

"It is my hope that someday," said William, "you will see your beauty and rejoice in it, and display it proudly, unashamed, brazenly even, excited by it, that you will be no longer an imitation man but an authentic woman, true to your deepest nature, joyous, welcoming and acclaiming, no longer repudiating, your femaleness, your womanhood, your sexuality."

"Being a female," wept Hamilton, "is to be less than a man!"

William shrugged. "If that is true," he said, "dare to be it."

"No!" said Hamilton. "No!"

"Dare to be a female," said William.

"No!" said Hamilton. "No! No!"

Brenda Hamilton ran in misery to the wall of her quarters. She put her head against the white-washed plaster, the palms of her hands.

She sobbed.

"Very feminine," said William.

She turned to face him, red-eyed.

"You are doubtless playing a role," said William.

"Please be kind to me, William," she begged.

William rose from the chair.

"Don't go, William!" she cried. She put out her hand.

William stood in the room, in the light of the single light bulb. He did not move.

"Why am I being treated like this?" whispered Brenda Hamilton.

"The third series of tests will begin in a day or two," said William.

Brenda Hamilton said nothing.

"The second series will terminate tomorrow evening."

"Why am I being treated like this?" demanded Brenda Hamilton.

William did not speak.

"Bring me my clothing, William," begged Hamilton.

"You are wearing it," said William.

"At least bring me my brassiere," she begged.

"You do not need it," he said.

She turned away.

"Your other clothing," said William, "has been destroyed, burned."

Brenda Hamilton turned and faced him, aghast.

She shook her head. "Why?" she asked.

"You will not be needing it," said William. "Furthermore it is evidence of your presence."

She shook her head, numbly.

"All of your belongings have been disposed of," said William. "Books, shoes, everything."

"No!" she said.

"There will not be evidence that you were ever within the compound."

She looked at him, blankly.

"You have never been outside of it, except once in the Rover with Gunther and me," said William. "You can be traced to Salisbury," said William, "that is all."

"But Herjellsen," she said.

"The Salisbury authorities know nothing of Herjellsen," said William. "They do not even know he is in the country."

Brenda Hamilton leaned back against the wall. She moaned.

William turned to go.

"William!" she cried.

He paused at the door.

"Free me," she said. "Help me to escape!"

William indicated two buckets near the wall. He had brought them earlier. "One of these," he said, "the covered one, is water. The other is for your wastes."

"William!" wept Hamilton.

William indicated the tray, untouched, on the bed. "I recommend you eat," he said, "that you keep up your strength."

"I do not want to be a woman," said Hamilton. "I have never wanted to be a woman! I will not be a woman! Never!"

"You should eat," said William. "It will be better for you."

Hamilton shook her head. "No," she said. "I'll starve!"

With his foot, William indicated the cardboard shoe box on the floor. "Here is a brush and comb," he said, "and cosmetics."

"I do not wear cosmetics," said Hamilton.

"It does not matter to me," said William. "But you are expected to keep yourself groomed."

Hamilton looked at him with hatred.

"Is that understood?" asked William.

"Yes," said Hamilton. "It is understood perfectly."

Just then Hamilton and William heard the two heavy locks, padlocks, with hasps and staples, on the door being unlocked. William, while within the room, was locked within.

"Who is it?" asked Hamilton.

"Gunther," said William.

"He must not see me like this!" wept Hamilton.

The door opened. One does not knock on the door of a prisoner.

Gunther entered. Hamilton backed away, against the opposite wall.

Gunther looked at her. His eyes prowled her body. Gunther had had many women.

His eye strayed to the cot, to the untouched tray. He looked at Hamilton.

"Eat," he said.

"I'm not hungry," whispered Hamilton.

"Eat," said Gunther, "now."

"Yes, Gunther," she said, obediently. She came timidly to the cot.

William was irritated.

"Herjellsen is nearly ready," said Gunther.

"All right," said William.

Hamilton sat on the cot and, looking down, began to eat.

"No," said Gunther to Hamilton. She looked at him, startled, frightened. "Kneel beside the cot," he said.

Hamilton knelt beside the cot, and, as she had been bidden, ate from the tray.

"She must be habituated," said Gunther to William. "You are too easy with her."

William shrugged.

"When a man enters the room," said Gunther to Hamilton, "you are to kneel, and you are not to rise until given permission."

Hamilton looked at him, agonized.

"Do you understand?" asked Gunther.

"Even if it is one of the blacks?" asked Hamilton.

"Yes," said Gunther. "They are males." He looked down at her. "Is this clearly understood?"

"Yes, Gunther," said Brenda Hamilton. She dared not question him.

Gunther indicated the cardboard box. He kicked it toward her.

"She does not use cosmetics," said William.

"Tomorrow night," said Gunther to Hamilton, "adorn yourself."

He then turned away, and left the room. "Do not lock the door," said William. "I am coming with you, presently."

Hamilton leaped to her feet, angrily.

"You obey him very well, Doctor Hamilton," said William. She blushed.

"Adorn yourself!" she mocked.

"I would do so, if I were you," said William.

"I do not like this dress!" said Hamilton.

"Then remove it," said William.

Brenda Hamilton's hand lashed forth to strike William, but he caught her wrist, easily. She struggled to free it, and could not.

He forced her, she resisting, again to her knees.

"One thing you must learn, Doctor Hamilton," said William, "before you think of striking with impunity, is that men may not choose to permit it. Further, such a blow might have consequences. You might be beaten, and perhaps severely." He looked down at her. "It is important that you understand, Doctor Hamilton," he said, "that men are stronger than you."

At his feet Brenda Hamilton, for the first time in her life, understood truly what this might mean, that men were stronger than women.

"You are angry with me," she said, "William."

He looked down on her, furious.

Unable to meet his eyes, she put her head down.

Then he turned away, and left the room.

She looked up, at the door. She knelt on the planks of the room. She heard the two hasps being flung against the staple plates, angrily. She heard two heavy padlocks, one after the other, thrust through their staples, and snapped shut.

She leaped up, and ran to the door. She put her fingernails to its crack, futilely.

She turned away from the door, and looked back into the room.

She saw the cardboard box, lying near the cot on the floor. She saw her reflection, red-eyed, across the room.

Slowly she went to the box and knelt beside it, taking a brush and comb from it and, with the brush, slowly, watching herself in the mirror, began to brush her long, dark hair.

The work in the experimental shack was apparently not going as well as it might.

The days passed slowly for Brenda Hamilton. In the morning, with a broom, she swept her quarters, and, when she had finished sweeping, with a cloth, dampened with water, on her hands and knees, she mopped the boards of her floor. Similarly, once a day, she wiped down the walls of her cell, using the cane chairs, to the ceiling of corrugated tin. There was little point in this. It was merely Gunther accustoming her to servile work. Also, he insisted that the cot be placed at a certain place and angle in the room, aligned with certain floor boards, and that the mattress be straight upon it. Doctor Hamilton was being taught discipline. She was being taught, too, to comply perfectly with the arbitrary will of a male. But such work was finished by ten in the morning, when the heat of the day was beginning, and there was then little to do in the hot, stifling room, now her cell, and she spent much time on the cot, lying upon it, staring at the wall or ceiling. She was fed small meals, four times a day, the last at nine P.M. She had more water than she needed. The diet was high protein, with few fats or starches. William, she knew, was in charge of her diet. The meals, and water, and such, were brought now by blacks, those whom Herjellsen used to guard the compound and perform its duties. There were two of them. As Gunther had told her, when they were in the room, she knelt. The first day one of them had pointed at the wall opposite the door. Understanding, she had risen and gone to the wall and knelt there, across the room from him, away from the door. There seemed little point in this; there were always two of them, one who would bring the food, or whatever it might be, and the other who would stand by the door, watching, just outside. She could not run to the door and escape. After the first time she did not have to be again instructed but, when one of them entered the room, she would kneel across the room, unbidden, away from the door. In the afternoon, she would wash her body and her single garment, using a chipped wooden bowl, and a piece of toweling, supplied by William, and water from the drinking bucket. Each night, after her supper, as Gunther had commanded, she adorned herself. At first she was clumsy, but she was highly intelligent, and her small hands were sure. She taught herself to apply lipstick, which she had not worn since high school, and to apply powder and eye shadow. It seemed very barbaric, somehow, for her to do so, so primitive, this adorning of the body. Did it truly make her more beautiful, she wondered, or was it only a device to attract attention, to signal her sexuality, to proclaim her femaleness, to announce her eagerness for, her readiness for, her vulnerability to, male aggression. She shuddered. She removed two earrings from the cardboard box. They were golden pendants, with clips. She fastened them on her ears. Her ears had never been pierced. Doctor Brenda Hamilton would have scorned that very idea, so primitive, like an aboriginal sex rite. She regarded herself in the mirror. Yes, they were beautiful. She was beautiful. She regretted suddenly that she had never had her ears pierced. How exciting, she thought, the symbolism, the flesh meaning of such an adornment, the piercing of her softness by the hardness of the metal, the literal wearing of such an ornament, its beads or rings or pendant against the side of her throat, beneath the dark hair, their being fastened on her. I am beautiful, she thought. Kneeling before the mirror, she reached again into the box. In a moment she had opened a small vial, and touched herself, twice, with perfume. She lifted her hair and regarded herself. You are an exquisitely beautiful woman, she told herself. She regretted never having had her ears pierced.

She leaped to her feet and walked about the room, looking at herself in the mirror.

How beautifully she moved! And she found she could move even more beautifully if she wished. She noticed that she was graceful, and beautifully curved. She understood then, as she had not before, how beautiful a human female can be. For a brief instant she was not displeased to be such a creature, but felt an indescribable thrill of joy, of pride, that it was what she was, that that was she, so soft, so delicious, so alive, so vital, so marvelously beautiful. For an instant Doctor Brenda Hamilton was pleased that she was a female. Then as she looked at the softness, the beauty, the delicacy of herself, she was angry, frustrated, furious. Tears came to her eyes. It was so soft, so vulnerable, her beauty! She thought then of men, so hard, so large, so strong, so different and sometimes fierce, so different, so different from her. She wondered of the meaning of her beauty, its softness, its vulnerability. Perhaps, she wondered, it belongs to men. "No!" she cried. "No!" And then she hated the beautiful, soft, thing she saw in the mirror. "No!" she cried, looking into the mirror. "No!" She would have torn away the earrings, washed away the lipstick and cosmetics, the perfume, but she did not dare, for Gunther had commanded her to wear them, and she was afraid to disobey him.

But Gunther had not come the first night. He had been working in the experimental shack with Herjellsen.

When the door had opened, it had been William. Brenda was kneeling before the cot, as she had planned, the striped mattress to be seen behind her, transecting, at its angle, her body.

William had stopped, stunned.

Disappointment had been visible, though only for an instant, in Brenda Hamilton's eyes. William had noted it, with brief irritation.

"Stand up," had said William.

Brenda had stood up, and she, unconsciously, smoothed down the thin cotton dress. The movement, as she realized instantly, had accentuated her beauty, drawing the dress momentarily tight over the softness of her breasts. She flushed.

They stood apart from one another, regarding one another. Brenda Hamilton was timid, inspected. Then she saw genuine awe in William's eyes. She smiled.

"You are beautiful, Brenda," he said. He did not address her as Doctor Hamilton. That would, in the moment, have seemed foolish.

He was a male, confronting a beautiful female prisoner. That was all. One would not address such a prisoner by such a title.

"Hello, William," whispered Brenda Hamilton.

"Stand straight," said William.

He walked about her, viewing her. He stopped behind her, some seven feet away, on the other side of the cot. She did not turn to face him.

"Yes," he said, "you are a truly beautiful woman."

She lifted her head, not turning.

He ranged about her and stood again in front of her. "Truly beautiful," he said.

"Thank you, William," said Brenda Hamilton. It was the first time in her life that such a thing had been said to her. It was the first time she had acknowledged such a compliment. Deep within her there glowed a sudden, diffused warmth. Startled, she felt, within her, which she would not have admitted, a surge of pleasure.

A man had inspected her, candidly, as she had stood well displayed before him, as she had stood as a mere prisoner, and had termed her, objectively, with nothing to gain which

he could not have taken by his strength, beautiful. Brenda
Hamilton, the prisoner, knew then that she was pleasing to a
man.

This filled her, for no reason she clearly understood, with
incredible pride.

She had stood well revealed, captive, before a man, and
had been pronounced beautiful. But suddenly she felt very
helpless, very vulnerable.

To her terror she saw William's hand reach out and touch
her shoulder.

"No!" she hissed. She backed away. "Don't touch me!" she
cried.

William looked at her with fury. He did not advance toward her.

"I have come to tell you," he said, "that we are encounter-
ing difficulties in completing the second series of experiments.
There will be some delay."

"I demand to speak to Herjellsen!" said Brenda Hamilton.

But the door had shut.

She heard the hasps strike the staple plates, the locking
of the heavy padlocks.

Brenda turned away, agonized. She had wanted William to
stay. He seemed the only link with the outside. Herjellsen
had not so much as seen her since she had left in the Land
Rover with William and Gunther. Gunther had not visited
her since her first night in captivity. There had been only the
blacks and, from time to time, William.

Brenda Hamilton regarded herself in the mirror, in the
light of the single light bulb under the tin roof.

Tonight, she knew, she had attracted a man. She lay down
on the cot, twisting in the heat, unable to sleep. She got up
and walked about the room. She drank water. She desperately wanted a cigarette, but William would not allow her any.
"Tobacco must not be smelled on your breath," he had told
her. "A keenly sensed organism can detect such an odor,
even days afterward."

Brenda Hamilton had understood nothing of this. But she
had not been given tobacco.

Fitfully, in the heat, she slept.

Once she awakened, startled. She had dreamed that
Gunther had taken her in his arms, as she was, as she had
been when William had seen her, and forced her back on the
cot, his hands thrusting up the thin dress, over her breasts,
freeing her arms of it, until it was about her neck and that
he had then, with one hand, twisted it, sometimes loosening

it, sometimes tightening it, controlling her by it, making her do what he wished, while his other hand had forced her to undergo delights of which she had not dreamed. How she had writhed and struggled to kiss him as he had then, when her body uncontrollably begged for him, deigned to enter her. But then she screamed and awakened, the light of a flashlight in her eyes.

"Go to sleep," said a voice from the window, on the other side of the bars, the netting. It was one of the blacks, making his rounds, checking the prisoner.

She lay terrified on the cot.

She lay awake. She waited. In what she surmised might be an hour, the flashlight again illuminated her body on the cot. She pretended she was asleep.

When it was gone, she groaned. She had not dreamed they would be so thorough.

Then she understood, too, the order of entries into her room, during the day, their timing, when the broom was given to her, the water, the wastes emptied, the food brought, the late checking.

She was under almost constant surveillance.

She had no tool. She was helpless in the room. She could not pick the lock for the locks were on the outside. She did not even have a fork, or spoon. With her fingernails and teeth she could not splinter through the floor, nor dig through the wall.

And, even should she gain the outside, there were the blacks, at least one on guard, and the fence.

And outside the fence there was the bush, the heat, the lack of water, the dryness, animals, the distance.

Gunther, she knew, was a superb hunter. Tracks, in the sand and dirt, soft, powdery, dry, would leave a trail which she supposed even she, a woman, might follow.

She lay on the cot looking up at the dark ceiling. I would leave a trail, she told herself, that even I could follow, even a woman.

She feared Gunther.

Then she noted that she had thought of herself not simply as Doctor Hamilton, but as a woman. No, no, she wept to herself. I do not wish to be a woman. I will not be a woman! I will not be a woman!

She twisted desirably, deliciously, in the brief dress, and thought of Gunther.

Suddenly she said to herself, startling herself, I want to be a woman!

Yes, I want to be a woman!

I am a woman!

No, she cried, I will not be a woman! Never!

She realized, though she could not understand the motivations, that it was no accident that she had been dressed as she had, that there had been a mirror placed in the room so that she would be forced to see herself so clad, that she had been ordered to adorn herself with cosmetics, and, indeed, most brutally, most unfairly of all, that she had been forced to kneel in the presence of males, and could not rise until their permission had been given.

"I hate them!" she cried. "I hate men! I hate all of them! I do not want to be a woman! I will never be a woman! Never!"

But a voice within her seemed to say, be quiet, little fool, little female.

She rolled on her stomach and wept, and pounded the mattress. Suddenly she realized she had not removed the earrings, the makeup. She removed them, and, too, from her body, washed the perfume. Then she lay again on the cot. She was almost frightened to go to sleep. There was no sheet, no cover. She knew the blacks would, from time to time, during the night, check with the flashlight. Then she laughed to herself. "I am only a prisoner," she said, "what do I care if they see my legs?" It seemed to her somehow amusing that a prisoner might attempt to conceal her legs from her jailers. Every inch of her, she knew, was at their disposal, if they so much as wished.

She lay on her stomach on the cot, on the striped mattress, her head turned to one side. The mattress, she sensed, was wet with her tears. Her fists, beside her head, on each side, were clenched.

As she lay there, helpless, locked in the room, she knew that the men had won, that whatever might be their reasons, their plans or motivations, their intentions with respect to her, that they had conquered.

She knew that it was a woman who lay on the striped mattress on the small iron cot, in the hot, tin-roofed building in a compound in Rhodesia.

"I know that I am a female," she said to herself. "I am a female."

In her heart, in her deepest nature, for the first time in her life, Doctor Brenda Hamilton—the prisoner Brenda—the woman—acknowledged her sex.

She did not know for what reason the men had done what

they had done, but she knew that they had accomplished at least one of their goals.

They had forced her, cruelly and incontrovertibly, in the very roots of her being, to accept the truth of her reality, that she was a woman.

Brenda wondered what might be their further goals.

They had succeeded quite well in their first. They had taught her that she was a woman.

Brenda no longer had doubt about this. She was tired. Brazenly she took what position she was comfortable with on the cot. She no longer cared about the blacks and their flashlights. She was a female prisoner. Her entire body, she knew, each curvacious, luscious inch of it, should her jailers wish it, lay at their disposal. She stretched like a cat on the cot, in the heat, and fell asleep. She was mildly scandalized, as she fell asleep, to discover that she was not displeased to be a woman, that she was quite satisfied with the luscious, curved, sexy body which was she.

On the fourth night, at 10 P.M., Brenda Hamilton heard the keys turn in the padlocks outside the door, heard them lifted out of the staples and, on their short chains, fall against the door; then she heard the hasps flung back.

The door opened.

"Gunther," she whispered.

She fell to her knees, and looked up at him.

This was the first time since the first night of her captivity that he had entered the room.

She had adorned herself beautifully, even to the earrings and perfume.

Kneeling on the wooden floor of her cell, in the thin, white dress, she looked up at him.

It came high up her thighs.

He did not tell her to rise. She remained kneeling. He looked at her, for a long time.

It was the first time he had seen her adorned.

It was a quite different Brenda Hamilton on whom he now looked, than on whom he had looked before. It was a Brenda Hamilton who was now a woman.

"Hello, Gunther," said Brenda Hamilton.

He drew up one of the cane chairs, its back to her, and sat across it, facing her, looking at her.

He did not speak.

After a time, Brenda whispered, "Do you like me as I am now, as you see me now?"

He did not answer her. His face betrayed no emotion. He turned about. "Lock the door," he said to someone outside, one of the blacks.

It was shut and locked.

He regarded her.

"We are now alone," he said. "We will not be disturbed."

"Yes, Gunther," she whispered.

Gunther regarded her. "You are now, without inhibition," he said, "to do precisely what you wish."

She regarded him, startled. Then she smiled. "No," she said.

"What is it that you feel like doing?" he asked. "What secret thought do you fight? What impulse do you repudiate, rejecting it as too terrible, too degrading?"

"It is not terrible," she laughed, "it is only silly."

"What is it?" he asked.

"A silly impulse," she said. "You would laugh, if I told you."

"Tell me," he said.

"It is too silly," she laughed.

"Tell me," he said.

"I have a silly impulse," she said, "to crawl to you on my belly and kiss your boots." She laughed.

"Do it," said Gunther.

"No!" she cried. "No!"

"Do so," he said. His eyes were stern.

"No, please, no!" whispered Brenda Hamilton.

"Do so," said Gunther.

Brenda Hamilton, possessor of a doctorate in mathematics, a Ph.D. from the California Institute of Technology, slipped to her stomach. She approached Gunther. Her hair fell over his boots. She took them in her hands and, again and again, kissed them. She tasted the leather, the dust of the Rhodesian bush, in her mouth. Tears in her eyes, she lifted her head, helplessly looking at him.

"Go to the cot," he said.

"Yes, Gunther," said Brenda Hamilton. She went to the cot. She knelt on the cot. She waited for him to come to her.

He slipped from the chair and went to the cot, and sat on it, his body turned, regarding her.

He placed his hands on her upper arms, and drew her toward him.

"What do you want?" asked Gunther.

She turned her head away.

"Speak," said Gunther.

She looked at him. "Must I?" she whispered.

"Yes," said Gunther. "What do you want?"

"I'm a prisoner," she said. "I want to be fucked like a prisoner, used!"

"Oh?" asked Gunther.

"By you, Gunther," she whispered, "—by you!"

He said nothing.

"You are the most attractive man I have ever seen, Gunther," she whispered. "You see," she said, "as a prisoner I must speak the truth. Ever since I have seen you I have wanted you to take me. Fuck me, Gunther. I'm your prisoner. You can do with me what you want. Fuck me, Gunther, please! I beg you to fuck me!"

"You are an American," said Gunther.

"Please, Gunther," she whispered.

"Do you not want candlelight?" asked Gunther, amused. "Soft music, sentiment, romance?"

He held her arms, she in the thin, white dress, under the single light bulb, high over their heads, under the tin roof, on the flat, thin striped mattress on an iron cot, in a stifling cell in Rhodesia.

"No," she said, "Gunther. I want sex. I want you to be hard with me, show me no mercy. Throw me down on my back, you, loveless and powerful, and treat me as what I am, and only as what I am, your female prisoner. Please, Gunther!"

"You seem quite different from what I knew before," said Gunther.

"I'm begging you to fuck me, Gunther," pleaded Brenda Hamilton.

"You are a virgin," said Gunther.

Brenda Hamilton stiffened. This would have been established in London, in William's gynecological examination. Tears came to Brenda Hamilton's eyes. The results had obviously been made available to the men.

Doubtless they were familiar with all of her records, her measurements.

"Yes," said Hamilton. "I'm a virgin."

"And twenty-four years old," laughed Gunther.

"Yes!" wept Hamilton.

"Virgin," laughed Gunther.

"I give you my virginity, Gunther," she wept.

His hands were hard on her arms. She cried out with pain, he held her so tightly.

"You give nothing," said Gunther. "If I want it, I will take it."

"Yes, Gunther," she whispered.

Suddenly Gunther thrust her from him. She was startled. "Gunther!" she cried.

Gunther stood up. He seemed very tall.

"Please, Gunther!" she wept.

"Beg on your knees to be fucked," said Gunther.

Brenda Hamilton slipped to her knees, on the floor, before him. She lifted her head to him, tears in her eyes. "I beg to be fucked," she said.

"No," said Gunther. He laughed.

Brenda Hamilton looked up at him, in disbelief.

Gunther turned and stepped away from her. Near the mirror he bent down and picked up the cardboard box of cosmetics. He threw the brush and comb on the cot. The box, with the rest of its contents, he held in his left hand.

She had not moved. With his right hand, one after the other, he jerked the clip earrings, those with pendants, from her ears. "Oh!" she cried, her head jerked to one side. "Oh!" she wept, her head jerked to the other side. She put her fingertips to her ear lobes and felt blood. "Gunther!" she wept. He dropped the earrings in the box. He shook the contents of the box before her. "You will not be needing these any longer," he said. "They have done their work."

Brenda Hamilton shook her head negatively. "Gunther," she whispered. "I do not understand."

"Wash yourself," said Gunther. "Get rid of the powder, the makeup, the lipstick."

She looked at him.

"Hurry," he said.

Obediently, Brenda Hamilton went to the water bucket and filled the bowl. With the tiny sliver of soap, and the reverse side of the piece of toweling allotted to her, she washed, and wiped, her face.

She faced him.

"Again," he said. "And swiftly!"

She turned again to the bowl, the soap, the towel. Quickly, clumsily, she cleaned her face. She then turned again to face him, to be inspected.

"Come here," said Gunther.

With his hand in her hair, he inspected her. He bent to smell her shoulder. "The perfume," he said, "lingers, but it will dissipate in a day or so."

By the hair he threw her to the cot.

He went to the door and knocked twice, sharply.

Brenda heard the padlocks being removed from the staples, heard them fall on their chains against the door. Then the door was ajar.

"Gunther," she said.

He turned to face her.

"Why did you not rape me?" she asked.

"It is not mine to rape you," he said.

"Not—yours?" she asked.

"No," said Gunther.

She looked at him, not understanding.

He turned away.

Quickly she rose from the cot. She went to him. She put her hand on his arm. He looked down into her eyes. "Gunther," she whispered, looking down, "please, please do not tell anyone what occurred in this room tonight—"

"Kneel," he said.

She knelt, looking up at him.

"What do you mean?" he asked.

"Do not tell anyone, please," she said, looking up at him, "—how—how I acted."

"How you acted?" he asked.

"What I said—what I did!" she whispered.

"On my honor as a gentleman?" he asked.

"Yes," she said, fervently, "on your honor as a gentleman!"

"I am afraid," he smiled, "that I cannot comply."

"I do not understand," she said.

"Surely you must understand that a full report, a complete report, exact and detailed, must be made to Herjellsen and William?" he asked.

"Report?" she whispered. "No! No!"

Brenda Hamilton, aghast, kneeling, sank helplessly back on her heels. She knew she had exposed herself as a woman with sexual needs, publicly, incontrovertibly, as a woman with desperate sexual needs, exposed clearly, publicly, unrepudiably. She did not doubt that Gunther's report would be objective, complete, accurate. She put her head in her hands, weeping.

"You are coming around beautifully, Brenda," said Gunther. "In my opinion you are, even of this instant, quite ready."

She lowered her hands, lifting her tear-stained face to him. "Ready?" she said, numbly.

"Yes," said Gunther, "quite ready."

"I do not understand," she said.

"Go to the cot," he said. "Stand beside it."

She did so.

"I do not understand," she said.

"Sit on the cot," he said. She did so. "Sit prettily," he said. "Put your knees together. Put your ankles together, and to one side. Turn your body to face me." She did so.

"What did you mean 'ready', Gunther?" she asked. "I do not understand."

"You are stupid," he said. He regarded her sternly.

She put her eyes down. "Yes, Gunther," she said.

He smiled, and turned away.

"Let me have the cosmetics," she begged, suddenly, looking up. "Let me keep them here."

They were tiny articles. She had little else to cling to.

Gunther turned to face her. He regarded her evenly. "You will not need them," he said. "They have served their purpose."

"Please, Gunther," she begged.

"When you are transmitted," said Gunther, "surely you must understand that you will be transmitted raw."

"Transmitted!" she cried.

"Certainly," said Gunther. "You are essential to the third series of experiments."

"Oh, no!" she wept. She slipped from the cot, and fell to her knees on the floor. "No!"

Gunther laughed.

Wildly, desperately, Brenda Hamilton looked about, like a caught animal, terrified.

"No!" she cried, as Gunther snapped one of his handcuffs on her left wrist, and, pulling her, threw her half back over the cot.

"You will try to escape," he told her.

He then snapped the other cuff about the curved iron bar at the head of the cot, securing her to it.

"This will discourage you," he said.

Brenda Hamilton leaped to her feet, pulling at the cuff, jerking the iron cot. She was perfectly secured to it. Bent over, her hand at the curved iron bar, cuffed to it, she watched Gunther leave.

"There is no escape," said Gunther, closing the door behind him.

She heard the locking of the door.

With the frenzy of a caught she-animal she jerked at the cuff. She was held perfectly. Moaning she threw herself on the cot, her left wrist on the mattress, just below the bar. She heard the cuff slide on the iron. She jerked at it. And then she lay still, weeping.

There was no escape for Brenda Hamilton.

◊ **5** ◊

"Where is the fork?" asked the black.

Brenda Hamilton, no longer handcuffed, kneeling across the room from him, away from the door, looked at him blankly. "There was only the spoon," she said. She was never given a knife. The black looked at the tray on the cot, the tin mug, the crumbs, the spoon.

He had not been the one who had brought the tray.

He regarded her, suspiciously. She saw the pistol, strapped in the holster at his side.

He walked toward her, across the wooden floor. She did not raise her eyes.

Suddenly she felt his hand in her hair, and she felt herself half lifted, twisted, forced to look at him. "Please!" she wept.

"Where is the fork?" he asked. She could not meet his eyes.

"There was only a spoon!" she wept. "Stop! You're hurting me!"

He pulled her to her feet, bent over, she crying out, and with two strides, she running, to ease the pain on her head, dashed her, jerking her head to one side at the last moment, against the wall. His hand had not left her hair. She slumped against the wall, weeping. Then she cried out as he jerked her again to her feet and, with quick strides, ran her against the other wall, again jerking her head back at the last instant. She struck the wall with force, her head jerked sideways, twisted. The top of her head screamed with pain. She reached up to his hand, her small fingers at his wrist. She could not dislodge his hand. He twisted her hair again and she quickly drew back her hands, submitting to the lesser pain, acknowledging to him his control.

"Where is the fork?" he asked.

"There was only a spoon," she wept. "Please! Please! Ask the boy who brought it!"

"Boy?" he asked.

"The man!" she cried. "Ask the man who brought it!"

He pulled her to her feet, and, she weeping, ran her against the far wall, and then back again, each time forcing her to strike the wall with great force, jerking back her head. Never did his hand leave her hair. Then, angrily, he threw her to the floor, releasing her. She lay on her stomach, her hands covering as best she could her head and hair, weeping. She sensed his boots on either side of her body.

"Where is the fork?" he asked.

"The man didn't bring one!" she wept. "Ask him! Please ask him!"

He stepped over her body. She heard him leave the room. Her thin, cotton dress was soaked with sweat. Her body ached. She sensed it would be bruised. Her head, her scalp, still shrieked with pain.

But she lay on the floor, and smiled.

She had gained time. The black might not ask the other about the fork. The other might not remember. And for the whites, William, Gunther, Herjellsen, it would be only their word against hers.

With the fork, splinter by splinter, working within the closet, cutting through to the outside, she might escape!

The closet was never opened. She would put the tiny pile of debris within it and then, after dark, try to open the stucco, slip through, and get to the fence. It would not take long to dig under it, the ground was soft and dry. And then she could run and run, and run, and come, with luck, sooner or later, to a bush road, a strip road, or a graveled road, and be picked up, and carried to safety.

In the daylight, in a few hours, she might, without water, without shelter, collapse in the heat, perhaps die, but in the night, in the comparative coolness, she might be able to make several miles.

It might be enough. It must be enough!

She thought of the leopard, and was frightened, and of snakes.

But there were things she feared more then leopards, or snakes, or the blacks. She feared Gunther, and Herjellsen, and the experimental shack.

She must escape!

With the fork she had the chance!

She smiled.

She heard someone on the porch, three people. Quickly she looked up, startled.

Her eyes furtively darted to where she had hidden the fork.

She knew her story. She would stick to it.

She heard the padlocks being opened, removed from the staples, heard the locks falling on their chains against the wood of the door.

Quickly she knelt, assuming the position of submission before men.

But this time she felt a surge of joy she tried to conceal. She might be a woman, and a prisoner, but she, too, was a human being, and could be clever and cunning. She was a woman. She had been taught her femaleness. But she was not a simpleton, not a fool!

She was clever, cunning. She would fool them all and escape!

The door opened.

Brenda Hamilton was startled. Herjellsen stood in the doorway. It was the first time since her captivity that she had seen him. She gasped.

She looked at him.

He regarded her. She knew it was the first time he had seen her dressed as a woman, and as a woman prisoner of men.

"Please get up," said Herjellsen. He blinked through the thick lenses of his glasses, glanced about the room.

Gratefully Brenda Hamilton rose to her feet.

Herjellsen returned his attention to her.

"You are an extremely attractive young woman, Doctor Hamilton," said Herjellsen.

"Thank you," said Brenda Hamilton.

"You have been crying," he said. "Please, if you would, wash away your tears."

Gratefully, Brenda Hamilton went to the water bucket, and with water, and a towel, washed her face.

"I do not like to see a woman's tears," said Herjellsen.

Brenda Hamilton said nothing.

Herjellsen looked at her.

"Please brush your hair now," said Herjellsen.

Obediently, Brenda Hamilton, while Herjellsen, and the two blacks watched, brushed her hair.

Then she turned to face them. "Ah," said Herjellsen, "that is better."

They regarded one another.

"Now," said Herjellsen, "where is the missing implement?"

"What implement?" asked Brenda Hamilton.

"The missing fork," said Herjellsen.

"There was no fork," said Brenda Hamilton. "One was not brought with the tray." She looked at the large black, who had abused her. "I told him that," she said. "But he did not believe me." Her voice trembled. "Look," she said, indicating a bruise on her arm, where she had been hurled into the wall. "He was cruel to me!"

But Herjellsen did not admonish the black.

"He hurt me!" said Brenda Hamilton.

"At the least sign of insubordination," said Herjellsen, "you must expect to be physically disciplined."

"I see," she said.

"Now," said Herjellsen, "where is the fork?"

"One was not brought," said Brenda Hamilton.

Herjellsen regarded her.

"Look!" she said, angrily. "Search the cell. I do not care!"

"That will not be necessary," said Herjellsen.

Brenda Hamilton looked at him.

"You will lead me to it," he said.

The golden light of the late Rhodesian afternoon filtered into the room, between the bars, through the netting.

"Approach me, my dear," said Herjellsen.

Hesitantly, Brenda Hamilton, barefoot, in the thin, white dress, sleeveless, approached him.

He then stood slightly behind her, to her left, and placed his hand on her arm, above her elbow.

"There is nothing mysterious," he told her, "in what I am now going to do."

Brenda Hamilton was terrified.

"It is a simple magician's trick," said Herjellsen. "It is called muscle reading. The principle is extremely simple. You will find that you are unable to control the subtle, almost unconscious movements of your arm muscles."

"No!" she cried. She felt his hand on her arm. His grip was not tight, but it was firm, and strong. She knew herself held.

"You must not, of course," said Herjellsen, "think of the location of the missing implement."

Immediately the location of the hidden fork flew into

Brenda Hamilton's mind, the inevitable response to the psychological suggestion of Herjellsen's remark.

She felt herself helplessly, uncontrollably, pull away from its location.

"It seems," said Herjellsen, "that it is on this side of the room," indicating the direction she had pulled away from.

Brenda Hamilton moaned. She tried to clear her mind.

"We must find it, mustn't we, my dear?" asked Herjellsen.

Again its hiding place darted into her mind.

Herjellsen guided her in the direction she had pulled away from.

She tried to relax her body, her arm, to think nothing. "Please," she said.

Herjellsen stopped. "Excellent," he said. "We must not be tense."

Immediately Brenda Hamilton's body, helpless under the suggestion, tensed.

"Ah," said Herjellsen. He led her to the corner of the room.

She trembled. She stood in the corner, where the two walls joined. There was only the bleakness of the white plaster. "There was no fork," she said. "You see?" She looked at Herjellsen, her lip trembling. "There is nothing here," she said.

"Get the fork," said Herjellsen to the black, the large fellow. He came to where they stood.

Herjellsen released her. Brenda Hamilton ran to the center of the room.

The black reached up to where Herjellsen indicated, where the walls stopped, and the sloping, peaked, tin corrugated ceiling began, with its metal and beams.

He took down the fork, from where Brenda had thrust it, at the top of the wall, under the tin.

He put it in his shirt pocket.

"Lie down across the cot," said Herjellsen to Brenda Hamilton, "head down, hands on the floor."

She did so.

"At the least sign of insubordination," he said, "you must expect to be physically disciplined."

Herjellsen turned away. "Two strokes," he said to the guards.

He left the room.

Brenda Hamilton, fighting tears, felt the dress thrust up over the small of her back, heard the rustle of the heavy belt pulled through its loops. It was doubled. She was struck twice, sharply.

Then they left her.

Brenda Hamilton crawled on the cot and stretched out on it, red-eyed, humiliated.

The room was now half dark as the dusty afternoon faded into the dusk. She heard insect noises outside.

She did not turn on the electric light bulb.

It was an unusually docile Brenda Hamilton who was served her meal that evening.

When the black had left the room she lifted her head and sped to the tray.

Her heart leaped. There was again both a fork and spoon with the mug and tray.

William, if the usual routine obtained, would pick up the tray.

She washed her body and her face, and even the garment and put it quickly back on. In the hot Rhodesian night it would dry in minutes on her body. She combed her hair, and brushed it until it was glossy. Then, a few minutes before ten P.M. she bolted down her meal. She thrust the fork into her mattress.

At ten promptly, as was usual, William entered the room. He didn't look at her.

"You heard what happened?" she asked.

"I heard you were foolish," said William.

"Look at me, William," she said.

He did so. She smiled.

He seemed angry with her. She flushed slightly. Doubtless Gunther had made his report.

But she smiled her prettiest and lifted the spoon left on the tray.

"I tried to hide a fork today," she said. "And now look," she pouted, "I have only this spoon to eat with. I feel silly, eating meat with a spoon. They treat me like I was a child."

"Oh?" asked William. He looked at her, closely.

"See if you can't get them, tomorrow, not tonight, to let me have a fork again."

"You don't need it," said William.

"Don't be cruel to me, William," she said.

"Herjellsen must have given them their orders," he said.

"See if you can get him to change them tomorrow, when he is in a better mood," she wheedled. She smiled at him.

William basked in her smile.

"You are quite beautiful," he said, "when you smile. Very well, tomorrow I will ask Herjellsen to permit you to have the proper utensils."

"Thank you, William," she breathed.

"But no knife, mind you," laughed William.

"Oh, of course not," she laughed, "—Master!"

"You make a pretty slave, Brenda," said William.

Brenda Hamilton fell to her knees before him, and put her head to his feet. "The slave is grateful to her master," she laughed.

William looked down at her. "I see," he said, "that it is a social misfortune that the institution of female slavery was abolished."

Brenda looked up at him, deferentially. "Yes, Master," she said.

"Last night," said William, suddenly, angrily, "you were on your knees before Gunther."

She looked up at him, agonized.

"Don't get up," said William.

She put her head down.

"Beg me to fuck you," said William.

"Please, William," she whispered.

"Do it," he said, "you little whore."

"No!" she wept. "I wanted to be had by Gunther. I wanted it! I needed it!"

"And you don't need it from me," said William.

"Please, William," she said, "I like you—you're the only one who is kind to me. I like you. I do like you!" She lifted her eyes to him.

"Say it," said William. "I want to hear it."

"I—I beg you to fuck me, William," whispered Brenda Hamilton.

"Slut!" said William.

He picked up the tray and mug, and spoon, and angrily left the room.

He did not look back.

Elated, Brenda Hamilton ran to the light switch and turned it off, and went to the mattress and took the fork from it. The first check, she knew, would not come until eleven o'clock. She counted the minutes, as carefully as she could, while she worked in the closet, as silently as she could, digging at the plaster, flaking it away. Giving herself a margin of safety she went and lay down in the cot, as though asleep. She hated each wasted minute lying there, but, at last, some ten minutes after she had lain down, she sensed the flashlight in the room, through the window, and falling on her apparently sleeping body. When it had left she leaped to her feet and began her work again. It was shortly before midnight, and the second check, when she came to the coating of stucco that formed the outside of the hut. She returned to the cot, a sleeping prisoner. When the light had passed again, she returned to the work. It took only some fifteen minutes to work away enough of the stucco to make a hole large enough for her to crawl through. This would give her, if she were successful in escaping the compound, a lead of only some forty-five minutes. She slipped from the building. She looked back. She must leave the hole exposed. There was nothing with which to conceal it. She hoped it would not be noted. The compound was lit by the four lights on poles, illuminating the dirt grounds, making them seem hard and yellow. The hole was on the side of the building, away from the light. She hoped it would not be noticed.

She went to the end of the small building. Then she fell to her stomach in the shadows at the side of the building.

Between her and the fence one of the blacks was walking his rounds, his rifle over his shoulder.

She remained lying there for some minutes. She counted the seconds between his rounds. She was in tears. She would not have time to get to the fence and tunnel under the wire. Then, in her counting, the guard did not pass when she expected him to. Her heart leaped. Perhaps he had stopped somewhere, to relieve himself, or drink, or smoke, or chat with his partner, perhaps at the gate.

She scurried from hiding and began, with her hands and her fork, to dig frenziedly at the wire. The ground was dry and soft, powdery. In a matter of two or three minutes, on her stomach, she slithered under the hanging wire. A barb ripped through the shoulder of her dress and she cried out half blinded with sparks and pain. There had been a crack-ling, and her inadvertent cry of terror and pain. She scram-bled to her feet, stunned, sick, her vision swimming with blasts of light, and vomited in the dust, and then, stumbling, fled into the darkness.

Apparently her cry and the crackling of the sparks had not been heard.

Outside the compound, sick, some hundred yards away, she collapsed in the brush and looked back.

No one was coming. There was no pursuit. The compound was large. No one had apparently heard her.

She threw up again from the shock of the fence. She wanted only to lie down and rest.

She staggered to her feet.

She began to stumble through the brush.

It had been a nightmare of running, but Brenda Hamilton, at three forty in the morning, reached a road, her legs bleeding, dust in her hair, her body coated with dirt.

She lay beside the road, gasping, on the side away from the direction from which she had come.

She could scarcely breathe, she could scarcely move her body.

The dress was half torn from her.

What now if there were no vehicle? There might not be any. This was not a commonly traveled road. It was late at night. When she had been with Gunther and William in the Land Rover, in all their driving, they had passed no vehicle.

She moaned.

She would die in the bush, without food and water. She feared leopards, and snakes.

She knew no way to a village.

She could walk the road. It would lead somewhere. But she, having stopped, found it almost impossible to get to her feet. She closed her eyes.

Then, from the distance, she heard a vehicle, coming down the road.

Her heart leaped, and she crawled to the side of the road.

She saw the two headlights. She heard the engine. The vehicle was coming with rapidity.

What if it would not stop for her?

Painfully she stood up, on the surface of the road, gasping. The gravel hurt her feet.

They must stop for her!

The headlights were approaching rapidly.

They were hurrying. They would not stop!

But they would! She would flag them down! They must stop! They must!

The headlights were now looming, like eyes. She heard the grinding of the gravel under the wheels of the vehicle, the thick roar of the engine.

She stood out, almost in the center of the road, and lifted her hand.

She waved wildly.

She lifted both of her arms and ran toward the headlights, weeping.

They must stop!

To her joy she heard the driver remove his foot from the accelerator and heard the scattering and crunching of gravel under the tires as the vehicle began to slow down.

She ran toward it, illuminated in its headlights, as it ground to a halt.

"Help me!" she cried.

She stopped.

The Land Rover was stopped now, the motor still running. Gunther leaped out, onto the road.

She screamed and turned, and streaked into the brush. She ran and ran.

She heard the Land Rover start again, turn off the road. She saw it plowing after her.

She darted through the brush, crying.

It dodged small trees, suddenly bright in its headlights, it rode over brush, through dips and high grass, jolting, falling and climbing.

Running, she heard the engine behind her, the breaking of brush, the sound of the tires.

Suddenly she was illuminated in the headlights.

She was terrified they would run her down. Then the Land Rover turned to one side, her left, as she ran, and was behind her and on the left.

She ran, stumbling. She felt herself caught in the blaze of the hand searchlight mounted near the front, right window.

"Wir haben sie!" she heard Gunther cry, elated. He almost never spoke German.

She heard the crack of the compressed-air rifle and was suddenly stung in the side. She was knocked off her feet by the impact and rolled for more than a dozen feet. Then she scrambled to her feet again, and began to run again, stumbling. She heard the Land Rover following her, slowly. She ran for perhaps a hundred yards, and then fell, and got up and, slowly, began to stumble away again. The Land Rover seemed to move almost at her very side. She was conscious of the headlights on the brush. She was aware that she, herself, was illuminated in the hand searchlight at the side of the vehicle. With her fingers, reeling, she felt the dart sunk in her side. It had penetrated the thin cotton dress and had fastened itself deeply in her flesh. She stumbled, and fell. She heard the Land Rover stop. She tried to crawl away, and then fell to her stomach. She fought to keep conscious. She knew she lay in the light of the hand searchlight. She heard the door of the Land Rover open. She heard booted feet leap to the ground. She heard the booted feet approach her. Her right hand, first, was dragged behind her body and snapped in a handcuff, and then her left. She lay cuffed. A hand forcibly jerked out the dart. She heard it placed in the pocket of a leather jacket. Then she felt herself being lifted lightly to a man's shoulders, her head over his back, and carried to the Land Rover.

She moaned, and fell unconscious.

◊ **6** ◊

Dr. Brenda Hamilton awakened.

She lay on her side on the cot. Her left hand, extended, lay under the curved iron bar at the top of the cot; her right hand lay beside her face; she looked at the slender, small fingers; it seemed so small, so delicate compared to that of Gunther, or William, or Herjellsen, to a man's hand.

The half light of late afternoon, golden, hazy, filtering, dimly illuminated the room.

The white-washed interior seemed golden and dim. She looked up at the arched roof, its beams, the corrugated tin. It was hot, terribly hot. She remembered that she seldom spent time in her quarters before sundown. She remembered that she had, once, awakened similarly. She remembered then that she was a prisoner.

She tried to move her hand, her left hand. Something jerked at it. She heard a steel cuff slide on iron. She sat up. She was handcuffed to the iron bar at the head of the cot.

She sat wearily at the edge of the cot. She wanted to relieve herself. She looked across the room to the wastes bucket.

She got up, to pull the cot to the side of the room. It remained fixed.

It had been bolted to the floor. It was aligned with the floor boards designated by Gunther. She smiled. The alignment of the cot was no longer her responsibility.

She considered, briefly, urinating on the floor, or soiling the mattress.

She would not do so.

She knew she was, at the slightest sign of insubordination, subject to physical discipline, and that it would be, unhesitantly, administered. She wondered what they would do to her for having attempted to escape.

How foolishly she had run to their arms. How easily she had been recaptured.

She remembered the Land Rover pursuing her, terrifying her, loud and roaring, through the midnight bush, the glare of its lights, the sting of the anesthetic bullet, Gunther's cuffs.

She looked at the girl in the mirror, facing her, sitting on the edge of the cot, a steel cuff confining her to it. The girl was weary, filthy, her dress torn, her hair awry and filled with dust; her face was dirty; her hands were dirty, and there was dirt, from digging, black, under the fingernails; her legs were covered, too, with dirt, and scratches and blood.

They had brought her in as she was, from the bush, thrown her on the cot, handcuffed her to it, and left.

She was hungry, and thirsty, and wanted to relieve herself, and clean her body.

She lay back, on her side, her legs drawn up, on the striped mattress, on the cot, her left hand under the curved iron bar at its head.

She smelled her body. She smelled, too, fresh plaster. The hut, she conjectured, where she had broken through it, through the closet, had been repaired.

She closed her eyes against the heat.

Then, almost against her will, she opened her eyes, wanting to look again in the mirror. Lying on her side she regarded herself, her head and hair, her figure, the curve of her hip and waist, the dress well up her thighs, the curves of her legs and ankles. She looked at herself, sullenly. She did not jerk at the handcuff. She lay quietly, secured. She had not escaped.

At six P.M. the door was unlocked.

The large black, who had beaten her, entered. His companion entered behind him.

Behind them came Herjellsen, and Gunther and William.

Brenda sat up.

Gunther came to her and unlocked the cuff from her left wrist.

Hamilton rubbed her wrist.

Herjellsen motioned for Dr. Brenda Hamilton to lie across the cot, as she had before, her hands on the floor, her head down.

The smaller black then dragged the dress up over her body, and half over her head, confining her arms in it.

"Beat her," said Herjellsen.

While the men watched, the larger black, with his belt, doubled, struck her, sharply, below the small of the back, fifteen times.

The beating, Hamilton knew, was not intended to be physically punishing. It was intended to be emotionally humiliating. It was. But, too, it stung, terribly. She could not keep tears from her eyes. She felt like a child. She knew it was not a man's beating, but a woman's beating. In tears, she realized it was more in the nature of a severe rebuke for naughtiness than anything else. It meant, clearly, that they were not particularly annoyed with her, that she had not worried them, that her escape attempt had not been, and was not, taken seriously. Her effort, to herself, though foiled, had been momentous, desperate. Now it was being punished, sharply, but trivially. She supposed she was being punished at all, only because she had been insubordinate, and they felt that something in response, however trivial, should be done to her. She asked herself if this was all her escape attempt was worth to them, all it had earned her.

The beating also told her that she was a woman, not worth the severe discipline that might be accorded a male.

That, too, humiliated her.

It taught her in a new way that she was a female, only a female.

She wept, too, because Gunther and William were watching. How could she face them again?

The last blow fell.

Gunther pulled her, she still tangled in her dress, sobbing, to her side. Her left wrist was jerked to the vicinity of the iron bar at the head of the cot. She felt it locked again in the cuff that dangled there.

She was confined as before.

The men left.

She, furious, frustrated, helpless, felt like a punished child. She wept. She was furious at what men could do to women, if they wished. She hated their strength, and her own weakness. They can treat us like children, she wept.

"I hate you!" she cried.

Then she was afraid that they might hear her, and return to punish her again. "I hate you," she whispered. "I hate you." But mostly she hated herself, that she was a woman.

How could she ever again face Gunther and William?

Then she knew how she could face them again, and only how she could face them again, only as a woman—a woman —and one they had seen being beaten.

Then, after a time, she no longer hated being a woman. She lay on the thin, flat, striped mattress, on her side, her wrist helplessly handcuffed to the iron bar at the head of the simple cot, and looked at herself in the mirror. Her small, luscious, curved body, captive, formed a remarkable contrast to the thin, flat mattress, its linearity, the plainness of the iron cot, on which she was confined. She studied herself in the mirror, her head and hair, the deliciousness of her body, her legs, the slenderness of her ankles. Then no longer did she hate that she was a woman. She found it again, strangely perhaps, a precious thing to be. And she found herself, too, strangely enough, pleased that men were strong enough to do to her what they had done. She found herself, for some strange reason, pleased that one sex was so much weaker than the other. And, perhaps most strange of all, she found herself pleased that she was of the weaker sex.

She found, as she lay on the cot, captive, handcuffed to it, that the strength of men excited her, that she found it profoundly and unaccountably exciting.

I love it that there are men, she whispered to herself. I love it. I love it!

At ten P.M. the door was again unlocked.

The large black, he who had beaten her, again entered. Lying on the cot, she cringed. But he carried a large piece of bread in one hand and a tin mug of water in the other. Brenda saw, briefly, his companion behind him, before the door closed.

He approached her.

She regarded him with fear.

"Sit up," he said.

She did so. She winced.

"Open your mouth," he said.

She did so.

He thrust the bread into her mouth, whole.

He waited until she had, half choking, swallowed it down. Then he held the tin mug for her. She drank.

Before he left, with his foot, he shoved the wastes bucket to the cot.

For four days Hamilton saw no one but the blacks, and her feedings consisted of bread and water, each given to her as they had been the first time.

Sometimes, smiling, she tried to engage them in conversation, but they did not speak to her.

Once, angrily, she cried out, "Speak when you're spoken to, Boy!"

He turned, slowly, toward her.

"I'm sorry," she whispered. "I'm sorry!"

His hand struck her, knocking her forcibly to her right. She was jerked up short by the handcuff, taut, on her left wrist. He pulled her to her knees at the side of the cot, facing him. "I'm sorry!" she cried. Her lip was cut on her teeth. He pointed to his feet. She kissed them. "I'm sorry," she said. "I'm sorry!"

"Very well," said he, "—Girl."

He left.

On the fourth night, she said to him, "Please tell them I'll be good! I'll be good!"

"All right," he said.

"Thank you," she said.

The next morning Gunther and William arrived at the time of the first feeding.

Gunther carried a short length of chain, and two padlocks, and William a bowl of warm water, with a towel and soap, and a clean, folded garment.

"Lie on your stomach on the cot," said Gunther.

"Yes, Gunther," said Brenda Hamilton.

She felt one end of the heavy chain looped about her left ankle, snugly, and fastened with one of the padlocks. The loose end of the short chain was then looped about her right ankle, snugly, and fastened with the second padlock.

Gunther then removed the handcuff from her left wrist, and also from the iron bar at the head of the cot.

"Kneel," he said.

Free of the cot, she did so. She heard the heavy links of the chain confining her ankles strike the floor.

"You will wear the cuff at night," said Gunther.

"Yes, Gunther," she said.

Gunther slipped the handcuffs, together, into a small leather case, worn at his belt. He buttoned shut the case.

"And during the day?" she asked.

"You are shackled," he said.

"Yes, Gunther," she said.

"Is that not the answer to your question?" he asked.

"Yes, Gunther," she said.

"The experiments are progressing," said Gunther. "You will shortly be needed."

She looked up at him.

"You will not receive the least opportunity for escape," said Gunther.

She put down her head.

"Do you understand, Brenda?" he said.

"Yes, Gunther," she said.

He then turned and left.

William smiled, and put down the bowl of warm water, with the towel, and soap, and laid beside them the small, white, folded garment.

She looked at it.

"It is identical to the one you are wearing," he said, "only, of course, it is not filthy, not torn, not marked with blood. It was not dragged through the Rhodesian bush in the middle of the night."

"I did not know there was more than one," she said, numbly, looking at it.

"You are permitted, of course," said William, "only one at a time."

She looked up at him, then understanding better than before the planning that had taken place.

"When was it purchased?" she asked.

"With four others," smiled William.

"When?" she asked, looking at him.

"When you accepted the retainer," he said, "to come to Rhodesia."

"I see," she said.

"These garments were here," he said, "folded and waiting, packed, before your arrival."

"When I walked in the gate," she said, "they were waiting for me."

"Yes," smiled William.

She put her head down.

"Don't put it on," warned William, "until you are clean and fresh."

"Very well, William," she said.

"When you are finished," he said, "knock on the door. I will then bring you water and a shampoo, to wash your hair."

Brenda looked at him, gratefully.

When he left the room she knelt by the bowl and threw off the soiled, tattered garment she had worn. Rejoicing, she cleansed her body of the dirt, the filth, of the bush. She wrapped the towel about her head, to keep her hair from her body. She slipped on the new, fresh, pressed, crisp white frock. It was identical to that which she had first worn, thin, very brief, sleeveless. She knocked on the door. "William," she said.

The door opened and William entered, with two buckets of water, and a shampoo, and a fresh towel.

He sat in one of the cane chairs, straddling it, its back to her, watching her wash her hair.

"The brush and comb," he said, "when you want them later, are where you left them."

They lay at the side of the wall.

She knelt before the mirror and ran the comb through her hair, straightening it. She would comb and brush it later, fully, when it was dry. It lay wet and black, matted, straight, beautiful, down her back.

When she looked at him, he said, "Shave your legs, and under your arms." He handed her a safety razor, containing a blade.

She used the soap and water, and the blade, and shaved herself.

Then she returned the razor, and the blade, to him.

William picked up the materials he had brought, the buckets, the bowl, the two towels, the other things.

She stood and faced him.

"You are very beautiful, Brenda" he said.

She said nothing.

"If you are good," he said, "you will be fed well."

She did not respond.

"Well, Brenda," he said, "it seems that things are much as they were before."

"Yes, William," she said.

"Except," smiled he, "that your ankles are chained."

She did not answer him.

"You have very pretty ankles, my dear," he said. "They look well in chains."

There were only eight inches of chain separating her ankles.

"Keep yourself clean, neat and well groomed," he said.

She said nothing.

"Kneel," he said.

She did.

"Do you understand?" he asked.

"Yes, William," said Brenda Hamilton.

He turned to leave and then again, for a moment, faced her.

"Tonight," he said, "you are to be interviewed by Herjellsen."

"What are you?" asked Herjellsen, sharply.

"A woman," said Brenda Hamilton. "A woman!"

"What is your name?" demanded Herjellsen, sharply.

"Brenda," she said. "Brenda!"

Herjellsen leaned back in the cane chair, satisfied. It was only then that Brenda Hamilton realized how different her responses were to such questions than they would have been only two weeks ago. Before, she would have responded, unthinkingly, to the first question, "A mathematician!" and, to the second, "Doctor Brenda Hamilton."

She knelt before Herjellsen. Her ankles were still chained. But now, too, by Gunther, her wrists had been handcuffed behind her.

Gunther and William, also on cane chairs, sitting across them, sat to one side, listening.

"The interview is over," said Herjellsen, getting up.

Brenda Hamilton looked up at him, astonished.

"What do you think of men?" asked Herjellsen, looking down on her.

"I—I think they are very strong," said Brenda Hamilton.

"Do you desire sexual experience?" asked Herjellsen.

"No!" cried Brenda Hamilton. "No!"

"Gunther's report," said Herjellsen, "suggests otherwise."

Brenda blushed scarlet. She recalled she had, on her knees, begged Gunther to fuck her.

"That you desire, or do not desire, sexual experience," said Herjellsen, "is doubtless less relevant to the success of the experiment than whether or not you, yourself, are, by others, found sexually desirable."

"Others?" asked Brenda Hamilton.

"But," said William, "when a woman does desire sexual experience she becomes, surely, subtly, physically, more desirable."

"You have in mind," asked Herjellsen, "subconscious body signals?"

"Yes," said William, "but even more obvious than that such things as smiling, inadvertent posings and touchings, approaching the male more closely than the culturally accustomed distances."

"How do you read her?" asked Herjellsen. He again took his seat on the cane chair. He looked at Hamilton.

"I have studied her," said William, "and I read in her body great conflict between resistance and yielding."

"I do not find conflict," said Gunther. "If I snap my fingers, she will lay for me."

Hamilton put down her head.

"I mean more generally," said William. "For example, today, while I watched her comb her wet hair before the mirror, she was obviously holding herself differently than if I were not present."

Hamilton swallowed. She realized she had performed this act differently, when under the eyes of William. She had done it more slowly, more luxuriously, more beautifully, than she would have otherwise.

"That is natural," said Herjellsen. "It is only a young female posing before a young male."

"Look at her now," said Gunther. "See the shoulders, back, the belly tight. She is presenting herself to us, even now, as a female."

Hamilton put down her head and wept.

"Do not weep," said Herjellsen. "It is natural female display behavior. It is quite healthy."

Hamilton looked up at him.

"The only thing to be ashamed of," said Herjellsen, "is the guilt."

Hamilton regarded him, red-eyed.

"You are really quite beautiful," said Herjellsen. "Straighten your body, put your shoulders back, draw in your stomach, thrust out your breasts."

Tears in her eyes, Hamilton did so.

William whistled. "A beauty," he said.

And suddenly Hamilton was no longer ashamed to be beautiful before men. That right was hers. She was a female. She would be beautiful, boldly.

"A true beauty," said William.

Hamilton looked at Gunther.

"A slut," said Gunther.

Hamilton tossed her head, and did not retreat. She looked

away from him, her head in the air. She remained beautiful.

"Excellent," said Herjellsen.

He turned to William.

"How do you read this woman's attitude toward Gunther?" he asked.

"She desires him, intensely," said William. His voice was flat.

Hamilton did not look at Gunther.

"Some women," said Gunther, "who do not desire sexual experience, are extremely attractive. Their very coldness, their haughtiness, is a taunt to the blood, a challenge. It is great sport to take them, and reduce them to whining, panting whores, to break them to your will, to make them beg for your touch."

Hamilton swallowed, painfully. Her shoulders fell forward. She bent forward, her head was down. She was again only a chained, handcuffed girl kneeling before men, at their mercy.

"Weakness, and fear, too," Gunther was saying, "can enhance a woman's sexual attractiveness."

"Among mammals," said William, "one is the aggressor, one the aggressed upon. This is the sexual equation. In most species of mammals, if not all, it is the male which is the aggressor. Sexual aggression in the female commonly neutralizes male aggression and makes consummation of the sexual act impossible. It is a common device used by women hostile to men, to prevent intercourse and insult and punish the male. In their own mind, and in his, if he is uninformed, she appears to be eager for sexual experience and he appears to be unable to satisfy her, or to be impotent. With another woman, of course, he functions normally."

"I encountered, twice, such women," said Gunther. "I beat them."

"Scarcely gentlemanly of you, old man," said William.

"After they were beaten," said Gunther, "they responded perfectly."

"Abjectly?" asked William.

"Yes," said Gunther, "and with numerous orgasms." He looked at William. "They only wanted to find a man stronger than they were. Strong women, they wanted stronger men, men strong enough to make them women, strong enough to subdue them, completely."

"And you were that man?" asked William.

"Yes," said Gunther. "In their hearts, like all women, they wanted to submit."

"And you made them submit?" asked William.

"Yes," said Gunther, "I made them submit." He looked at William. "I made them submit to me—completely."

"And doubtless they loved it?" asked William.

"That was not my concern," said Gunther.

"What was your concern?" asked William.

"Their submission," said Gunther.

"Did they seem pleased?" asked William.

"They were obedient," said Gunther, "and had numerous orgasms. They wished me to keep them with me, on any terms. One was rich."

"You see, Gunther," said Hamilton, "I am not the only woman who is attracted to you."

"You were not spoken to," said Gunther.

"Forgive me, Gunther," whispered Hamilton.

"Weakness and fear, as I said," said Gunther, "can enhance a woman's attractiveness."

"They provoke the aggressor," said William.

"What of servility, and submissiveness?" asked Herjellsen of Gunther.

"Yes," said Gunther, "particularly if they are enforced upon her—if she is given no choice." Gunther regarded Hamilton. "Women revel in groveling," he said.

"That is not true!" cried Hamilton.

"Be silent," said Gunther.

Hamilton put down her head. Something deep within her stirred. Though she hated the thought, she knew that she was pleased to have been so sharply commanded. Gunther had given her an order, a strict one. It excited her to obey him.

"What of helplessness?" asked Herjellsen of William.

"Yes," said William, "helplessness in a woman tends to provoke sexual aggression; it stimulates the male. This expresses itself, of course, in countless ways. She needs him, say, to open a window, carry a bag, move a heavy object. Both he and she are conscious of her weakness; she must ask his favor; he readily performs the tasks; she now owes him, and she, being weak, being a woman, has only her body with which to pay him. She responds with sexual favors; in the civilized situation, these are trivial—smiles, words of gratitude, an entire body attitude of gratefulness. That the male wants these favors is indicated by his customary fury, should she offer monetary payment. It is her 'thanks' alone he wants. Naturally. Her 'thanks,' of course, are a culturally accepted, little understood, muchly desired by the male display of her femaleness before him. Symbolically, he has had

her; winning her smile is for him surrogate for the possession of her body."

"Interesting," said Herjellsen.

"A most obvious example," said William, "occurs when
the woman must take the automobile, in need of repair, to
a mechanic. Though her socio-economic status may be far
above his she must, in her ignorance, her helplessness, approach the mechanic with typical female submission behavior. Moreover, he will exploit this situation, by being
patient, by looming over her, by listening to her attempt to
explain the problem of the engine. Very few individuals,
incidentally, can speak clearly of a complicated piece of
machinery, or even know more than a few names for parts.
Yet the mechanic's attitude will make her feel inferior,
ignorant, stupid, and he, by contrast, large and wise, efficient
and strong. Soon she will be laughing at herself, and pretending she knows even less than she does. She finds herself
forced into acting like a fool, petitioning for a favor. She
smiles, she laughs uneasily, she moves her body, she is
embarrassed, she blushes, she looks up at him. He agrees to
repair the vehicle. He will find out what is wrong, and whatever it is he, the noble fellow, will fix it. She leaves. He has
had a sexual experience. Similar exploitative matrices may
exist in the context of the female student and male teacher,
or the female employee and the male employer. Females
are forced, in thousands of ways, to be pleasing to men,
and, as they struggle to smile, and be pleasing, he symbolically enjoys her, has her, accepts her, for the time, as
one of his women."

"What do you think of this, Gunther?" asked Herjellsen.

"I think it is true," said Gunther. "Further, perhaps to
your surprise, I do not disapprove. Rather I approve. Wom-
en should smile, should be forced to engage in submission
behavior before men."

"Why is that?" asked Herjellsen.

"Because men are dominant," said Gunther. "And it is
right that women should submit to them." He looked at
Herjellsen. "Women do not smile and move provocatively
because society forces them to do so; they do so because
they are women; they are not the dominant sex. Display
behavior, and submission behavior, is always displayed,
throughout the animal kingdom, before the dominant organisms. It is natural for the dominant organism to elicit, or
enforce, this behavior. Your mechanic, he in William's anec-
dote, is dominant. It is thus natural for him to elicit, or en-

force, display behavior, submission behavior, in your upper-middle-class woman. She is, after all, whatever might be her socio-economic class, only a female."

"I'm afraid you are a male chauvinist, old man," said William.

"As a scientist," said Gunther, "I attempt to ascertain the truth. I do not respond like a slavering dog to political stimuli." ·

"When I spoke of helplessness," said Herjellsen, "I did not have in mind such things as being unable to locate one's car keys." ·

The three men looked at Hamilton. She had her head down. She knelt, the short white dress well up her thighs. Her ankles, each snugly, were confined in the short, chain shackle. Her wrists, behind her back, were locked in Gunther's cuffs.

"Brenda," asked Herjellsen. "Are you helpless?"

"Yes," said Brenda. She lifted her head, and looked at them, red-eyed. "How could I be more helpless?" she asked.

"If you were nude," said Gunther.

She put down her head.

"She is powerless, and at your mercy," said Herjellsen. "You are young males. Does that enhance her sexual attractiveness?"

"Yes," said Gunther.

"Yes," said William.

"It is natural," said Gunther, "for a man to want complete power, absolute power, over a woman."

"This has to do, perhaps," said William, "with the aggression-submission equation. For the male, maximum power facilitates total aggression; for the female, utter powerlessness gives her no alternative to complete submission."

"More important than such trivialities as handcuffs and ankle chains," · said Gunther, "is to force the female's psychological submission."

"Of course," said Herjellsen, "we are creatures with minds."

"The best lay that I ever had," said Gunther, "was a girl given to me for the night by a friend, four years ago, a Bedouin chieftain."

"What was she like?" asked William.

"Juicy, cuddly," he said, "brown, quick, large dark eyes, long black hair. When I pulled away her silk I saw that he had had her branded."

"Oh," gasped Hamilton.

"She was a slave girl," said Gunther, looking at her.

Hamilton averted her eyes. "Oh," she whispered.

"Yes," said Gunther, "a superb female slave—simply superb. When she entered the tent we both knew that she was in my absolute power. The psychological dimension was perfect. She stood there, waiting to be commanded. I could do with her what I pleased, and whatever it was that I pleased that is what I did with her. It was a most interesting evening."

"What did you do with her?" asked William.

"I could do with her what I pleased," said Gunther.

"And what did you do with her?" asked William.

"Exactly what I pleased," said Gunther.

"I see," said William.

"It was a most interesting evening," said Gunther.

Hamilton did not look up. She wished she had been that female slave.

"This seems practical," said Herjellsen, "only where there is an institution of female slavery, socially accepted, societally enforced."

"It is practical," said Gunther, "wherever men are willing to make slaves, and have the opportunity."

Hamilton wished that she were Gunther's slave.

"For example," said Gunther, "this compound is isolated." He gestured to Hamilton. "We could, if we wished, make her a slave."

Hamilton looked at him. She was frightened.

"Do not be afraid, Doctor Hamilton," said Herjellsen, "it is not we who will make you a slave."

"I don't understand," she whispered.

Herjellsen rose to his feet. "It is late," he said. He nodded curtly to Brenda Hamilton, kneeling before him. "Good evening, my dear," he said.

Then he, followed by William, left the room.

"Stand," snapped Gunther, "back to me."

Brenda Hamilton, shackled, looked up at him. "Please help me, Gunther," she said.

He placed his strong hands beneath her arms and lifted her lightly to her feet.

She stood close to him; shackled, wrists fastened behind her. She looked at him. "Please, Gunther," she said. She lifted her lips to him.

"Turn," he said.

She did so, and he, with his key, unlocked the handcuffs, and removed them from her wrists.

"Use the wastes bucket," he said. "I will return in five minutes."

"Yes, Gunther," she said, head down, blushing.

In five minutes he returned. She was sitting on the cot. He looked at her. Quickly, she knelt.

"Lie on your stomach on the cot," he said, "and place your left wrist under the iron bar."

She did so, and he approached her. She felt one cuff locked on her left wrist, and then the other she heard snapped about the iron bar at the head of the cot.

He then bent to her ankles.

He removed the chain that confined them.

She rolled to her back, suddenly, sliding the handcuff along the iron bar, twisting the links, and faced Gunther.

She laughed with pleasure.

She lifted one leg, and then the other. They were long, slender, shapely, lovely. She had her eyes closed. She moved them, slowly, exulting in the luxury of the movement. She lay then on her back, and opened her eyes. She stretched her left leg, and bent the right, knee lifted, heel on the mattress.

Gunther was watching her.

"It feels so good to move," she said. She smiled at Gunther.

He looked at her, angrily.

"You do find me attractive, don't you, Gunther?" she asked. She was smiling.

"Whore," said Gunther.

"Yes," laughed Brenda Hamilton, looking at him, "Doctor Brenda Hamilton is a whore."

Gunther regarded her, puzzled.

"I'm your whore," she said.

"I do not understand," he said.

"Every woman," said Brenda Hamilton, "if she is vital, for some man or other, would be his willing, eager whore."

Gunther looked at her.

"I'm yours," she said. She laughed.

"Whore!" he snapped.

"Only to you," she laughed. "Not to William, or Herjellsen, or the blacks."

He looked at her, not speaking.

"Sit beside me, Gunther," she said. "Please."

He did so. He sat on the edge of the cot, looking down on her, his left hand across her body, resting on the left side of the cot.

"I'm in your complete power, Gunther," she said. She

jerked at the handcuff, indicating that she was secured. She smiled. "You have absolute power over me," she said. "Does that not excite you?"

He said nothing. His eyes were expressionless.

"You can make me do anything you want," she said. "I will obey you, perfectly, completely."

With his right hand, he touched her head, and then, holding her face, turned it from one side to the other, looking at it.

"Perfectly, completely," she whispered.

He removed his hand from her face.

"Was the brown girl so marvelous?" she asked him.

"The slave?" asked Gunther.

"Yes," said Brenda Hamilton, "—the slave!"

"Yes," said Gunther.

"I can be better," she said.

"Oh?" asked Gunther.

"Try me," she said.

Gunther smiled.

"Have me stand before you," said Hamilton, "as she did, not knowing what you will command. See which of us is better!"

He put his hand at the neckline of her thin, cotton dress. She felt his fist in its fabric.

"Strip me!" she begged.

He looked down on her.

"I'm in your complete power, Gunther," she said. "You have absolute power over me! You can do with me what you want! Anything! Whatever you want! Does that not excite you?"

"Yes," he said.

"Too," she whispered, "it excites me! I have never been so excited in my life, Gunther!"

She tried to sit up on the cot and hold him with her right arm. With his left hand he forced her right wrist down, and pinned it to the mattress. The handcuff on her left wrist confined her hand at the bar. The steel slid on the iron. She could not rise. She was held. Gunther's right hand was still at the neckline of her frock.

She looked up at him.

"Could I not be your slave, like that brown girl?" she asked.

He did not answer her.

"Caress me, Gunther," she begged.

Gunther stood up, releasing her. "Others will caress you," he said.

"Others?" asked Hamilton.

"Yes," said Gunther.

"But what if I do not want others to caress me?" she asked.

"It does not matter," said Gunther. He bent down and picked up the chain and the two padlocks from the floor at the foot of the cot, and went to the door.

Brenda Hamilton rolled to her stomach, and screamed and sobbed, thrusting her mouth against the mattress. She squirmed and struck at the mattress, kicking it with her feet, pounding it with her right fist. She bit at it, sobbing, and scratched at it with the fingernails of her right hand. She turned on her side, and held out her hand to Gunther, who stood by the door.

"Gunther!" she wept.

"Tomorrow night," said Gunther, "we will attempt to initiate the final test sequence of the second series of experiments. Herjellsen has told me that you will be permitted to watch.

Hamilton regarded him, red-eyed.

"You yourself, as you have been informed," said Gunther, "will figure essentially in the third series of experiments."

"Why will you not make love to me?" asked Hamilton.

"Herjellsen has decided," said Gunther, "that you are to be transmitted as a virgin. He expects that it may enhance your value, if trading is pertinent."

"Value?" breathed Hamilton.

"Too, Herjellsen supposes," said Gunther, "that they might be less likely to slay a virgin. A virgin might be something of a prize."

"Who are—they?" asked Hamilton.

"We do not really know," said Gunther. "But we suspect that they will have some connection with the Herjellsen artifact."

"No!" cried Brenda Hamilton. "No! No!"

"There is some danger, of course," said Gunther, "in transmitting a virgin."

Hamilton looked at him.

"The sacrifice of virgin females may be practiced."

Hamilton regarded him with horror.

"But, in your case," said Gunther, "this seems unlikely. Lovely as you are you are in your twenties, and this, we conjecture, will be sufficient to remove you from this danger. Furthermore, such sacrifice, commonly, involves tribal girls of high station in the group, such being regarded as the fittest gifts for the gods." Gunther looked at Hamilton. "You, not so much a girl as a woman, a stranger, ignorant, one foreign to ·them, one with no standing, no status, we conjecture will stand in little danger of being regarded as a desirable sacrifice."

Hamilton sat now on the edge of the cot. She was aghast. She trembled.

"Furthermore," said Gunther, "we commonly associate the sacrifice of virgins with agricultural economies, where men are more dependent on factors outside of their control, the weather, for example, than with hunting economies, where the nature of acquiring food, and the efforts relevant to its acquisition, are more clearly understood. Perhaps more importantly in agricultural economies the population is larger and the social institutions and structures more complex. A larger population is doubtless more willing to expend certain of its members; further there is in a larger population, naturally, less personal contact among all members, and this makes the sacrificial expenditure of a given member of the group a much more impersonal matter; furthermore, in the agricultural economy, with its larger population, you have, doubtless, an extensive, complex cult tradition, perhaps with its professional witch doctors or priests, providing the population with an elaborate justification for ritualized homicide. Social developments of this complexity would be less likely to occur in a hunting group. Furthermore, in a hunting group, where life would be more precarious, it seems likely to suppose that it might also be regarded as more precious. Women would be needed to bear children and carry burdens. It is not likely that they would be used as the victims in ceremonial homicides."

"Oh, Gunther," wept Hamilton. "Help me to escape!"

"Hunting groups, we conjecture, too," said Gunther, "would, if they are to survive, be dominated by strong men, large men, rugged men, intelligent men, energetic, cunning and swift, men of much stamina, of sound constitution and hardy appetites."

Gunther looked at Hamilton, and she shuddered.

"Such men," said Gunther, "are likely to relish and appreciate, robustly, the bodies of their women. They will have better uses to put the bodies of their women to than human sacrifice."

· "You must help me to escape, Gunther," wept Hamilton.

"With the conquest of agriculture, as you may not be aware," said Gunther, "there was a concomitant degeneration of the human stock. This can be established skeletally, and also by cranial capacity. Modern man is smaller, and quite possibly intellectually inferior, to these free hunters. We have now, of course, in compensation, numbers and technology. We have libraries, and a complicated culture. We are much more advanced, inferior, but much more advanced. We do not know what direction the race will take. As we are to the hunters, future man may be to us, miserable, petty and neurotic, or, perhaps, we shall grow again, toward the hunters—and the hunters will come again, from us ourselves—for surely we are their descendants, and surely we, somehow, somewhere, hidden within us, hold their promise—latent in our genetic codes the hunters may not be dead, but only asleep." Gunther looked at Hamilton. "The race," said Gunther, "is divided into the farmers and the hunters, those who grow millet and barley, those who trudge in the mud and dig in the soil, the swarming mobs in the river valleys, scratching with their sticks and carrying their water, and the hunters, the lonely ones, the swift ones, the solitary ones, not understood, who will not dig in the soil, the ones who know the smell of the forest, the burrow of the ermine, the track of the caribou, who rise at dawn, in the cold, who can run fifty miles in one day, who can shoot the bow and hurl the spear, and live for weeks on the land, the cunning ones, the dissatisfied ones, the pursuers of meat."

Hamilton looked at Gunther, strangely. Never had she heard him speak like this. He was usually silent, arrogant, taciturn.

"The world," said Gunther, "is divided into those who fear, those who seek security, those who do not dare to lift their eyes from their narrow fields, and the other—the hunters." Gunther was quiet for a moment, and then he spoke again. "Do you know where the hunters have gone?" he asked.

"No," said Brenda Hamilton.

"The farmers, in their numbers, have killed them," he said.

Hamilton regarded him.

"But they may not all be dead," said Gunther. "Some may be only asleep."

Hamilton said nothing.

"There has always been war," said Gunther, "between the hunters and the farmers." He smiled. "And I suppose there always will be."

"There is nothing left to hunt," said Hamilton.

"Mankind's greatest game is now afoot," said Gunther. He

frowned. "The farmers will do what they can to prevent its pursuit."

"What game, Gunther?" asked Hamilton.

"Meat!" said Gunther. "Meat fit for the gods!"

"What meat, Gunther?" asked Hamilton.

"The stars," said Gunther. "The stars."

She looked at him. She shook her head. "No," she said. "There is nothing more to hunt."

"There are the stars," he said.

Then he left her alone.

Gunther is mad, thought Brenda Hamilton, he is as mad as the others. She lay back on the mattress and twisted in the heat. She jerked at the handcuff and cursed, and then tried to find a comfortable position in which to sleep.

◇ **7** ◇

Brenda Hamilton, fascinated, watched the leopard in the translation cubicle.

It was a beautiful, terrible beast.

It lay on its side on the smooth plastic of the cubicle. Its four feet had been tied together. Its jaws were muzzled. It was helpless. It had been drugged. It was now recovering. It whined, and struggled.

Hamilton recalled how she had first seen it in the wild, in the branch of a tree, lying across the carcass of a slain calf. Gunther, while William had distracted it, had struck it with an anesthetic bullet.

It had been captured.

Brenda, with fascination, watched the twisting beast, growling, whining.

She wore the white dress.

She sat in a cheap, kitchen chair, made of metal. Her hands, in Gunther's handcuffs, were fastened behind her back. The cuffs had been placed before two of the narrow metal back bars of the chair and then pulled through. They had then been behind the chair.

"Sit in the chair," Gunther had said.

He then pulled her wrists behind the chair and locked them in the cuffs, confining her to the chair.

The chain he had removed from her right ankle, looped it twice about the metal rung between the front legs of the chair, and then, snugly, fastened it once more about her right ankle. Her ankles were held back, close to the metal rung; fastened to it.

She was thus, doubly, confined to the chair.

Brenda watched the leopard. It was a capture.

She felt the handcuffs on her wrists, the chain on her ankles. She knew that she, too, was a capture.

Herjellsen sat beneath the steel hood, bent over, his fists clenched.

This night there was no play of light.

This night there was no dislocation of her time sense.

She watched the beast in the cubicle. It was uncomfortable, rebellious, growling, helpless.

Herjellsen sweated, fists clenched, bent over beneath the steel hood.

William and Gunther stood in the background.

Suddenly it seemed all strange to her, impossible, insane. She knew that what they were attempting to do could not be done. Even a child would know that.

It is insane, she felt. Insane! And she was locked in a shack, cuffed and shackled, with madmen!

The experiments, she knew, did not always go well.

She wondered if they ever had.

She recalled William and Gunther discussing Herjellsen, and fraud, and illusion, and madness, in the Land Rover.

She surely could not have seen once what she thought she had seen.

It could not have been true.

Then she was terrified.

She saw Gunther looking at her.

Herjellsen, at last, worn, exhausted, bent, withdrew from under the hood and, painfully, wearily, straightened his body. He looked at her blankly, his eyes blinking behind the large, heavy convex lenses. Then he left the shack.

Gunther turned off the equipment.

William left the shack.

It had been a failure.

The beast still lay, helpless, twisting, on the floor of the cubicle.

They had not transmitted it.

Gunther opened one of the cuffs and freed Hamilton's wrists from the metal back bars of the chair, then closed it again on her wrist, keeping her hands cuffed behind her. He then freed her left ankle from the chain, disengaged the chain from the metal chair rung, and then, with the padlock, again fastened the chain about her left ankle, freeing her now completely of the chair, keeping her shackled.

He then lifted her small body lightly in his strong arms and carried her to her cell, where, after permitting her to relieve herself, he briefly withdrawing, he cuffed her to the cot, freed her of the shackles, and left her for the night.

She heard the padlocks locking the door.

"Gunther!" she cried, jerking against the handcuff.

But there was no response. She heard his feet leaving the porch.

"Gunther," she wept, "what if it doesn't work? What will they do with me?"

She lay in terror, handcuffed to the cot, looking up at the corrugated tin roof.

"Lie on your stomach on the cot," said Gunther.

"Yes, Gunther," said Brenda Hamilton.

It was now the night following the failure of the experiment with the leopard.

Hamilton had already placed her left wrist under the iron bar at the head of the cot. She felt Gunther lock the cuff on her wrist. How snug, and inflexible, it felt. Then she heard the other cuff closed about the iron bar. Then Gunther bent to free her of the shackles. She knew it would now be ten thirty P.M. At this time she was put to the cot.

"Gunther, she whispered, prone, the left side of her face on the mattress.

"Yes," he said. He removed the chain from her ankles. He stood up.

"What—what if the experiment does not go well?"

He looked at her.

"What if it doesn't work—if Herjellsen is not successful?"

"You mean if he cannot transmit you?" asked Gunther.

"Yes," she said, "—if I cannot be transmitted."

"Surely you understand," said Gunther, "that you cannot be released."

She turned, wrist back, lying on her side. She looked at him, fearfully. She, dragging the handcuff along the iron bar, sat up on the edge of the cot, her body twisted, turned to face him.

"You know too much," said Gunther. "You could put us in prison for years." He regarded her. "If the experiment is unsuccessful, if you cannot be transmitted, you will be disposed of in the bush."

"I do not want to die," she said, "Gunther." She sat on the edge of the cot. She shook her head. "You would not kill me, would you, Gunther?" she asked.

"Yes," said Gunther.

She put her right leg on the cot, beneath her; her left leg was not on the cot; the toes only of her left leg touched the floor; her left leg was flexed; her body faced Gunther; her left wrist was back, handcuffed to the iron bar at the head of the cot.

She shook her head. "Don't kill me," she said.

He regarded her, unmoved.

"Sell me," she whispered.

He did not speak.

"I am a Caucasian," she said. "William says that I am beautiful."

Gunther said nothing.

"Surely you could get a good price on me," she said.

"Do you know what you are speaking of?" asked Gunther.

"There are markets, are there not, secret markets, where white women are sold?"

Gunther looked at her. He did not speak for a long time. Then he spoke. "Yes," he said.

Hamilton looked at him, agonized, pleading.

"I have been in two such markets," said Gunther.

"You?" she said.

"I am trusted," he said.

"Don't kill me," said Hamilton. "—Sell me."

Gunther smiled. "What do you think your body is worth?" he asked.

"I—I don't know," she said.

"It might be interesting to see you on the block," he said.

Her lower lip trembled.

"Can you smile?" he asked. "Can you pose? Can you excite the interest of buyers? Can you move your body in such a way that it suggests that it could be a source of incredible pleasure for a man?"

She looked at him with horror.

"If you do not perform well," said Gunther, "you will be whipped."

Hamilton said nothing.

"There are difficulties in transportation," said Gunther. "You would have to be smuggled across borders in a truck, perhaps at a given point carried northward in a dhow."

"Drug me," said Hamilton. "I do not care if I do not awake until I am dragged naked before the buyers."

He looked at her, carefully. "It could be done with you, I suppose," he said.

"Yes, Gunther," she said, "yes!"

"It would be simpler," said he, "to dispose of you in the bush."

"No, please, no," she wept. "Sell me! Sell me!"

"Perhaps," said Gunther, "perhaps." He looked at her. "I shall take it under consideration," he said.

He went to the door.

"Gunther," she said.

He turned.

"What is done to such women?" she asked. "Where are they kept?"

He shrugged. "In isolated villas," he said, "in desert palaces, in luxurious slave brothels, catering to a rich clientele."

"I see," she said. Then she said, "Gunther, you have denied me sexual experience. I gather that if I were a slave, I would be granted such experiences."

Gunther threw back his head and laughed. "Yes," he said, "your master, or masters, and their guests, or clients, would see that you served them well."

She put down her head, blushing furiously.

"Even superbly," he added, smiling.

She clenched her small fists.

"You said," said Gunther, "that you were my whore."

"I am," she said, "Gunther." She looked at him. "Any time you want me, I'm your whore."

"A slave girl," he said, "is the whore of any man who buys her."

"I know," she whispered.

He laughed. "Any man," he said.

"I know," she whispered.

"You know nothing," he said.

She looked at him, puzzled.

"A whore," he said, "is a thousand times above a slave."

"No!" she cried.

"Yes," he laughed.

"Is it true, Gunther?" she begged.

"Men care more for their dogs, than for their female slaves," said Gunther.

"No," she whispered.

"It is true," said Gunther. "I know." He looked at her. "Would you not prefer to be disposed of in the bush?"

"No, Gunther," she said. "Sell me."

"Then," asked Gunther, looking at her evenly, "you are truly willing to be a female slave?"

"Yes, Gunther," she whispered.

He regarded her, half kneeling, half sitting on the cot, in the brief white dress, facing him, on the striped mattress, her hand back, handcuffed to the iron bar at the head of the cot.

"I always thought you were a slave," he said.

She looked at him, angrily.

"Slave," he sneered.

"Yes—slave!" she said.

He left.

◈ 8 ◈

"I see that you are still a virgin," said William.

Hamilton was silent.

•She stood before the two men, under the light bulb, barefoot on the floor of her cell, the cot and mattress in the background, stripped, freed of the shackles, wrists cuffed behind her back.

"Is your examination finished?" she asked.

"I would have thought that Gunther would have used you by now," said William.

"She is for others to use," said Gunther.

Hamilton's physical examination had been thorough, including blood and urine samples taken earlier in the day.

William's black bag lay beside his cane chair.

When they had entered the room together this evening, she had been startled. William was a physician. Gunther was not.

She had not wished to strip herself before Gunther, not in the presence of another man.

"Remove your clothing," had said William.

"No," had said Hamilton.

"Are you being insubordinate?" had asked William.

"No," she had whispered.

Gunther's eyes had met hers. He had snapped his fingers. Clumsily, quickly, she had pulled the cotton shift over her head.

"Turn about," he had said.

He had put her wrists in handcuffs, thrown her to the cot, removed the shackles from her.

"Stand," he had said.

She did so.

"Come here, dear," had said William, opening his kit, removing a stethoscope.

"Must Gunther be present?" she had begged.

"Is a slave modest?" asked Gunther.

"No!" she said, angrily.

She had approached William. The examination had begun.

William now snapped shut his kit, but left it on the floor. He, sitting, Gunther, too, to one side, regarded her.

"Is the examination finished," she asked.

"Come closer," said William.

She did so.

He looked up at her. She looked away.

"Do you find that you desire sexual experience?" asked William.

"No," she said.

"It does not matter," said William. "That you yourself are found sexually desirable will be more than sufficient."

Hamilton looked at him with horror.

"We shall now conduct a small experiment," said William. He placed his hand, gently, cupped, between her legs. He lifted his hand, pressing it gently against her delta.

Hamilton looked away.

"Now say aloud, slowly, five times," said William, "the name Gunther."

She looked at Gunther. She did as she was told.

To her horror she felt her body, her hair, press into William's hand. She wished it was Gunther's hand.

William lifted the hand. He held it before Hamilton, who quickly turned her face away. For the first time, she had smelled the odor, her own, of an aroused female.

"For all practical purposes, Gunther," said William, "this woman belongs to you."

"I can have many women," said Gunther.

Hamilton closed her eyes.

"Of course," said William.

Hamilton opened her eyes, furious. "Are you quite finished with this examination?" she asked, icily.

"The medical portion is completed," said William.

She looked at Gunther.

"Gunther," said William, "was requested to be present by Professor Herjellsen. He is supposed to render something in the nature of a consulting opinion, though not precisely from the medical point of view."

Gunther went behind Hamilton, and removed the cuffs from her.

She stood across the room from them.

"He is to render something in the nature of a flesh assessment, or appraisal," said William.

Hamilton blushed.

"I informed Herjellsen I am fully capable of rendering such an opinion myself," said William, smiling.

"I'm sure you are," said Hamilton.

She looked at Gunther. His eyes frightened her. He had looked, she knew, on countless women. He had even looked on them in slave markets.

"How do you find her?" asked William.

Gunther did not answer him.

He continued to look at Hamilton, until her eyes fell, acknowledging his dominance, her femaleness.

"Do not, William," said Gunther, "interfere with me in what I am going to do."

"Very well, old man," said William.

Hamilton looked at Gunther, angrily.

"You will follow my instructions implicitly," said Gunther to Hamilton, "without question, without hesitation, and in your mind and imagination, as well as in your body."

"No," whispered Hamilton.

"A slave obeys," said Gunther. His hands went to the buckle of his heavy belt.

"I will obey," said Hamilton.

"A slave," said Gunther, "is given no place to hide. Her entire person is her master's. She is totally open to him. You will follow my instructions, accordingly, in your mind and imagination, as well as in your body."

"I am not a slave," said Hamilton.

"For the next four minutes," said Gunther, "you are a female slave."

"Gunther," protested William.

"Do not interfere," said Gunther.

William shrugged, angrily, and returned his attention to Hamilton.

"For the next four minutes," said Gunther to Hamilton, "you are a female slave—only a female slave."

Hamilton looked at him. "Very well," she said, "—Master."

William breathed in, sharply.

"Close your eyes," said Gunther.

Hamilton did so.

"Think now," said Gunther, "think deeply, of yourself as a slave."

"Very well," said Hamilton.

"It will be impossible for this to be simulated," said Gunther, "for there is a congruence between the thought and the behavior, and if this congruence is not present, betrayed by the slightest, most subtle, unconscious inappropriateness of behavior, you will be beaten."

She looked at him, frightened.

"Close your eyes," he said.

She did so.

"You are familiar, surely, with Stanislavsky's theories of acting?" he asked.

She nodded, terrorized.

"Think of yourself now," he said, "profoundly, as a female slave."

Hamilton, frightened, dared to do so.

Suddenly she felt herself slave. Her body shuddered. She moaned with misery.

"You are now a slave," said Gunther, "a slave girl, willess and rightless, completely at my bidding."

Hamilton's body shook.

"Do you understand?" asked Gunther.

"Yes," she whispered.

"You are owned," said Gunther. "You may be bought and sold. You may be whipped or slain. You are branded. You must do what men command you."

Hamilton, in misery, slipped to her knees, her head down.

"Before," said Gunther, "you were acting, but you are not acting now."

She shook her head.

"Now," said Gunther, "the acting is finished—what are you now?"

"A slave," she whispered, "—Master."

"To the block, Slave," said Gunther.

Brenda Hamilton stood on the slave block, her body reflecting the torchlight. She felt sawdust beneath her feet. She felt herself turn and felt the auctioneer, his hand on her arm, exhibiting her. She heard the cries, the bids, of the men.

"You have been sold," Gunther informed her.

She stumbled from the block. She felt her wrists locked in slave chains. She felt herself hooded.

When the hood was torn away, in a large, marble-floored room, with rings set in the floor, she first saw, clearly, the features of her master.

She had been fastened by the wrists to one of the rings.

"He beats you," said Gunther.

She writhed beneath the blows of the whip.

Sobbing in pain she felt her wrists unfastened from the ring.

"You are eager to please him," said Gunther.

She danced her beauty before him, to placate him, pleadingly, piteously.

"He consents to let you please him," said Gunther.

Hamilton crept to the cushions and arched her body for the kiss and touch of her master.

Suddenly she felt her left hand handcuffed and heard the other cuff closed about the iron bar at the head of the cot.

Her face was slapped to one side.

"You are no longer a slave," said Gunther. "You are the female prisoner, Doctor Brenda Hamilton."

"Yes, Gunther," she said. She turned her head to one side.

William was standing, watching her, in awe. "Fantastic," he said.

"That is how an assessment is made of a woman, short of using her," said Gunther.

"What is your opinion?" asked William.

"What is yours?" asked Gunther.

"Incredible, fantastic," breathed William.

Gunther looked at Hamilton. "She is satisfactory," he said.

With his foot he shoved the wastes bucket to the side of the cot.

They had not put the shift on her again.

The men turned to leave.

"Gunther," said Hamilton.

"Yes?" he said.

"Why was I examined today?" she asked, red-eyed.

"Did William not tell you?" asked Gunther.

"No," she said.

"Yesterday evening," said Gunther, "quite late, we managed to transmit the leopard."

She looked at him.

"You understand what this means?" he asked.

She shook her head.

"We can now transmit an animal of that size and weight," he said.

She looked at him.

"Nothing now stands in our way," said Gunther. He regarded her. "The third phase of experiments can soon begin." He looked at her. "How much do you weigh?" he asked.

"One hundred and nineteen pounds," said Hamilton.

"The leopard," said Gunther, "weighed one hundred and forty pounds."

"It seems, then, Gunther," she said, "that I need not fear either the bush or the slave markets of the north and east."

"Not our bush," said Gunther, "not our markets."

She looked at him.

"Doubtless there are other wildernesses," said Gunther, "other men, other markets."

She pulled at the handcuff, defeated.

◊ 9 ◊

"More wine, Doctor Hamilton?" inquired Herjellsen.

"Yes," said Brenda Hamilton.

Herjellsen nodded, and one of the blacks, in a white jacket, stepped discreetly forward and filled her glass.

"Thank you," said Brenda Hamilton.

The black did not reply.

"May I smoke?" asked William, drawing out a cigarette.

"Certainly," said Hamilton.

He lit the cigarette. "Would you like one?" he asked.

"No," said Hamilton.

They sat at table in Herjellsen's quarters, where, in earlier weeks, they had commonly dined together, a continental supper, served at nine P.M., after the heat of the day.

Herjellsen, and William and Gunther, wore evening clothing, black tie.

Brenda Hamilton wore an evening gown, a slim, white sheath, off the shoulder. She had never worn such a gown before. It fitted perfectly. Except for a string of pearls, and two pearl earrings, it was all she wore. Gunther, standing behind her, had put the pearls about her neck.

Her ankles, her wrists, were free of fetters.

Hamilton looked down at the white linen tablecloth, the napkin, the silverware.

There was candlelight.

The evening was comfortable.

The conversation, mostly unimportant talk, had not been unpleasant.

Hamilton sipped the wine.

"A toast," said Herjellsen, lifting his glass toward Hamilton. "I had forgotten until now," he said, "how beautiful a European woman could be." He used "European" in the African sense.

Gunther, with William, and Herjellsen, lifted their glasses to her.

"Thank you," said Hamilton.

She blushed, and lowered her head, pleased in spite of herself, in the depth of her new-found womanness, which they had released in her, at being the object of their admiration. William, she had seen, had not taken his eyes from her all evening. Even in Gunther's eyes she had detected a grudging admiration. This had stirred her, helplessly, deeply. He was the most exciting man she had ever seen. She knew she was his for the asking, even though she knew he despised her, and had, as her jailer, treated her with contempt, with harshness, and even cruelty. She sat among them as a slim, erect, elegant young woman, educated, beautiful, and civilized, in a white sheath gown and pearls, but she knew that if Gunther wanted her, she would yield to him on his own terms, whatever they might be. If he so much as snapped his fingers, she would prepare herself, eagerly, for him. She wanted to serve him, intimately, desperately, at length, even if he, in his cruelty, forced her to take payment for doing so, a cigarette, or a shilling. She sat across the table from him, looking at him, over the candlelight. "Do you know, Gunther," she asked him, silently, to herself, "that I, sitting here, elegant in my white silk and pearls, am your whore?" She regarded him. He smiled. She put down her head. She knew that he knew.

She sipped her wine, finishing it.

"More wine?" asked Herjellsen, attentively.

"No, thank you," said Hamilton.

"Coffee," said Herjellsen to one of the blacks, standing nearby, in his white jacket. The fellow left the dining area.

"I had thought," said Hamilton, to Herjellsen, "that I was not to be permitted cosmetics, perfume."

Tastefully, and fully, beautifully, she had adorned herself this evening. She had, of course, been instructed to do so.

"Tonight," said Herjellsen, "is a night on which we are celebrating. We have worked hard. We have been successful. You would not begrudge us our wine, surely, our supper, the stimulation of your lovely presence."

"Of course not," she said. She smiled.

"We have treated you rather harshly," said Herjellsen, apologetically. "But we have done so in the hope that we may have, thereby, increased your chances of survival."

"I find it difficult to follow your reasoning," said Hamilton.

The coffee was brought, black, hot, bitter, in small cups. On the tray there was a small container of assorted sugars, with tiny spoons.

"I have made a positive identification," said Herjellsen, "of the rodent, which you observed being brought into the translation cubicle. The family is obviously Muridae. It is a species similar to, but not precisely identical to, the widely spread, cunning, vicious, highly successful Rattus norvegicus, the common brown rat, or Norway rat. It is doubtless an ancestral form, the only actual difference being that the teeth are more substantially rooted."

"Does this identification have significance?" asked Hamilton.

"Of course," said Herjellsen. "It is a commensal."

"I—I do not know the word," said Hamilton.

"A companion at meals," laughed William.

"A commensal," said Gunther, "is an animal or plant that lives in, on or with another, sharing its food, but is neither a parasite to the other, nor, normally, is injured by the presence of the other."

"It thrived in the Pleistocene," said William, "and thrives

today, one of the most successful forms of life the world has ever seen."

"It supplants allied species," said Gunther. "It is a swift, curious, aggressive, savage animal, with the beginnings of a tradition, older animals instructing the younger, particularly in avoidance behaviors, as in preventing their consumption of dangerous or poisoned food."

"A very successful co-inhabitant of our Earth, my dear," said Herjellsen, "but, more importantly for our purposes, a commensal."

"It entered Western Europe from Asia in prehistory," said Gunther, "as an accompanier of migrations."

"The current brown rat," said Hamilton, "is a commensal of man."

"Precisely," said Herjellsen. "And so, too, was it in the beginning."

Hamilton could not speak.

"You see now the significance of the catch?" he asked.

She shook her head, not wanting to speak.

"It gives us the coordinates of a human group, a living human group," smiled Herjellsen.

"This is much more accurate than a stone tool," said William. "Such a tool, particularly if adequately protected from weathering, and patination, might have been abandoned or dropped hundreds of years ago, or years earlier."

"Where the brown rat is found," said Herjellsen, "there, too, will we find man. They are companions in history."

"You said," said Hamilton, "that you treated me harshly, that my chances of survival might be improved."

"Yes," said Herjellsen. "It is our anticipation that these men do not live in an environment so hostile and cruel that they need fear, in practice, only the scarcity of game, or so remote and impenetrable that no others would care to live there. Eskimos, for example, are a kindly people, trusting, helpful, affectionate, and, in a very different environment, so, too, are the Pygmies of the Congo."

"Such peoples, you note," said Gunther, "have been driven from choicer lands by more aggressive competitors."

"What are you trying to tell me?" asked Hamilton.

"Xenophobia," said Herjellsen, "or the hatred of the stranger, is an almost universal human phenomenon, at one time, judging by its pervasiveness, of important evolutionary import. Groups who did not distrust strangers were either destroyed, or driven into the remoter and harsher portions of the Earth. Too often, in the history of the world has the stranger meant ambush, treachery, disaster."

"Interestingly," said William, "this suspicion tends to be somewhat reduced during the prime mating years, particularly those of adolescence and the early twenties."

"That, too, doubtless," said Herjellsen, "has played its role in mixing and distributing genes among diverse populations."

"Why don't you transmit a man?" begged Hamilton.

"We think," said Herjellsen, calmly, "they would kill a man."

"Kill?" asked Hamilton.

"Surely," said Herjellsen.

"That is why we are transmitting a woman," said Gunther, "and one who is young and not unattractive."

Hamilton looked down. It was the closest Gunther had ever come to complimenting her.

She looked up at Herjellsen. "How do you know they will not kill me?" she asked.

"We do not know," said Herjellsen.

"What do you expect them to do with me?" asked Hamilton.

"If they have a language," said Herjellsen, "you will not be able to speak it. You will be to them a stranger. You will not be known to them. You will have no kinship ties, no blood ties, with the group. You will be to them an outsider —a complete outsider. You will not be a member of their group." Herjellsen smiled at her through the thick lenses. "Do you understand, my dear," asked Herjellsen, "what that might mean—in a primitive situation—not being a member of the group?"

"What do you expect them to do with me!" demanded Hamilton.

"You will be transmitted naked," he said, "and, as Gunther has observed, you are not unattractive."

"What will they do with me?" whispered Hamilton.

"Make you a slave," said Herjellsen.

Hamilton looked down, miserable.

"Drink your coffee," said Gunther. Hamilton sipped the coffee.

"If you were a man," said William, "they would probably kill you."

"I do not want to be a slave," whispered Hamilton. Then she looked up. "Slavery," she said, "is a complex societal institution. Surely it could not exist in such a primitive society."

"Apache Indians," said Gunther, "in your own country, kept slaves."

"Semantics is unimportant," said Herjellsen.

"You will be an out-group female," said Gunther. "Doubtless you will live, if you are permitted to live, on their sufferance, depending presumably on how well you please and serve them. You would be, of course, subject to barter and exchange."

"—I would be a slave," whispered Hamilton.

"Yes," said Herjellsen.

"You have been training me for that?" asked Hamilton.

"When a man enters your room, what now is your inclination?" asked Herjellsen.

"Unthinkingly," said Hamilton, "I feel an impulse to kneel." She reddened. "You have made me kneel, as a prisoner, in the presence of males," she said.

"This is to accustom you to deference and subservience to men," said William.

"You must understand," said Herjellsen, "that if you were transmitted as a modern woman, irritable, sexless, hostile, competitive, hating men, your opportunities for survival might be considerably less."

"We do not know the patience of these men," said Gunther. "They might not choose to tolerate such women."

Hamilton shuddered.

"We have tried to teach you various things in your training, my dear," said Herjellsen, not unkindly. "First we have tried to teach you that you are a beautiful female, which you are, and that this is a glorious and precious thing in its own right, and that being a woman is not the same as being a man. Each sex is astonishing and marvelous, but they are not the same. We have tried to teach you the weakness, the beauty, the vulnerability, the desirability of your womanhood. We have tried to teach you that you are a woman, and that this is deeply precious."

Hamilton, though she did not speak, knew that in her incarceration, she had, for the first time in her life, accepted herself as a woman, and had found joy in doing so.

These men, cruel as they might have been, had given her to herself.

She was grateful to them. She was no longer the little girl who had wanted to be a little boy, nor the young woman who had pretended her sex was unimportant, and had secretly wanted to be a man. She was now a woman happy in her womanhood. She looked at Gunther. She rejoiced that he was a man, not she. She wanted to be held by him, and had, helplessly, yieldingly. She wanted to be a woman in his arms.

Herjellsen put down his coffee. "It is our hope," said Herjellsen, "that we have improved your chances for survival in an environment of primitive realities."

"Other aspects of your training," said William, "were reasonably straightforward. For example, the cleaning of the floor and walls of your quarters accustomed you to manual labor. The alignment of the cot was intended to induce discipline, attention to detail, neatness, compliance with the arbitrary will of a male."

"Your punishments," said Gunther, "have taught you to expect humiliation and pain if you are disobedient or insubordinate."

"You have been very thorough, Gentlemen," smiled Hamilton.

"We have perhaps saved your life," said Herjellsen.

"It might all have gone for naught," said Hamilton, "if I had escaped."

"You had no opportunity to escape," said Herjellsen.

Hamilton looked at him, puzzled.

"You were given utensils," he said, "that you might attempt escape."

"Oh," said Hamilton.

"The first time, of course, we did not permit you to escape. I used muscle reading to locate the missing utensil. This was to induce a feeling of psychological helplessness in you. We were interested to see if this would crush you. Happily, it did not. That very evening, with a second utensil, you attempted your escape. You are a brave, fine woman, intelligent and resourceful. We were proud of you."

"I told William, that night," she said, "that no fork had been brought with the tray."

William smiled.

"I thought I had fooled him," she said.

"You were an excellent actress," said William. "I had been informed, however, that your escape attempt would take place that night. Indeed, that is why the second fork was provided with your food that evening."

"How did you know I would try that night?" asked Hamilton.

"It was simple, my dear," said Herjellsen. "You were

anxious to escape. You did not know how long you might have, before your portion of the experiment began. You would attempt to escape as soon as possible. Further, you would know that the missing fork would be noted, at least by morning. You would know, too, that its location, if hidden, could be revealed by the technique of muscle reading. Thus your attempt to escape, and a brave one it was, to essay the bush at night, alone, would take place that night."

"We heard you digging out," said William.

"We even interrupted the guard in his rounds," said Herjellsen, "that you would have time to dig under the fence."

"I hoped you weren't shocked too severely," said William.

"No," she said. She looked at Gunther. "I was clumsy to touch the wire, wasn't I, Gunther?" she said.

Gunther shrugged.

"We thought you would strike out for the road," said Herjellsen.

"But Gunther, with a dark lantern, followed the trail for some time, to ascertain this," said William.

"You followed me, Gunther?" she asked.

"For a time," he said. "I then returned to the compound."

"It was not difficult to pick you up in the Land Rover," said William.

"I left the road," she said. "You followed."

She recalled the frantic flight through the bush, the headlights of the Land Rover, the searchlight on its side, the sting of the anesthetic bullet.

"You were not difficult to take," said Gunther. "But the hunt was enjoyable."

"I'm pleased," she said, acidly, "that I gave you sport."

"It is pleasant," said Gunther, "to hunt women."

She recalled falling in the bush, crawling, being unable to crawl further, then being captured, her wrists dragged behind her, their being locked in Gunther's cuffs.

She recalled being lifted, thrown, secured, over his shoulder, and being carried to the Land Rover. She had then lost consciousness.

"And, doubtless," she said, "it is pleasant, after bringing your catch home, to make them slaves."

"Yes," said Gunther, "doubtless that would be pleasant."

"You are a beast, Gunther," she said.

He smiled. He shrugged. "I am a man," he said.

"Finish your coffee, Doctor Hamilton," suggested Herjellsen.

Hamilton finished the small cup of bitter, black fluid.

Brandy was brought for the men. Herjellsen, and William and Gunther, lit cigars.

"Would you like a liqueur?" asked Herjellsen.

"Yes," said Hamilton.

It was brought. It was thick, heavily syruped, flavored with peach.

Hamilton sipped it.

"The escape phase of the experiment," said Herjellsen, "permitted us to test your cunning and your initiative. Both proved themselves satisfactory."

"Thank you," said Hamilton.

"In the bush itself, of course, as we expected," said Herjellsen, "you behaved like a frightened, ignorant woman."

"I suppose," said Hamilton, sipping the liqueur, "that my 'training' was also enhanced in some way by my escape attempt?"

"Yes," said Herjellsen. "We regarded it as important to give you the experience of being a fleeing, hunted, then captured woman."

"It is a very helpless, frightened feeling," said Hamilton.

"We wished you to have it," said Herjellsen.

"The most important lesson of the escape phase, or perhaps I should say, the 'failure-to-escape' phase," said Gunther, smiling, "was to imprint, and imprint deeply, in your consciousness the incontrovertible recognition that you had not escaped—that you had been caught—and were once again, and more securely than ever, the prisoner of men."

Hamilton recalled the misery with which she had understood this.

She had been, thereafter, their experiment finished, shackled during the day, handcuffed to the cot at night. They had needed no more data. She was held, perfectly.

And Brenda Hamilton knew, deeply within her, that her futile escape attempt, summarily punished by a brief humiliating beating, stinging, trivial, a woman's beating, had never been realistic. She would have left a trail. To a practiced eye it could have been followed. She knew then that, even if the Land Rover had not been used, she could have been retaken, and almost at their leisure. How female she had felt, how helpless. She was angry. And how swiftly, in a matter of days, the short rations, the bread and water, had brought her to her knees before them, promising compliance.

She had come to understand, as it had been intended that

she should, that men were dominant, and, if they chose, women were at their mercy.

The room seemed dark at the edges.

She sipped again the liqueur.

She had failed to escape. She remained the captive of men.

"We had difficulty, as you may recall," said Herjellsen, "in transmitting the leopard."

"Yes," said Hamilton, shaking her head.

"It is interesting," said Herjellsen, "but I met resistance."

"How is that?" she asked.

"I felt it," said Herjellsen. "Earlier we had failed to transmit the beast when it was unconscious. When you observed, it was conscious—but resisting."

Hamilton recalled the animal, twisting, growling.

"It could know nothing, of course, of what was occurring," said Herjellsen, "but still it was distressed, angry, displeased, resistant."

"You failed to transmit it?" said Hamilton.

"Later, when it was partially anesthetized, we managed to transmit it," said Herjellsen, "when the resistance was lowered."

Hamilton steadied herself with a hand on the tablecloth.

"Interesting that a beast could resist," said Herjellsen. "Fascinating."

"I will resist you!" suddenly cried Hamilton. "I will resist you!"

The room seemed to be growing darker.

"It seems unlikely," said Herjellsen.

"I do not feel well," said Hamilton.

Herjellsen appeared concerned. He glanced at William. "It is a temporary effect," said William.

"When is your experiment to take place?" asked Hamilton.

"Tonight," said Herjellsen. "Now."

She shook her head.

"Strip her," said Herjellsen.

She felt Gunther removing the pearls from the back of her neck.

She could not resist.

"The liqueur has been drugged," explained Herjellsen. "You will not resist." Then he spoke to Gunther and William. "Remove her clothing and clean her," he said, "and then place her in the translation cubicle."

"Please," wept Brenda Hamilton. "Please!"
She felt Gunther remove the earrings from her ears.

◇ 10 ◇

Brenda Hamilton, raw, lay on her stomach in the translation cubicle.

She heard the men outside.

"No," she wept. She struggled, weakly, to her hands and
knees, her head down, hair falling forward. She tried to lift
her head.

"Raise the power," she heard Herjellsen say, the voice
seemingly far away, on the other side of the plastic.

"No," she wept, and again sank to her stomach. She lay on
the cool, smooth plastic, almost unable to move her body.
She tried to close her hand into a fist. It was difficult to do
so. She only wanted to lie still, to rest, helpless, on the
plastic.

"It is beginning," she heard William say.

She opened her eyes. To her horror she saw, at one corner
of the cubicle, a tracery of light, darting, swift.

Herjellsen sat before his apparatus, his head beneath the
hood, his fists clenched.

Slowly, muscle by muscle, she moved her body, raising
herself again to her hands and knees. She tried to lift her
head.

She saw a tendril of light appear now to her right.

She lifted her head. She looked out through the plastic.
It was heavy. She saw that it had been, on the outside, reinforced with metal piping.

She rose to her feet. Light played about her ankles. "No,"
she whispered. She could not feel the light. She was conscious only of a tiny coolness.

A set of beads of light darted from one side to the other
of the cubicle.

She stumbled against the plastic wall and, weakly, tried

to beat on it with her fists. "Please!" she wept. "Let me out! Let me out!"

Tears streamed down her face.

She saw Gunther and William, impassive, on the other side of the plastic.

"Gunther!" she wept. "William! William!"

Suddenly it seemed a tendril of light moved about her leg. She kicked wildly at it. She tried to thrust the light from her body. She could not see the floor of the cubicle now, though she felt it, as firm and cool and solid as before, beneath her bare feet.

"Let me out!" she wept.

It seemed to her suddenly that she was a little girl in a closet, crying to be let out, pounding on the wood in the darkness. The voice that seemed to cry within her was that of a child.

Then she saw again William and Gunther outside, and Herjellsen, under the hood.

She shook her head, wildly, having sensed the dissociation which, as a psychological concomitant, occasionally accompanied the presence of the Herjellsen phenomenon.

She must resist, she knew. She must resist!

Her body, her will, was weakened, but she would fight. She could fight, and would!

She stood in the center of the cubicle, bent over, fists clenched, hair wild. "No!" she cried. "No! No! No! No!"

It seemed that light, wildly, swirled about her; for an instant she feared she might drown in light, but then she realized that there was no impediment to her breathing, indeed, that the very phenomenon of light itself depended on some reaction with oxygen in the cubicle.

"No!" she said.

Then she felt herself, as though being buffeted, reel in the cubicle. But she knew that no blows were struck upon her body. Yet it seemed she was struck, as though by sound that could not be heard, but felt.

She felt herself weakening, and fell to her knees at the plastic wall, almost lost in light. She piteously scratched at the plastic, trying to find a crevice, a flaw, that might admit of her access, secure her release.

Outside she saw Gunther and William. Their faces wore no emotion.

She shook her head, and fell half backward from the wall and rolled to the center of the cubicle. Then she could see nothing, nothing but the light, which like a brilliant, luminous, sparkling golden fog almost blinded her. She shut her eyes. "No!" she said. "No!" She rose again to her knees. She clenched her fists, now tightly. "No!" she cried.

When she opened her eyes again, to her astonishment, her relief, the light was gone.

She was alone in the cubicle.

Outside she saw Herjellsen, no longer beneath the hood. He was standing outside, looking at her. Gunther and William stood to one side.

"You have failed!" she cried.

Her heart bounded with elation. They had been unable to transmit her. They had failed.

"I have resisted you!" she cried. "I have resisted you!" She laughed. "You have failed!" She looked at Gunther. "You will have to sell me, Gunther!" she cried. "You will have to sell me!"

Herjellsen, she saw, picked up a small microphone from the table, near the hood.

"Can you hear me?" he asked.

She nodded. She heard his voice, quite clearly. The speaker was fixed in the ceiling of the cubicle.

"Turn their eyes," he said, "to the stars."

She looked at him, puzzled.

Then she said, "You have been unable to transmit me. My will was too strong for you. You have failed."

"Turn their eyes," said Herjellsen, "to the stars."

"It will not be necessary to dispose of me in the bush, Professor Herjellsen," she said. "There is an alternative. I realize you cannot simply release me. But there is an alternative, an excellent one, to consider. I have discussed this with Gunther, and he informs me it is practical." She drew a deep breath. "I can be sold," she said. "Please, Professor Herjellsen," she said, "do not kill me." She looked at him. "Instead let me be sold."

"We have no intention of killing you, my dear," said Herjellsen, "nor, indeed, of having you sold."

"I—I do not understand," she said.

"Retrieval of living material, once transmitted," said Herjellen, "is apparently impossible. Retrieval was attempted with the leopard. We received only certain fragments of bone. These have been identified as those of a contemporary species of leopard, but the dating has fixed the acquisition at better than twenty-eight thousand years ago."

"I do not understand what you are saying," said Hamilton.

"I am saying," said Herjellsen, "that it seems that retrieval is impossible."

"Retrieval?" she asked.

"Yes," said Herjellsen.

"What has this to do with me?" she whispered.

"Surely you must understand," said Herjellsen, "that the chamber is now open."

She looked about herself, in terror. Everything seemed the same.

"Don't kill me," she said. "Sell me!"

"It will be necessary neither to kill you nor sell you, my dear," said Herjellsen.

"I don't understand," she said.

"The chamber is now open," he said.

"You are mad, mad!" she screamed.

"Turn their eyes," said Herjellsen, "to the stars."

Hamilton threw back her head, and threw her hands to the side of her head, and screamed.

◊ 11 ◊

Brenda Hamilton knelt, head thrown back, hands pressed to the sides of her head, screaming, in cold, wet grass, in the half darkness.

"No, no, no!" she wept.

She threw herself to her stomach in the cold grass, and clawed at it, and pressed the side of her cheek against it. She felt her fingers dig into the wet mud at the roots of the grass. "No," she wept. "No!"

A light rain was falling. "Herjellsen," she wept. "No!" She felt cold. "Please, no!" she wept.

She rose to her knees, shaking her head. She felt the cold, wet grass, flat and cutting, on her legs and thighs. She was cold. "No," she wept. The sky was dark, except for a rim of cold, gray light to her left. "No!" she cried.

She rose to her feet, unsteadily, cold, in the half darkness. She felt mud with her right foot.

The rain, slight, cold, drizzling, fell upon her. She cried out with misery.

"Herjellsen!" she cried. "William! Gunther! Take me back! Take me back! Do not send me away! Please!"

She screamed to the dark, gray, raining sky, standing in the wind, the cold rain.

"Take me back!" she cried. "Do not send me away! Please! Please!"

She knelt down and seized the grass with her hands. "I'm here!" she cried. "I'm here! Take me back! Please!" Then suddenly she screamed, and fled stumbling from the place. "It seems retrieval is not possible," had said Herjellsen. All that had been recovered of the leopard had been crumbled bone, indexed by carbon dating to a remote era, more than twenty-eight thousand years ago.

She looked at the place, in the early, cold light, where she had lain and knelt.

It seemed no different than other places she could make out, except that the grass had bent beneath her weight, wet, crushed.

She crept back to it, and put her hand timidly to the grass. Suddenly there was a stroke of lightning, broad and wild, cracking in the sky, and she screamed and fled away, falling and getting up.

In that stroke of lightning she had seen illuminated what seemed to be an open field, of uncomprehended breadth.

Thunder then swept about her, a pounding drum of sound, a stroke, rolling, of great depth and might, and suddenly the rain, wild with wind, following the turbulence in the sky, lashed about her.

She looked up, crying.

Again and again lightning split the darkness. She stood alone. Thunder smashed the world, pounding about her. Rain lashed her body.

"Herjellsen," she cried, "I am here!"

Then she threw herself down on the grass, naked, terrified of the lightning, whipped by the rain, covered her head with her hands, and wept.

In a few moments the storm had abated, and there was again only a light drizzle of rain. It was lighter now, and there was, all about her, the gentle, cool, gray of dawn. She could see the field extending away from her, on all sides.

The light was substantially to her left, which direction she surmised was East.

She stood up, in the drizzling, cold dawn, and looked about.

She tried to find where she had first knelt, but could not do so.

She was hungry.

She took grass and sucked rain from it. The grass had a sweet taste. The drops of water were cold.

She looked up into the sky. The clouds were vast, the sky was vast. The rain had almost stopped falling now.

"I am here, Herjellsen," she whispered.

Then she remembered that in the human reality, in time as it could only be understood by humans, Herjellsen, and Gunther and William could not hear her.

They had not yet been born.

She kept the sun on her left and began to walk, generally south.

◆ 12 ◆

Tree's nostrils flared.

He smelled female. And it was not one of the group. The other men did not notice. Several were sleeping. One was working a peeled, slender shaft, holding the wood over a small fire, softening it, and then inserting it through one of the holes in the drilled board, then bending the shaft carefully, straightening it.

Tree looked about the camp. It was a trail camp, a day's trek from the flint lode, two days' trek back to the shelters, a half day's march from the salt. Tree had found the salt, following antelope. But Spear had said he had found the salt. Spear was first in camp.

Tree rose to his feet, and stretched.

It was not an attack, for a female would not come in the attack.

The attack would not come from upwind.

It was not the Ugly People. The smell was not the Ugly People.

An ugly girl was in camp, who had been captured when
Spear and two others had killed her group. She was short,
and stooped and had large bones. Her head did not sit on
her shoulders as did that of the Men; it leaned forward,
looking at the ground; it was hard for her to lift her head;
she had a squat body; her knees were slightly bent. The
Ugly People, though, were good hunters. They could follow a
trail for days, by smell, loping, heads down, like hunting
dogs, on the scent. But Tree was a greater hunter. He did
not envy the Ugly People. They were not of the Men. In the
camp, only Runner could outdistance Tree, and Runner
was slight, but heavy chested. Tree was stronger, and could
throw further. Tree was strongest in camp, except Spear,
who was first.

Tree did not count as we would, nor was there need for
him to do so. We would have found that there were forty-
seven individuals in the camp. If Tree had spoken of
this, and he might have, for he had a language, the language
of the Men, he would have told us that there were two
hands in camp, for there were ten men, and it was these
that were counted. But he would have grasped the concept
of counting beyond this, if it had seemed important. If
there had been eleven men in camp, he would have said
there were two hands and one finger in camp, for that would
be eleven individuals. Further, if one had asked him, if all
in the camp were men, how many men would there be, he
would have thought and said, then there would be nine
hands and two fingers, or forty-seven individuals, only, of
course, that there were really only two hands, for there
were only ten men. If Tree's group had dogs, or goats, for
example, it would not have occurred to him either to
count those, but he might have done so, if asked. For
example, if each dog was also a man, then how many men
would there be, and so on. But Tree's group did not have
dogs, or goats. They did have, though, like other groups,
children and females.

There were ten men in Tree's group; there were sixteen
women; a woman is a female who can or has borne young;
there were twenty-one children; a child is a female who is
too young to bear young or a male who is not yet able to
run with the hunters. There was only one woman in camp
who was too old to bear young. Such women were rare.
She was Old Woman. There were no old men. There had
been one, but when he had gone blind, Spear had killed
him.

The men in the camp were Spear, who was first, and then Tree, finest of the hunters; Runner, who could single out an antelope and, in hours, run it to death, until it fell, gasping, and he would cut its throat; Arrow Maker, whose hands were the most cunning of all; Stone, who never laughed; Wolf, who did not look into one's eyes, and hid meat; Fox, quick, shrewd, who had once come from far away to trade flint for salt, and had stayed; he could speak the hand language of the Horse Hunters and Bear People; Spear had not killed him; he stole meat from Wolf; Knife, ill-tempered, cruel, the son of Spear; Tooth, a large man, fearsomely ugly, with an atavistically extended canine on the upper right side of his jaw, teller of stories, popular with children; and Hyena, whose brother was said to be a hyena, who spoke to him in dreams; the medicine of Hyena was thought to be the most dangerous in the camp.

There were sixteen women in the camp, but few of them are important. We might remark, at this time, Short Leg, docile with men, fierce to the women, dominant among the females; Old Woman, who tended the night fires; Flower, sweet-hipped, blond, sixteen years of age, most avidly sought, most frequently used, of the camp women; and Nurse, a large woman, fat, whose breasts had not been permitted to dry, whom the camp keeps to give suck to the young.

There were, too, twenty-one children in the camp, nine boys and twelve girls, ranging from infancy to the age of fourteen. These knew their mothers, but not their fathers. The others were only the Men. Kinship lines were simple because of the small size of the group, and relationship was traced through the female. This was not a matriarchy, if that implies that women had power, for the women, being women, had no power. We may, however, perhaps speak of the group being matrilineal, meaning by this only to denote the fact that kinship ties, such as they were, were, and, under the circumstances, could only be, established through the mother. The men, of course, stood in awe of the growth of a child and its bringing forth. They, too, of course, stood in awe of the growing of the moon, the coming of grass in the spring, the appearance of fruit on hitherto barren branches. Specific paternity, puzzling as it may seem to us, was not of great account with them. But that the group should have young, that it should continue, that there should be new hunters, was for them a matter of great concern. Fertility was of great moment. It was not that the men did not know the connection between conception and birth, for it was familiar to them, but rather that the family, as we often today think of it, insular and monogamous, was not yet an economic or social practicality. There might, under such circumstances, be women who did not bear young; and there might be men who, protecting or defending a given woman or given set of children, would not stand with the group, and the group might thus perish. One might say either that the family, as we know it, did not then exist, or that the group, the whole, was the family. It is somewhat misleading to speak in the latter sense, however, for the emotions of men and women being what they are, one could not, in the group, under the circumstances, have the same sense of love or loyalty that can bind together smaller social structures. There was, in Tree's group, little love, save that of mothers for their children, a phenomenon of significant evolutionary consequence, pervasive among primates. There were, of course, in the group, shifting couplings, and favorites. The instinct to pair bond, strongest in the female, who needed a protector, was present; she had a biological desire, constantly rebuffed, to attach herself to a given male, thereby assuring her his attention and her feeding; he, the hunter of meat, was less instinctually driven to pair bond, but he, too, when the female was pleasing and served him well, was not unaverse to maintaining, at his will, a longer-term relationship. But the facts were simple. The female needed the male. The hunter did not need the female. The hunter could choose his women. No one in the camp would starve, but to be fed well, if one were not a child and not pregnant, it was well to be a hunter's woman.

To be a hunter's woman meant, in effect, to be his favorite. This did not preclude the hunter using the bodies of other women for his pleasure, as the whim or urge came upon him. He could do what he wished, for he was a hunter. If he were a successful hunter, he might add to the number of women he fed. Spear fed five women. Tree, greatest of the hunters, fed what women he wished, when he wished. He had not permitted any of the women in the camp to kneel regularly behind him at the feeding, at his shoulder. Out of the relationship of favorite to hunter, and jealousy, and pride in one's children, not yet understood, would come in time marriage, intragroup mating restrictions.

In short, the women belonged to the men, but relationships were in actuality much more complex than this. Each woman did not, so to speak, belong to each man in the same way. Women, in whom the pair bonding instinct is stronger than in males, tended to attempt to become the females of given hunters, their favorites; and among the men, too, there were those who felt more attracted to one woman than another, and, accordingly, tended, as one would expect, to feed her more often, or regularly. If she should displease him, he would then throw her no more meat, and then, if she were not pregnant, she would try to please another hunter, to be fed. If she were pregnant, of course, she would be well fed. But, interestingly, after the child was cast, she would again have to compete for food, with the other women, trying to please a hunter. If she was unsuccessful, she would have to creep to the bones when the others were finished, and scavenge what she might, for herself and the child. There was usually little left. It was important to a woman to be pleasing to a hunter, if she would eat.

Tree bent down and picked up his pouch, his spear and rawhide rope.

Arrow Maker looked up.

"I am going hunting," said Tree.

He took his way between the huts, which they built far from the shelters.

These huts, most of them, consisted of poles and branches. First a round pit was scraped, a foot deep, some eight feet in diameter. In the center of this circle a rooftree was planted, a peeled pole, with projecting, peeled branches. Other poles then, planted in the rim of dirt about the edge of the circle, the dirt from the pit, leaned against the center tree. They were, further, tied in place with root and vine. This framework of poles completed, branches were then interlaced among them. Then, beginning at the bottom, that each layer overlap the lower layer, a thatch of broad-leaved branches was woven into the lateral branches, those placed in and about the pole framework. Rain, thus, falling from one thatch of leaves, dripped to the next, and did not enter the hut. The rim of dirt provided not only an easy foundation for the poles, even and soft, but kept rain from entering the house pit. In the front of the pit, in front of the tree, was the cooking hole. There were six such huts, round huts, and two others, built quite similarly, except that they were rectangular in shape and had two rooftrees, and a roof beam between them, consisting of a long pole. The poles of the side walls leaned against this elevated, central pole, running the length of the hut. The back poles, closing

the rear of the hut, leaned against the back rooftree. Both
sorts of huts, the round huts and the rectangular huts, were
open in the front. In the rectangular huts the cooking hole
was in the center. The rectangular huts had a width of some
eight feet, and a length of some twelve feet. The group had
made only round huts, but Fox, who had come from far
away, had introduced the rectangular hut. Spear had had
Hyena dream on the matter before permitting Fox's wom-
en, those he fed, to build according to his directions.
Hyena's dream had been favorable. The Horse Hunters built
such huts, and there was luck for horse hunting in them.
Spear wanted his hunters to be able to hunt not only
antelope, and moose, and elk, but, if the need should arise,
horse, too. No one in the group knew the horse prayers,
but this did not mean they might not, if the need arose, be
able to hunt horse. The horses might be fooled by the
rectangular huts. Too, Hyena could make horse prayers, and
if they were good prayers, maybe the horses would let themselves be killed. If one who was not a Horse Hunter killed a
horse, of course, there could be danger. If the horse was
angry, the men might die from the meat. But if the huts
were rectangular and the prayers were flattering, perhaps
trouble could be avoided. The horses might be gracious, and
the group could feed. There was no reason why horses
should let themselves be killed only by the Horse Hunters.
Spear's hunters were good hunters, and it was not dis-
honorable for horses to let themselves be killed by them.

"Where are you going?" asked Spear.

"I am going hunting," said Tree.

He continued on.

To one side he saw Knife, who was the son of Spear. His
descent was figured through Crooked Wrist, a woman who
had died many years ago from the bites of a cave lion, who
had hunted men in the vicinity of the shelters. But there
was no doubt that he was the true son of Spear. The
resemblance was clear, the same narrowness of eyes, the
same heaviness of jaw, and so it was known that Knife was
Spear's son.

Tree did not know if any of the small children in the
camp were his. He had had, since beginning to run with the
hunters, seventeen years ago, all the women in the camp,
except Short Leg, Old Woman and Nurse. And he had not
wanted them.

The woman who had borne Knife had originally been
called Fern. She had once displeased Spear. He had broken

her wrist. It had not healed cleanly. She had come to be
called Crooked Wrist. Nine months after her wrist had been
broken, the boy, to be called Knife when old enough to
run with the hunters, had been pulled bloody from her body.

The cave lion had killed four members of the group before it had been caught in a pit and killed with stones.

Spear had been fond of Fern. The cave lion, dying under
the stones, had died slowly. Spear had not seen fit to hurry
its death. Sometimes even now, many years later, Spear
angrily called the name of Fern in his sleep. This did not
please Short Leg, lying awake beside him, who was now
first among the women whom he fed.

No one now in the group, except Stone and Spear, knew
what the pit had been like or how it had been baited. Old
Man would have known, but, when he had gone blind, Spear
had killed him. Old Woman was old, but she had been purchased from the Bear People after the lion had been killed,
for two sacks of flints. In those days she had been called
Pebble; the man who had bought her had been called
Drawer, because he made marks in the sand with sticks.
Later he had been called Old Man.

Spear, who knew Knife as his son, coming to understand
this as the boy had grown, was proud of him, in a way
many of the Men, not knowing their own sons, found it
hard to understand. But Tree thought he understood. Tree
thought it would be good to know one's son. One could
then teach him to be a great hunter. And one could be his
friend. But though Spear was proud of Knife, he was not
his friend. Spear feared Knife, for he thought Knife would
supplant him, and become first in the group. Knife had already killed one man, fighting over meat in the winter, and
was much feared in the group. Many of the Men, Fox, and
Wolf and Stone, chief among them, did not understand why
Spear, fearing Knife, did not kill him. But Tree thought he
understood. One could not kill one whom one knew was
one's own son. It would be worse than the killing of one's
self. It would not be a good thing. Many of the men did not
understand this. But Tree understood it, and he thought
Arrow Maker, too, might understand it. If Tree had a son,
he would not kill him. He would teach him to be a great
hunter. And he would be his friend, and, sometimes, when
the fires were small, he would talk with him.

And so Spear waited for the time when Knife would kill
him, and become first in the group.

"Where are you going?" asked Knife. He was lying in the

grass behind one of the huts, on one elbow, pulling at a piece of dried meat with his teeth.

"I am going hunting," said Tree.

At Knife's feet lay Flower. She was licking slowly at his ankle. He pulled off a piece of dried meat in his teeth and, with his hand, held it down to her. She took it in her teeth, and began to chew it, moving slowly, with her lips and hands, up his leg.

At the edge of the camp there were two sets of poles. The first set of poles was a meat rack, consisting of two upright poles and, lashed across them, several small poles, over which were hung strips of meat, drying in the sun. The other set of poles was a game rack, or skinning rack. It consisted of two crossed poles at each end, bound together at the top, and a lateral pole, set in the joinings of the end poles. From it, upside down, hind feet stretched and bound to the pole, hung a small deer. Its throat had been cut that morning and the blood, dripping, had been caught in a leather piece, fitted into a concave depression in the ground. The hunters, as was their wont, had drunk the fresh blood. That it was a source of iron to them they did not know; they did know that it gave them strength and stamina. Blood was prized. Many of the women did not know its taste. None of the children knew. A boy was not permitted blood until he had killed his first large game animal. Then it was his right to drink first. The deer had been killed by Stone, who had driven it into a thicket and then broken its neck.

Ugly Girl whimpered and cowered away from Tree as he strode past.

He looked down on her. She crouched, bent over, her thick-legged, squat, round-shouldered body shaking. She looked up at him, her hair like black strings, her eyes stupid and frightened, like those of an animal.

Tree despised those of the Ugly People, though he had never killed any of them.

Spear, with Knife and Stone, had surprised Ugly Girl's group and had killed them all, with the exception of Ugly Girl.

In camp Spear had tied a short rawhide strap on her ankles, shackling her in leather. She could move about the camp, but clumsily, and slowly. She could not run. When she had been brought to camp the children and women had much beaten her with switches. Then, when they had tired of this, they had put her to work, carrying water in the hide buckets from the stream, gathering stones for the cooking holes, gathering wood for the fires. She was still much beaten, for the Men did not care for the Ugly People. Her heavy, clumsy fingers could not easily untie the rawhide. When Spear had caught her doing so, he had switched her until she had howled and covered her head with her hands. She then knew she was not permitted to touch the rawhide shackles. She knew she might, in time, untie them, but now she was afraid even to touch them. In her simplicity and stupidity, she remained shackled. She looked away from Tree, down at the dirt, whimpering. Had she been able to reach the leather with her teeth she might have bitten through it, tearing it in her teeth, but she could not reach it.

Tree did not kick at her nor cry out at her, to frighten her. He ignored her. He did not know why Spear, and Knife and Stone, had not killed her as well as the others. She was not a woman. She was a female of the Ugly People. Tree would not have wanted her, any more than a doe or a mare. She could not even speak, though, he knew, the Ugly People did make noises which, among themselves, somehow, they found intelligible. It did not occur to Tree that they, like the Men, and like the Horse Hunters and the Bear People, might have a language. He knew, of course, that he, and the others, even Fox, could not understand her noises. Nor, as Fox established, did she know the hand sign of the Horse Hunters and the Bear People. Thus Tree inferred that Ugly Girl could not speak. Or, more exactly, he inferred that she was unable to speak until she had been brought to the camp of the Men. Here the children had taught her certain noises, which she could, in her guttural, half inarticulate way, imitate. Tree thought that Ugly Girl should be grateful to the Men, for they had taught her to speak, if only a few words. But Ugly Girl did not seem grateful, only miserable and frightened. The children of the Men, Tree noted, learned the words more swiftly than Ugly Girl. She was stupid, not of the Men. One could see that she was dull, that she understood nothing, that she was only an animal. Sometimes at night she cried.

Tree turned and looked back at Knife and Flower. Knife had now taken her by the hair and drawn her between his legs, where she, laughing and kissing, sought to please him.

Elsewhere he could see Feather, a thin woman, grooming Stone, taking lice from his hair, eating them.

She would lick sometimes his neck with her tongue, and whimper.

The women groomed the men. Men did not groom women. Women groomed one another, and the women, too, groomed the children. Children were permitted to groom one another, until the boys became old enough to run with the hunters.

Now Feather lay on her back before Stone, whimpering, and lifting her body to him.

Stone regarded her for a time, and then he crawled to her, and, as she cried out with pleasure, locked her helplessly in his arms.

It was the Capture Position, holding the female down, confining her movements, making her helpless.

Feather cried out her pleasure to the camp.

Flower, angrily, broke away from Knife, and lay before him, lifting her body to him.

He went to her, and took her in his arms.

Soon, she, too, cried out with pleasure.

The women of the Men had two hungers, each as open, direct and piteous as the other. For the one hunger it was common to open the mouth and point a finger to it, and then extend the hands, palms up; for the other hunger it was not uncommon to do as had Feather and Flower, to lie before the hunter and, sometimes piteously, lift her body to him.

Again, from upwind, came the scent of female to Tree, and not one of the group.

In the camp he heard one woman, and then another, cry out her hunger, excited doubtless by the cries of Feather, and then Flower. He had seen this happen before in the camp. Soon, like a contagion, the manifestation of their need might spread, woman to woman, each in her moaning and whimpering stimulating the other, and then they would approach the males, timidly, fearing to be struck, and creep to their feet, begging to be touched. There were ten hunters in the camp, and sixteen women.

Tree caught the scent again, but it was fainter this time. He must hurry.

"Tree!" cried a woman, seeing him, standing between two huts. There was another woman behind her. They were Antelope and Cloud. He had often fed them.

Tree looked to Flower, still wrestling, laughing, in the arms of Knife, who was once more refusing to release her.

He would have liked Flower, but Knife now held her. He did not want to fight Knife.

"Tree!" cried Antelope. She was tall, dark-haired, young.

Cloud was shorter, more timid, thick-ankled, younger than Antelope.

Tree's eyes warned them not to approach.

"Tree," called Antelope. She fell to her knees. So, too, behind her, did Cloud. Either, or both, was his for the asking.

"I am going hunting," said Tree.

He was aroused. He was angry. He thought he would take Antelope, but then he might lose the scent.

Antelope kicked well, he enjoyed her.

"Tree," called Antelope.

"I am going hunting," said Tree, angrily, and turned, and left the camp.

Once outside the perimeter of the camp he stopped and, nostrils distended, drank in the scent. He had not wanted to do this in the camp, for fear another hunter would see, and, too, test the wind. Tree's senses were sharpest of the hunters, but the senses of these men, on the whole, would have seemed incredible to later, smaller men. There was not one of them who could not smell deer, in a favorable wind, at a thousand yards, or locate the droppings of small animals in high grass, by scent alone. They could see squirrels against a network of branches at two hundred yards, observe clearly the bright eyes of circling eagles, and mark instantly the place where a paw had minutely pressed aside a bit of leaf mold. The breathing of a human being they could hear at fifty feet, that of the cave lion at one hundred. Tree, alone of the hunters, could follow a trail by night, by smell.

He was angry, for in the camp the women had been becoming aroused. Soon they would be much in their need. Tree enjoyed seeing them in their need. He enjoyed seeing them come to him, creep to his feet and, whimpering, lift their bodies to him. Then he would take which one he wished. When their need was upon them they kicked well, any of them. But Tree had his favorites. His favorites were Flower, and Antelope and Cloud. Flower was quick to arouse, but she did not, Tree thought, kick as well for Tree as for Knife. This made Tree angry, and made him desire her more. Flower, he knew, wanted to be the woman of the leader. Tree would not be the leader. Knife would be the leader, when he had killed Spear. But Antelope and Cloud, Tree admitted, kicked well for Tree, very well. Even when their need had not been upon them, it would become manifest when he touched them. He had only to take them in

his arms to make the desire-smell break forth from between
their thighs. The desire-smell excited Tree. It made him
want to have the women. Old Woman, when he had become
old enough to run with the hunters, had showed Tree how
to make the desire-smell come in any woman, if he wished.
She had also showed him how to touch, and be patient, and
wait, like a hunter, caressing and licking, until a woman,
even one resistant, could not help but kick for him. "I did
not want to be the woman of Drawer," Old Woman had
told the youthful Tree, "but he made me kick for him."
Her eyes had been shining, in the wrinkled skin. She had
cared much for Drawer. But when he had become Old
Man, he had gone blind, and Spear had killed him. But it
took time to do with a woman what Old Woman had shown
him, and Tree, like the other hunters, seldom had such
patience. It was usually not as Old Woman had told him.
When the members of the band were in their need things
did not usually proceed as Old Woman had recommended.
The woman, if in her need, usually came whimpering to the
hunter, lifting her body to him; she would then be used at
whatever length he might please; the hunter, in his need,
no other hunter intervening, usually took what woman he
wished, swiftly, then discarded her. Often, of course, the
women, even if not in need, would lift their bodies to the
hunters. They would do this to please them, and to be fed.
It was well to be pleasing to a hunter, if one were not
pregnant, if one would eat.

In the feeding, Spear cut meat first, for he was the leader.
He would give meat, then, to the hunters. Later they would
cut their own meat. Pieces, then, by Spear, or Tooth, or
others, would be thrown to pregnant women, and to the
children. The smaller children were thrown separate pieces,
that they might eat; the older children were thrown a larger
piece of meat which the oldest and strongest, who might be
male or female, but was usually female, for at this age the
females tended to be larger than boys of comparable age,
would divide among them. The leader of the older children
in Spear's group was the girl, Butterfly, who was not popular
with the children, for she played her favorites in the distri-
bution of the meat; the young boys hated her, for she made
them beg her for meat; in time, of course, as she grew
older, and the young boys grew tall and straight, and strong
beyond her, and she became a woman and they became
hunters, their situation would be, to the pleasure of the
boys, well reversed. She would learn to lift her body to them.

As the men were eating, and the meat had been thrown to the pregnant females and the children, the other females would creep nearer, for the men, if they wished, to feed them. They might not steal meat or take it for themselves, for they were women. The only exceptions to this were Old Woman and Nurse, who took meat when they wished, neither challenged. Old Woman was simply Old Woman; and Nurse was important for the small children, the infants. Sometimes a mother did not have milk. In some human groups, the Bear People, for instance, nursing mothers were extended the same meat rights as pregnant females, but this was not so in Spear's group. In Spear's group such women obtained their meat like other women, by begging and by being pleasing to hunters. Spear had discovered that a woman who needs meat to make milk in her body for her baby will kick well. After the hunters were finished, of course, anyone, woman or child, might fall on the remains of the repast, to pick what bones might be left, to poke about in the ashes for bits of gristle or to lick grease from the charred wood of the fire. After these were finished, Ugly Girl would, the others not stopping her, creep to the fire, scratching and smelling for what might be left. It was not always the case, of course, that a woman would beg for meat, or lift her body to the men to be fed. Such women, though rare, often wandered away from the groups. Usually they died; if they did not die they did not have children. Women who wished the touch of hunters, who accepted being owned by them, who willingly, eagerly, lifted their bodies for meat, would be those women who would survive, whose children would be born, whose young would take in time their place, in turn, as hunters and the women of hunters.

Tree now circled the camp, not losing the scent. It was not difficult to follow.

He carried his pouch, his rope, his spear.

◇ 13 ◇

For four days Brenda Hamilton had wandered in a generally southward direction, in the morning keeping the sun on
her left and, in the evening, on her right.

At the end of the second day she had come to the end of
the rolling grassland in which she had first found herself.
She had dug roots and found wild strawberries, and had
drunk at small pools of rain water. Once she had come to a
larger watering hole, near which were the prints of numerous animals. The water had been muddy there, and she had
not drunk. She had gone around the hole and continued on
her journey. She saw only one herd of animals, a herd of
some twenty horses. They were the size of large ponies, and
had an unusual mane, stiff and erect, like a brush. They
were tawny in color, and kept well away from her, even
when she attempted to approach them more closely. She
did not know, but they had been hunted. They knew the
smell of men. If she had gone further to the north she
would have found more animals, herds of bison and smaller groups of aurochs. In the mud at the watering hole she
had found no prints of paws, except those of tiny animals,
rodents and insectivores, with one exception, those of a
pair of apparently large animals, feline, it seemed, who had
come to the water to drink together. The great majority of
the prints at the watering hole were those of small, hoofed
animals, doubtless mostly those of horses, of the sort of
which she had seen one herd. There were other prints, too,
hoofed, which, being smaller, she conjectured were those of
various, lesser ungulates. The larger paw prints had frightened her. She had not lingered at the watering hole. They
were the prints, though she would not learn this until later,
of one of the most beautiful, and dangerous, animals of
the Pleistocene, the giant cheetah.

In the late afternoon of the second day she had come to
what seemed to be an endless, linear stand of deciduous

134

trees, oak, elm and ash, and yew and maple, and others she did not recognize, stretching northeast by southwest. Entering the trees she discovered a long, swift stream, quite cold, flowing southwestward. She drank at this and, finding a wide place, using a pole to thrust ahead of her to test her footing, she forded it, and then, on the southern bank, followed it southwestward. Within an hour the grasslands, at first visible through the trees on her left, had disappeared, to be replaced with darkly green, forested country. By night-fall she could no longer, either, through the trees, see the grasslands on her right.

She had left the fields.

She had come to the forests.

The forests, with their darkness, and their sounds, frightened her.

She tried to make a fire by rubbing sticks together, and striking rocks, and failed.

It was cold at night.

She slept fitfully. Once she awakened and screamed. Not more than twenty paces from her, in the moonlight, she saw the dark forms of more than a dozen doglike creatures, curious, watching her. When she screamed, they moved away, scurrying, but then continued to watch. She wept and screamed and threw rocks and sticks at them. Two snarled, but then the pack turned, and, as one, faded into the trees.

Weeping, Hamilton climbed a tree, and clung to the branches.

They had been wolves.

Man is not, and has never been the natural prey of wolves, a quadruped that strikes for four-footed game. Her erect posture might have saved her. Or her smell, which was not the game smell of wolves. The wolf, in its pack, like the hunting dog, is a tireless tracker and hunter, and a success-ful pack killer, and ruthless, and savage, but it is not, and has never been a predator on man. Had it been so the dog, derivative from wolf stock, doubtless would never have been domesticated. And, too, perhaps, man would not have sur-vived. Wolves, however, are curious animals, a trait indica-tive of animal intelligence. Human camps were often objects of curiosity to them, and it was not uncommon for them to scout them, and prowl them. Wolf eyes beyond the fire-light, almond and gleaming, were not unusual. Humans did not, however, fear wolves, for the wolf did not hunt them.

It was sometimes otherwise with the cave lion, if the animal were old or crippled, or with leopards.

Hamilton, who did not know the hunting habits of wolves, was terrified.

She determined to leave, if possible, the forest, but she did not wish to return to the grassland. The prints of the large felines she had seen by the watering hole still frightened her. She reasoned that if she continued to follow the stream she might remain indefinitely within the forest, for it might, even to the sea, margin the waterway, broadening, too, as other streams fed into it, or it, itself, became a tributary to some larger flow of water, perhaps a great forest-encompassed river. Too, she wished to move generally southward, rather than southwestward. The terrain and vegetation about her reminded her strongly of that of the temperate zones, and this made her afraid of what winter might be like. The season of year in which she found herself in this fresh, frightening world seemed surely to be late spring or early summer. The grass in the fields had reached generally halfway up her calves. The trees were not budding, but openly and richly leaved, and still a rich green. The season was not dry as she would have expected in late summer. She went south, rather than north, correctly ascertaining by the stars, their familiarity to her, their difference from the African night, that she was in the Earth's northern hemisphere. Had the night sky been that of the southern hemisphere, she would have trekked north. She began to go south immediately, for she had no idea how long it might take to reach a climate which might remain mild throughout the year. She lacked clothing; she lacked shelter; she lacked, as far as she knew, the skills even to make a fire; she did not believe she would survive in the winter; there would be little to eat, if anything; and there would be the cold. She trekked south.

Her main motivation to follow the streams and rivers was to keep close to drinkable water, though she would, when possible, drink from rock pools, filled with rain water, rather than from the streams, which were often dark with mud, washing silt down to the sea, draining basins perhaps hundreds of miles wide. Small, clear forest streams, emanating from springs, much pleased her. River water frightened her. Still she must, at times, drink. It would take weeks, she knew, to die by starvation; but she could thirst to death in less than four days.

Still she had made her decision to depart from the stream, which was moving southwestward.

She feared the forest; she did not know the habits of wolves; she did not wish to be led by the streams too far west, for she wished to move more directly south. There were two other reasons, too, why she elected to move more directly south, though she scarcely dared to consider them explicitly. The first was that she suspected that men might exist in this time, in these countries, and follow the rivers, or make their habitations near them. The last thing she wanted, perhaps paradoxically, for she was inutterably lonely, was to encounter men. She did not even know if they would be human. Her imagination was terrified. She wondered if they might appear subhuman primates, with great jaws and long arms, or, if they seemed human, if they might have, in effect, the minds of apes. At best, she knew, they would be ruthless, and savage. She did not wish to fall in with such. With uneasiness she recalled Gunther's speculations as to whether or not they might sacrifice virgins. He had speculated that they, being hunters, would not. Herjellsen had said that they were sending a woman, because a man would be killed. But, might they not kill a woman, too, especially if she were not a member of their group, if she were an utter stranger? At best they might keep her as an oddity, or, more likely, as a pet or, if they found her body of interest, as a slave. She would, at all costs, avoid men. Brenda Hamilton smiled to herself. She was beautiful, sophisticated, and highly intelligent. She had a Ph.D. in mathematics from the California Institute of Technology. She had no intention of becoming the slave girl of savages. The second other reason for moving more directly south than could be achieved by following the stream was that she feared reaching the sea. The sea on one side would be a wall. She knew she might be hunted, or pursued, from the forest, and, across the beach, driven against that wall. Against the sea she could be trapped. Gunther had told her that in fenced game preserves lions had learned to drive antelope against the wire fences, trapping them for the kill. She had no wish to be in a position where she might be so trapped. She feared to be hunted, by whatever might hunt her, whether it might be animal or human, or near human. She did not want the sea closing off one hundred and eighty degrees of an escape route. Also, of course, she feared that, at the edge of the sea, there might be men,

either in their habitations or using the relative openness of
the beaches for trekking.

Accordingly, Brenda Hamilton left the stream. If she did not
find fresh water after one day, it was her intention to return to the stream, and again follow it.

On the third day of her trek, however, the first day of
leaving the stream, she discovered, to her pleasure, that
her southward journey transected various small brooks, and
that rock outcroppings, in which water could be found, were
relatively plentiful. Less to her pleasure, she did not discover the trees thinning, or giving way, as she had hoped,
to either grassland or savannah country; sometimes she
walked on a carpet of leaves, between tall trees, whose
canopied branches all but obliterated the light of the sun;
sometimes, in the heat, naked, feet and ankles scratched,
her body struck by branches, she forced her way, foot by
foot, through what seemed to be an inclosing, almost impenetrable thicket of trees, brush and fallen timber. Once
she came to a broad, scarred, half-blackened belt of stumps;
it took her more than half an hour to traverse it; it was
now scattered with patches of green, and tiny shoots of
trees, bright, in the grayish earth, where rain had mixed
with ashes and soil; the cause of the fire, she conjectured,
would have been lightning; it would have taken place, presumably, in the last dry season, late in the preceding summer or early in the succeeding fall. She thought that she
was entering ever more deeply into the forest, and to some
extent she was, but, when the evening of the third day fell,
she was startled to discover a stream that was flowing not
from her left to right but from her right to left, and, to her
dismay, she found the evening sun on her left, rather than
her right. Her path, described, would have resembled a
large hook; she had not circled, but she had, in the thickets,
during the time of high sun, turned gradually back on her
path; it was difficult in the forests, for one who could not
read the forest, and Brenda Hamilton could not, to keep a
straight direction; the common stratagem of marking out
distant landmarks and trekking to them was not available
to her; and her stride, even if it had not been for the forest,
was not even; few humans, not trained in the military,
can maintain an even stride; over a period of hours, and
miles, the unevenness tends to bring about, unless com-
pensated for, say, by noting directions or landmark trekking, a gradually curved path, not the desired linear pro-
gression. Accordingly, on the third day, Brenda Hamilton,

though moving generally southward, had gone far less far to the south than she would have hoped. She had, on the third day, in twelve hours of trekking, reckoning in time, moved only some three or four hours, or some eight or ten miles, further to the south. She did not, of course, know that she had done even this well. She knew only that she had discovered herself, toward the evening of the third day, moving northward, rather than southward, that she had been moving in the direction exactly opposite to that in which she had intended to move. This discovery terrified and shattered her, for, to the best of her understanding, she had been, continually throughout the day, moving as she wished, southward. Suddenly she no longer had confidence in her ability to find her way as she wished. What had seemed simple to her no longer did so. She now knew she might, stumbling and pressing through thickets, when the sun was high, lost among the branches and leaves, unknowingly, unwittingly, lose her direction. If the touch of the winter extended, from her latitude, some hundreds of miles to the south, and she could make only a few miles a day in her trek, it was not unlikely that she would be trapped in the forest. She imagined herself caught in the first snows, naked, perhaps still unable to make a fire, without food. She wept with misery. For the first time since her first hours in the grassy field, she felt utterly helpless, utterly alone. She realized now that it was not impossible that she, alone, unable to help herself, might die in the forest. That evening she found a handful of nuts to eat, which she picked from the ground. She broke them with rocks, and ate their meat. She lay on her belly, on the gravel, beside a small stream, and drank. She crawled into some brush, and pulled it about her. She lay on her side, and moaned. She now knew, clearly, that she lay at the mercy of her ignorance and the elements. And, too, she feared beasts, wolves, or unknown beasts, such as might have made the large paw prints at the watering hole, which might hunt her, and bring her down with their teeth, as easily as a doe. Toward morning, after much weeping, she fell asleep. She had decided, however, that she must continue to attempt to travel directly south. If she stopped and followed a stream generally southwestward, it might take hundreds of extra miles to reach a warmer latitude, even assuming the sea itself, or an arm of the sea, did not, when reached, itself present an obstacle to that advance, and the winter might overtake her. She must try to move, she reasoned, difficult though it might be, directly to the south. She did not know how many days there might be until the onset of winter; more importantly, she did not know how far she would have to travel to reach a mild climate, nor how much of this distance she might be able to cover in a given day. On this day, the third day of her trek, she knew only she had discovered herself, in the evening, moving in the wrong direction; she did not know if she had covered even a mile of her projected journey in the past twelve hours of trekking.

One other decision Brenda Hamilton had reached before she fell asleep.

If it came to a choice between death by starvation or exposure, or at the fangs of beasts, and presenting herself to a human, or humanoid, group, she would do the latter. She would take her chances with them, that they might kill her. She hoped that Herjellsen, and Gunther and William, were right, that such groups would not kill a woman. They had speculated, however, that another fate would be likely to be hers, that she would be made a slave. "Very well," thought Brenda Hamilton, angrily, "I will let them make me their slave." She twisted, angrily. "I do not care!" she whispered to herself. "I would rather be the slave of apes, than die," she said to herself. She lay on her back, looking up at the brush about her. She recalled how she had begged that, rather than be disposed of in the bush, she be sold as a slave. But that slavery would have been quite different, from that she now considered. That would have been a silken, perfumed slavery, with little fear, perhaps, other than the master's whip. But this other slavery would doubtless be quite different. Doubtless there might be physical labor, even burdens to carry. And what if she did not sufficiently please a brutish master? Would he simply kill her? She shuddered.

She fell asleep.

On the morning of the fourth day, it was bright, and hot, when Brenda Hamilton awakened. She had slept until well into the morning, and felt rested. She was not particularly angry at having slept longer than she had intended. She had come to two decisions, that to attempt to continue in a direct southward direction and that, as a last resort, if absolutely necessary, she would make contact with a human, or humanoid group, though she was confident that if she did this, she would be placed in bondage.

She reached up to pick some fruit from a branch.

"Yes, Gunther," she said to herself, "you were right—I am a slave."

She laughed, and took the fruit, and bit into it. "Does that shock you, Gunther," she asked, speaking as if he might be present, "that I would rather be the slave of apes than die?" She chewed some fruit, and swallowed it, spitting out some seeds. She felt the juice on her wrist. "You are such a prude, Gunther," she said. She laughed. "I would have made you an excellent slave, Gunther," she laughed, "but you missed your chance!"

She went to the stream, and drank, and then noted her directions, judging from the course of the stream and where the sun had set the evening before.

She knew that now, in the beginning, at least, she was moving south.

She again began her trek.

◇ **14** ◇

Tree, facing upwind, observed the female. She was naked. This pleased him.

Her legs were shapely.

She was not as tall as most of the women of the group, but she was not short, either. She was taller than Cloud.

Her body seemed very white, which surprised Tree, not tanned like the women of the group.

Her breasts were ample; her hips were wide; her ass excited Tree.

He decided he wanted her.

From his pouch he removed a short length of rawhide rope, some eighteen inches in length. He looped this twice about his wrist and knotted it loosely, a knot that he might pull free with his teeth. He then, carefully, set his pouch to one side, and the long rope he carried, coiled, over his shoulder, and his spear. He then, staying downwind of the female, moved to be in a position such that she would approach him.

Brenda Hamilton picked her way carefully, for the ground, here and there, was soft.

A quarter of an hour ago there had been a light shower, muddying the ground, but now the sun had broken through the clouds. The leaves and the grass were wet and sparkling.

She picked her way carefully, for she was fastidious, and did not wish to muddy her feet.

It happened swiftly.

Brenda Hamilton scarcely saw him. It was suddenly something moving toward her.

She cried out, and turned to flee. Her foot slipped in the mud. She began to run. She had gone no more than three or four paces when he was upon her; his shoulder struck her behind the back of the knees; her head and back snapped back and then, after a sickening instant, she momentarily conscious of his arms locked about her legs, she, her entire body, helpless, propelled by his weight and hers, snapped forward again, pitching headlong, violently, forward through the air. She landed, skidding in the grass and mud. She thought, momentarily, her back was broken. She gasped for breath. Dimly she was aware of herself, prone, her belly in the mud, his knees now on either side of her body. She tried to breathe. She felt her wrists jerked behind her and fastened together, with great tightness. She gasped, struggling for breath. She felt herself then turned on her back. "Oh!" she cried. "Oh!" She could scarcely believe the magnificence of the creature who had taken her. "No," she cried, then, "No, please!" She struggled, but it was to no avail. He thrust apart her thighs. He thrust to her. She closed her eyes in pain. "Please!" she wept. She saw his eyes, puzzled, angry. He had never had a virgin. Always it had been the older men who had taken them. He looked at her, partly not understanding, for the woman was clearly too old to be a virgin; in the group it was Spear who decided when a girl was too old to be a virgin, then ordering her to take her place with the other women, to beg meat from the hunters; this took place sometimes when a girl was as young as twelve, at other times as old as fifteen. A law had been made in the group that no hunter might take a girl until she had begun to beg meat; Spear had made this law; it was he, too, who had made the law that children and pregnant women must be fed, even if sometimes the hunters must do with less. Tree did not understand all of Spear's laws, but he obeyed them, for he did not wish to be killed. It was good he understood that the children and the pregnant women would be fed,

though, for without them there would be no group, no growing. The other law Tree did not understand so clearly, but he
did not object. Old Woman, when he had asked her of this,
had said that the children of girls too young to beg meat
were small and weak, and often died; and, too, girls who
were made to kick too early were sometimes injured, and
frightened, and they might not kick so well later. Tree had
shrugged. The law did not matter to him, for he was not
interested in girls too young to beg meat. When they put
away their bone and skin dolls, and began to look sideways
at the hunters, that was time enough for them to learn to
beg meat. When a girl did take her place with the women,
behind the men at the cutting of the meat, it was usually
Spear, or Stone, or sometimes Arrow Maker, who used them
first, always one of the older men. Tree had never had a
virgin.

Brenda Hamilton struggled back, pushing with her heels
in the mud, backing away from him.

"No," she said. "No."

Tree grinned at her.

He took her by the right ankle and pulled her again to
him. "No!" she cried.

Again her thighs were spread.

She cried out with pain.

When Tree had finished with her there was blood on the
inside of her left thigh, smeared to the side of the knee.

She lay on her side, her wrists still tied behind her.

Tree took a bit of the blood on his finger and licked it. It
tasted of blood, but there was other fluid, too. He found the
taste of interest.

She looked at him with horror.

He took some more blood on his finger and held it to her
lips, that she might taste. This was done in the group, that
the girl, too, might know the taste of the blood of her
deflowering. In the group they were eager to know the taste,
for they experienced the world richly, sensuously, knowing it
not only by sight and concept, but by touch, smell, feel and
taste. The Bear People, Tree knew, even had a ceremony in
which the girls were deflowered. The Men, though, had no
ceremony for this. They did have a ceremony when the boy
began to run with the hunters. He drank first blood of his
first kill, the other hunters, even the great ones, waiting to
drink after him.

Brenda Hamilton cried out with misery, and turned her
face away.

This angered Tree, and he thrust her mouth open with his left hand and thrust the bloodied finger across her lips and tongue.

Brenda Hamilton, forced, tasted and smelled Tree's trophy of her ravished virginity.

She looked at him, with fury.

Tree's hand again went forth to touch her ankle. She pulled away. "Please don't hurt me again," she wept.

Tree reached to her and, taking her by the hair, pulled her to her feet. He led her beside him, bent over, holding her by the hair, to where he had left his pouch, and his rope and spear. There he sat her down, regarding her.

"What is your people?" he asked.

Brenda Hamilton did not understand him, for he spoke the language of the Men.

"I cannot understand you," she said.

She did not speak the language of the Men. Tree had not expected her to be able to do so, of course, though Old Man, long before Spear had killed him, had told him that there were other groups who did speak the language of the Men. Old Man had also told him of a great trek, which had lasted, in the telling of it, for five generations, in which the Men had moved westward. In this trek different groups, from time to time, had split away, seeking a territory sufficient for hunting. This had been, however, even before Old Man's time. Old Man had known many stories. Tree was sorry that Spear had killed him. Tree had liked Old Man, and, too, he had liked the stories he had told. He had even told of beasts, large and hairy, as large as huts, or larger, with great, long curved teeth, and of black rocks that, when lit, would burn like wood. Spear had said Old Man was a liar.

Tree was not disappointed that the woman could not speak the language of the Men. He was glad.

It meant one could do with her what one wished, completely. One, of course, did much what one wished with the women of the group, using them, and beating them, and such, but one was not supposed to kill them. They, though women, were of the group, its followers, and breeders and workers. Tree looked at the helpless, desirable, bound body of his catch. She was not of the group. If one of the hunters wished, she might even be killed.

She did not speak the language of the Men. Tree was glad.

She would learn, of course, to speak the language of the

Men, and learn it quickly. The women would see to that. She must understand the orders that would be given to her.

Tree looked at his catch. She was just that, totally rightless.

"You will belong to the Men," he told her.

Hamilton looked at him blankly.

Tree wondered if she could speak in the Hand Sign, that used by the Horse Hunters and the Bear People. Only Fox, in his group, was fully conversant with Hand Sign, but Tree knew the Hand Sign for the Men, and knew, too, how to ask for another's group, or people, and how to make the more general question sign. He also knew the hand sign for the Horse Hunters and the Bear People, and for salt and flint. That was the extent of his vocabulary. But Fox could speak fluently in Hand Sign.

Tree took his long rope, and with one end of it, lashed together Brenda Hamilton's ankles.

He then untied her hands.

She sat and faced him, her hands free, her ankles crossed and tied together.

Tree pointed to her, and then held up his left hand, palm facing to the right, and then placed his right index finger upright with the upright fingers of his left hand, one among others. "To what people do you belong?" he had asked in Hand Sign.

She shook her head, she understood nothing.

Tree frowned and touched his left hand to his head, as though puzzled. Then he held his right hand forth, palm to the left, thumb folded in, four fingers pointing down toward the earth. "Are your people the Horse Hunters?" he had asked.

She shook her head, trying to indicate that she understood nothing.

Tree was patient. He knew, of course, that females, even in the Horse Hunters and Bear People, were not generally taught Hand Sign, being women, but he was sure they would know at least how to respond to certain simple signs. They would know, certainly, the sign for their own group.

But this woman was apparently completely ignorant of Hand Sign.

Tree touched his head and frowned, and then lowered and raised his hand in a cupped fashion, as though he might be scooping something from the water. "Are you of the Bear People?" he asked. He then moved his hands, as though striking flint, the sign for flint. No recognition came into her eyes. He then licked his upper lip, in the sign for salt. She did not respond. He then pointed to himself and raised his right fist, as though it might hold a spear. "I am of the Men," he had told her.

She shook her head. "I do not understand anything," she said.

Tree took her ankles and turned them, throwing her to her stomach. Then he knelt across her body and, again, tied her hands behind her back.

When he had done so, she turned, and struggled to a sitting position, and again regarded him, her captor.

He removed the rope from her ankles, tied one end of it about her neck, and tied the other end about a tree and over a branch some five feet from the ground. He regarded her, his captive.

She looked upon him. Never before in her life had she seen such a male. He made even Gunther seem a lesser man. Her imagination had not even dreamed that such a man could exist. The men she had known earlier, even Gunther, had been no intimation that there might be such males as these. Such men, she thought, could not exist in her time. In her time there was no place; there could be no place, for such men as these.

Before him she felt, as never she had in her own time, even before Gunther, a complete female. Never before had she understood the import of two sexes, as she did now. It suddenly seemed to her, as it had never before, radically and explosively significant that there were two sexes. And how overjoyed she was that she was one of them. But, in fear, and still feeling pain, she drew back from him, for he had hurt her.

And, too, she was a woman of another time. Such a man terrified her.

And suddenly she understood that the cost of civilization, and the ascendancy of women, was the crippling of such men, or their destruction.

They were like great beasts that must be broken, or killed, that there might be the triumph of mildness, the victory of plows and religion, of fears and superstition, of complacency, of contentment, of smallness, and being afraid and mediocrity, and keeping in one's place and being polite, of camouflage and invisibility, of passionless comraderie, of achieving prescribed adjustment, of smiling normality, and being safe, and indistinguishable from others, and quiet, and then dying.

She looked upon him.

He was not such a man.

Tree did not try to speak further to her. He sat across from her, observing her.

"Please do not hurt me," said Brenda Hamilton to him. She knew it was foolish to try to speak to him, but she could not stand the silence, his watching her. In the group, men and women often looked at one another, sometimes for minutes at a time, simply seeing one another. In Hamilton's time men and women looked at one another, but they seldom saw one another. There is a great difference. Hamilton was uneasy, and wanted to cry out. She had never, in this way, been seen.

In his eyes, and the carriage of his head, and body, the subtle movements of his face, Hamilton sensed, even though he was a gross savage, little more than an animal, great intelligence. She sensed, somehow, looking at him, that his intelligence was far greater than hers, or perhaps even Gunther's, or Herjellsen's, in spite of the fact that, doubtless, he could not read nor write, in spite of the fact that he must be little more than a primeval barbarian, ignorant, uncouth, illiterate. And in looking at him she understood sharply, with devastating force, for the first time, the clear distinction between learning and intelligence. He could not be learned, certainly not in the senses in which she understood that word, but she knew, and felt, looking upon him, that he was of incredible intelligence.

But his hands, too, seemed strong and cunning, supple and powerful, like the rest of his body.

It startled her to find, conjoined with intelligence, such strength, and power, such size, such supple muscularity. The mighty brain she sensed had in such a body its mighty throne.

He seemed one thing to her, though, not a brain and a body, but one thing, somehow, a complete, and magnificent animal, whole, no part of him questioning or despising another part, not divided against himself, not diverted into attacking himself, not set at war with himself. There was no war here between this man's brain, and his glands, and blood, no more than between the left hand and the right hand, no more than between the beating of the heart and the breathing of the lungs. In him Brenda Hamilton sensed a terrifying unity, as simple as that of the lion or leopard. In his eyes she read power and intelligence, and lust and cruelty, and the desire for her body, and she read these things not as furtive glimmers but as a snared hind might read them in the eyes of the tiger, sinuously approaching, preparing to feed.

"Don't hurt me!" she begged.

Tree had not moved. He had not yet seen her, as he wanted to see her. When he had seen her, and wanted to, then he would move.

Hamilton turned her head away from him. She could not bear to look at him. She could not meet his eyes.

She knew now why civilization had no option but to break or destroy such creatures.

It had no place for them. It had no place for hunters. It needed diggers, not hunters.

Such a man, she knew, would never dig. There would always be another mountain, another horizon.

He would never make a civilization. It did not interest him.

Others would make a civilization, and breed in their hundreds, and thousands, and then millions, and the world of the hunters would be smothered, and the planet would be covered, and crowded, with the diggers. The giant cheetah would be extinct; the mammoth would no longer roam; the steppes would no longer shake to the charge of the wooly rhinoceros; and where the horses had run there would triumph the fumes of the internal combustion engine; the cave lion would be dead, and the cave bear, and there would be no striking of flints and hunting salt, for the hunters, too, like the lion and the bear, would have gone.

But Gunther had said that the hunters might not be dead, but only sleeping.

And Herjellsen had said to her, "Turn their eyes to the stars."

"There is nothing more to hunt," Hamilton had told Gunther.

"There are the stars," had said Gunther.

Hamilton again looked at Tree.

The hunters would rule the world for thousands of years, and the diggers, perhaps, for little more than some dozens of centuries.

The longer triumph would be that of the hunters, and the beasts.

And they might not wish to share the digger's world.

But Gunther had said that the hunters might not be dead, but only sleeping.

"There is nothing more to hunt," Hamilton had told Gunther.

"There are the stars," had said Gunther.

"Turn their eyes to the stars," had said Herjellsen.

But Herjellsen was mad, mad!

Tree had decided that he would not, this day, take the

white-skinned slave girl to the camp. He would take her to the camp tomorrow. He had never seen a woman like this. He did not wish, immediately, to share her with the others. For the time he would keep her for himself.

He looked at her. Her wrists were bound behind her back. She was sitting, with her knees bent. She seemed very much afraid of him. His rope, knotted about her neck, tethered her to a tree.

He was hungry. From his pouch he took a strip of dried meat, antelope meat, and chewed it.

He did not offer the slave any.

He was puzzled. She did not lie before him and lift her body. She did not beg meat. Perhaps she was not hungry. It did not occur to Tree that she did not know how to beg meat. He thought all women knew how to beg meat.

"Please," she said. "I am hungry."

He swallowed the meat. Then he got up to look about, for three suitable roots.

"What are you going to do?" asked Brenda Hamilton.

He found three roots, of the sort he wished, sturdy, properly placed. From two, he scooped out dirt beneath them, exposing them. The third was already fully exposed. They formed the points of an isosceles triangle, whose longer sides were something over a yard in length.

He then returned to Brenda Hamilton, and regarded her. She was filthy, from when she had been caught, tied, turned and raped in the mud.

Tree untied the rope from the tree and, approaching her, coiled it in his hand. When he stood over her he pulled her to her feet by the end which was still knotted about her throat.

"He is taking me to his camp," thought Brenda Hamilton.

She followed Tree, his hand holding the rope, about a foot from her throat.

At a stream he stopped and tied the rope about a small tree.

He then, to her surprise, untied her wrists. He then, with a gesture, ordered her to the center of the stream. She stood there, shuddering in the cold water, it swirling about her waist. She looked at Tree. Her neck was tethered to a small tree on the bank.

He, making scooping motions with his hands, and rubbing his body, instructed her to wash herself.

She stood there, looking at him.

Tree wondered if she were stupid. Then he would wash her. He waded toward her.

"No!" she cried. "I will do it!"

Although the water was cold, Brenda Hamilton cleansed her body, and hair.

It pleased her to do so. She washed the dirt from her body. She washed, too, the blood from her leg.

She thought how ironic it was, the concern of Gunther and Herjellsen, and William, for her precious virginity. It had meant nothing. They could not have known, of course. She had lost it. Lost? She smiled to herself. It had been ripped from her. She stole a glance at the bronzed giant sitting on the bank, watching her. She had scarcely seen him before she had been caught, hurled to her belly and bound helplessly, then turned on her back. She had looked into his eyes, had been startled, had cried out with astonishment, seeing the magnificence of the creature that had caught her. Then, within the minute, that virginity which she had hoarded, protected and prized, and had hitherto been willing to surrender only to Gunther, had been, she helpless, unable to resist, torn from her. When Tree had caught her, she had been a girl; when he had pulled her, bent over, by the hair to his accouterments, she was a woman. She looked again at Tree. She was not sorry that it had been he, not asking, predatory, arrogant, insolent, her captor, like an animal, who had torn her virginity from her. She was pleased that she had not been invited to surrender it, or bestow it on some nice fellow as a gift; she could scarcely admit the thought to herself but she was pleased to have lost it as she had; she had not had to beg him to take her virginity, as she had Gunther; he had simply wanted her, and taken it; startled, protesting, shocked, suddenly she had found herself a captive; she had been powerfully desired; her virginity, at his will, by storm, had been removed from her. She looked once more at Tree. She was not displeased that it had been a man such as he. How many women, she wondered, could boast that they had inspired such a desire in such a man as he. But she again looked at him. But he might have taken any woman in such a way, she told herself. Any other woman he had fallen in with, she told herself, might have suffered the same fate. And she knew this was true, but still she was much pleased that on this signal occasion, when first her body was forced, completely, to serve a man, that the man had been such as he. To her horror, and pleasure, she realized she would not have wanted it otherwise. It had been, for her, a fantastic experience. Yet he had hurt her, and she feared him.

"He is having me clean myself," she said to herself, "to take me to his camp, to show me to his people."

Doubtless they would be thrilled to see her.

She felt the leather leash pull on her neck and she stumbled through the water, toward him.

Tree was not fastidious, but he did not wish the female, whom he intended to enjoy, covered with dirt. He did not wish grit between his strength and her smoothness. Too, he was curious about the whiteness of her skin, and wished to see it more clearly. Too, he was learning the female, and he wished, when he had her in his hands, to experience her sweat, her secretions, her odors, freshly broken from her body. A rich dimension of Tree's world was that of scent, which, to modern man would become largely a lost avenue of experience. Brenda Hamilton did not know it but her scent, to those of the Men, was as distinctive as a fingerprint, as individual as the lineaments of her face. Any of the Men, once smelling her, could, even in the darkness of a cave, even if she huddled among other women, find her, put their hands upon her, and pull her out from the others.

Brenda Hamilton saw that her master had already untied the rope from the small tree by the bank.

The rope was looped twice in his hand. He did not retie her hands. He turned about and went back to the place where he had left his accouterments.

She followed him, docile, tethered.

She expected to be led to his camp.

But when he reached his accouterments, he motioned for her to sit down, within the isosceles triangle he had formed of roots, facing the two exposed roots which formed the limits of its base.

She did so, puzzled.

Suddenly he took her wrists and bound them together again, behind her back, tightly, but this time ran the rawhide twice, too, under the exposed root. She was tied half back; she could not sit upright.

She realized then that she was not to be taken immediately to his camp. He had other plans for her.

She struggled.

He removed the rope from her neck and tied it about her right ankle. He then ran the rope from her right ankle under the exposed root at her right, that forming the right termination of the base of the triangle. He then took the rope up and through the exposed root to which her wrists were tied, and brought it down to and under that root which formed the termination of the left side of the triangle's base. He then tied it securely about her left ankle.

"You beast," she hissed.

Old Woman had taught him the tie. The girl is tied down by the wrists, yet able to half rear to a sitting position. If her right leg is extended her left knee is sharply bent; if her left leg is extended her right knee is sharply bent; if tensions are equal, both knees are slightly bent. She cannot, in either case, because of the roots, close her legs. She remains deliciously, vulnerably, open to her captor. The tie, by intention, permits her to struggle, but the limits on such movements are so strict, their extent so precisely regulated, that the result of her movements induces in her, almost immediately, as a psychological consequence, a feeling of being trapped, of complete inability to escape, of utter helplessness.

"Beast!" cried Brenda Hamilton. "Beast!"

She struggled to sit up. She realized now she had been forced to wash herself not to be presented to his camp, as a rich prize, but simply that her body would be more pleasing to him. She jerked at the bonds; she moved her legs. She lay back, and moaned. She felt herself being lifted for his penetration.

"I cannot escape," she thought to herself. "I cannot escape!"

"Please don't hurt me," she begged him. "Please don't hurt me!"

She remembered the pain, and closed her eyes, tensing herself, but this time there was no cutting pain, no sharp pain, no tearing of her softness. Her body's resistance had been ruptured. Never again could it oppose itself to a man. She put her head to one side. She was now only another opened woman, no different from any other, once again being used. She felt his manhood, urgent and vital, and gasped as her body, in a shameless spasm, a reflex, closed about him, and he cried out with a sound of animal pleasure that thrilled the womanhood of her to the quick, and then her body was struck by his ten to a dozen times, causing her to lose her breath, almost tearing her from the rawhide bonds, and then, so quick, he had pulled away from her, and stood up, looking down on her, wiping sweat from his upper lip. She looked up at him angrily, fighting for breath. He had finished with her too soon. She felt unsatisfied, cheated. Now, too, she became aware of a soreness, irritation from her earlier penetration.

"You could at least let me heal, you beast," she said to him. "What do you care for my pleasure?" she demanded.

But he had turned away from her now, and, picking up his pouch, and his spear, disappeared among the trees.

"Don't leave me!" she cried. "Please don't leave me!"

And as she lay there, tied, she realized that he did not care for her pleasure. It was of no interest to him. And that, if he wished, he would leave her, lying behind him bound, helpless, alone in the forest.

With horror she suddenly understood that she had met a man to whom she was nothing, a man who cared nothing for her will, her desires, her feelings. Her delicacy, her sensibility, were not of interest to him. She knew she could expect nothing from him. From her, she knew, he would expect everything. She lay back, knowing that she was the helpless property of such a brute, and moaned.

When he returned to her the moon was full.

She struggled to sit upright, but could not do so. She rose on her elbows, knees bent, and looked at him.

He carried a fruit, a yellowish, tart applelike fruit, which he held for her. Gratefully she fed on the fruit. When she had eaten around the core he threw the core away. He then gave her a piece of dried meat from his pouch. It was tough and dry, and gamy, but she chewed it, and, with pleasure, swallowed it.

"Thank you," she said.

He then bent toward her, to put his mouth to hers. She shrank back in the thongs. She tried to turn her head to one side, but he held her mouth to his.

Then she understood, suddenly, that he held water in his mouth, that he was bringing her drink.

Lifting her head she took the water from his mouth.

She lay back.

"Thank you," she said.

Tree looked down at her, lying bound in the moonlight.

She looked up at him. It had pleased her to take water from his mouth. She had touched her teeth to his, and they had seemed hard, and strong.

Tree wondered about this woman. She did not kick well. She seemed a cold fish.

"You will learn to kick well," he said to her, "if you would eat."

Brenda Hamilton looked at him blankly.

He looked at her intently. He put his hand gently on her left breast. She was very beautiful, this woman. She was more

beautiful than the other women in the camp, except perhaps
Flower. It was too bad she did not kick well. She would be
used to do much work. Perhaps she could be tied at night
with Ugly Girl.

He looked down at her.

"You will learn to kick well," he said to Brenda Hamilton.
"You will learn to kick well, if you would eat."

◆ 15 ◆

They were near the village now. She could smell the
smoke. She was frightened.

She pulled back on the tether, shaking her head, wildly.
"No, please!" she said.

The leather, one end knotted about her neck, the other end
in Tree's fist, was taut between them.

"No, please," she said.

Tree jerked the rope toward him and Brenda Hamilton
stumbled forward, half strangling, and fell on her left shoulder
at his feet, her wrists, tied behind her, unable to break
her fall. He jerked her to her knees by the leash, at his thigh.
She looked up at him, tears in her eyes. "Please do not take
me to them," she begged.

He jerked her to her feet and she stood again, his rope
on her neck, facing him.

Then he turned and walked toward the village.

She felt the tug of the leash, and followed.

This morning, she had slept, fitfully, twisted on her side,
still bound as she had been the night before, and then, at
dawn, when the dew was still dark on the leaves, and there
was only a half light, he had slapped her awake, and her brief
dream of clean sheets, and her bedroom in her former apartment in California, vanished, and she found herself, face
stinging, startled, cold, lying in wet grass, bound in the thongs
of a primeval master.

He fed her as he had the night before, and then, when the
warmth of the food was in her body, he used her briefly,

she weakly trying to resist, knowing its futility, and then unbound her ankles from the roots, freeing his rope. She felt
the rope then tied about her throat. He then released her
hands from the root and the rawhide thong which, during the
night, had so perfectly imprisoned her wrists. She was then
led quickly to the stream, and thrust into the water, to wash
herself. She shuddered, but cleaned herself. She then felt,
again, her hands tied behind her back. He led her again to
where he had left his pouch and spear. Gathering these, he
had turned and, she following on the tether, had disappeared
into the trees.

They had not walked more than half an hour before she
had smelled the smoke. She knew his people were near.

She had pulled back on the tether, shaking her head wildly.
"Please, no!" she had begged.

She had then been briefly disciplined by the leash, taught
its power to control her.

Then she had stood again, facing him, and he had turned
and walked toward the village. She, terrified, miserable,
obedient now to the leather collar of her leash, followed him.
She had no choice.

Four times during the night had Tree used her body, once
awakening her to his long, pounding thrusts.

The fourth time, in spite of her stiffness, her soreness, to
her astonishment, and fear, she had sensed the beginning of a
strange sensation in her body; she did not know whether it
was painful or pleasurable; it was very different from anything she had felt before; she was terrified of the sensation,
rudimentary and inchoate, incipient, because she sensed that
she might be swept helplessly away from herself before it,
that it might, if unchecked, transform her from a human person with dignity, though abused, into a degraded, uncontrol-
lable, spasmodically responding female animal. "I must never
let them take me from myself," she told herself. "I must always retain my control. I must always keep my dignity. I must
always remain an intelligent, self-restrained, dignified human
being, a true human person." But she had feared that if the
sensation had not been checked, she would have, had his
touch continued, been literally forced to succumb to it, that
it would have reached a point where she could not have
helped herself, that it would have been entirely in his hands.
She had sensed then that, had he wished to do so, he could
have made her an animal, that animal she feared most to be,
a beautiful, helpless, responding female beast, the uncontrol-
lable, yielding prize of a greater, a stronger beast. She had

closed her eyes, and turned her head to one side, and gritted
her teeth, and fought the sensation, trying to keep her body
inert, trying, desperately, not to feel. Then, when she sensed
that she would lose the battle, and she wanted to cry out,
"Don't stop! Please don't stop!" he had finished with her, and
had withdrawn, to roll to one side, to sleep.

"I hate you," she whispered. "I hate you. I hate you!"

Then she had resolved to resist more mightily than ever,
to yield never to such a beast, or to others like him. "I will
never permit them to rob me of my dignity," she told herself.
But she was afraid, for she recalled the beginning of the
strange sensation. It kept recurring to her, even as she followed him on her tether, and it made her belly and inward-
ness grow warm, and excited. Once he stopped and turned
and regarded her. She stopped, and looked down, blushing.
She had seen his eyes, and the slight flaring of his nostrils. She
knew in the heart of her that this strange man, whose very
life in this fierce time might depend on the sharpness of his
senses, had literally smelled her desire, the secretions that
acknowledged her body's receptivity, its readiness. He had
walked toward her. "No," she had said, turning away. "Go
away. Go away!" She felt his hand on her, and she shuddered.
"Go away!" she cried.

He had turned from her and again taken his way through
the trees, she, leashed, following.

"I will resist you!" she cried.

She was furious with him.

Now, outside the tiny village, the trail encampment, Tree,
with his caught female, stopped.

He was downwind of the camp, that he might approach it
sensing, rather than being sensed. If anything was amiss in
the camp, in particular, if there were the odors of strange
men, it would be well to know. The Weasel People were
enemies of the Men. They and the Men did not sell women or
salt to one another. Antelope had originally been of the Bear
People. But Wolf and Runner had stolen her from the Weasel
People, who had taken her, with others, in a raid. The Men
and the Bear People and the Horse Hunters did not steal
from one another. They would sell women, or flint or salt to
one another. But Antelope was not returned to the Bear
People. They had not taken her from the Weasel People.
The Men had done this. Besides she was comely. The Men
kept her. Antelope did not mind. The Men were fine hunters.
She and her friend, Cloud, were often fed by Tree. Both of
them were good females, good kickers. The white-skinned

slave girl, the girl he had taken in the forest, was a cold fish. But she would learn to kick, if she would eat. Antelope was not kept as a slave. That was because she was of the Bear People, who were friends of the Men. But she was not permitted to return to the Bear People. She belonged, now, to the Men. Though not a slave, the Men kept her as they did the others, as a woman. Ugly Girl was kept as a slave, which was like being the woman of a woman; she was not of the group, or of a friendly group; she was simply slave; the white-skinned female, Tree's catch from the forest, too, was not of the group; she, too, thus, like Ugly Girl, or a girl of the Weasel People, would be kept as a simple slave; she must take orders from anyone in the group; she would be much beaten; she would have no rights, not even the life right, that accorded to members of the group; if she did not work well, or was not pleasing, she might be killed. Tree tested the odors, and found that all was well in the camp.

He would now circle the camp and approach from upwind, that they would know his approach, and that he brought with him a female. That would give the camp time to gather, and greet him. It would please Tree's vanity to bring her in, presenting her as a new slave to the men.

They would be much pleased to see the new acquisition.

In Tree's opinion she was more beautiful than the other women of the camp, with the possible exception of Flower. Tree smiled to himself. He did not think this would make the life of the new slave any easier.

Tree circled about the camp, for what reason Brenda Hamilton did not understand. She thought that perhaps it was customary to enter it from a given direction. But if that were so, why had he approached it from the opposite direction? It did not occur to her at that time that the difference was an important one for Tree, and other Hunters, the direction of the wind.

Soon she heard shouts in the camp, the cries of children and women.

Then, to her surprise, Tree took her in his arms and lowered her to the ground. Then, from his pouch, he took a length of rawhide, similar to that which now so tightly confined her wrists, some eighteen inches in length, and crossed and tied her ankles, tightly. She looked up at him. He then removed his rope from her neck, and, carefully, looped it about his body.

He looked down at her.

His pouch was slung at his side, the rope was looped about

his body, some four times, from the right shoulder to the left hip. His spear, hafted, the flint point bound in the shaft with rawhide, lay beside him on the grass.

His legs were long and powerful, and bronzed: He wore a brief skin about his waist. His belly was flat and hard, his chest large, his shoulders broad, his arms long and muscular. He had a large head. About his neck there was a tangle of leather and claws. His dark hair, black, jagged, was cut back from his eyes, and cut, too, roughly, at the base of his neck.

Brenda Hamilton looked up at her master.

Then, lightly, he picked her up, and threw her over his shoulder.

He bent down and picked up his spear, and turned toward the camp.

The shouting, and the cries, were much louder now.

Brenda Hamilton would not be permitted to enter the camp on her own feet, even wrists bound, and tethered.

She would be carried, trussed, over the threshold of the camp, as meat or game.

She would be thrown to its ground at the feet of the skinning poles.

She was slave.

Brenda Hamilton, bound hand and foot, was carried lightly, helplessly, into the camp, over the shoulder of Tree, the Hunter.

She became aware of men, and women and children, crowding about her.

She was aware of huts, and smells.

She was aware of two sets of poles, one set consisting of two upright poles and several small, slender poles, lashed horizontally between them, from which hung strips of drying meat; the other set consisting of two crossed poles at each end, bound together at the top, with a lateral pole set in the joinings of the end poles; from this lateral pole, on the one set of poles, there hung, upside down, hind feet stretched and bound to the pole, a small deer, its head dangling peculiarly, its throat opened. There was dried blood matted in the white fur at the bottom of its head, beneath its mouth.

Tree stopped with his prize before this latter set of poles, from which hung the deer, which had had its throat cut, that the hunters might have the blood.

Brenda Hamilton was conscious of the ease with which she was carried, that she was so slight a burden for his strength, and of his arm, bronzed and muscular, holding her on his shoulder.

Tree stood with his prize before the skinning rack, to which is brought meat, and game, and slaves.

Over his shoulder, head down, Brenda Hamilton felt the inhabitants of the encampment press about her, eager, excited, talking, curious, commenting, speculating, some feeling her body and hair. Then she felt Tree's body stiffen. And the crowd of women, children and men, fell back, and was silent.

Someone, she knew, had approached.

She heard voices.

"Where have you been?" asked Spear.

"I have been hunting," said Tree.

"What have you caught?" asked Spear.

"This," said Tree.

Rudely Brenda Hamilton, bound hand and foot, was thrown to the dirt of the camp, at the foot of the skinning rack.

She lay on her side, as she had been thrown. Her shoulder hurt.

She was conscious of the feet, and knees and legs, of those about. Some of the women wore strings of shells about their left ankles. They made a sound when they moved. She wondered at how far they might be from the sea.

She would learn later that these shells had been obtained in trade, exchanged for flints at the shelters, in barter with traders who had come from the world's edge, scions of the Far Peoples.

She heard a man's voice, harsh, direct.

"String her on the rack, that we may look at her," said Spear.

Brenda Hamilton felt her hands being untied, and then, by two men, she was lifted into the air, and, by two others, with rawhide thongs, was bound, wrists apart, hands over head, to the lateral pole set in the joinings of the crossed end poles. Her feet did not touch the ground. She hung suspended, in rawhide thongs. Her ankles were untied. To her left, tied upside down, bound by its spread hind legs to the same horizontal pole, hung the carcass of the bloodied deer.

Spear, and the others, regarded the slave.

Brenda Hamilton saw women and children standing behind and among the men. Most of the women were bare breasted. Almost all of the women wore necklaces of leather, claws and shells.

Tree did not think Spear would order her slain. She was

comely. If he did order her killed, he would fight Spear. But
Spear would not want her killed. He would keep her for
working, and kicking.

Brenda Hamilton looked into the large, stolid face that regarded her. She looked away, terrified. The face frightened
her, more than had that of her captor. The eyes, particularly, frightened her. They seemed at odds with the face, and
the largeness of the man. They were narrow and shrewd,
cunning, sharp. The body and the face, together seemed only
large, and slow, heavily muscled, thick, heavy, particularly
the jaw, but the eyes were bright, seeing, observant. The man
moved his head slowly, and his body, but she sensed in this
a deception, one belied by the eyes. This creature, seemingly dull, shambling, she sensed, could, if need arose, move with
the swiftness of a snake, the purposiveness of a panther.

She sensed this was the leader.

She would learn later his name was Spear.

Closely behind him she saw a younger man. She saw clearly that he was the son of the other, from the narrowness of the
eyes, the heaviness of the jaw, but there were two differences;
the younger man's body was more alert, more supple, less
heavily muscled; but his eyes, though cruel, were simpler,
more arrogant, less cunning. She sensed greater intelligence
in the older one, and, too, quickness, that he might, if he
wished, strike before the younger could move.

Spear's hands felt her body, the firmness of her breasts, the
curvatures of her ass.

"She is pretty," said Spear to Tree.

She felt Spear's hand at her delta. She closed her eyes,
and gritted her teeth.

"She does not kick well," said Tree.

Spear stepped back and regarded her. He shrugged. "She
is pretty," he said. "We will keep her." Then he said, "She
can carry flint."

She saw Tree's body relax.

She understood very little of what was going on.

Tree was pleased. He did not now have to fight Spear.

She did not even understand that Spear had decided that
she would be, at least for the time, permitted to live.

A woman with a limp, and a scar beneath the left cheek-
bone, began screaming.

"Kill her! Kill her!" cried Short Leg. She was first among
the women of the Men, dominant among the females. She
was, too, the first fed of Spear's five women. Indeed, so high
she stood with Spear that, for more than two years, none of

the other hunters had used her. Some of the hunters wondered why she should stand so high with Spear. Only Spear knew. She was shrewd, and highly intelligent. She gave him many good ideas. She knew much. And, in the camp, she was an extra pair of eyes and ears for Spear. She made him more powerful.

But still she was only a female.

Spear's left hand flew back, cuffing the screaming female back.

Brenda Hamilton saw blood leap from the face of the struck woman, who reeled back.

"Throw the sticks!" cried Short Leg. "Throw the sticks!"

"I have decided," said Spear.

Brenda Hamilton saw hostility in the eyes of the women, as they regarded her.

"Throw the sticks!" screamed Short Leg.

Spear's eyes met those of a small man with a twisted spine, with narrow ferret eyes, whose head was turned to one side. "Get the sticks," he said.

Hyena sped from the group and went to one of the huts. He returned with a leather wrapper and, when he unfolded it, within it, Brenda Hamilton saw more than a dozen sticks, painted in different colors, some in rings. The colors were mostly yellows and reddish browns, the rubbings of ochers into the peeled wood.

The group fell back and, with another stick in the wrapper, a larger stick, with a feather tied to it, Hyena, to one side, drew a circle in the dirt. He then brought five rocks, and put them in the circle, too. Then with his stick, he drew lines from one rock to another. Two of the women gasped. Where before there had been only rocks there was now a star, and the rocks were its points.

Hyena gestured for silence.

He looked at Short Leg, and the women. He seemed nervous. "Throw the sticks," said Short Leg.

He looked at the men. They did not look upon him pleasantly. He began to sweat.

He went to Brenda Hamilton and, head twisted, bent over, looked up at her.

Then he went back to the circle and picked up the sticks. He looked at Knife.

He looked at Spear, and at Stone, and Tree, and the others. "Throw the sticks," said Spear.

More than ten times Hyena lifted and dropped the sticks, watching carefully, studying carefully, sometimes on his hands and knees, the way they had fallen, their angles, their relationships to one another.

Then he stood up. "The meaning is clear," he said. "It is always the same."

"What do the sticks say?" demanded Short Leg.

"They say Spear is right," said Hyena.

Spear's face did not change expression. Short Leg turned about in disgust, and left the group.

The women, other than Short Leg, seemed satisfied. The men seemed pleased.

The sticks had confirmed the decision of Spear. The female strung on the skinning pole would be permitted, at least for the time, to live.

She looked from face to face. There was the leader, narrow-eyed, heavy jawed, who was Spear; there was, near him, the one she recognized as his son, who was Knife; to one side stood a large man, heavy faced and dour, Stone; then there was a spare man, lean and large handed, Arrow Maker; and a smaller man, heavy chested, short-legged, long armed, Runner; standing together were two men, a small, quick man, grinning, furtive, who was Fox, and a larger fellow, slower witted, secretive, who would not look into her eyes, Wolf; then she almost cried out in fear, as her eyes fell upon Tooth, so ugly, so large jawed, with the extended upper right canine tooth; he approached her; "Do not be afraid," he said to her, in the language of the Men; then he turned away, followed by two children; the small man, with the twisted back, who had thrown the sticks had taken his sticks back to the hut; before he had done this he had erased his circle and lines, and thrown the stones into the brush; he was Hyena. Then, too, there was the tall, black-haired fellow, bronzed, in the brief skins, who had taken her captive, and muchly raped her, and brought her to the camp, as his bound prize; his name, she would learn, was Tree.

She gasped.

Two women stood beside him, a shorter woman, blond, and a taller woman, dark-haired. She saw the shorter blond women slip to her knees beside him, on his right side. There, kneeling by his right thigh, she took his leg in her hands, and, softly, began putting her lips to his leg. The darker woman rubbed her body against his, and began pressing her lips to his body. Then, too, she sank to her knees beside him, docile and delicate, holding his legs, kissing at him.

Brenda Hamilton, suspended by her wrists from the pole, could scarcely believe her eyes. How shameless they were!

Yet there was something so open, so frank, so organic, so honest, so uninhibited, so ingenuously sensual and vital in their behavior that she found herself, in spite of herself, and her shock, indescribably thrilled. And then she was furious. She hated them! How shameless they were! And she knew that she, too, wanted to kneel beside him, as they did, competing for his attention.

"Get away from him," she wanted to cry. "I am his prize, not you!"

She had never seen a man such as he.

But she said nothing. She was silent.

To her fury, Tree turned away from her and went back among the huts, followed closely by the two females, holding to him, pressing themselves against him.

"I hate him," said Brenda Hamilton to herself.

She struggled, but could not free herself. The members of the group looked at her, curiously.

Then she hung again, quietly, wrists lashed apart over her head, helplessly.

Horror came into her eyes. She saw another face among the others. But it was not a human face. She cried out in fear, seeing Ugly Girl.

The members of the group turned to see at what she might have cried out.

Ugly Girl, frightened at seeing the eyes upon her, turned away, her head low on her shoulders, her dark hair like strings, her rounded shoulders cowering, and tried to shuffle away. She was naked and squat, thick legged, long armed. No ornaments had been given to her. Brenda Hamilton saw, startled, that her ankles were fastened together, about a foot apart, by a knotted rawhide strap. One of the children, the leader of the children, a blond girl, comely, one developing, one perhaps some fourteen years of age, one Brenda Hamilton would later learn was Butterfly, reached down to the strap on the ankles of the shambling girl and jerked back on it, throwing the girl to the dirt, and then she leaped over her and began to strike her, repeatedly, with her open hands. Four other children then, two boys and two girls, began to follow her lead. Ugly Girl rolled on the ground, covering her head and face with her arms, howling, and then, breaking away, followed, crept whimpering between the huts.

Brenda Hamilton felt sick. Never had she seen anything as repulsive as Ugly Girl.

She was horrid.

She found herself pleased that the strange girl, so horrifyingly ugly, was not of the group.

She would avoid her, continually. She made her sick.

She heard again the screams of Ugly Girl, now from between the huts. Then she saw the homely fellow, with the large tooth, still followed by children, go to drive the other children away from the squat, hideous creature. She heard him cry out angrily at the children, and heard their shrieks and protests; he must, too, judging from the cries, have struck one or two of them. Soon, the blond girl, and the other children, came back to the rack. The fellow with the tooth turned away, and went to the other side of the camp. He seemed angry. The two children still followed him.

Spear turned away from the rack. He nodded with his head toward the other set of poles, from which hung strips of meat. "The meat is almost dry," he said to Stone, and the others. "Tomorrow we will go for salt and flint, and then return to the shelters."

The men nodded.

Brenda Hamilton saw that the younger man, who resembled the leader, could not take his eyes from her body. She hung, wrists apart, frightened, scrutinized. Then she saw a blond girl, lovely, bare-breasted, with a necklace of shells and claws, hold him by the arm, trying to pull him away. He thrust her to one side. The girl looked at Brenda Hamilton with hatred. It was Flower. Then she approached the young man and knelt before him, and with her lips, began to touch her way upward along the interior of his thigh, timidly, and then she thrust her head up, under his skins. He laughed and seized her, and dragged her from the group, back between the huts, pulling her by the wrist, she, laughing, pretending to resist.

Flower, boldly, had won his attention away from the new slave.

Brenda Hamilton shuddered.

"Old Woman," said Spear.

Brenda Hamilton saw a hag emerge from the others. She was partly bent, white-haired. She wore skins covering her upper body as well as her lower body. There was much wrinkled skin about her eyes. The eyes, however, were sharp and bright, like those of a small bird.

She was the only one among the women who did not seem to fear the men, or show them deference.

Spear pointed to Brenda Hamilton.

"What do you think of Tree's catch?" he asked. "Can she bring children to the men?"

The old woman's hands were on Brenda Hamilton's hips. Brenda felt her thumbs, pressing into her flesh, feeling her body, measuring it. "Yes," said Old Woman, "she has good hips, wide hips. She can bring to the Men many children."

"Good," said Spear. His own woman, his first woman, Short Leg, had had only one child, and that had been delivered stillborn. Life in these times was precarious, and a good breeder, one who could bring many children to the group, was highly prized. Without such breeders groups died.

Brenda Hamilton felt the old woman's hands on her breasts. She looked away, miserable.

Spear looked at Old Woman.

"When the time comes," said Old Woman, "she will not need Nurse."

Spear nodded. That was good. Some of the women in the group did not have enough milk, and there was already much work for Nurse.

It was important for a female, if possible, to give suck to her own young.

"It is too bad," said Spear, "that she does not kick well."

The old woman turned to Brenda Hamilton. "Is it true, my pretty," she asked, in the language of the Men, "that you do not kick well?"

Brenda Hamilton looked at her blankly. Her shoulder hurt, where she had been thrown to the dirt by Tree. And, too, her wrists hurt from the thongs. She could scarcely move her fingers.

Old Woman repeated her question in the language of the Bear People, which she had never forgotten. Many years ago she had been purchased from the Bear People by Drawer, who had become Old Man, whom Spear had killed when he had gone blind. Old Woman had been fond of Old Man.

"You must learn to kick well, my pretty," cooed the old woman, kindly, to Brenda Hamilton.

Brenda Hamilton struggled, trying to escape the old woman's hands. But she could not do so. With her left arm, the old woman held her still, and, with one finger, not entering her, very gently, on the side, tested her.

Brenda Hamilton hung miserably on the pole.

"Well?" asked Spear.

Old Woman removed her hands from Brenda Hamilton, and turned to face Spear.

"Her body is alive," said Old Woman. "I do not understand why she would not kick well."

Then she turned again to Brenda Hamilton, puzzled.

Brenda Hamilton looked at the other women standing about
Never had she seen such women. They seemed vital, sensual,
alive, half animal. Their femaleness seemed one with their
person, as much as a smell or a pigmentation. How different
the men and women seemed, the men hard, strong, tall, the
women so much smaller, so lusciously curved, so vital, so
shamelessly female.

These, of course, were women from before the agricultural revolution, before a man became bound to a strip of
soil, and became obsessed with the ownership of his land, the
authenticity of his paternity, the reliability and legitimacy of
inheritances. These were times before a man owned, privately, his land, and his children and his women. The economic system was not yet such that, before effective birth-
control procedures, it was desirable to inculcate frigidity in
females, a property useful in the perpetuation and support of
patriarchal monogamy. The cultural conditioning processes,
abetted by religions, whose role was to support the institutions of the time, had not yet been turned to this end.

Brenda Hamilton, looking on the women of the Men,
realized that they had not been taught to be ashamed of
their bodies and needs.

They are like animals, she thought. Brenda Hamilton,
though enlightened, though informed, though historically
aware, was yet a creature of her own times and conditionings, of a world in which her attitudes and feelings had, without her knowing it, been shaped by centuries of misery, un-
happiness and mental disease, thought to be essential in
guaranteeing societal stability, thought to be the only alternative to chaos, the jungle and terror. Fear and superstition,
often by men whose gifts for life were imperfect or defective,
and hated or feared life, poured like corroding acids into the
minds of the young, had been a culture's guarantee that men
would fear to leave their fields, that they would keep the
laws, that they would pay the priests and the kings, that the
hunters would not return.

But the women, and the men, on whom Brenda Hamilton
looked, had not felt this oppressive weight.

They were free of it, simply free of it.

They still owned the world, and the mountains, and hunted
the animals, and went where Spear decided they would go.

They were as free as leopards and lions, as once men were,

as once men might be again, among new continents, among
new mountains, once more being first, now among the stars.

"Her body is alive," said Old Woman, looking up into the
face of Brenda Hamilton. "I do not understand why she
would not kick well."

Brenda Hamilton looked away from her.

"You must learn to kick well, my pretty," said the old
woman to her. "You must learn to kick well for the men."

Brenda Hamilton turned to her, miserable, looking down
into her face.

The old woman looked up at her, and cackled. "You will
learn to kick well, my pretty," she said, "if you would eat."

Then she turned away.

Spear looked at her. Then he said to the men, "Let us go to
the men's hut."

The men turned and went between the huts, leaving the
women and children at the rack.

Spear was the last of the men to leave.

Before he left he faced Brenda Hamilton. "You are a
slave," he told her. She looked at him, blankly. Then he said
to the women and children about, "Teach her that she is a
slave." Then he, too, walked away, following the men, between the huts.

The women and children pressed closely about her, poking
at her, smelling her, feeling her body.

"Please untie me," begged Brenda Hamilton.

One of the women struck her, sharply, across the mouth.

Brenda Hamilton hung, wrists apart, hands now numb,
from the pole, her feet some six inches from the ground.

She tasted blood in her mouth, where the blow had dashed
her lower lip against her teeth.

She closed her eyes.

Suddenly, from behind her, she heard the hiss of a switch
and she cried out in pain, the supple, peeled branch unexpectedly, deeply, lashing into the small of her back, on the
left side; she twisted in the thongs, agonized, to look behind
her, and another switch, swiftly, cut across her belly; she
cried out in misery, writhing in the thongs; first on one side
and then the other, and in front and back, and the length of
her body, the women and the children, chanting, circling her,
leaping in and out, struck her.

Brenda Hamilton saw the ugly girl, the stupid, horrid one,
crouching, naked between the huts, watching her.

Then the switch fell again, and again.

Then she saw, limping from between the huts, the woman

with the scar, who had screamed something before, and had later, after the sticks had been thrown, left the group. She demanded a switch from one of the other women. It was immediately given to her. And then the others fell back. Short Leg looked at Brenda Hamilton. Then she lashed her with the switch, making her cry out with pain. She lashed her methodically and well, with care and strength, and then Brenda Hamilton, broken, blubbering, wept in the thongs. "Please stop," she wept. "Don't hurt me," she wept. The older woman with the scar, Short Leg, held her face to hers, by the hair. Brenda Hamilton could not meet her eyes, but looked away.

She knew that she feared this woman terribly, that she was dominant over her.

Short Leg, angrily, threw away the switch, and limped away.

Hamilton saw another woman pick up the switch, a dark-haired woman, one of the two women who had left with the hunter who had captured her. It was Antelope. Behind her was the shorter woman, blond, thick-ankled, who had accompanied them, Cloud.

Antelope strode to her and struck her five times, and then gave the switch to Cloud, who, too, lashed her five times. Antelope smiled at her over her shoulder, as she walked away. She had the hip swing of a woman who has been muchly pleasured by a man.

A little later the young, blond girl, who had left with the other hunter, Flower, strolled to the rack, and she, too, smiling, lashed Brenda Hamilton.

"I don't want him!" wept Brenda Hamilton. "Don't beat me! He's yours! He's yours!"

Flower threw away the switch and strolled from the rack.

Then the old woman was among the other women and the children.

She pushed them away, and they, weary now, from striking, and taunting and chanting, left the pole.

Brenda Hamilton hung, beaten, alone. Her body was a welter of lash marks.

To her left hung the deer, hind feet apart, tied upside down, with its cut throat.

The sun passed the noon meridian, and none paid more attention to her. She watched the shadows of the poles then creep across the ground.

Her hair was half across her face. In the early afternoon she fell unconscious.

She awakened in the late afternoon, when the shadows were long.

She saw most of the men sitting cross-legged, watching her. Among them, though, were not the hunter who had captured her, nor the small man who had thrown the sticks. Too, the small, quick man, Fox, was not among them. He was to her left, beginning to skin the deer. He began at the bound foot to his left, cutting around the leg with a small stone knife, and then made a deep vertical incision down the animal's body. In a few minutes he had freed the skin from the meat.

The men watched impassively.

When he had jerked the skin free and thrown it to one side, to the grass, he looked at Brenda Hamilton, who regarded him, numbly.

Then, to her horror, with his knife he reached up to her bound wrist, that on his left and laid the knife against it.

"No!" she screamed. "No! No!"

The quick man, with a wide grin, took the knife away, and the other men, all of them with but one exception, the heavy-jawed, dour man she would learn was Stone, roared with laughter. And across even his face there was the trace of a smile.

She blushed, so completely had she been fooled. She was still shuddering, when she was lifted in the thongs, untied from the pole, and carried to a place on the grass.

She was sat on the grass, naked, the men about her.

The one who was their leader handed her a broken gourd, filled with water.

Gratefully she drank.

She was then handed small bits of meat, dried. She ate them.

She saw some of the women now untying the skinned deer from the pole. Others were preparing a large, rectangular fire in a clearing between the huts. Poles would be set up; it would be gutted and roasted. Another woman had picked up the skin, and was taking it away with her.

Her body felt miserable, from the beating. She could scarcely move her hands; she could not feel her fingers. Her wrists bore deep, circular red marks, where the thongs had bitten into them.

She was given more water, more pieces of meat. She drank, and ate.

The men sat about, watching her.

She felt less frightened with them than with the women.

She knew that, to them, she was an object of curiosity, of interest, of pleasure. To the women she sensed she was only another woman, a rival, competitor. Moreover, she had recognized, with a woman's swiftness and awareness, that she was among the most delicious of the females in the camp. She had seen only one she had felt was her superior in beauty, the young, blond girl, whom she would learn was Flower. It was not without reason that the new slave feared the other women in the camp. She hoped the men would protect her from them. She sat now among them, naked, shielded from the women. She could see that they were pleased that she had been brought to the camp, that they were pleased that she was theirs.

She felt some strength coming back to her body. She looked about herself, at the men.

Suddenly she realized that they would have nothing to do until the women prepared the meat.

She leaped to her feet, but one of the men, the dour-faced, heavy fellow, Stone, seized her ankle, and she was hurled to the grass, again among them.

Spear pointed to a hide spread on the grass, that she should take her place upon it.

The men were watching her.

"Please, no," she said.

Spear pointed again to the hide on the grass.

She crept to it, and sat upon it.

"No," she whispered, "please, no."

She saw them inching toward her. She tried to move back on the hide.

With a sudden cry, as of animals, they leaped upon her, she screaming, and thrust her shoulders back to the hide. She felt her ankles being jerked apart, widely, the hands and mouths of them eager and hot all about her body, holding her, caressing her, licking at her, biting at her, pinioning her.

The first to claim her was Spear, for he was the leader.

Brenda Hamilton thrust her fingers in her mouth. They were still sore from the blow of Old Woman's stick. She did not know whether or not they might be broken. She had tried to take a piece of meat. Screaming, striking her again and again with the stick, beating her on the back, Old Woman had driven her away from the roasting meat. Then Hamilton had fallen, stumbling, her ankles fastened, one to the other, with about a foot of play, like those of Ugly Girl, with rawhide. Spear had done this, when the men had finished with her, then turning her loose. Hamilton had fallen to the ground, helpless under the blows of Old Woman's stick. And then two other women, too, attacked her, striking at her with their hands, kicking her with their feet. Even a child hit her. Hamilton had knelt down, head down, her hands over her head, crying out in misery. Then Old Woman had said something, and the blows had stopped. And Hamilton had crawled, abused, from the light of the fire. She had learned that she could not take meat. She was a female. But she had seen Old Woman take meat, and the large, heavy-breasted woman, too, take meat. She had learned now that they were special, and that she was not. She was only another female. Old Woman, in the cooking, was assisted by two other women, but, like the other women of the Men, they, too, were not permitted to feed themselves. The meat, like the women, belonged to the hunters. It was theirs to dispense. The only exception to this practice was that taken, usually in the course of the cooking, by Old Woman and Nurse. Old Woman did much what she wanted, and few interfered. Nurse, too, was privileged. Without Nurse some of the young might die. Nurse and Old Woman were not thought of by the Men, perhaps strangely, as being of the women. They were women, but somehow not the same, not in the same way of the women.

Brenda Hamilton knelt outside the circle of the firelight. The smell of the roasted deer was redolent in the air, with the smell of ashes and fat, and bodies.

"They are fools," thought Brenda Hamilton. "Anyone could untie the knots on my ankles. When I wish to do so, I will, and run off."

A few feet from her, crouching in the darkness, round shouldered, head set forward on her shoulders, eyes peering at the roasting deer, was the squat, clumsily bodied girl, with the blank, vacant eyes, the slack jaw, the hair down her curved back like strings.

Brenda shuddered, repulsed, and edged to one side, to be farther from her.

She was terribly hungry, for she had had little during the day, only the fruit and meat which her captor had given her, she bound, in the half darkness of the morning, and the bits of meat given to her by Spear before the men had put her to their pleasure. And that meat, both that of the morning and that given her by Spear, had been insufficient, and had been terribly dry, almost like cubes of leather.

She could see the fat dripping from the roasting carcass of the deer into the fire, sizzling and flaming.

She moved her fingers. She was pleased to see that Old Woman's stick had not broken them.

This afternoon, after the men had finished with her, some more than once, she had lain on her stomach, dry eyed, miserable, on the hide that had been the bed of her masters' pleasure, for better than an hour. She had scarcely been aware, lying on the hide, that, when the men had finished, Spear had tethered her ankles, fastening on them that knotted rawhide shackle; she had known it had been done; her ankles had been handled roughly; but it had seemed almost as if it might be happening to someone else; dully only, she had comprehended that her slim ankles were now bound in leather restraints; had the men not taken much pleasure from her; was this her only reward; she hoped that they did not think of her as they did the ugly girl; but that she, and the ugly girl, were identically shackled, told her much; that whatever status in the camp might be that of the ugly girl, that that status, too, was hers.

I am a slave, she had said to herself, lying on the hide, her ankles shackled in leather, I am a slave!

After an hour she had risen stiffly to her feet, and looked about herself.

She had been forgotten. The slave was no longer of interest to those of the camp.

She smiled to herself, ironically. Your conjecture, Professor Herjellsen, she said to herself, was correct. Your experiment is eminently successful. Unfortunately you do not know how successful it was, nor how accurate your speculations were regarding my probable fate.

Naked, hobbled, her body switched and much abused, a woman of our world, and our time, Brenda Hamilton, intelligent, sophisticated, sensitive, looked about herself, finding herself the slave of savages in a primeval camp.

But she stood erect, her head up.

I am alive, she told herself. I am alive.

She moved her body, slowly. It hurt her to do so. She had been suspended, for hours, from the pole, her entire weight on tightly knotted wrist thongs, and she had been, at length, and viciously, as she had hung helplessly, switched by the women and children. And her body, too, was stiff and sore, from the attacks of her captor yesterday, and during the night, and this morning, and from the rude, prolonged attentions of her other masters this afternoon.

But I am alive, she told herself. I am alive!

She breathed in the fragrant air of the woods, of the trees and grass.

She smelled the roasting meat, the mingled odors of the camp.

She heard the cries of children, naked, running about. One was pursuing the others, and then, when he would touch one, that one would turn about and, in his turn, pursue the others, or any one of them, until he managed to touch one, and that one would then take his place.

It is tag, thought Brenda Hamilton. They are playing tag!

She saw one of the men drawn into the game, the large fellow with the prognathous jaw, and the fearsomely extended, atavistic canine tooth on the upper right side. With the children he seemed playful and gentle, even foolish. But she recalled he had used her as brutally as had the others, and not long ago. He was almost instantly "it," and, though he was doubtless a swift, and dexterous, hunter, he seemed clumsily unable to touch the children, who, sometimes, would even run quite closely to him, taunting him, and then dart away swiftly when he leaped toward them.

Brenda Hamilton turned away, looking about the camp. She noted the number of huts, and their construction. When she tried to look inside one, a woman had screamed at her and raised her fist, and Brenda Hamilton had, stumbling, turned away.

One of the huts, one of the two with a rectangular pit, and the side poles laid and tied about a horizontal pole, had sewn hides stretched across the openings at either end, that none might look within. Though Brenda Hamilton did not know it that was the Men's hut. No female might enter it, not even Old Woman or Nurse. Even to look inside, if one were female, was to risk a severe switching. It was a mysterious place to the women. Sometimes the men met within to make medicine, but generally it was only a place to talk, a place to be where women might not come. One other hut, a smaller round one, which lay at the outside edge of the camp, separated from the others, also had hide across its opening. Brenda Hamilton would learn later that it was the Bleeding Hut, to which women, caught in flux, were banished by Old Woman, driven there if necessary with a stick. Old Woman, Brenda Hamilton would learn, could drive even Short Leg to the Bleeding Hut. In the hut, it was Old Woman who brought them water and food. As Old Woman had grown older her senses were not as keen as earlier, and she could not smell the bleeders as readily. It was dark, and lonely and hot in the Bleeding Hut. Many of the women, to fool Old Woman, stanched their flow with a tiny roll of hide, sneaking away and cleaning and washing themselves once or twice a day. Old Woman, as she had grown older, was less zealous in her policing of the females. The Bleeding Hut was often empty. Last to be sent to it, howling and protesting, had been the girl, Butterfly, who cut the meat for the older children. She had been within it only a day.

At the outside of the camp, outside of its perimeter, a line scratched in the dirt with a stick, was the midden, where bones and waste were thrown. Brenda Hamilton looked at it for some time, but she saw no signs of brownish rats, similar to that which Herjellsen had had caged in the translation cubicle in Rhodesia. Such rodents, she did not know, did not follow men in their marches, but remained at the greater middens, near the shelters. Only if the men failed to return, and the edible waste at the greater middens became exhausted, would the rodents again follow the men, picking up their trail, following it, reappearing at the new middens, at the new shelters, wherever they might be.

She turned about, and, following the interior perimeter of the camp, circled the huts. In a little way, also outside the perimeter, was a waste ditch, a narrow trench, some two feet deep, some nine feet long. The dirt dug from the trench lay at its edges. The camp had two such ditches, one for the Men, the other, on the other side of the camp, for the women and children. When waste was deposited in the ditch, a small amount of the dirt from the edges of the ditch was thrown into the ditch, to cover the waste and eliminate the odor of spoor. When the ditch was filled a new ditch was dug by the women, with sticks and the flattishly curved hip bones of antelope. This trick had been learned by many of the primeval peoples. It had been learned from the great, predatory cats, who bury their wastes, thus concealing evidence of their presence in the vicinity from quarry, which might take flight, terrified by the odor of the predator. Certain human groups who had not adopted this, or a similar custom, had perished of disease. Unknown to the Men this custom, borrowed from the great cats, had, particularly in camps of long standing, sanitation values which far outweighed the concealments of scent. Another practice with indirect hygienic value was the washing of the body. Among the Men, and among their properties, their women and children, this was done with some frequency. It was done primarily that animals, either game or predators, be less easily apprised of the presence of the Men. It, like the covering of wastes was, too, in its way, an attempt at concealment. Too, it was done, particularly by the women, for cosmetic purposes. They were far more pleasing to themselves, and to the Men, when their bodies were washed free of acrid, fetid and stale odors, leaving their natural scents, exciting, sexually provocative, fresh and stimulating. The great associated advantage of washing, of course, was unknown to them, the sanitary advantage, the ridding of the body of sometimes dangerous, exodermically lodged bacterial cultures. The greatest sanitary protection of the various peoples, of course, was their isolation from one another. In these times a disease that might have later swept across continents, felling its millions, destroyed or decimated only a handful of victims. Indeed, we may surmise that many noxious mutations of bacteria or viruses did arise in these times, as in later times, but that having done what damage they could they either burned themselves out, dying themselves in dying bodies, or perished, leaving behind them only the immune, the survivors. Under such circumstances it is not unlikely that many a typhus, many a cholera, perished, unnoted in medical annals, never to reappear. Microscopic organisms, like their macroscopic brethren, too, may know extinction. Of starvation virulences and plagues, like men, may die.

That small hunting group, that band, calling itself the Men, was, from the standpoint of modern medical science, incredibly healthy. None of that band had ever had a disease. No child of that band had had a disease, no man of it, no woman of it. None of them had suffered from so much as a common cold. Subjected at times to exposures which would have induced pneumonia and death in other organisms they survived. There was no mystery in this. It was simply that, among them, disease did not exist. Disease requires its organisms. The organisms were not present. One cannot be eaten by a tiger if where one lives there are no tigers.

In a time Brenda Hamilton had circled the camp, discovering even, on its other side, the second waste ditch. She would learn later that that was the ditch for the women and children, and slaves. She noted at this time only that it was not as well dug, as long or deep, or sharp sided, as the other. There was a reason for this. The women who dug the Men's ditch knew they would be beaten if the Men were not pleased with it. Accordingly, they dug it well. It is one thing to be switched by a woman; it is quite another, ankles tied together,

to be switched by a man. But the women who dug the
woman's ditch were not subjected to the same discipline. The
Men did not care much about the woman's ditch, except that
the wastes deposited in it, too, be carefully covered, to conceal the scent of the spoor. Too, the women did not take
much pride in their own ditch. They knew that they were only
women.

Brenda Hamilton turned about, and again faced the center
of the camp.

The ugly fellow, with the extended canine tooth, was, sitting cross-legged, arms wide, sweeping, regaling the children
with a story. They sat clustered about him, listening, sometimes crying out, sometimes clapping their hands with pleasure.

Two women, elsewhere, were scraping a skin. Another
pair, working together, was removing, unlacing, another skin
from a drying frame of peeled, notched, green-wood poles.
Green wood was used that the skin, in drying and growing
taut, would be less likely to tear loose from the lacings or
snap the wood. The green wood provided a constant tension,
keeping the hide taut, and yet was sufficiently resilient to
preclude damage to the skin or the destruction of the frame.

One of the men, Wolf, was cutting an odd piece of hide
into thin strips which he would later braid into a flexible rope.

Two of the women were giving suck to infants.

Spear was talking to Stone.

Brenda saw that the skinning rack and the meat-drying
rack had been dismantled. She also recalled that the women
had been unlacing a hide from a drying frame.

If she had been able to read these signs she would have
understood that tomorrow, at dawn, the camp was to be
broken.

One man, carefully, was feathering an arrow. He used a
resinous substance, which he chewed soft, for glue, and, for
twine, strands of human hair, woven into a strong thread.
Another man, squatting, long-armed, heavy-chested, power-
ful-legged, watched him. It was a skill Runner would like to
acquire, the delicacy of the feathering, the placement of the
feathers, that the shaft, guided, might fly true. All the Men
knew how to do this, but it seemed that the best arrows
were always those made by Arrow Maker. What all knew
how to do, Arrow Maker, somehow, did better. He would
sometimes reject an arrow with which the others could find
no fault, until they had loosed it from the bow. Sometimes
Arrow Maker would tap the wood and listen to it; sometimes

he would balance it on a finger and see how it rested. The shafts which inclined downward slightly were usually chosen, unless a larger arrowhead were to be used. The shaft, the point, the feathers, must all be matched. Each arrow was a work of art, calling for judgment and skill. Sometimes Arrow Maker named his arrows. He had his favorites. Sometimes, as he worked, he talked with the wood, explaining to it what he was doing, and what was to be expected of it. And, as the Men said, the wood must often have listened, for Arrow Maker's arrows were almost always the best. He knew, it was said, the language of the wood. He was a good craftsman, and the wood would listen to him.

Knife, whom Hamilton knew only by sight, as the son of the leader, slept. Fox, too, whom Hamilton knew as the fellow who had pretended to put the knife to her body, when she had hung on the rack, slept.

Most of the women sat or knelt together, some yards from the fire. They were closely grouped, almost huddled. Some groomed one another. Others talked. Two played Shell, a guessing game in which a tiny shell is held in one hand, and the other player guesses in which hand it is held. Score was kept with pebbles, placed to one side. One woman was cutting hide with a tiny piece of sharp flint. Another, carefully, was piecing together two pieces of hide, folding their edges within one another and puncturing through the folds with a bone awl, then threading sinew through the holes. She pulled the sinew tight with her teeth and fingers, taking its tip first, as it was thrust through from beneath, in her teeth and then, when she had pulled it through, in her fingers, then turning the hide for the reverse stitch. One pregnant woman was being groomed by two other women, who would sometimes rub their bodies against hers.

Hamilton regarded the group of females. A single net might have been thrown over them all.

How different they are from the men, she thought.

Short Leg, whom Hamilton knew only as the leader of the women, she to whom they all deferred, stood up, angrily, and regarded her. Hamilton saw the scarred face, the crooked shoulder, the result of the shorter leg. Their eyes met. Hamilton averted her eyes, quickly. Short Leg terrified her. It was not simply that Short Leg was powerful, and free, and Hamilton was slave, or that Short Leg had, earlier, beaten her viciously; it was deeper and more terrifying than that; it was the recognition on the part of one female that she is hated and despised by another, who is quite capable of killing her, and is, in every way, totally dominant over her. Hamilton did not fear the men, who seemed so rough and fierce, a thousandth as much as she feared Short Leg. Hamilton was certain she could please the men. They wanted her body. She need only, with them, she knew, work hard and be perfectly obedient. With them, she knew, her femaleness, and its desirability, would protect her. But she knew she could not please Short Leg and the other women with such ease. They did not want her; they did not want her body. To them she was a competitor, a rival, in some sense a threat. She recalled that it had been the scarred woman who had demanded the throwing of the sticks, and that something, concerning her, had been decided, or confirmed, in the throwing of the sticks. The preferences of the men had been clear; the preference of the scarred woman, and certain of the others, opposing preferences, had also been clear. But the men had won the throwing of the sticks. And, Hamilton realized, she was still alive. Suddenly she realized that the scarred woman had wanted her dead. Hamilton felt sick. Suddenly she saw Short Leg before her. Quickly Hamilton fell to her knees, and put her head to the ground.

Then Short Leg had turned away, and returned to the women. She was, now, no longer looking at Hamilton.

Hamilton, red-eyed, angry, stood up.

She knew that she must, if she remained in the camp, try to please Short Leg. If she did not, she knew, she would suffer greatly; indeed, she might even be killed. She sensed Short Leg had power in the camp, even with the men. Even the leader, the heavy-jawed, narrow-eyed man, had listened when she had spoken. He had not complied with her wishes, but he had listened. She sensed that the men seldom listened to the women. That the leader had listened to the scarred woman was evidence of her power. Hamilton shuddered.

But when she had groveled before Short Leg, kneeling and putting her head to the ground, Short Leg had not struck her, or even spoken to her. She had only turned away, and returned to the women.

Hamilton was much relieved. She still feared Short Leg, and terribly. But Short Leg had not harmed her. Hamilton sensed that she would be unlikely to kill her, particularly if given no provocation. Hamilton would be zealous to see that Short Leg was given no provocation. She would try to be completely pleasing to her, ingratiating, obedient, servile, and give her no cause for anger. Already she had, in kneeling and putting her head to the ground, acknowledged Short

Leg's complete and absolute dominance over her. And Short Leg had turned away, satisfied.

This made Hamilton feel strong. She now felt she might, if she were careful, control Short Leg.

If she posed no threat to Short Leg, she might be safe.

Hamilton's face clouded with anger.

Too, Short Leg might be pleased at her absolute power over such a beautiful woman. Short Leg might be pleased with the beautiful new slave's deference to her. Would it not make Short Leg seem even more impressive and formidable among the men, to see the new slave, their prize, so small and helpless before her, so desperate to please her.

"I hate her," said Hamilton to herself. "I hate her!"

But then she smiled. There were others in the camp beside Short Leg. Doubtless Short Leg could not do precisely as she wished. Doubtless she might not, simply, destroy her, even if she wished. There were, after all, men in the camp. The men would not want her killed. Hamilton laughed to herself. The power of the men, if she were careful, would protect her. The men would be her champions, protecting her from the women. She realized, of course, swallowing hard, she might have to be pleasing to the men. "Well," she said to herself, defiantly, "I can please a man, if I must, as well as any other woman." She was angry. "It is my intention to survive," she told herself. But she told herself that she would not really have to please men to survive, only submit to them. The use of her beauty, even she inert, not responding, would be more than enough for them. "I am beautiful," she said to herself. "That is sufficient."

She looked about herself.

She smelled the meat cooking.

To one side, some yards away, before a hut, the small, twisted man, who had thrown the sticks, was kneeling in the dirt arranging small shells in geometric patterns, muttering to himself. He was the only one of the Men who had not used Hamilton.

She watched him for a time, he picking up and laying down shells, forming patterns, intent, muttering.

Idly she wondered if he were insane.

She saw the short blond woman, Cloud, emerge from one of the huts, brushing back her hair from her face. The taller woman, Antelope, had been with the other women, being groomed.

Brenda Hamilton slowly approached the hut from which the short, blond woman had emerged.

Her heart was beating rapidly.

She took short steps, the rawhide shackle confining her movements, and pretended to be looking at the sky. As she passed the hut she would, casually, inadvertently, glance inside. She was angry with the short, blond woman, but she was gone now, and so, too, was the dark-haired woman.

Suddenly her legs, backward, flew out from under her, jerked back by the rawhide strap, and she pitched forward into the dirt. She heard a squeal of laughter.

The young blond girl, Butterfly, stood over her.

Brenda Hamilton, the slave, on her side, kept her head down, and did not dare to rise.

She remembered Ugly Girl.

She hoped she would not be switched.

With a laugh, Butterfly turned about and, stepping over Hamilton, left her.

Angrily Hamilton got to her feet. She was relieved, however, that she had not been beaten.

The animosity, she suddenly realized, which the group felt for the ugly girl, doubtless in part a function of repulsion and fear, they did not feel for her. She, slave though she might be, was, if not of their group, of their kind. The ugly girl was not. Hamilton was pleased that there was one less than she in the camp. Hamilton was pleased that she was better than the ugly girl, for she, at least, was human. The ugly girl, it was clear, was not.

From where she stood, Brenda Hamilton could see the deer roasting on a long spit. It made her hungry. She was angry at the young blond girl who had tripped her.

Then, looking about, she approached the hut from which the short blond woman, Cloud, had emerged.

She looked within.

Inside, he was sleeping.

He had not taken her with the rest of the men, on the hide between the huts.

"You beast," she said, "I hate you."

It was he who had captured her. It was he who had brought her, slave, to this camp. It was he who had taken her virginity, she recalled angrily, and within moments of seizing and binding her. And, too, she recalled, how he had tied her down at the wrists, and had spread her legs, securing them, and had, at his leisure, taken her, again and again during the night, and again at dawn. She was furious. How casually, how arrogantly, he had used her for his pleasure.

Then he had brought her to the camp as a slave.

On the hide she had learned that she belonged to all the men, as, too, she suspected, so did the women.

But she thought of one as more her master than any other, and she now looked upon him, sleeping, lying on his side, his head on his arm.

"I hate you," she said, "you beast."

Then she turned about and looked up at the clouds, and the sky. She drew a deep breath. She inhaled the odors of the camp, the smoke, the smell of fat and the meat.

She looked about the camp, and at its inhabitants.

They were people, clearly, of her race, and of her kind. Yet here they were clearly savages, as much or more so as any isolated, deprived or benighted group in any jungle or mountain remoteness of her own time, and these people were not remnants of competitively unsuccessful groups, driven to, or fleeing to, wildernesses, unable to withstand the onslaughts of harsher, stronger groups. These men, she understood, were as strong, or stronger, as formidable, or more formidable, than any other human groups of their time. Indeed, their hunting terrain, she suspected, might be extensive, and rich in game. It was probably no accident that they hunted the forests they did. She regarded them. They were larger and stronger, and better looking, generally, than modern men, and, too, she suspected they were, human by human, more natively profound, more quickly witted, more intelligent than their later counterparts, the results of large, indiscriminately mated gene pools, and an environment in which the harsh strictures of nature, due to an advanced technology, were largely inoperative. In these times she realized that foolish or stupid men might not live; in her times she realized that such might thrive, and be encouraged to multiply themselves, providing useful and exploitable populations for their more clever brethren. Here there was little place for the foolish, the ignorant, the gullible and the weak; there were no votes to be cast, no products to buy, no institutions to support, no uniforms to wear, no rifles to bear; if these men fought, or killed, they would do so because it was their own will, and they saw the reason; they would decide themselves, if they would trek, or fight, or kill. They did not thrash in traps constructed by ambitious men; they did not salivate on signal, at the will of psychologists, the employees of invisible potentates.

They were people, clearly, of her race, and of her kind, but they were very different.

Their technology was one of stone.

"They are at the beginning," said Brenda Hamilton to herself.

In a way, this was true, but the Men, whose property she was, stood not at the beginning, but far along an ancient journey, a trek of life forms. There had been manlike things for thousands of years before them, and before such things, other successions and journeys, and even the tarsiers, and the tiny shrews, whose viciousnesses and tempers are so like our own, lay late along this journey. It was a journey that extended back to distant, turbulent seas, whose saline ratios we carry still in our blood, and to growths and movements scarcely to be distinguished from simple chemical exchanges, the rhythms and affinities of oxygen, and nitrogen and hydrogen, and, crucially, the instabilities and complexities of carbons. It was a journey that had seen worlds and climates wax and wane, which had witnessed stones boiling like mud and the endless, falling rains; it had witnessed the first stirrings in the slime; it had noted the track of the trilobite; it would remember the grandeur of the fern forest and would not forget the tread of the stegosaurus; and sometime, somewhere along this journey, a hominid creature had discovered what a noise might mean; and what a frightening illumination that might have been for a small, dark brain; and it may have lifted its teeth and eyes to the stars, for the first time, snarling, challenging, but frightened, wondering at the reality, the mystery, which had spawned it; and in that tiny, dark-brain the reality, the mystery, itself, may first have wondered at its own nature; in that snarling hominid, frightened, reality may have first asked itself, "What am I?"

And so the Men were not truly at the beginning, but were, truly, only yesterday. The beginning which was theirs, for they were a beginning, however, was the human beginning, the truly human beginning, for the Men, and other groups like them, were among the first of the truly human groups.

Brenda Hamilton, a woman of our time, the slave girl of savages, naked, her ankles linked by a rawhide thong, stood erect in the primeval camp. She looked up at the sky, and then again at the huts, and at the men and women. She smelled the fragrant air, the meat roasting on its spit. Incredibly, and she did not understand the emotion, she felt a surge of joy. Although she did not comprehend how it might be true, she knew that she was happy to be where she was, that she did not wish it otherwise. "I am at the beginning," she told herself. "I am at the beginning of human beings."

Herjellsen had told her, she recalled, "Turn their eyes to the stars."

She laughed. She was only a slave. She knew that she would be expected to work, and work hard, and serve the pleasures of her masters.

But, incomprehensibly, she was not unhappy. She did not wish to be other than where she was.

"I am at the beginning," she told herself. "I am at the beginning of human beings."

"Turn their eyes to the stars," Herjellsen had said.

She laughed.

She could not turn their eyes to the stars.

She was only a slave.

Hamilton cried out with humiliation and pain as the switch struck her, unexpectedly, below the small of the back. And then another switch, too, struck her.

She fell to her knees, her head down, covering her head with her hands, as she had seen the ugly girl do, earlier in the day.

Again and again the switches fell, two of them.

Hamilton tried to crawl away, but she was held by the hair. Then the switches stopped.

She looked up, through tears, to see the two women, the dark-haired woman, and the shorter blond woman, who had accompanied her captor earlier in the day.

They stood between her and the entrance of the hut in which he who had captured her slept. They were angry, and raised their switches. They motioned her away.

She had been caught dallying in the vicinity of the hut of the handsome hunter.

Hamilton, with difficulty, rose to her feet.

They took a quick step toward her, and Hamilton, trying to move away, but confined by the thong tying her ankles, fell. They were on her, striking her again.

Hamilton crawled from their blows and, when they had stopped hitting her, she rose again to her feet, and moved away. But as she did so, on some impulse she did not fully understand, but could not resist, looked at them, over her shoulder, and smiled, the smile of a female who well understands the motivations of other females, but is aware of the power of her beauty, and does not care for their wishes. Her smile said to them, "I am beautiful, and if he wants me, he will have me, and you will have nothing to say about the matter." She felt an incredible female thrill as she did this, an emotion so deep and primitive she would not have known

she could feel it, the elation and pride of the competitor female, but then, almost instantly, she regretted her action for,
like she-leopards they were on her again with the switches.
Brenda Hamilton howled for mercy before they stopped beating her. She fled, crawling, before them, driven on her hands
and knees from the hut of the handsome hunter. When they
stopped beating her, she stopped crawling, and head down,
concealing it, smiled. Her body hurt, and muchly, laced by
stinging stripes, but she knew she had, as a female, inspired
fear and hatred in the two women. It had been their intent,
clearly, to drive her from the hunter. She told herself they
had misjudged her motives. Then she asked herself why she
had been lingering in the vicinity of his hut, and had crept
to it, to look in upon him, for she had no interest in him,
and, indeed, hated him, for what he had done to her. He had
abused her and it was he, too, who had brought her to the
camp as a slave. "I hate him," said Brenda Hamilton to herself. "But he is rather handsome," she said to herself. And,
too, she remembered the beginning of the strange sensation,
which he had, in the darkness of the night, when she had
lain bound at his mercy, begun to induce in her, that sensation
which she had, with closed eyes and gritted teeth, fought,
but to which she had known she must shortly yield, when he
had finished with her, withdrawn and rolled to one side, to
sleep. She had lain there bound in the darkness, miserable, hearing the sounds of his breathing. "I hate you," she
had whispered. "I hate you. I hate you!" And she had resolved
to resist more mightily than ever, and never to yield to him,
or such a beast as he, but forever, proudly, to keep the
integrity of her personness, her independent selfhood, her
dignity. Never would she permit such a beast to transform
her into a beautiful, helpless, spasmodic, yielding female animal, only a surrendering prize, his conquest. She was, after
all, a full and complete human being. She would at all costs
protect her self-respect. They would never make her yield.
Never! But never, too, had she forgotten the sensation.

Slowly, painfully, Brenda Hamilton rose to her feet.

She was, somehow, rather proud of herself.

Then she stood very straight, very beautifully, very proudly, almost disdainfully, for she saw him, standing before
his hut. She was thrilled, but did not show it, seeing the
strength, the leanness, the bronzedness of his body, so tall,
so lithe and yet mighty. Never in her life had she been such a
man. She wondered how much of her beating he had witnessed. Doubtless the blows and her cries had aroused him.

He was eating a yellowish fruit, biting into it with his strong, white teeth, looking at her. She did not care what he thought but she hoped he had not seen her howling and being beaten. That would have been embarrassing. He grinned at her, his mouth filled with the white meat of the fruit. She turned away, disdainfully, and tossed her head.

She made her way between the huts, away from him.

"If he wants me," she said to herself, "he may have me, for he is a man. And I may not resist him, for I am a woman."

She stopped some yards from the group of women, to which the dark-haired woman, and the shorter, blond woman, had now joined themselves.

Several of them looked at her with hatred.

Brenda Hamilton turned away.

"Those women with switches have misjudged my motives," she said to herself. "They may have him if they wish. I have no interest in him. He is only a beast, a savage. I do not even find him attractive. He bores me."

But Hamilton, in the heart of her, not nicely perhaps, was quite pleased with the jealousy she had induced in the two other women. Clearly, they regarded her beauty as a serious threat, that they would not even let her linger near his hut, and this Hamilton found exquisitely flattering, even though she was not, she told herself, in the least interested in the hunter. "Perhaps I could smile at him sometimes," she said to herself, "if only to drive them wild. That might be amusing. But, of course, I do not wish to be switched again." Then she grew angry. "Who are they to say whom he picks for his pleasure?" she asked. But she did not wish to be switched. That hurt. She felt a violent surge of hatred for the two other women.

"I cannot help it," she said to herself, "if he simply takes me and rapes me. They must surely understand that. That is not my fault. It is nothing I can help."

Then she smiled to herself. "I am beautiful," she thought, "and I cannot help it if he desires me, and that he, being a beast, will simply take what he desires. That is not my fault. It is nothing I can help. Surely they must understand that."

Brenda Hamilton then understood the adversary relationship in which the unusually beautiful woman stands to other women, that they hate her, and that such a woman then, alienated from other women, has no choice but to turn to men, and is pleased to do so, for among them she finds herself exquisitely prized.

She looked back at the closely grouped women.

"I do not wish to huddle with the women," said Brenda Hamilton to herself. "I would find the company of the men more congenial."

"The women," thought Brenda Hamilton to herself, "are my enemies." And then she thought, soberly, "And the men are my masters."

Brenda Hamilton thought of the tall, lean, mighty hunter. She smiled to herself. "If one must have a master," she said to herself, "it might as well be one such as he." And she regretted that she was not his alone, but, apparently, the common property of all the males, as, too, she gathered, in effect, were the other women. We are all slaves, she thought, all of us. "In this time women are held in common, all of them as slaves of the men." She thought of the men she had seen. "How dominant they are," she thought, "how unassuming, how arrogant, how masculine, simply keeping their females as slaves." She was scandalized, horrified, but, too, somehow, indescribably thrilled. Men were stronger, and could do what they wished. And here, in this primitive camp, she realized, shuddering, they did. "If I were a man," thought Brenda Hamilton, scandalizing herself, "I, too, would keep women as servants and slaves. Such weak, desirable, pretty things! I would be a fool not to do so!" And then she recalled that she herself was such a thing, desirable, weak and lovely, and would, accordingly, by men such as these be kept, like other women, as a slave.

Hamilton asked herself if she feared the switches more than she desired the hunter. "I am not afraid of the switches," she said. "Too, if I am pleasing, the men will not let them switch me. Let them, then, dare to switch me, when the men are about. They would then be beaten!" Hamilton smiled to herself. "I will survive here," she said to herself. "I need only please my masters."

Hamilton stood straight.

She put back her head and, hands at the back of her neck, shook out her hair, long and dark, over her back.

She saw the old woman, with a stick, poking at the meat, it hot and dripping, roasting on the spit.

Two other women, under her supervision, had been turning the spit. The heavy, large-breasted woman stood nearby.

With her stick the old woman, poking and tearing, ripped free a chunk of hot meat. It was torn from between the animal's ribs. It emerged, hot, half-cooked, thrust on the stick.

The old woman and the heavy-breasted woman, the meat between them, began to bite at it, tearing it away from the stick. The other two women, who had been turning the spit, stood to one side, watching them.

Hamilton approached the fire.

She became suddenly aware of how hungry she was. All day, she had had only a bit of meat and fruit, near dawn, and, later in the day, before the men had raped her, their new slave, on the hide, some tiny pieces of meat.

She was ravenous.

She noted that, hanging loose, dangling by a thread of meat, torn almost free by the old woman's stick, there was a handful of meat, popping and hot with fat. There would be no difficulty in taking it, for it was hanging there, like fruit, ready for the seizing. The fire pit was rectangular and narrow, and Hamilton need only reach over the flames and pull it free.

The old woman and the heavy-breasted woman had now torn the meat from the stick. Each now had her own piece. The old woman, her eyes closed, was sucking on fat from the meat. The heavy-breasted woman was thrusting her piece of meat into her mouth, ripping at it, moving her head in doing so. Hamilton saw juice running at the side of her mouth.

Hamilton went to the side of the fire, to the meat.

The two women who had been turning the spit took no note of her, they conversing.

Old Woman opened her eyes, looking at Hamilton.

Hamilton smiled at her.

Old Woman did not smile, but watched her, carefully.

Hamilton thought her fingers were broken, so savagely had the old woman's stick struck them!

Hamilton screamed with pain, and twisted, and, stumbling, fighting to keep her balance, fled, driven, from the meat, she crying out, the old woman screaming, the stick lashing her, hot on her back, and then, her ankles caught up by the rawhide shackle, sprawling, she fell to the ground.

"Please!" she cried.

The old woman's stick was merciless. Hamilton, kneeling, head down, hands covering her head, wept with misery.

The two other women, those who had been turning the spit, leaped to her, striking her with their hands, kicking her with their feet. Even a child ran to her, striking at her.

Then the old woman said something, sharply, and the blows had stopped.

Hamilton, abused, crawled from the light of the fire.

She now knelt outside the ring of the firelight, in the falling dusk. She sucked her fingers, and then, carefully, painfully, moved them. They had not been broken.

She had learned that she could not take meat. She was a female.

Her back was sore from the beating of the stick. Her ankles were chafed by the rawhide shackle.

But she had seen Old Woman take meat, and the large, heavy-breasted woman, too. She had learned now that they were special, and that she was not. She was only another female. Even the two women who assisted the old woman, she had noted, now, did not take meat. They, too, were not permitted to feed themselves. The meat, like the women, Brenda now understood, belonged to the hunters. It was theirs to dispense. The only exceptions were apparently the old woman and the heavy-breasted woman. They were privileged. Hamilton would learn that Old Woman did much what she wanted, and that Nurse, too, did much as she pleased. Nurse and Old Woman, Hamilton conjectured, though women, were somehow not in the same way as she, and the others, of the women. Those two were special. The others, and she, were not.

Hamilton was furious, kneeling outside the circle of the firelight.

She moved her ankles.

"They are fools," she thought. "Anyone could untie the knots on my ankles. When I wish to do so, I will, and run off."

A few feet from her, crouching in the darkness, round shouldered, head set forward on her shoulders, eyes peering at the cooking deer, was the squat, clumsily bodied girl, she with the blank, vacant eyes, the slack jaw, the hair down her curved back like strings.

Hamilton shuddered, repulsed. She edged to one side, to be farther from her.

Hamilton was terribly hungry.

She smelled the roasted deer. She could see the fat dripping from the roasted carcass of the deer, dropping into the fire, sizzling and flaming.

She moved her fingers again. She was pleased that Old Woman's stick had not broken them.

The old woman said something to the two women who had been cooking the meat, turning the spit.

Those two women then, under the supervision of the old woman, now, one at each end, lifted the green-wood spit on which, impaled, hung the roasted carcass. They lifted it from the fire slowly, heavily, and sat it down on a large, flat, gray rock, on which it would be cut. The green-wood spit was left in the meat.

All day Hamilton had had only a bit of meat and fruit, near dawn, and, later in the day, some tiny pieces of meat.

She was ravenous.

"Feed me, you beasts," she said to herself, "I'm starving."

The old woman cried out a single word, loudly, shrilly. Immediately the women, who had been clustered together, got to their feet and came forward. The children, too, came forward. They all stood in a circle, about the flat rock on which the meat lay. With her stick the old woman pushed back some children, and one of the women. The women and children now stood in an open circle about the meat, it forming the center of the circle. Then the women parted and, between them, tall and mighty, the masters, strode the men. "How small and weak women are beside them, the uncompromising beasts," thought Brenda Hamilton. First among the men came Spear, with his narrow eyes, his easy movements. Hamilton noted that there was gray in the shaggy dark hair at his temples. Behind him, first, came the one she knew must be his son, for he had the same cruel features, the same shape and heaviness of jaw. Then came the others, among them the tall, handsome hunter who had taken her, who had made her a slave. "How incredibly handsome and strong he is," she thought, in spite of herself, "what a magnificent male!"

Her hunter, with the others, squatted down about the meat. He was between her and the meat; too, there were others between them. Brenda stood up, so that she could see better. The women then, to her interest, separated from the children. The children went to one side, foremost among them the young, blond girl, who had tripped her and, earlier, the ugly girl. The women, Brenda noticed, aligned themselves about, and behind, various hunters. She was sure that this was not a random dispersal, but that there was an order involved. She saw the two women, the taller, dark-haired girl, and the shorter, blond girl, kneeling closely behind her hunter. They were too close to him! The blond girl put her lips to his shoulder. Hamilton was furious.

Spear's flint knife, some eight inches long, the handle wrapped in leather, taken from a rawhide belt, thrust down into the hot meat.

It was the first time, of course, that Hamilton had witnessed a feeding.

She was startled at much of what she saw. The first piece of meat Spear lifted to the sky and the directions, and then threw into the fire, that it might be destroyed.

There were many meanings in this, and various groups did this differently. There seemed nothing in this of childish magic, like the throwing of the sticks. In its way it seemed simple and profound. It was a gift to the power, and showed both the gratitude and generosity of the Men. Part of what they had been given they would give back, for they were the Men. The power was in the trees and the water, and in the wind and the budding flower, the curling leaf, the stone, the tiny branch, in the swiftness of the fish, in the flight of the bird, the stealthy padding of the lion's paw, and in the Men; it was in all things. In Spear's act there was little of superstition, but little, too, of reverence. It was rather a celebration, and acknowledgment, of the aimless, random grandeur of the power. The power, as conceived of by the Men, had no greater love for them, nor should it, than for the blade of grass or the beasts they slew for food. No more than the rain and the sun could the power be placated, for it was the power. It gave not only life but it destroyed it as well; meaninglessly it bestowed all things, misery and joy, and life and death; with equanimity it looked on the recurrent cycles of growth and decay; it delivered men into the hands of age and blindness and antelope into the hands of the hunter; Spear had heard it in the scream of the murderess and in the cry of the newborn child; he did not prostrate himself before it, nor did he reverence it; but, in his way, he acknowledged it, and, perhaps, did it honor, for, without the power, there was nothing. Men, in these days, were not so foolish or arrogant as to create deities in their own image; they were too close to the power, in its terribleness, too close to the reality, for such invention to be taken seriously; only too obviously was the power not a manlike thing; only a fool could think so; one who did not sense the nature, the pervasiveness, the mightiness, the amorality, of the power; but, without the power there would be nothing; without the power there would not be the grass, or the antelope or the men; without the power there would be nothing; but Spear, and the others, did not grovel before the power, for they were men; they were grateful when the hunt went well, and part of the kill they would return to the power; this showed gratitude, but, too, in its generosity, that they returned a portion of this gift, it showed the mightiness of the hearts of the men; not even the cave lion would be so proud, so arrogant, that it would dare to exchange gifts with the power; Spear, and the others, did not love the power, nor did they reverence it, but they acknowledged it, and, in their way, honored it. They would not worship it, of course, for the power was not so trivial or petty, so childish, that it either required, or demanded, worship; it would simply have been pointless to worship it, for it was not that sort of thing; and, had the power been a man, if it were not psychotic, worship would have simply embarrassed it; and so Spear, on behalf of himself, and the others, not reverencing and not worshiping, but acknowledging, and, in his way, honoring, did, with a good heart, lift unto the power meat, and then burned it.

Spear's flint knife, some eight inches long, the handle wrapped in leather, taken from a rawhide belt, thrust down into the hot meat.

It was the first time, of course, that Hamilton had witnessed a feeding.

Piece by great chunk was ripped and pulled from the roasted carcass and thrown to the hunters who, squatting down, with both hands, began to feed on it, tearing it apart with their teeth and fingers.

Spear cut a huge chunk away and threw it to Tooth, the hunter with the prognathous jaw, the atavistically extended canine on the upper right side of his mouth. The children clustered around him.

Then Spear cut pieces of meat for those females who were pregnant, their bellies heavy with child beneath the skins, their breasts already swelling with milk. There were four such females, slow, and awkward, who took the meat and began to chew on it.

The man with the large tooth cut small pieces of meat for each of the tiny children, those walking, those less than some five years of age. The small ones would be guaranteed food, and the pregnant females. It was the law. Spear had made it. The man with the large tooth then gave the rest of that chunk of meat to the young, blond girl, she who was some fourteen years of age, and she it was who would distribute it among the older children. She took the first piece herself, and ate it, they watching, eyes wide, waiting for her favor. Some of them whimpered, and put out their hands, and she struck them away. Others pointed to their mouths. One boy, Hamilton noticed, did not beg, but stood with the children, sullen, angry. He, too, might have been some twelve or fourteen years of age, but whereas the blond girl was lusciously, incipiently a female, he was only still a boy. He was not yet old enough to run with the hunters. He did not have the great leap of growth yet that would bring his body to the pitch at which he might follow the pace of the older men, in their long hunts, hanging behind them, learning the smells and signs of the forest. He was two inches shorter than the girl, and less heavy. He was still slight, still a boy. But Hamilton saw that he was proud, defiant. The girl, arrogantly, threw the meat to the other children, giving more or less as the child was or was not one of her favorites. Much of the meat she ate herself. The younger children leaped and cried, and she would throw them a piece of meat. The boy cried out angrily, demanding food. She paid him no attention. She ignored his outstretched hand. Then, angrily, he tried to snatch a piece of meat and she struck him, screaming, and drove him from the meat, hitting him, kicking at him. He fell to the ground. She kicked him and turned away from him. She returned to the meat and, pulling it apart, ate some herself, and threw other pieces to the children. One piece, dark with gristle, she threw to the dirt before the boy, and stood up, head high, wiping her hands on her thighs.

Hamilton saw that there were five women behind the leader, and first among them was the lame, scarred woman, who had so terrified her.

The leader, over his shoulder, handed back meat to the lame woman, who took it, eating some, distributing other portions to the other women. Behind each hunter there knelt one or more women, waiting to be fed. After a time the hunters, growing heavy with food, grease on their hands and bodies, juice at their mouths, began to hand meat back to the women. Some of the women, from time to time, would whimper, and point to their mouths, indicating their hunger. Most of the women seemed to have hunters who fed them. The young man who was the son of the leader gave meat to the older blond girl, who was muchly beautiful, and clung much to him, she whom Hamilton would learn was Flower. Her own hunter, to her anger, was feeding the dark-haired woman and the shorter blond woman. Sometimes he would hand them meat, sometimes he would hold it in his hand, or mouth, and make them take it in their teeth. He did not so much as look at Hamilton. "I am hungry," she thought. "I am hungry."

She saw that two of the women were nursing infants. They, like the others, knelt behind men, begging their food. Hamilton saw two other women, to her irritation, lying on their backs, holding out their hands to hunters, lifting their bodies to them. "Filthy bitches," thought Hamilton. "Prostitutes! Whores!" She was furious that they would offer their bodies to the hunters' pleasure, merely to be fed. "Whores!" thought Hamilton. Then Hamilton saw, too, that now one of the mothers, her infant in the arms of another, was lying before a hunter, lifting her body. Hamilton turned away. "I hate men," she thought. "I hate them."

She saw meat thrown to the women who lifted their bodies. Other women, still hungry, now lifted their bodies to the men. Some others crawled to them, and kissed them, about the ankles. Many had meat thrust in their mouths.

Hamilton turned away, disgusted. "They are slaves, the females are slaves," she thought.

But the high females, like the lame woman, and those others, behind the leader, seemed to feed well. Their importance, their prestige, Hamilton thought, is a function of the males with whom they associate themselves. If one would be a high female, one must well please a high male. But the lame, scarred woman was not truly attractive, and yet she knelt behind the leader himself, behind his left shoulder. In some important way, Hamilton thought, she must serve him well. She shuddered as she thought what must be the menace, the power, of the lame, scarred woman.

She saw the young blond girl, Butterfly, walking among the group. She saw the leader's eyes, narrow, watching her.

She did not think it would be long before the young blond girl would be told to take a new place in the feeding, among the women.

She saw the boy gnawing on the gristly meat he had been thrown.

Almost unaware of it, Hamilton discovered she had edged closer to her hunter.

Different hunters now were cutting into the meat, feeding themselves, and the women about them. The first pieces of meat had been cut by the leader, and distributed by him, for he was the leader, he was the one who gave meat.

The old woman and the nurse, too, were pulling at the meat, as though they might be hunters.

Hamilton saw the old woman take some meat and give it to one of the nursing mothers.

She also saw the heavy-bodied man, with the extended canine tooth, give a tiny piece of meat to a toddling child, who put it in his mouth and ran to his mother.

Hamilton edged closer to her hunter.

Then he faced her.

"I'm very hungry," said Hamilton. "I know you cannot understand what I'm saying, but I trust that my need, and my condition, are sufficiently obvious. I would appreciate receiving some food."

He turned away from her, eating.

"Please," said Hamilton.

He paid her no attention.

She rose to her feet, and, hunter by hunter, asked to be given meat. Most looked up at her, and then looked away. She was not a woman they had elected to feed. She saw the women exchanging glances, and smiling. "Please," said Hamilton. "Please!" She was becoming more desperate. She did not ask meat from the leader. She was too terrified of the lame, scarred woman behind him. Sometimes when she approached a hunter, the other women behind him would motion her away, angrily. But most to her consternation was the fact that the hunters did not seem much interested in her. Suddenly Hamilton was frightened. Was she not beautiful? Should they not be eager to please her? Her heart sank. She suddenly understood that she stood in a competitive situation, she against other females, even to be fed. "No!" she wept to herself. But the men had used her. But now they did not seem interested in her. "Oh, no," she said, sinking to her knees, "oh, no, no." She had not sufficiently pleased them. What could she do to please them? What must she do? "No, no," she wept to herself.

Anxiously she returned, ankles thonged, to behind the tall, lean hunter, he who had brought her captive, slave, to this camp.

She knelt behind him. "Please," she begged him. "Feed me!"

The dark-haired girl, and the blond girl, chewing, looked at her.

There was no interest in their eyes.

"Feed me!" wept Hamilton.

The hunter did not look at her.

Hamilton felt her wrists being drawn behind her back. She looked over her shoulder. It was the leader. She felt her wrists tied together, tightly, with a rawhide thong. He then untied the rawhide from her ankles and, crossing her ankles, used it to secure them. He then lifted her lightly and carried her from the fire. Before one of the small, round huts, he paused, and then, easily, threw her within. She landed in the hut pit, on her shoulder, a foot below the surface of the surrounding soil, in the dirt, in the darkness. She struggled. She could not free herself. She could not rise to her feet. For more than two hours she lay on the sunken floor of the hut, in its pit, bound. She wept, she struggled. Her body was hungry, and ached from the beatings she had been given.

Outside the hut she could hear a pounding on sticks and something like singing, and laughter.

She did not know but tomorrow, at dawn, the people would go for salt, and then to the flint, and then, when ready, return to the shelters.

When the camp was quiet Brenda Hamilton heard something coming, slowly, shuffling, animallike, toward the hut. In the darkness, she struggled to sit up. It was coming closer. Brenda shrank back against the side of the hut pit, pushing back against it.

A head appeared in the entrance to the hut.

"Stay away!" screamed Hamilton, suddenly terrified, knowing she was helpless, and could not defend herself.

The creature entered the hut, stepping down, its head low on its rounded shoulders.

"Stay away from me!" screamed Hamilton. "You're not human! You're hideous! Stay away!"

Ugly Girl, her ankles in their leather shackles, but otherwise free, peered down, in the darkness, looking at Hamilton.

She thrust her wide, round head toward Hamilton. Hamilton felt the greasy, stringlike hair on her shoulder.

"No! No! No!" cried Hamilton. "Help! Help!" She tried to turn away, trapped against the side of the hut pit.

The creature looked at her, quizzically.

"Stay away from me!" screamed Hamilton. "You're a monster! You're repulsive! You are hideous! Keep away! Keep away!"

Ugly Girl backed away, squatting down.

"You haven't the intelligence of a dog!" screamed Hamilton. "Keep away from me!"

Ugly Girl made no noise, squatting in the darkness, near Hamilton.

"Stay away!" hissed Hamilton. "Stay away!"

Ugly Girl did not move for some time but then, slowly, neared Hamilton. "Stay away!" screamed Hamilton.

Ugly Girl, steadily, not listening to Hamilton, disregarding her cries, her movements, thrust her mouth against Hamilton's. Hamilton tried to twist her mouth away, terrified, hysterical, almost retching, but Ugly Girl persisted, forcing her mouth to Hamilton's. Suddenly Hamilton realized that there was something in her mouth.

It was meat.

Hamilton suddenly took it and chewed it, and swallowed it. Ugly Girl pulled back her head.

There was a long silence.

"Thank you," said Hamilton.

Ugly Girl's hand reached out, tenderly, and touched Hamilton's cheek, and then she went to the other side of the hut and lay down.

In a few moments Hamilton heard the breathing of her sleep.

During the night, at times, Ugly Girl whimpered, and twisted.

"How hideous she is," thought Hamilton. "How hideous."

◆ 16 ◆

Brenda Hamilton struggled, tied back to back with Ugly Girl, her hands tied behind her, about Ugly Girl, fastened in front, tightly, of Ugly Girl's belly, Ugly Girl's hands similarly in front of her own belly. The two girls knelt, their ankles tied together, Ugly Girl's left ankle to Hamilton's right, Hamilton's left to Ugly Girl's right. They could not rise. They saw the ovoid eyes gleaming in the darkness, like fiery copper.

They were in the vicinity of the shelters.

Yesterday the animal, in the morning, had dragged one of the women into the brush. That same afternoon it had killed a child.

It was a lone animal, like most who would prey upon human groups, taking them as game when, being too old or too ill, it could not pursue and slay its more accustomed quarry.

But men were dangerous game.

That afternoon and morning, in a narrow place between thickset trees and brush, the women, Brenda and Ugly Girl among them, had, with stones and sticks and shells, dug the pit, lifting the dirt from it in leather sacks on rawhide

TIME SLAVE   197

ropes. In the bottom of the pit Spear and Stone had set a large number of sharpened stakes, at intervals of some six inches from one another. The pit was some sixteen feet deep, some ten by five feet wide. It had been covered with light sticks, over which leaves and grass had been spread.

Ugly Girl's breathing seemed almost to stop. Her back felt cold against Brenda's.

Hamilton threw back her head and screamed, and struggled. The eyes came a foot closer. By their movements Hamilton could see it turn its head from side to side. It was a large shadow, lithe and sinuous. She heard the breathing, and smelled the animal.

It was ten days after Brenda Hamilton had first been brought by Tree to the camp of the Men. The morning after her arrival in camp the camp had broken and the Men had trekked to the salt. It was only a half day's trek from where the game camp had been set.

Once in the vicinity of the salt the women, and the children, with Brenda and Ugly Girl, were herded between some trees. There they were made to huddle, closely together. A thin strip of rawhide was stretched about the trees, like a tiny string fence. The women and the children, and the two slaves, must remain within this perimeter until the men returned with the salt.

The location of the salt was a secret of the Men. Women must not know its whereabouts. Women might be stolen, and were subject to barter. They were exchangeable. If a woman knew the location of the salt, a most precious commodity, more valuable than themselves, they might reveal it to others. A male, of course, when he became old enough to run with the hunters, when he became of the Men, would be taught the location of the salt. He, in learning it, would not be sworn to secrecy, sworn to keep it from the females. That was not necessary. Any male knew that females might not know the location of salt. They were females.

It was said in the group that Spear had found the salt, but there were those among the Men who remembered that it had been Tree. He had found it while following antelope.

Brenda and Ugly Girl had waited with the women. Their ankles were no longer thonged. That was impractical in the trek. But they were tied together by the throat, by a length of rawhide some five feet long.

In the trek the women had, on their heads, carried hide bundles. Ugly Girl had held hers on her shoulder, for it was painful for her, with the placement of her neck to support

weight in that fashion. Hamilton balanced the bundle she
was given by Short Leg on her head, in the fashion of the
other women. Hamilton was human. The bundle she carried, though perhaps heavier than most, was not particularly
heavy. She was not permitted to carry food or water. The
possessions of the Men, other than the women and the children, were few. The men traveled lightly. Hamilton's bundle,
like that of Ugly Girl, consisted of several skins, prepared
during the sojourn at the game camp.

About the huddled women, inside the rawhide string,
strode one of the men, Fox, with a switch, to be assured
that they did not attempt to follow the Men and learn the
whereabouts of the salt. Even Short Leg, to her irritation,
must remain within the string. She, too, was only a woman.
Even Old Woman did not complain. She had long since
resigned herself to the fact that salt must remain a secret of
the men. Too, she did not much care any longer where the
salt might be. Free salt was of great value, far more than
gold or diamonds would have been, but it was not essential
for life, for it could be obtained in the tissues of slain
animals, in meat. Still it was a great luxury. Free salt was a
trading commodity *par excellence*.

By nightfall the men had returned with four sacks of
salt.

The group had camped in the open that night, and, in
the morning, had continued the trek, to the flint lode.

The next evening, at dusk, they had come to the flint
cliffs.

Although Hamilton did not understand it, there was much
anger, much fury, among the men. Clearly the flint cliffs had
been worked in their absence.

Furthermore, to their outrage, in a deposit of clay thrust
between two stones, was drawn a sign, the meaning of
which was clear to the Men. It was the sign of the Weasel
People. And it meant that they claimed the flint as their
own.

Spear scratched away the sign of the Weasel People and,
in its place, with his knife, cut the sign of the Men. It was
an angled line, surmounted by a straight line. At the tip of
the straight line, to the left, was a point. It was a representation, crude, of an arm hurling a spear.

That night guards were set.

For four days the Men worked the flint. Skins were sewn
into long bags, five feet in length, a foot wide. The men,
with green sticks, and picks of antler horn, and rocks,

cracked and prïed the flint from the cliff. When a piece of suitable weight and size was obtained, it was put into a bag. Little of the flint was shaped at the lode. The amount of flint taken was a function of the number and strength of the females, who would carry it.

At the lode Brenda Hamilton had not been fastened to Ugly Girl, but had been free, though she was set much work. She carried water in skins to the men, and carried flint down to the sacks, and gathered wood for the night fires. She was also taught to dig roots and gather fruit and vegetables. There was no hunting done at the lode, for the men were concerned with the flint. Dried meat was eaten, together with vegetables and fruits. Hamilton also noted that certain insects, and grubs, were eaten. She would not eat such. She was not given meat, but she fed well enough, on roots and fruits, and vegetables, of the sort which she was instructed to gather. The children also joined in such work. Hamilton was, to some extent, pleased, because she now realized how much more free with food was the land than she had realized. There were many things to eat which she had not understood heretofore as being edible. She realized she might have starved in the midst of plenty. Among other things she learned were edible was the inner bark of the white birch tree, and pine nuts and rose hips. During the first two days at the lode Hamilton had tried to remain in the vicinity of the hunter who had taken her slave, bringing him water, gathering his flint, but he had paid her little attention, and, some four times, with the stroke of a switch, wielded by either the dark-haired girl or the shorter blond girl, she had been driven from his vicinity. "I do not care," she had said to herself. "He is nothing to me." But she hated the dark-haired girl and the shorter, blond girl.

They did not want her near the hunter. They would beat her when she lingered near him.

The switch stung her and made her angry. She fled from it. It hurt her.

After four days at the lode the flint sacks were filled with what rock a human female could carry.

The sacks were then lifted by the beasts of burden, the females. They were slung about the neck, the weight falling to each side.

Even Short Leg carried flint. So, too, did the older children, though in lesser amounts. Of the women, only Old Woman did not carry flint. "I am too old to carry flint," she said. The bags given to Hamilton and to Ugly Girl were especially heavy, for they were slave. Hamilton could scarely believe that she was expected to carry it. Fox, with his switch, gestured that she lift it. She, now thonged again by the neck to Ugly Girl, struggled to lift the sack. Suddenly stung by Fox's switch, she stood erect, feeling its weight. She almost fell. Fox's switch tapped her in the small of the back, indicating that she should stand straight. She then felt the switch tap her under the chin, twice, indicating that she should hold up her head. She stood, a beautiful, erect slave girl, under her burden. Spear cried out, from the head of the column. The Men, carrying their weapons lightly, preceded the column. The switch struck twice, along the column. Fox strode on one side, Wolf on the other. The women, struggling under the weight of the stone, stumbling, followed the men. With them, leashed by the throat behind Ugly Girl, went Brenda Hamilton. She, too, like the others, though a woman of our time, though the holder of an advanced degree from a prestigious institution of higher learning, barefoot, sweating, carried flint.

On the morning of the third day of the trek, unexpectedly, the beast had struck. Hamilton did not even see it, though she did hear the screams of the woman being dragged by the shoulder through the brush.

Spear had not permitted the men to follow. It was his belief the female would be dead before she could be reached. Further, it was dangerous, with the primitive weapons at the disposal of the men, to cope with such a beast. To attack it as one might a cave bear would be to invite the loss of three or four men, or perhaps more. Such an animal, stone-tipped spears hanging from its haunches, bleeding, maddened by the bruising of rocks, could, frenzied, attacking, with the blows of its paws and the lockings of its great jaws, destroy an entire hunting party. Such a beast must be met with guile.

That afternoon the beast had struck again, this time seizing a child in its jaws and padding away, white-muzzled, into the brush. The child had been taken not more than twenty yards from Hamilton. Its back had been broken in the first bite. Its eyes open it had dangled in the jaws, lost in shock. It would not live more than a few moments. Hamilton had screamed and tried to flee. Ugly Girl, jerked about by the leash, had held her, not letting her run. Hamilton, wildly, sank to her knees, and held Ugly Girl. They clung together. The women began to weep and cry out. One woman, the mother, tried to run into the brush after the animal but Spear followed her and, striking her again and again, tried to beat her unconscious. To Hamilton's amazement he, with his strength, could not do so, but, at last, dazed, and in shock, the woman sank to the ground and Spear carried her back to the old woman and to the heavy-breasted woman. Another child, too, ran to her and she took it in her arms, holding it closely, weeping, rocking back and forth, trying to sing to it.

That night many fires had been set about the group and the women, Ugly Girl and Hamilton, too, and the children, were put in the center of the group. The men crouched about the outside of the circle, where they might reach brands from the fire.

Wolves circled the group late, in the darkness, but they were merely curious.

The beast did not return. Somewhere, gorged, it slept. It might not wish to feed for another two or three days. It might wish to feed again by tomorrow nightfall. The men did not know its hunger.

The next morning, the tenth after Hamilton's arrival in the Men's camp, in a suitable place, the pit was dug. It was some sixteen feet deep, some five feet wide, some ten feet long. While the women dug and carried away dirt, the men constructed the runway. It was done with naturalness, with branches and sticks and thorn brush. In was widest at the point at which the beast would find it most convenient to enter, narrowest before the pit. It would be difficult to approach, except from one direction. Spear and Stone, in the bottom of the pit, when it was ready, at roughly six-inch intervals, set many sharpened stakes. The intervals were narrow for the beast, though large, was lithe, sinuous. If it were not impaled it would have little difficulty climbing from the pit. Furthermore, if it survived, it would be doubly dangerous, for it would now be wary of its approach and its footing. It would have profited, unfortunately for the Men, from a lesson that would not need to be repeated, a lesson which the men, in effect, had the opportunity to administer only once. When the stakes had been placed, Spear and Stone, on ropes, scrambled from the pit. Then the light network of branches was placed over the pit, and covered with other branches, and grass and broad leaves.

Behind the pit, leading to it, a path, approximately a foot wide, had been left in the thorn brush.

Brenda Hamilton wondered with what the pit would be baited.

She felt the hand of Stone on her arm.

"No!" she cried.

She saw Spear held Ugly Girl, who was whimpering, her simple, vacant eyes filled with terror.

The rawhide thong which linked the two slaves by the throat was removed.

For an instant Hamilton was elated. They would use Ugly Girl, not her!

But Spear gestured that she, too, should edge between the narrow walls of thorn brush leading to the back of the pit.

"No!" she cried.

She fell to her knees.

"Use her! Not me!" cried Hamilton. "I'm human! I'm like you! Use her! Not me! Not me!"

But Stone, rawhide strips in his teeth, pulled her up by the arm and, painfully, thrust her through the narrow opening in the brush.

At the back edge of the pit Brenda Hamilton and Ugly Girl were forced to kneel. There they were tied back to back, their arms about one another, the wrists of each, behind them, tied about the belly of the other. Then their ankles were tied together, right ankle to left, left to right. They knelt then at the back edge of the pit; they could not rise to their feet.

Through the opening in the brush Hamilton saw the women. Several of them were smiling, in particular the dark-haired girl, and the shorter, blond girl. She saw, too, her hunter. He was looking at her, impassively. She moaned. She struggled in the bonds, perfectly secured. Then she saw, thorn bush by thorn bush, the narrow opening, from the edge of the pit backwards, being filled with brush, walling them in. There was a ledge about a yard wide between the wall of thorn brush and the edge of the pit. It was here that the bait would wait, kneeling.

"Come back!" cried Hamilton. "Come back!"

But the Men had gone.

The eyes of the animal, ovoid, gleaming, came a foot closer.

Brenda Hamilton threw her head back and screamed, struggling in the rawhide thongs.

It was some ten yards away.

It paused, testing the wind, lifting its head. Then it entered, back low, head down, between the walls of brush at the open end of the funnel.

Ugly Girl was, head turned to one side, watching it.

The beast, low, dark, tail moving back and forth, was suspicious.

Now Brenda Hamilton was too terrified even to scream. It seemed she could not move her body. Her world seemed limited by the dark walls of brush, the shape, the gleaming eyes.

Then the beast, low, tail switching, ears' back, crept a foot closer, then stopped.

Then Ugly Girl began to whimper, but it was not a fear whimper, it was a tiny noise.

Brenda Hamilton did not know the noise but it was the rooting noise of the small-tusked bush pig.

The beast, an old one, may not have caught such a swift, erratically running, delicately fleshed animal in more than a year.

The leap of the beast begins with a short run, but the leap is timed, always, to fall just short of the game, and it is on the bound, following the leap, when earth is again struck, and the great coiled springs of the back legs unleash themselves at point-blank range, that the game is seized. Just as the bullet has its greatest speed and power at muzzle velocity, so, too, the strike of the beast is most terrible at the instant that it has just left the earth. Accordingly, it strikes the prey, when possible, on the upbound. It takes its run, leaps, hits the earth a yard before the prey, and then, with its full ferocity and strength, on the upbound, strikes it, biting and tearing. The weight of the beast was some six hundred pounds, its length was some ten feet. Its strike, if made immediately from the ground, could knock a water buffalo, rolling, from its feet. It could break the back of a small horse laterally, snapping the spine. The pit the Men had dug was ten feet in length. It was thus almost certain that the termination of the approach leap, the striking of the earth immediately prior to the killing bound, would be at the pit's edge.

Ugly Girl continued to make the small noises of the bush pig.

Then, suddenly, she stopped. To Hamilton's amazement then, after an instant's silence, Ugly Girl uttered a tiny, inhuman squeal of fear. It was the warning signal of the bush pig. It is a genetically linked terror signal which also, genetically, releases the fear and flight response in other pigs.

In the old brain of the beast this was a sound it well remembered.

It preceded momentarily the almost instantaneous, terrified scattering of the pigs.

Suddenly, without an instant's hesitation, the dark, low shape, swift and terrible, sprang up, bounding forward. At the edge of the pit it sprang into the air.

Hamilton and Ugly Girl threw themselves back against the brush.

There was a sudden snapping of light branches, and a scream of rage.

For a wild instant Hamilton saw the copperlike eyes blazing not more than a foot from her body, and one paw, extended over the edge of the pit, and then the beast, twisting, fell sideways, down, away from her, disappearing in the darkness. There was a horrid scream of pain and rage, and she heard stakes snapping and the ripping of the body of the animal. Then she heard movement in the pit and more cries of rage and pain. The animal, she knew, with a sinking feeling, was among the stakes, injured, terrible, maddened with pain.

She heard it scratching at the sides of the pit. She could not see its head.

Then she heard it leap up, and saw the head for an instant, wild, frothing, bloody, and then it fell back. Again it screamed with pain.

Then again it leaped, and she saw its head, huge, broad, and the teeth, fangs white in the night. The head was more than a foot wide. Two mighty paws, claws extended, caught to the earth not more than five inches from their bodies, and the animal tried to scramble up, back feet digging at the side of the pit, snarling, roaring. Hamilton saw that it was now blind in one eye. There was blood, black against the side of its head, on the left side of its head. The left ear was torn.

The animal, partly out of the pit, regarded them.

It held, precariously, to the side of the pit. Then, suddenly it pitched backward into the darkness.

Its six hundred pounds fell from some sixteen feet backward onto the stakes.

Hamilton heard a sudden whimpering. Hamilton did not know the sound. It came from the pit. It was that of a cub crying for its mother.

Then there was silence. The pit was dark, and very quiet. Hamilton, tied against Ugly Girl, lost consciousness. Ugly Girl,

bracing her body, held Hamilton and herself upright. Ugly
Girl began to make a low, crooning noise with her mouth, a
repetition of some four or five notes. She repeated this over
and over, happily, to herself. It was the Ugly People's way of
singing. She, and the human slave girl, were alive.

◆ 17 ◆

Brenda Hamilton laughed.
She had made good her escape.
Yesterday night she had fled from the group. The group
had come, in the late afternoon, to a group of high, almost
sheer cliffs. In them, here and there, high, some of them
more than two hundred feet from the ground, there was a
set of openings, leading to deep caves.
These were the shelters.
They were the home of the Men, and of their properties,
their skins, their flints, and their women and children.
The cliffs, with their height, and the dark openings, had
frightened Hamilton.
She was afraid to be owned in them.
Camp had been made at the foot of the cliffs, for the men
must investigate the caves again, many with torches, to make
certain that the cave bear had not, in their absence, claimed
them as his own.
The group was in good spirits. The cave lion had been
killed, and such beasts, preying on humans, were extremely
rare. Many hides and much meat had been taken at the game
camp, and the men had found salt; and much flint had been
carried to the foot of the cliffs.
Brenda Hamilton, naked, thonged to Ugly Girl by the
throat, her body aching from the weight of the flint sack,
had, with the other women, thrown down the flint, and knelt
with them, at the base of the cliffs, exhausted. No longer
were she and the others hurried forward by the switches of
Fox and Wolf. Her body had been struck many times. The
other women, except Ugly Girl, were happy; they were

home; Brenda Hamilton, her body aching from the weight of
the stone, and stinging from the blows of switches which
had encouraged her to carry it more swiftly, looked up at
the cliffs; she was afraid; they were very high, and the dark
openings frightened her; some of them were more than two
hundred feet high in the cliff. Ugly Girl did not seem happy
or unhappy; she seemed only stupid, docile, vacant; she
would do whatever her masters told her; Brenda Hamilton
would not; she was determined to escape. She no longer
wished to carry flint as a slave; she did not wish, again, to
be used as a piece of meat, living meat, to bait a trap. Many
of the women had smiled, when she had been tied with
Ugly Girl, particularly the dark-haired girl, and the shorter,
blond one. And the hunter had looked upon her, when her
eyes had pleaded with him, impassively. She would flee.

Her opportunity had come much earlier than she had
hoped. The men had gone up the cliffs, to investigate the
caves. The women and children, thus, had been left below.

Before the men had left, dried meat had been distributed.
Brenda and Ugly Girl had had four cubes apiece. It had been
held in the palm of the hand of Runner. They had taken it,
as kneeling women often did, in their teeth, directly from his
hand.

At the flint lode, in gathering fruit, and roots and vegetables, and watching what was eaten, Brenda Hamilton had
learned much.

She was confident she could now, in one way or another, survive.

She must make her way to the south before the onset of
winter.

When it grew dark, and the others were asleep, the men,
not wishing to descend the cliff at night, in the uncertain
light of torches, camped in one of the shelters, Brenda
Hamilton, carefully, silently, began to chew on the rawhide
thong that tethered her to the slack-jawed, vacant-eyed, inhuman Ugly Girl. Ugly Girl approached her, whimpering, and
tried to push her hand from the thong, but Hamilton,
frenzied, furious, struck her back. "Stay away!" she hissed.
Whimpering, Ugly Girl withdrew to the end of her tether.
In time, biting and pulling and scratching with her fingers,
she managed to part the thong. "What fools they are not to
have bound me hand and foot," she laughed to herself.

Then she had crawled from the group, slowly, silently.
When she had cleared the area of the bodies, and the low,
dim light of the dying fire, she leaped to her feet and ran.

She had escaped.

She had run for many hours, until she had gone so far no one could follow her.

Then she had slept. In the afternoon she had arisen, and, finding some nuts and roots, had fed; had, with the aid of a small stick, sharpened with a rock to a point, removed the remains of the tether from her throat, which had fastened her to Ugly Girl; and had then continued on her way.

"No more will I be subject to their switches," she laughed. "No more will I have to eat like a female animal from their hand. No more will I have to carry flint. No more will I have to see that hateful hunter!"

Suddenly Brenda Hamilton threw her hand before her mouth. She saw the eyes, briefly, in a flash, between bushes. It was not an animal the size of the cave lion. It was much smaller. But it was a sinuous, stealthily moving animal. It weighed perhaps only forty or fifty pounds more than Hamilton, but it was quite capable of taking prey twice its weight or more. It was a strong predator, which could pull its prey, even if heavier than itself, high into the branches of a tree, to keep it from scavengers. It was the most agile of the large cats, and, to men, perhaps the most dangerous. Hamilton had seen one of its descendants in Rhodesia, smaller, but still quite dangerous. To her horror, it was stalking her.

She remembered the body of the calf, half torn, lying over the limb of the tree in the Rhodesian bush. She recalled the great care of William and Gunther, even armed, in approaching it, even when it was sleepy, somnolent and gorged. Gunther, who was a remarkable hunter, with excellent weaponry, would not have followed it into the bush.

"Oh, no!" wept Hamilton.

Sometimes she thought that she had lost it, but then, again, shifting in the darkness, almost indistinguishable among shadows, she would see it again.

Once she picked up a rock, and hurled it at the shape.

She heard only a snarling, and saw it crouch down. She sensed its nervousness. She remembered the cave lion.

She was terrified that she might provoke its charge. She moved a little away, and it moved a little toward her. She ran, shouting, toward it, but it did not retreat. She saw it gather its hind legs, like springs, ready to leap.

She stood still, terrified.

It hesitated, and lay down, tail slashing, watching her.

She looked about. It could be upon her before she could climb a tree. She sensed that it would charge when she turned her back. And, too, she knew, a tree would not be likely to much protect her. It was a far more swift, expert climber than she. If she were already in a tree, and had perhaps a heavy branch, she might perhaps, striking and thrusting, be able to keep it away, as it tried to approach, scrambling after her, but she was in no such position, and had no such implement.

The beast, eyes blazing, snarling, crept toward her.

Hamilton began to back away.

She wanted to turn and flee, but she knew that it, bounding and leaping, would be on her in a matter of seconds.

Hamilton backed into a grassy clearing, moving back, step by step. Her eyes were wide. Her hand was before her mouth.

The beast, creeping, eyes blazing, every muscle of it excited, tail switching, followed her.

Hamilton tripped over a root and, crying out with misery, fell.

In that instant the leopard charged. In less than the time it took Hamilton to see it clearly it was across the clearing and, snarling, leaping toward her. She saw the heavy shaft, not realizing at the time what it was, strike the beast in its leap and saw the flailing paws, claws exposed, striking toward her. Another body leaped over hers and she cried out in fear and, her weight on the palms of her hands, saw the leopard biting at the shaft protruding from his side, and the other shape, human, but bestial, ferocious, like nothing she had ever seen that was manlike, hurl itself on the spotted beast, a knife of stone in its hand. He clung to its back, one arm about its throat, rolling with the animal, jabbing and pulling the knife again and again across the white, furred throat. The great, clawed hind feet raked wildly but could not find their enemy. The blood flooded from its lungs, sputtering out like hot red mud, and then the blood, no longer flowing from its mouth, burst from its throat and the assailant, his fist and knife red to the wrist and hilt, drew his hand from the beast's body.

The beast then lay at his feet, the arterial blood throbbing out, a pulsating glot to each beat of the animal's heart. To Brenda's horror the assailant then knelt beside the beast and, catching its blood in his hands, held it to his mouth, drinking. Then the glots became smaller, and their expulsions weaker, as the heart slowed, and then stopped. The assailant, dipping his finger in the throat of the animal, then drew signs on his own body with the blood, luck signs and courage signs and, among them, the sign of the Men.

Tree rose from beside the beast and looked down at the lovely naked female on the grass, whom he had saved.

Brenda Hamilton felt her ankles tied tightly together. Her hands were left free. She did not try to free her ankles.

Tree lifted the leopard.

Hamilton was indescribably thrilled, for what reason she knew not, to see that the stone tip of the spear had emerged, inches of it, from the right side of the leopard. She could scarcely conceive of the incredible strength of such a cast.

Tree, placing the butt of the spear on the ground, forced the shaft through the leopard completely, thus freeing the weapon and protecting the bindings which fastened the long stone point to the wood.

Then, spear in hand, he stood over her. He was breathing heavily. She had seen him drink the blood of the leopard. And its blood, too, in strange signs, he wore on his body.

Her ankles were bound. She could not run. She lay at his mercy.

She could not even thank him for having saved her life. She only hoped that he would not kill her. She could not meet his eyes. Such a man, so mighty, so frightening, terrified her. She knew she would do whatever such a man commanded her, unquestioningly, even eagerly.

She dared to look up, to look into his eyes. Never had she felt so helpless, so much a mere female.

Quickly she looked down at the grass.

How miserable she was. She had been caught.

He went to the leopard and began to gut the beast, saving meat and skin, the head and claws.

When he had finished he untied her ankles, and gestured that she should stand.

When she did so he put the leopard over her shoulders. It was heavy, even bled and gutted. She felt the stickiness of bloody hair on her back, and the softness of the fur, and the heavy paws, with their claws, limp and weighty, touch her body.

She looked again into his eyes. She suddenly realized she was a runaway slave. She looked down again. She knew she would be beaten.

He then turned away and she, carrying the carcass of the leopard, followed him.

She understood then only too well, though she did not understand how it could be, that such men could follow her like dogs, that they might pick up her trail and, with ease, when they wished, pursue and retake her. "There is no escape for me," she whispered to herself. "There is no escape." And too she had learned that the primeval forests would offer her small refuge. She looked about herself now in terror, for the first time better understanding the ferocities and perils of her environment. Within twenty-four hours of her escape she had nearly fallen to a leopard. Had it not been for the intervention of the hunter she would, by now, have been half eaten. A lone female in these times, she realized, had need of the protection of a man. Without the protection of men she could not survive. The choice was simple for the female. Either serve men on their own terms or die.

Staggering under the burden of the leopard, Brenda Hamilton, the slave, followed the hunter back to the shelters.

Brenda Hamilton scrambled to the back of the cave. She put her cheek against it, the palms of her hands. It was rock. She could go no further.

She did not look over her shoulder.

She knew he crouched in the entrance, the switch in his hand.

"Please don't hurt me," she begged. "I'm sorry I ran away. I will not do it again!"

He, of course, could not understand the strange noises she made, not of the language of the Men, nor, if he could have understood, would he have listened.

She was a girl to be disciplined.

Brenda Hamilton's fingernails scratched at the rock. The cave, for a full day now, twenty-four hours now, had been her prison. The entrance, for the caves, was a large one, though it had appeared much smaller from far below. It was some four feet in height and three feet wide, irregular. Outside it was a narrow ledge, not more than two feet in width. The fall from the ledge to the valley below, Brenda Hamilton had seen in terror, was better than some one hundred and seventy-five feet, approximately that of a seventeen-story building. Above and below the cave, and to the sides, the cliff was sheer. It was reached from a ledge above, by a knotted rawhide rope, which, when the hunter left, he drew up after him. Inside the cave there was a gourd of water, and two frayed, worn hides. There were also some pieces of fruit, and rinds. The cave, within, was much larger, like many of the caves, than one would have expected from the outside. It was roughly some eight feet in height and width, and some forty feet deep. It was lit by light from the entrance and, overhead, in the ceiling, some fifteen feet in, by a long, narrow cleft in the rock, extending some fifty feet upward, diagonally, too small to admit a body.

She had been brought to the cave blindfolded, that she might not struggle in terror. Her wrists had been tied together and placed about his neck and shoulder. He had, after lowering them both to the ledge, disengaged her arms from him and thrust her into the cave. There he had removed the blindfold and wrist thongs and left her, taking them with him, thrust in his belt, climbing the knotted rope, which he drew after him.

She had run to the cave entrance and, dropping to her hands and knees, had entered into the sunlight, and screamed, seeing the drop below her.

She heard a scrambling above her and saw the hunter attain the ledge above, some twenty feet higher. Then the rope was jerked up, following him.

"Don't leave me here!" she screamed. "Please! Please!"

But he was gone.

Sick, she inched herself backward, timidly, and lay down inside the entrance, helpless, surrounded by the walls of stone.

She felt certain that she had been abandoned, but, in the morning, on the ledge outside, she had found the gourd of water, and some pieces of fruit.

Now the hunter crouched in the entrance. She saw the switch, and knew she was to be disciplined. She was naked.

She had scrambled to the back wall of the cave. Her fingernails scratched at the stone.

She heard him behind her.

She did not look back.

Suddenly the switch struck, wielded with a man's strength. She screamed in pain.

She turned to face him, to plead with him, and the switch struck again.

She fell to her knees and again, this time across the shoulder, the switch fell.

She leaped to her feet, trying to escape, and ran to the entrance. She dropped to her hands and knees and crawled onto the narrow ledge. She cried out with misery. By the ankle she was dragged back into the cave. Four times more fell the switch. She rolled, and scrambled again to her feet. He struck her again. Weeping she tried to escape him, but there was no escape. Twice, by the arm, he threw her against one of the walls, beating her at the foot of it. Then he took her by the hair and hurled her back to the rear of the cave. There she fell to her knees and covered her head. Ten more times the switch fell on her body. Then the hunter threw her to her back, on the hides, weeping, and swiftly raped her, after which, she moaning in terror and misery, he left her. "I won't try to run away again," she wept, eyes glazed, looking after him through her long, dark hair. "I will not try to escape again," she wept, "—Master!" She was startled that this word had involuntarily escaped her. She lay there in misery, wondering at what it had meant. Could it be, she asked herself, in horror, that, subconsciously, the lean hunter had been truly, incontrovertibly, acknowledged as her literal master? "No!" she wept. "No!" But she could not forget what she had said. Not meaning to, unintentionally, in misery, she had called him "Master." She lay in the cave, sullen, in pain, knowing she had, unconsciously, unable to help herself, called him "Master." "He will never master me," she wept. "Not Brenda Hamilton! No savage, no barbarian, will ever master Brenda Hamilton!" But she could not forget that she had called him master. This troubled her greatly. And, too, it made her furious. "No savage, no barbarian," she hissed, "will ever master Brenda Hamilton!"

"Old Woman," said Tree, "I would talk with you."

"Talk," said Old Woman. She was sewing, poking holes through hide with a bone awl, then pulling a thread of sinew after it, through the hole. She worked carefully. Old Woman's eyes were still sharp. It was a winter garment for one of the children, the oldest boy. He would soon be able to run with the hunters. Old Woman was fond of him. He was the son of a woman who had been her friend. She had been killed in an attack of the Weasel People, some ten years earlier, on a game camp.

Tree did not speak, for Nurse was walking by. She held at her breast one of the camp's infants.

On a ledge nearby Tree could hear Fox and Wolf arguing. Wolf had hidden meat and now could not find it. Fox was asking him where he had hidden it. Wolf would not tell him, only that it was gone. "You should not hide meat," Fox was telling him. "It is not good to hide meat. "Where do you hide meat?" "I will not tell you," said Wolf. "I am your friend," said Fox.

"Talk," said Old Woman to Tree, regarding her sewing.

It would not have occurred to Tree to talk to the women, except to give them orders, but he did not think of Old Woman as being of the women. She was different. She was independent. She was shrewd. She was ill-tempered. She was wise.

"You know the pretty bird I brought to camp," said Tree.

"Stupid little thing," said Old Woman.

"Yes," said Tree, "she is stupid."

"But pretty," said Old Woman, pulling the sinew tight with her teeth, still, in spite of her age, sharp and white.

"Do you think she is pretty?" asked Tree.

"Yes," said Old Woman, "more pretty than Antelope, more pretty than Cloud."

"But not so pretty as Flower?"

"No," said Old Woman, "not so pretty as Flower." Old Woman looked up. "How long are you going to keep your pretty little bird on her perch? She has been there for four days. There is work for her to do down here."

"I will keep her there as long as I please," said Tree.

"Poor little slave girl," grinned Old Woman.

Tree, squatting beside Old Woman, looked out the entrance of the shelter. Fox and Wolf had gone.

"I am angry with her," said Tree.

"Why?" asked Old Woman.

"I do not know," said Tree.

"Does she know?" asked Old Woman.

"I do not know," said Tree.

"She is stupid," said Old Woman. Anyone knew that when a man was angry with a woman she would lift her body to him, to placate him, and beg to kick for him, that in the pleasures of her body, he would forget his anger. Else she might be beaten. Any woman with half a brain knew that.

"It is too bad that she does not kick well," said Tree.

"Why?" asked Old Woman.

"She is pretty," said Tree, "very pretty. She should be a good kicker."

"Does this woman trouble you?" asked Old Woman.

"Yes," said Tree.

"Do Antelope and Cloud trouble you?" asked Old Woman.

"Not like this woman," said Tree.

"She is not of the Men," said Old Woman. "She is a foreign female, she is a slave."

"I know," said Tree.

"Take her," advised Old Woman. "Use her as much as you wish. Tire of her." She grinned. "That is the cure for sickness over a woman," she smiled, "use her repeatedly until you weary of her."

Tree smiled. "I want more from this woman," he said.

"Ah," smiled Old Woman. "She has stung your vanity. You want to make her kick for you."

"Perhaps," said Tree.

"The poor little thing has been abused enough," grinned Old Woman. "You surely would not be so cruel as to make her yield to you?"

"You are a wise old woman," said Tree.

"Poor little slave girl," cackled Old Woman.

"It takes time," said Tree, irritably.

Old Woman laughed. "A little patience is a small price to pay for a night of pleasure," said Old Woman. "Be patient, great hunter," she advised, "until you catch her." She pointed the sewing awl at Tree. "What you catch," she laughed, "I assure you will be well worth the wait."

Tree rose to his feet.

"Remember all that I have taught you," said Old Woman. "Any woman—any woman—can be made to kick."

"I will make her kick and squeal like a rabbit," said Tree.

"Poor little slave girl," said Old Woman.

Tree turned about, and left Old Woman.

Old Woman looked after Tree. She was old and wise. She had not come on this sort of thing often, but she knew of its existence. She remembered Drawer, whom, when he had become Old Man, and when he had gone blind, Spear had killed. She continued her sewing, crooning to herself a little song.

Old Woman was happy.

It was noon, and the sunlight was hot on the cliff, when Tree slipped down the knotted rawhide rope to the ledge outside the cave where the lovely slave girl was kept.

He dropped to the ledge.

She moved back further, within the cave. She put out her hand, and shook her head. Her eyes showed fear. She said something in her barbarous tongue, unintelligible to the Men.

Naked, defenseless, slight, the stone wall at her back, she was quite beautiful.

Tree leapt forward and thrust her, standing, stomach to the stone, against the wall.

Then, with a length of rawhide, he fastened her wrists behind her back, and turned her about to face him.

Her back was now against the stone. She looked up at him, frightened. He touched her hair. She said something in her barbarous tongue. He lifted her from her feet and put her, bound, on the two hides.

Though the sun outside was hot, the cave was cool. Tree went to the water gourd and took a drink. He ate one of the pieces of hard fruit at the side of the cave. Twice a day he had fed and watered the slave.

He then turned and looked at her, hands tied behind her back, sitting on the hides, looking at him.

He approached her, and sat, cross-legged, beside her. She tried to edge back, but the wall prevented her retreat. The stone was at her back.

She spoke again in the barbarous tongue, questioningly, fearfully.

He made no move toward her. For a long time he looked at her, carefully, relishing the delicious, captive curves of her slave body.

She said something to him, pleading, obviously begging him to go away.

He spoke to her in the language of the Men. "I am going to make you kick," he told her. "I will teach you what it is for a female to kick for a man. I will teach you to kick as you have never kicked before. I am going to make you kick superbly."

Then he reached down and took her right ankle in his hand.

The lovely slave looked at him with horror.

"Go away!" cried Brenda Hamilton. "Go away!"

She tried to free her hands, but she, tied by a hunter, could not do so. She moaned. She was defenseless. Her entire body, each inch of it, curved and vulnerable, lay open to his tongue, his teeth, his fingers, his hands, his forces and pressures, his touch.

She tried to pull her ankle away but could not do so.

He seemed amused that she, with only the slightness of the female, should try to pit her strength against his.

She saw the dilation of his pupils, and knew that she was beautiful to him.

A tremor of sensation coursed from her ankle up her leg. She shuddered.

"Rape me swiftly, you beast," she begged. "Be done with it!"

His hand still on her ankle, he reached to her hair and pulled her head forward, exposing the back of her neck. She felt his teeth, gently, biting at the back of her neck. Once she felt his jaws half close about the back of her neck. She knew he could, if he wished, with those strong jaws and white teeth, that large head, bite through the neck, breaking it. Then she was on her side, his hands moving on her body, with the full liberty of those of a master on the body of his female slave, in long, possessive, stimulating caresses. She moaned, and tried to pull away, but his hands held her. Then she was put on her back. He delighted himself with her breasts. She closed her eyes and gritted her teeth. For a long time Tree, slowly, tenderly almost, but with the underlying hardness of a master who, ultimately, will permit no compromise, and this the girl knows, kissed and touched her. He avoided only the delicacies of her delta, which she feared most, shuddering, he might touch. Should he do so, could she resist him?

Brenda Hamilton lay miserably on two hides, on the stone floor of a primeval cave, her hands tied behind her with a rawhide thong.

She looked up at her master.

Her body was helpless. In it stirred tumults of sensation. But he had not yet even touched her most intimately.

He was the most magnificent man she had ever seen, and she was helplessly his. But he was only a savage, a barbarian! She was a thousand worlds and times his superior. She was sensitive, intelligent, educated, civilized! She jerked at her wrists, trying to free them. But she looked up into his eyes. She saw that he was mighty; she sensed, too, in his eyes that his intelligence, in its raw, untutored power, was far greater than even hers, greater even, she suspected, than that of Gunther, who had been the most brilliant man, saving Herjellsen, she had ever known. She looked up at him, and knew that he was her superior in every way. She turned her head miserably to one side. And this was his world, not hers. She was not a thousand worlds and times his superior. No. He was a thousand worlds and times her superior! She, in this world, naked, bound, lying at his mercy on hides in a primeval cave, was no more than a slave, only a slave.

His hand moved toward her helplessness, but he did not touch her.

She looked at him, in terror, her body charged with blood, hurtling in the rapids of her beauty.

This was the beast who had taken her in the forest, who had brought her slave to his camp. How she hated him! She had been forced, as a beast of burden, to carry flint. He had looked on, impassively, when she had been tied as bait, to lure a predatory beast to a trap. She, and Ugly Girl, too, for that matter, might have been killed! She hated him! And she had fled, but he, like a dog, had followed her, easily. There had been no escape from him! She looked up at him. She knew she could not escape him. She shuddered, remembering the leopard. She had fallen. It had leaped toward her. The great shaft, tipped with sharpened stone, had struck it from her. Then he, seemingly as terrible, as fierce, as inhuman and bloodthirsty as the beast itself, had fallen upon it, and, striking again and again, had killed it. She remembered the grass, the night, the blood pulsating from the beast's throat, and the killer hunching beside it, drinking its blood, and then, as a man, drawing signs upon his body, and among them, the sign of the Men.

And then standing over her, she only a naked, frightened female, from another time, at his feet, with the great, stone-tipped spear.

The leopard, gutted and bled, he had forced her to carry back to the caves, his trophy, borne on the shoulders of the recaptured female slave.

Then he had put her in this prison, in this cave, where she, nude, confined by the steepness of the cliffs, must, helpless, await his pleasure.

And then, the day after her incarceration, he had, viciously, with his man's strength, laid the switch richly to her beauty, well disciplining the slave for her flight. She had cried out to him that she would not run away again. She had, inadvertently, to her astonishment, and horror, in English, addressed him as "Master."

"No man will ever master Brenda Hamilton," she said. And then, helplessly, closing her eyes, she lifted her body to him.

She, body arched, heard his great laughter in the cave, and, opening her eyes, saw him sitting beside her, his head thrown back, roaring with laughter.

She lowered her body, and turned her head to one side.

When he had finished laughing, she again regarded him.

"Yes, I'm yours," she said, "Master." She again lifted her

body. "I am not ashamed. You are my master. Do with me what you will. I am your slave."

Tree saw the lovely slave girl lift her body to him, as though she might be of the women.

He knew then that he could make her kick, and make her kick superbly.

He threw back his huge head and laughed.

When he looked again upon her, she again, pleadingly, lifted her body to him. She said something in her barbarous, unintelligible tongue. Tree did not precisely understand what she said, of course, but he understood clearly the submissiveness of her tone of voice. She was asking him to use her as a female. She was submitting herself to him.

Gently with tongue and fingers he fell upon the most vulnerable delicacies and beauties of her helplessness.

She began to writhe and scream with pleasure.

But Tree did not forget the lessons of Old Woman for he, in his strategems, had only begun to arouse the lovely, helpless slave. When he finally entered her she was quivering and crying and biting at him, but even then he, following the advice of Old Woman, resisted her pleadings, and the piteous, supplicatory movements of her body, sometimes, by sheer force, holding her, weeping, immobile. But at last, after more than a thousand, varying stabs of pleasure, swift, and slow, and gentle, and fierce, and sweet and hard, he, as she screamed with pleasure, rearing under him, shattered her, exploding within her the long-withheld tenseness, the force, of his manhood. He did not then withdraw from her either, for Old Woman had told him to stay with the woman, and hold her, and caress her, or it would be like taking food from her mouth, leaving her half hungry.

"Don't leave me!" wept Brenda Hamilton. "Don't leave me!" She fought the thongs that bound her wrists behind her back. She wanted to seize the hunter, and hold him, tightly, in her arms, never letting him go. But her wrists were behind her back, fastened tightly in rawhide loops. He could leave her with ease, should he wish.

"Please don't leave me!" she wept.

And the hunter continued to hold her, small, soft, yielded, piteously his, against the now-relaxed gentleness of his leanness, his supine might, his hardness, now suddenly gentle, now unbent like a great bow.

Though she knew he could not understand her, Brenda Hamilton, in English, softly, her head against his chest, spoke to the hunter.

"My name is Brenda Hamilton," she said. "You could not perhaps understand my world. It is very different from yours. I come from a different time. On my own world I am of some small importance. There I am a respected person, highly intelligent and well educated. I have an advanced degree in a technical subject from a great university. Here I am only a naked female, and even my wrists are bound. Here I am only an outsider, and a despised slave, but here I am in your arms. My world, in many ways, is empty. This world, in many ways, is much more real. I suppose I should be horrified that I lie here a slave in a primeval cave but I am not, dear hunter, dissatisfied. I would not have it otherwise, dear hunter. Do you know why that is? Do you think it is simply because you have mastered me, and made me behave as a slave in your arms? Because you have made me truly a slave? Oh yes, dear hunter, I acknowledge that I am your slave, completely. You have given me no choice in that. But is there not more to it, dear hunter? It is not that I am simply a slave girl. I am rather a slave girl who helplessly loves her master. Did you give me choice, either, in that? No, you did not, you beast." Then Hamilton, gently, kissed the hunter. "The slave girl loves her master," she whispered. "I love you, my master."

It was late afternoon when the hunter left the slave. Before he left, he untied her hands. But he did not let her touch him; rather he thrust her back, stumbling, tears in her eyes, for she was, after all, only a slave.

Then his lean body, hand over hand, disappeared up the knotted rawhide rope, which he drew up after him.

Brenda Hamilton extended her hand after him. "Come back to me, Master," she cried. "Come back to me, soon!"

In the cave Brenda Hamilton threw herself on the hides and cried out for joy. "I love him!" she cried. "I love him!" And then she moaned, "Come back to me, soon, Master!"

Not only had the incompleted sensation in her body, which the hunter had long ago induced in her, been completed, but it had led to a thousand other rhapsodies of pleasure, dimensions of feeling, of emotion, of tissue sentience, of body awareness, of which before in her life she had never suspected the existence. Her body, for the first time, seemed rich and glorious, and saturated with excitement and feeling. She wanted to kiss his hands and lips and

manhood for what they had done to her. For the first time
in her life she felt the fantastic sentience of an owned, loving female. And, too, she had begun to suspect, in his
touchings and lovings, that even beyond these dimensions of
joy, like thousands of doors and horizons, there might lie
others, and more. She wanted to train herself, and to grow,
from day to day, from year to year, eagerly exploring and
learning, in sentience and feeling. She knew women could
improve themselves in such matters, as in any others. She
must give attention to them. She must train herself to become more responsive, perhaps more swiftly reflexive, to
feel more rapidly and more deeply. She had just begun to
sense the possible depths of her feelings, the possible heights
of her ecstasies. She had just begun, under the hands of a
primeval hunter, to learn the possibilities, the capacities, of
her femaleness.

"I love you, Master!" she cried.

That night, bringing a piece of hot meat in his teeth,
Tree returned to the lovely slave.

He did not tie her hands.

He offered her the meat. She threw it aside and fell to
her knees before him, thrusting her head beneath his skins,
kissing his manhood.

Tree took her in his arms and, laughing, threw her back
to the hides on the floor of the cave.

Four days more was the lovely Brenda Hamilton kept a
helpless love slave in the primeval cave.

In this time the hunter spent much time with her, day
and night, only leaving her to fetch food and water. When
he returned she would welcome him, helplessly, deliciously,
and melt into his arms.

"Tree keeps his little bird long on her perch," said Spear
to Old Woman.

"He is training her well," said Old Woman.

Spear had laughed, and turned away.

Old Woman smiled to herself. She remembered that, years
ago, though it was still fresh in her memory, when she had
been a young and beautiful woman, Drawer had similarly
trained her, and superbly.

Above, in her high, prison cave, Brenda Hamilton lay in
the arms of her hunter. "I love you, Master," she whispered
to him. "I love you."

Had she known of the conversation of Spear and Old
Woman, and could she have spoken the language of the

Men, she would have stood brazenly before Tree, laughing, her hands behind her head, her body thrust toward him. "Yes, Master," she would have laughed. "You have trained me well. I am now a well-trained slave."

And Tree would have seized her by the ankle and again pulled her to the hides, laughing, and she, in his arms, looking up at him, a lovely, eager slave, would, lifting her lips and body again to his, have again addressed herself to her duties, those of his pleasure.

"Thank you, oh thank you, Master!" cried Brenda Hamilton. She reached out and took the rectangle of soft deerskin, about a foot wide, and some two feet long, beveled inward on each end. Both edges, and the beveled sides, were turned and sewn, and through the top edge, through perforations, was drawn, as though stitched through, a slender rawhide strap, serving as a belt. Delightedly she wrapped this simple skirt about her, and tied the ends of the strap belt, as she had seen the women do, over her left hip. Because of the inwardly beveled edges, her left leg was muchly revealed, and thrust provocatively from the skirt. Many of the younger women wore such garments. Flower, and Antelope, did. Cloud did not.

Brenda Hamilton, delighted, proud, walked and posed, and turned, before her hunter, her master.

He, she saw, was startled to see her thusly.

Then she walked before him as one of the women, as she had seen the women walk, displaying themselves in their walk to men.

She saw him grin widely.

He gestured her to him, and she ran, barefoot, to him.

He jerked on the knot at her left hip. It could not be immediately loosened.

"Tie this properly," he said to her in the language of the Men.

"Yes, Master," she said, in English, shyly, well understanding him. Obediently she tied the knot in the fashion of the younger women. She lifted her lips to him, and kissed him. "You beast," she whispered. Now, at a single tug, she could be stripped. "You make your slave feel very vulnerable, Master," she whispered to him. She kissed him again, excited. Then she darted away, and turned to face him. She then, in her movements, well displayed her legs. They were marvelous. Tree regarded them as the best legs of any female in the camp, except perhaps those of Flower or Butter-

222   JOHN NORMAN

fly. "The slave thanks her master for her beautiful gown,"
said Brenda Hamilton. She then, looking demurely down, her
left index finger beneath her chin, holding with her right
hand the deerskin from her right thigh, curtsied to him.

Tree had never seen such a movement. It made him
laugh.

"Come here," said he, in the language of the Men, gesturing to her.

Brenda Hamilton quickly sped to her master. She knew
that he, like any powerful male brute of these times, must
be obeyed swiftly and well by his females. Too, unaccountably perhaps, she found herself eager to be promptly
obedient to him.

From his pouch he drew forth a long tangle of claws,
shells and thongs.

He untangled it and held it out, up before his face, smiling.

It was an ornament, a necklace, of the sort that the females of the Men often wore about their neck.

Brenda Hamilton put forth her hand, but she did not touch
it. "It is beautiful, Master," she whispered.

"See," said Tree, in the language of the Men, pointing
to a small rectangle of leather, about an inch square, one
of five, threaded into the thongs, with the claws and shells.
Brenda Hamilton looked. On it she saw, drawn, scratched
into the leather and pigmented in red, the sign of the Men.
The same sign, identically, appeared on the other four rectangles. Tree turned her about and then, standing quite
closely behind her, wrapped the necklace, in four loops,
snugly, about her neck. He then tied it behind the back of
her neck, tightly. She knew it identified her, by means of the
rectangles, as a woman of the Men. She put back her head,
to touch the hunter. She wondered if this sort of thing were
the origin of the necklace, that it served in the beginning
not simply as an ornament but as, in its way, an identifying
slave collar. Tree turned her roughly about. Eagerly her
lips met his, those of her master.

She felt his hand reach to her hip.

An hour later, in his arms, pushing back his hair at his
neck, kissing him, Brenda Hamilton saw again the tiny,
strange mark on his neck. She had seen this before. It in-
trigued her. It was a birthmark. It was like a tiny bluish
stem, with branches reaching upward. It was from this mark
that her hunter had had his name, "Tree."

She kissed the tiny mark.

He smiled and pointed to the mark, and to himself. "I am Tree," he said, in the language of the Men. "Tree."

She kissed him beneath the chin. "I am Brenda," she said. She kissed him again. "Your slave's name is Brenda, Master, unless you wish to give her another name. Then the other name would be hers, and not Brenda."

"Brenda?" he asked, picking the name from her words.

She knelt beside him, and pointed to herself. "I am Brenda," she said. "Brenda."

"Brenda," he said. She smiled.

The word "Brenda," of course, in the language of the Men, had no meaning. Tree, or Spear, or one of the other men, could eventually give her a name in the language of the Men. In the meantime the noise "Brenda" would do. It provided a means by which, when she was wished, the beautiful slave could be summoned.

Tree rose to his feet. He indicated that the beauty should clothe herself.

Hamilton wrapped the brief skirt about her and tied it over the left hip, tying it as she knew her master desired, that it might be loosened with a single pull.

She stood across from him, some eight feet from him, on the floor of the high cave. She was barefoot. She wore a brief skirt of tanned deerskin. She was bare-breasted. Her hair was long, loose and dark. About her neck, twisted and looped, four times, was a necklace of claws, shells and thongs, and, threaded among them, part of the necklace itself, the small squares of leather, bearing on them, clearly, the sign of the Men. Brenda Hamilton stood proudly, a primeval female, one of the women, facing a primeval man, one of the Men, one of her masters.

"Come, female," said Tree, turning about and going to the ledge.

He grasped the knotted rope.

Brenda Hamilton came, too, to the ledge, and put her arms about his neck.

In an instant she was swinging, clinging to him, over a drop of more than one hundred and seventy-five feet. But she was not afraid. Quickly, seeming hardly impeded by her weight, he climbed up the knotted rope. He drew the rope up after him, freed it from a small, stunted tree, and looped it over his shoulder. Then, scrambling and climbing, moving from ledge to ledge, he gained the height of the cliff. To Hamilton the view was breathtaking, the sight of the fields and forests, and two rivers, extending to the horizon. Then, rapidly, she followed him. He was moving across the top of the cliff, one of a series of such, and, then, making his way downwards, in a roundabout fashion. In some places steps had been chipped from the stone. In other places a branch of a small tree provided a handhold. Taken with care, the descent was not dangerous.

Brenda Hamilton smelled meat cooking.

The slave, hungry, no longer fearful, delightedly, followed her master.

◆ 18 ◆

Tree, kneeling beside the roasted carcass, cut with the edge of his stone knife through the hot meat, fat streaking and bubbling at the edge of the flint blade, severing a huge, steaming chunk.

Antelope and Cloud knelt behind him. Then another woman thrust herself in front of them, kneeling behind the hunter.

Cloud, with a cry of anger, seized Brenda Hamilton by the hair and pulled her back. Like a tigress, screaming with fury, Hamilton turned on her, striking her with her fists across the face. Cloud stumbled back, startled, scrambling, and Hamilton followed her, striking her twice again, and kicking her. Then Cloud whimpered, and fell back, astonishment in her eyes, and tears, and fear. Hamilton took a step toward her and, crying out, Cloud, on her hands and knees, scrambled away. Then, seeing Hamilton did not pursue her, she crept away, shrinking back, driven from the side of the hunter.

Hamilton felt the swift, hissing slash of a switch on her back, and turned, wildly, in fury, to see Antelope, her hand again raised. Hamilton's back stung. But Antelope did not have time to strike again for Hamilton had leapt on her, and the two females rolled, screaming, scratching, biting, pulling hair, clawing, over and over, among the bodies, even to the edge of the fire. The men and women, and children, separated, to let the females fight. Then, panting, bleeding, hair awry, scratched, bitten, the two females, now naked, rose to their feet and circled one another. Then with a scream of rage Hamilton leaped on Antelope, and had her hands, both hands, in the other's hair. She jerked Antelope back and forth, and swung her about, while Antelope, screaming in pain, tried vainly to free Hamilton's hands from her dark hair. And then Hamilton threw her by the hair to her feet on her back and seized up the switch, and began to lash at her, and Antelope rolled to her stomach, weeping, head twisted, Hamilton's left hand still fastened in her hair, Antelope's hands futilely on Hamilton's wrist. Hamilton, with the switch, again and again, struck Antelope's extended, exposed body, and then Antelope, weeping, struggled to her knees and put her head down, her hands over her head. Twenty more times Hamilton struck her and then, by the hair, she hurled her to her feet. Then Hamilton stood over Antelope, her hand no longer in her hair, but the switch raised.

Antelope shook her head, tears in her eyes, and held her hands out before her, to shield her from any blows which might fall.

"Please," she cried in the language of the Men, "don't hit me again."

Hamilton lowered the switch.

Antelope, tears in her eyes, crept away.

Suddenly Hamilton saw Short Leg, first woman of Spear, leader of the women, facing her.

Short Leg put out her hand for the switch.

Hamilton, frightened, sought the eyes of Tree.

Hamilton put the switch into Short Leg's hand, and then Hamilton, naked and bleeding, knelt before Short Leg and, submissively, put her head to the ground, her hair in the dirt before Short Leg's feet.

Short Leg turned away, and threw the switch into the darkness, and returned to her place behind Spear.

Suddenly the Men, looking upon Antelope, and Cloud and Hamilton, began to laugh, with the exception of Stone, who, too, this time, once again, seemed amused. The women reddened, and were much discomfited. It pleased the men to see the women fight. They looked so foolish. Hamilton and Antelope tied their brief skirts about their hips.

Then Hamilton knelt down behind Tree, smoothing her hair.

Runner said to Cloud. "Kneel behind me. I will feed you."

Cloud went and knelt behind Runner. Runner had long had his eye on Cloud. He relished her short, thick body, her sturdy ankles. He found her juicy. He wanted to feel her hair on his manhood.

Antelope looked about from face to face. She seemed agonized.

"Lift your body to me," said Wolf, "and I will feed you."

Antelope lay before Wolf and lifted her body to him. He threw her a piece of meat.

"Come to my cave later," he said.

"Yes, Wolf," she said.

Behind Tree Brenda Hamilton knelt. She opened her mouth and pointed her finger to it. He held meat to her in his mouth and she, biting into it and holding it, tore free her portion.

The meat that the Men ate was always rare or almost rare. It was juicier that way, less crusted and burned. It was also, though they did not know this, more nutritious. Another thing that surprised Hamilton was the amount of fat eaten. The fat was very important, and she was hungry for it. She ate much of it. In her normal civilized diet fats had been available in dozens of sources, such as oils, milk, butter and cheese, but, among the Men these foods did not exist, and the essential need for fats must be, and was, satisfied by the fats of slain animals.

Hamilton also noted the Men, and their women and children, splitting bones, and scraping and sucking out the marrow.

Tree gave Hamilton a small piece of the animal's liver. This, though she did not know it, was a rich source of vitamin A.

Then Tree began to cut other meat from the carcass, and to gorge himself upon it.

He paid the slave little more attention.

"You beast," she said, "I am still hungry."

After a time, smiling, Hamilton began to whimper, as she had heard the women doing sometimes.

The hunter turned to regard her.

She opened her mouth and pointed her finger to it.

He turned away.

"You beast," said Hamilton. She really wanted more to eat. What did he want?

Then she lay on her back, and whimpered. He turned and regarded her. She lifted her body to him. "There, you beast," she laughed.

She felt a piece of meat strike her body, and she took it and began, getting up and kneeling, to feed on it.

He grinned at her, and she, chewing on the meat, smiled at him.

"I am a prostitute," she thought. "I, like the others, have lifted my body for a piece of meat." It was quite good.

She saw his eyes. She knew he would make her pay him well later, for such meat, given to a female, was not without cost.

She was not unhappy. She was, rather, much pleased. She knew she would be made to enjoy paying for it.

Then the hunter turned about and, flint knife in hand, again fell on the meat.

Hamilton looked about. She saw the men eating, and the women and children. The firelight cast wild shadows on the cliffs, containing the shelters, looming above them. The trees, behind her, the beginning of the forest, were dark. The men squatted, or sat cross-legged, chewing, their bodies large, their hair long, powerful, intelligent men, like animals. Their females, their properties, knelt behind them, chewing on meat given to them by the men, the masters. Here and there there wandered a dirty, naked child, holding a bit of bone or gristle. Several of them clung about the large, fearsomely ugly fellow, with the extended canine, and he gave them bits of food. The girl, Butterfly, had distributed the meat to the children, with the exception of what she kept for herself, which seemed considerable. The older boy, to whom she had been cruel, crouched to one side, watching the hunters. He seemed hungry. The girl did not share the meat with him. It was hers, as oldest of the children, to divide and give out, except for the very young children, who were fed separately. Butterfly wore a garment like a simple, brief dress of deerskin, which covered her breasts. Hamilton noted that her legs were trim and shapely. Hamilton also noted that Spear watched her. She had little doubt that the girl Butterfly would, by the spring, be told to bare her breasts and beg with the other women. She would no longer be a child. She would be then only another woman of the Men. Doubtless, then, a necklace, too, would be found for her, one bearing the insignia of the Men.

Hamilton studied the faces. She would learn later the names of Spear and Stone, and Wolf and Fox, and Arrow Maker, Runner, Knife, Tooth and Hyena. She already knew the name of Tree, though she knew only, of course, the sound in the language of the men, not what it meant. Too, she regarded Short Leg, whom she feared, and Antelope and Cloud, and Nurse and Old Woman, and the others.

She was startled, and troubled, to see the face of Knife, as he regarded Spear. She saw in his eyes envy, and hatred. Yet, clearly, Knife was the son of Spear. Hamilton wondered at the hostility. Spear, she knew, was the leader. The younger man, Hamilton supposed, wanted to be first in the group. Her own hunter, Tree, seemed unconcerned with such matters.

Hamilton saw Flower behind Knife, distracting him by caresses.

Flower looked angrily at Hamilton.

Hamilton looked away. She did not want Knife. He frightened her.

On the outskirts of the group, little more than a hunched, kneeling shadow, Hamilton saw Ugly Girl, waiting for the feeding to end and the group to disband, that she might creep forward and poke through the ashes for scraps of meat or drops of grease on the half-burned wood. Hamilton shuddered. How horrid Ugly Girl was.

Ugly Girl was not of the women. Ugly Girl was not even human.

Hamilton finished the meat.

Soon the fire was built up and the group cleared a circle about it. The men drew to one side and the women to the other. The children remained behind the women. Hamilton knelt with the females. None of them gave the least sign of objection. She realized, suddenly, she was accepted as a female among them. They were all slaves, and she among them, but she now no more than they.

Runner brought out two sticks and he beat them together. Arrow Maker had carved a flute. Tooth had a small hide drum. The men began to sing, a repetitive song, in which responses were sung to something shouted by Tooth. The women did not sing words, but they uttered noises, carrying, too, the melody. They swayed together at times and clapped their hands rhythmically. Later, Fox leaped to his feet and danced, to the clapping of hands and the slapping of knees. Then Wolf, too, joined him. Together they joined in a narrative dance, in which Wolf played the role, apparently, of a large bear, or some such animal, which Fox, after much moving about, and swaying and stalking here and there, apparently managed to confront and slay, but, when Fox turned his back, Wolf, to the delight of the children, leaped up, roaring, and chased him from the circle.

"Put the new female before the fire," said Spear.

Tree gestured that Brenda should stand before the group, in the open space, before the fire. She did so, erect and beautiful, a lovely, bare-breasted slave, in the necklace which proclaimed her as being a woman of the Men.

"What is her name?" asked Spear.

"She calls herself Brenda," said Tree.

"That is not a name," said Spear.

"True," admitted Tree. It was surely not a word of meaning for the men. Thus, for them at least, it was not a name.

"Give her a name," said Spear.

Tree rose to his feet and went to stand before Hamilton. She looked up into his eyes.

He then crouched down and, picking up a stick, drew a picture in the dirt.

It was the picture of an animal, as seen from above, a symbolic representation but clearly recognizable. Brenda looked down and saw the ovoid shell, the head and tiny tail, the four small legs sticking out at the sides of the shell.

Tree pointed to it. "It is a turtle," said Hamilton, in English.

"Turtle," said Tree, in the language of the Men.

"Turtle," repeated Hamilton, this time in the language of the Men.

Tree pointed to her. "Turtle," he said.

"No," she said, "please."

Tree again pointed to her. "Turtle," he said.

Then he forced her to her knees, and gestured that she should kiss the sign he had drawn in the dirt.

She fell to her knees before it.

Tree grinned at her. The name Turtle, to the men, was not a demeaning name. In fact, to them, it was a rather attractive name. They regarded small turtles as pretty little beasts. Tree made a motion with his mouth. Hamilton understood. Turtles, too, were delicious. And then Tree, grinning, put his hands together, and flipped them over, and wiggled them. Hamilton looked down, reddening. The turtle, too, when placed on her back, is almost helpless.

"Turtle," said Tree, pointing to her. Then he gestured that she should kiss the sign in the dirt.

Hamilton read his eyes, and put her head down, and kissed the sign.

She lifted her head.

"Tree," said Tree, gesturing to himself. He looked at her. "Turtle," said Hamilton, in the language of the Men, eyes down, referring to herself, touching her chest with her fingers.

It was thus that Brenda Hamilton was given the name Turtle among the Men.

Then she stood alone in the circle, a primeval female before her masters.

"How does she kick?" asked Spear.

"Splendidly," said Tree.

"Good," said Spear. Then he said, "Let the females dance for us. Then we shall retire."

Tooth began to pound on his small hide drum; Runner began to beat his sticks together, and a melody, to the touch of Arrow Maker's fingers, began to emerge from the long, narrow, wooden flute.

Flower was first to join Hamilton before the fire, and then Cloud and Antelope, and the younger women, and those not pregnant or nursing. Old Woman did not join them, nor did heavy Nurse. Short Leg, too, stayed kneeling to one side. Flower tore away her deerskin skirt and wrapped it about her left wrist. Hamilton, angrily, did so, too. And the others. Flower thrust her body toward Knife, and then, when he reached for her, leaped back. Hamilton, boldly, did the same with Tree. Antelope swayed before Wolf. Cloud, naked, moved slowly before Runner, who had fed her. And the women, to the drum, the beating of the sticks, the melody of the flute, danced before the men. The primeval female, Turtle, too, danced with them. She danced before all the men, but mostly before one, a lean, tall hunter, squatting, who watched her, with narrow eyes that caressed each swaying inch of her, with eyes that drove her wild with the desire to please him. For a time Hamilton, the primitive female, Turtle, one of the women of the Men, lost herself in the dance and music. She felt the dirt beneath her feet, and the movements of her body, the pounding of her breath and blood, the eyes of the men. To one side loomed the cliffs, containing the shelters, to the other loomed the dark forests, and, between them, in the light of the fire, uninhibited and organic, liberated in their sexuality, in this environment completely free to express the deepest and most profound needs of their female reality, danced the women. Hyena crept away from the fire. He was insane and sterile, and hated beauty. The men clapped and shouted. Never had Hamilton felt so female, so free. For the first time she felt she could move her body precisely as she wanted, and she did so. The agricultural revolution was, in its success, thousands of years in the future. With it would come concentrations of population, the seclusion and restrictions of women, human sacrifice, taxations, religions and laws, the victories of priest-hoods and oppressive traditions, and the organization of fear and superstition for the purposes of profit; in thousands of years would come the time of the haters, the Hyenas. The time had not yet come when it would be wrong for women to dance and men to be pleased in their beauty. The seeds of Eve's apple tree had not yet been planted.

But the agricultural revolution was essential for the development of technology, and the development of technology was essential for the opportunity to touch the stars.

No one knew how high might grow the branches of the apple tree.

No one guessed that men might return to paradise, and, once more, now ready, having once eaten, climb it.

Prometheus was tortured, but the Greek ships, carrying fire in copper bowls, colonized a world.

With a pounding Tooth's drum was suddenly silent, and Runner stopped striking the sticks, and the flute of Arrow Maker was silent.

Flower dropped to the ground before Knife, eyes hot, breathing heavily, blood pounding, and lifted her body to him.

Hamilton, joyously and brazenly, excited, gasping, wild, her blood surging, her heart pounding, flung her body to the dirt before Tree, and lifted it, supplicating him for his touch. Cloud fell before Runner, and Antelope before Wolf.

Hamilton felt herself lifted easily in Tree's arms. He was incredibly strong. She felt herself carried with incredible lightness. She put her arms about his neck, and kissed him.

Over her head she saw, bright and beautiful in the black, velvety night, the stars. "Turn their eyes to the stars," had said Herjellsen. "Turn their eyes to the stars."

She saw, too, as she was carried, behind Tree, among the shadows, hunched and timid, round-shouldered, now creeping forward to the dying fire, to hunt for food, Ugly Girl.

She again kissed Tree.

He carried her to his cave.

◇ 19 ◇

Hamilton, the woman called Turtle, one of the women of the Men, returned to the shelters, through the snow, carrying, bound in rawhide, on her left shoulder, a heavy load of wood, food for the cave fires.

She wore leggings and her feet were wrapped in hide, tied about her ankles and calves. She wore a tunic of deerskin, which fell to her knees, and, over that, a sleeveless, furred jacket, belted, which, too, fell to her knees. Her head was bare. Her hair was bound back with a string of rawhide and shells.

For five months Turtle had been a slave of the Men, and, in particular, of one called Tree. He had amused himself with others, as the whim took him, but there was no doubt that Turtle, dark-haired and lovely, was his favorite. The other males of the Men, too, often used Turtle, as it pleased them to do so, and she found many of them marvelous and strong, and it much pleased her, from time to time, to kick for them, and well. Sometimes, even when she had not wanted to kick, they had, as Tree had before them, given her no choice but to kick, and superbly. She was only a woman, and at their mercy. They would force her body, and then her will, by means of her body, to do what they wished, for they were men, and master. Spear, the leader, in particular, had been incredible. He was second in her opinion only to Tree. When he had left her she had lain on the hides, beaten with the weight and power of his thrusting, exhausted and stunned. She had then well understood how it was that such a man was the leader, and how it was that he could feed five of the vital, prehistoric females. But the heart of the lovely slave, Turtle, always, in its depth, lay only in the capture thongs of one hunter, and one hunter alone, he who had first taken her, he who had brought her slave to the camp of the Men, he who had first forced her, in a high, prison cave, to yield to him, to helplessly love him, Tree, of the Men.

She was, in a sense that the Men found hard to understand, Tree's alone. Even when she screamed with joy in their arms, they knew they had forced only her yielding, and not her love. Only the arms of Tree, and his touch, had been strong enough to force that. Each night, after the ecstasy they had induced in her, she would creep to the side of Tree, whose cave she kept, whose skins she cleaned, at whose side she slept. And once, a week ago, Tree had not permitted Knife to use her. She had been frightened. They had almost fought. There was bad blood between the two men. She had wanted to give her body to Knife, that Tree not be endangered, but Tree, violently, had struck her and thrown her to one side of the cave. She had crouched there, terrified, her mouth bleeding. Knife had drawn a stone knife. "Go!" had said Spear to Knife. Knife, angrily, had turned away. Flower had to run to him, to console him. Over his shoulder, angrily, she had looked back. "It is not the way of the Men," said Spear to Tree, "to keep a woman to oneself." "I do not want Knife to use her," said Tree. "Strip," had said Spear to frightened Turtle. She did so, immediately. "Watch," had said Spear to Tree. Angrily Tree sat down, cross-legged. Then Spear had taken Turtle, and slowly, making her yield to him, whimpering, trying to restrain herself. At last she had writhed under him, bucking, crying out in misery. Spear remained a time with her, and then, not looking at Tree, he left her. Tears in her eyes Turtle lay on her side and held out her hand to Tree. He rose to his feet, turned away and left her. She wept. The next day Tree said to her. "Go to Knife. Strip yourself and lift your body to him." "Yes, Tree," had said Turtle, in the language of the Men, which she had, in the last months, learned to speak. She went to Knife and did as she was told. Mollified, Knife used her, swiftly, casually. Holding her clothing Turtle then returned to Tree. "I have done what you told me," she said. Then she wept. "You are a woman," he said to her. "You are a woman of the Men. You belong to all of the Men. Do you understand that?" "Yes, Tree," she had said.

"But most," said Tree, grinning, "you belong to me!"

"Yes, Tree," said Turtle, and ran to him. And he used her better than Spear, or Knife, or any of the others, better than they might have dreamed of using a woman.

When she lay in his arms, afterwards, she spoke to him in English, as it pleased her, though he did not know the tongue. "In my heart," she whispered to him, "it is your's only whose slave I am, my master. I am your helpless, adoring slave. Do with me what you will. I love you, my master. I love you."

Knife, satisfied, seldom used her thereafter, and when he did so, it was only as he might have used Antelope, or Cloud, or any of the other slaves.

Old Woman smiled to herself. "It is well the way of the Men has been kept," she said. And then she remembered Drawer. Spear had killed him, when he had gone blind. Old Woman hated Spear, but she knew, as Knife did not, and many of the others did not, that he was a great and wise leader. There were few groups who had a man so great as huge, swift, ugly Spear to lead them.

Turtle, under the load of wood, trudged through the snow toward the shelters.

She was happy. This morning the hunters had taken meat. Tonight she would be well fed, and, after the dancing and singing, she would pay for her meat, lovingly, in Tree's arms. How far away seemed her old world, with its pollutions, its hatreds, its madnesses. How simple and deep and beautiful, and now, clear and cold, seemed this fresh, virginal world in which she, a burden-bearing slave, returned to the shelters of her masters. The snow clung to the branches, and, in the distance, rearing up at the edge of the forest, she saw the cliffs. How marvelous they seemed, with their numerous, deep, caves.

Too, some of the caves held marvels.

Once, Old Woman, when the men were away hunting, had taken her, with a torch, deep into one of the caves. Women were forbidden to go into this cave but Old Woman did not care, and Hamilton had followed her. In the light of the torches, Hamilton, in awe, had seen, drawn on the walls and ceiling, some places which must have been reached by a now-discarded scaffolding, paintings in reds and yellows, and browns, and blacks, of huge and beautiful animals. There were bison there, and running antelope, and the aurochs, and even the mighty mammoth. They were done with an expression, and a zest, and beauty and freedom, and joy, that was almost incomprehensible to her. Here and there, too, almost in caricature, compared to the animals, were sticklike figures of men, with bows and spears. Hamilton saw that all of the animals, within their bodies, projecting from them, bore the weapons of men. She supposed that hunting magic had been done here, sympathetic magic, but, too, with it, exceeding it, was the celebration of the vigor, the strength and beauty of the beasts which the Men loved and hunted. Hamilton had stood there, in the half darkness, suddenly seeing these shapes and colors spring into existence, under Old Woman's lifted torch. It was almost as if they were alive, moving on the walls.

"Drawer made these," said Old Woman, simply.

"How did you dare to come to this place?" asked Hamilton.

Old Woman smiled. "Drawer brought me," she said. "He showed me."

"Where is Drawer?" had asked Hamilton.

"Spear killed him," said Old Woman. "He went blind. Spear killed him."

Hamilton was silent.

"He was old," said Old Woman. "He was not good for much."

"But you cared for him," said Hamilton. "You liked Drawer?"

"Yes," said Old Woman. "I liked Drawer."

Hamilton lifted her head, and looked about herself, at the paintings.

Animals had made tools, and manlike things, before men, had made tools. Tools needed not be a sign of man. But where there was art then, incontrovertibly, stood man. It is not in the making of tools, but in the invention of beauty, in the gratuitous invention of art, that we have unmistakable evidence of the first presence of man. In the creation of beauty something which might before not have been human became human, and unmistakably so.

"They are beautiful," said Hamilton.

"Drawer made them," said Old Woman. "We must go now."

"What are these?" asked Hamilton. She indicated a number of hands, some outlined in color, some printed in color.

"I do not know," said Old Woman. "It is a secret of the Men."

Hamilton wondered about them, but did not ask further, for Old Woman apparently did not know.

"Look," said Old Woman. She picked up a flat, rounded stone from the floor of the cave.

Hamilton looked at it, carefully. It seemed at first, to her, only a maze of lines, unintelligible scratches. Then, suddenly, she saw, among the lines, a flowing, hulking torso of a bison. Following another set of lines, superimposed, she traced out a gazellelike creature, swift, horned; then she found the lineaments of the forequarters, head and paws of a cave lion; there were two other drawings as well; one of a deer and, to her delight, shaggy and tusked, that of a hairy mammoth.

The rock had been a good one. The drawer had used it, she supposed, as a sketchbook. It contained pictures which might even have been studies for some of the paintings on the wall.

Old Woman took the rock. She put it back down on the floor of the cave. "It was Drawer's rock," she said. "He gave it to me when he went blind. I brought it here, to be with his other paintings."

Then Old Woman, with the torch, turned about and led the way from the large room. She stopped at the threshold into the narrow passage which had led to the room. "I liked Drawer," she said.

"Why have you shown me these things?" asked Hamilton.

"Tree is Drawer's son," said Old Woman. Then she turned about, and led the way from the room, Hamilton following behind her, following the pool of torchlight cast, moving, on the walls of the passage.

Turtle slightly shifted the weight of the wood on her left shoulder.

The snow was four inches deep. Her breath hung before her face. Under her tunic and jacket she perspired. In the caves, she would, like many of the other women, strip herself, or discard her clothing to the waist. In civilization Hamilton, in the winter, had liked closed rooms and considerable warmth. But, with the Men, she had come to find overheating and closeness distasteful, and even extremely uncomfortable. Living outdoors had wrought changes in her body chemistry. Temperatures which she might once have found chilly, and which might once have made her miserable, she now found only refreshing, even zestful and stimulating. Her blood, because of the fresh air, was charged with oxygen. She had great vitality and energy. Too, she was aware, as she had never been before, of thousands of subtle gradations and fluctuations in air and temperature. She had become, for the first time in her life, fully alive to the world in which she lived.

Happily, she trudged ahead in the snow, carrying the wood.

Sometimes she found her happiness unaccountable, for

was she not only a female slave, as the thongs tied about her neck proclaimed her, forced to labor, subject to the least wishes, and the switches and commands of masters? Yes, but somehow, however unaccountably, she was happy. Never had she been so happy in her life. She began to sing.

Today, this morning, the hunters had taken meat. She could, even from where she trudged through the snow, smell it cooking. Tonight, she knew, she would be well fed. She laughed delightedly. After the singing and dancing she would repay her master well for the meat which he might have deigned to throw her. She would, eagerly, give him fantastic pleasures. "After all," said she to herself, "a girl must serve her master well."

She shook her head happily, to hear the shells on the rawhide string that held back her hair.

Then she, startled, tried to cry out.

The hand closed over her mouth. She felt herself pulled backwards.

Her hands were pulled behind her back. To her astonishment she felt steel close about them, and lock.

"Do not make noise," said a voice, in English.

Hamilton was turned about, the hand still tightly over her mouth.

Her eyes widened.

"Do not cry out," said the voice.

Hamilton nodded.

The hand was removed from her mouth.

"Gunther," she whispered. "William!"

"Has Herjellsen sent you to bring me back?" asked Hamilton.

"You do not seem pleased to see us," said William.

"No," said Gunther.

"You are engaged in another phase of the experiments?" asked Hamilton.

"No," said Gunther.

Hamilton looked at him, puzzled.

The two men wore boots, and heavy coats, and hats. They carried backpacks. Each, over his shoulder, carried a rifle. Gunther wore his Luger, holstered, at his side. William, too, wore a pistol.

"Tell her," said William.

"Herjellsen has mastered the retrieval problem," said Hamilton.

The men were silent.

Hamilton clenched her fists in the steel cuffs, confining her hands behind her back.

"Please free me, Gunther," she said.

"Be quiet," said Gunther.

Hamilton was silent. She had been well taught to obey men.

"Tell her," said William.

"I see you have made contact with a human, or humanoid, group," said Gunther.

"They are human," said Hamilton.

"What is your status among them?" asked Gunther.

"That of other women," said Hamilton.

"And what is that?" asked Gunther.

"Slave," said Hamilton.

"Excellent," said Gunther. "I like female slaves."

"These men are dangerous," said Hamilton.

Gunther slapped the holster at his right hip. "We do not fear savages," he said.

"These men are hunters," said Hamilton. "And sometime you must sleep."

"We come in peace," smiled Gunther.

"You are strangers," said Hamilton. "It will be best that you go away."

Gunther then took her in his arms, and pressed his lips to hers.

When he released her, he looked at her, puzzled, not pleased.

Hamilton backed away from him a step, angry.

"Are you not pleased?" asked Gunther.

"You are a man," she said, "and can do with me what you wish, of course."

"Of course," said Gunther.

"You must understand, however," said she, "that I am not the same female who groveled before you in Rhodesia."

"What is the difference?" asked Gunther.

"I have been in the arms of hunters," she said.

Gunther whipped the pistol from its holster. "This is mightier than your hunters," he said.

"Please free me," asked Hamilton.

"Kneel," said Gunther.

Hamilton did so.

"Put your head down," said Gunther.

Hamilton, kneeling in the snow, complied.

"When it pleases me," said Gunther, "I will teach you to forget your hunters."

The primitive woman, Turtle, one of the slave females of the Men, smiled.

Gunther struck her brutally to the snow.

"Do you speak the language of these hunters?" asked William.

"Yes," said Hamilton.

"On your knees again," said Gunther, "head down."

Hamilton complied.

"You may conjecture our situation," said William.

"Be silent," said Gunther to William.

"There is little to be gained by force," said William.

"I shall do the speaking," said Gunther.

"Very well," said William.

"Brenda," said Gunther.

Hamilton lifted her head.

"We are interested in making contact with a human group. You have apparently already done so. You will be our instrument of communication. You will lead us to this group, and make our demands known to them."

"These men are dangerous," said Hamilton. "It would be better that you go away."

"If we go away," said Gunther, "we will take you with us."

Hamilton was silent.

"Does that not please you?" asked William.

"No," said Hamilton.

"We may take you with us whether you wish it or not," said Gunther.

"Of course," said Hamilton, "but I would not do so. It may not be easy to keep me."

"What do you mean?" asked Gunther. "Do you think you could escape?"

"Quite possibly not," admitted Hamilton.

"What then do you mean?" asked Gunther.

"You will be followed, and, I would suppose, killed." She looked at him, unafraid. "These men are hunters," she said. "Their senses are incredibly keen. They are like eagles and dogs. They can see details that you, even with your fine vision, would require a telescope to discern. They can, like dogs or wolves, follow a trail by smell. They run with swiftness, and the wind of horses. They would follow you and in the end catch you. Then, I expect, they would kill you."

"We have guns," said Gunther.

"You would perhaps be able to kill one, or two, and then they would remain beyond range, until dark. Then they would hunt you by scent. And in the darkness they could from many paces detect your presence by your breathing. I would not wish to be their enemy."

"They will run at the sound of a gunshot," said Gunther.

"They do not run from thunder, or from lightning," said Hamilton, "though they take shelter."

"We will put fear into their simple brains," said Gunther.

"They are tenacious and intelligent," said Hamilton. "They are as likely to be curious, as fearful. If you make them angry, they are not likely to be afraid."

"They might envy us our weapons, and want them" said William.

"Be quiet!" snapped Gunther. He looked angrily at Hamilton. "We will teach them fear," he said.

"They will teach you terror," said Hamilton.

"Among such savages," snarled Gunther, "with these," indicating the guns, "we will be as gods!"

"As nearly as I can determine," said Hamilton, "these men do not have the concept of gods. They do regard the world as animate, and think of many things, strangely perhaps to us, as being individual and alive, trees, flowers, grass, stones, water, animals. They will speak to animals, for example, and sing to them, and sometimes ask their permission to kill them. Too, they sacrifice sometimes meat, though to what or for what purpose I do not know."

"Why do you not know?" demanded Gunther.

"Why should I know?" asked Hamilton. "I am only a female."

"What is your purpose in telling us these things?" asked Gunther.

"To suggest to you," said Hamilton, "Gunther, that they have few superstitions which you will be likely to be able to exploit."

Gunther glared down upon her, angrily.

"If you displease them," said Hamilton, "they are less likely to be frightened than angry. They will regard you as a problem to be solved, probably by killing you."

Gunther swallowed, uneasily.

Hamilton looked up at him and smiled. "Is it not the human way?" she asked.

"We have no intention of displeasing them," said Gunther.

"It seems to me you are already risking their displeasure," said Hamilton.

"How is that?" asked Gunther.

"You are holding one of their females," she said.

"Perhaps I should kill you here, now," said Gunther.

"They would still follow you," said Hamilton.

Hamilton looked into the muzzle of Gunther's pistol. She saw the finger tense on the trigger. Then Gunther thrust the pistol into the holster, and flung her to her feet, turning her about. He freed her wrists, and placed the handcuffs in the pouch on his belt.

"That you are here," said Hamilton, "indicates that Herjellsen has solved the retrieval problem." She smiled. "It would be one thing to maroon a female, a mere experimental animal, in time, but quite another to maroon his two esteemed male colleagues. When are you to be retrieved, and from what point?"

"Do you wish to be retrieved with us?" asked Gunther.

"No," said Hamilton.

"You are mad," said William.

"Perhaps," laughed Hamilton.

"You whore!" snarled Gunther.

"Perhaps," said Hamilton.

"We can take you with us by force," said Gunther.

"I would not advise the attempt," said Hamilton.

"Here," said William," "you are only a slave."

"Was I less a slave, even when putatively free, in my own world?" asked Hamilton.

"What if Herjellsen," said William, "Brenda, has not solved the retrieval problem?"

Brenda looked at him, puzzled.

"Your joke, William," said Gunther, "is a poor one."

William did not meet his eyes. He was silent.

"The retrieval problem, as you conjectured, Brenda," said Gunther, "is solved, else we would not have undertaken this journey."

"What is your purpose here?" asked Brenda.

"As a female, it is not yours to inquire into the purposes of men," said Gunther. "It is yours to obey. Do you understand, Brenda?"

"Yes, Gunther," she said.

"You will take us to your group," said Gunther. "In this we are determined. On this we will not compromise."

"And if I do not?" she asked.

"You will be stripped and tied to a tree in the snow, and lashed with my belt," said Gunther.

"And if, even then, I do not?" she asked.

"I shall strangle you," he said, "and leave you in the snow."

"Are bullets so precious?" she asked.

"Our supplies are limited," said Gunther, "until the rendezvous for retrieval."

"You leave me little choice, Gunther," she said.

"I leave you the choices of a female slave," he said, "which is what you are, absolute obedience or the shameful death of a slave girl who has failed to be pleasing."

"I shall try to be pleasing," she said. She smiled.

"Good," said Gunther.

"I will help you if I can, Gunther," she said, "but, truly, I think it would be best for you to avoid these men, at least those among whom I find myself slave. They are highly intelligent, dangerous men, and you, Gunther, and William, are strangers. I am a female. They found my body of interest, and so made me a slave, but you, you they might simply kill."

"She is right," said William. "Let us go away."

"But she will intercede for us," said Gunther.

"How weighty, Gunther," she asked, "do you feel will be the intercession of a slave?"

"We will shoot our way out, if necessary," said Gunther. Hamilton smiled.

"Let us go away," said William.

"She will speak for us," said Gunther.

"Your lives would be in my hands," said Hamilton, "for you do not know the language. Will I translate accurately for you? Will I tell them truly what you say, or you what they say?" Her eyes became hard. "Do not forget that it was you who by force cruelly exiled me to this time and place."

"Please, Brenda," said William. "Conjecture our situation."

"You two, too, are now exiles in time," said Hamilton. "Why should I help you?"

"Please, Brenda," said William. "Our ammunition and food is limited. If we cannot make contact with some self-sustaining human group we shall surely, sooner or later, die."

"No," said Hamilton, "you can learn to hunt, too, with primitive weapons. You, too, can learn to live in this world."

"But only as savages," said William.

"Yes," said Hamilton, "only as savages."

"You must help us, please, Brenda," said William.

Gunther again unsheathed the Luger. "Kneel," he said. Obediently, commanded by a man, Brenda knelt.

"Open your mouth, bitch," said Gunther.

She did so.

"Close your mouth," said Gunther.

She did so, on the Luger's barrel.

"You must clearly understand," said Gunther, "that you are to help us. You will take us to the human group of which you are a member. At the first sign of any insubordination or treachery you will be immediately shot. I will blast the back of your neck out. Is this understood?"

He permitted her to open her mouth, and he removed the pistol from her mouth.

"Perfectly," said Hamilton. "May I rise?"

"Get up," said Gunther.

Hamilton got to her feet.

"How did you find me?" she asked.

Gunther seemed angry. "We entered this time, this place, at coordinates similar to yours. We then assumed you would travel south. We followed, for two days, certain natural geodesics. We saw, from a distance, cliffs. We made our way toward them. We found a trail, a woman's trail, in the snow. We followed it. It was yours."

"We were incredibly lucky," said William.

"I hope so," said Hamilton.

"Lead us to your masters, Slave," sneered Gunther. He covered her with the pistol.

Hamilton did not respond to him but bent down, and, stick by stick, picked up the scattered wood, that which had spilled from her bundle when she had been seized.

"What are you doing?" asked Gunther.

"I was sent for wood," said Hamilton. "If I do not return with it, I will be beaten."

She reconstructed the bundle and threw it to her shoulder. She staggered slightly under it.

"Let me help you," said William.

"No," said Gunther.

Hamilton smiled at William. "Gunther is right," she said. "Manual labor, I discover, is for females. Men hunt and play."

"Hurry," said Gunther.

"The wood is heavy," she said. "If you do not carry it, you will have to make my pace yours."

"Bitch!" said Gunther.

She faced him, carrying the wood. She wore deerskin tied on her feet, wrapped and thonged about her ankles and calves; and deerskin leggings and a tunic of deerskin, and, over the tunic, a jacket, furred, belted, which fell to her knees. Her long dark hair was bound behind the back of her head by a string of rawhide, threaded through shells. Her eyes were saucy, alive and bright; her cheeks were red; her breath, like smoke, clung about the fire of her luscious lips, bruised and swollen from Tree's kissing of her last night.

"You find me different now, don't you, Gunther," she asked, "from when you knew me before?"

"Yes," said Gunther.

"And now you find me attractive," she said.

"Yes," said Gunther. He would not tell her but, suddenly, it seemed to him he had never before seen so attractive a female. She seemed so different. So primitive. So marvelous. So deep. So sexual. She seemed to him now so completely other than a modern woman, pinched, hostile, envious, constricted, tight, competitive, neuter, petty. She seemed to him deep and exciting, and intelligent and beautiful, joyously different from a man, completely free and happy in her femaleness, unapologetically, exultantly female.

"Your hunters," said Gunther, "have improved you."

"Perhaps, Gunther," she said, "you will have an opportunity to see just how well."

"I do not understand," said Gunther.

"You want me, do you not?" asked Hamilton.

"Yes," said Gunther.

"Then it seems not unlikely that you will have me," said Hamilton.

"How is that?" asked Gunther.

"A month ago," said Hamilton, "a trader from another group, the Bear People, came to my group. He was known and welcomed."

"I see," said Gunther.

"Yes," said Hamilton. "The males of my group are hospitable, and generous. While he stayed with us, he had his pick of the females."

"Did he pick you?" asked Gunther.

"No," said Hamilton. "There is one more beautiful than I in the group. Her name, in English, would be Flower. She it was whom the trader selected."

"Perhaps I shall pick her over you," said Gunther.

"Why not take us both?" asked Hamilton.

William gasped.

"And if I should choose you," asked Gunther, "in what way must you serve us?"

"In any way you wish," smiled Hamilton. "I am a slave." Then she turned and, carrying the wood, trudging through the snow, led the way toward the shelters.

Gunther sheathed the Luger.

"Of course," said Hamilton, "they might not welcome you. You would then be killed."

William moaned.

Gunther left open the flap on his holster.

"Have no fear," said Gunther, "my dear, if we are not killed, you at least will be chosen."

"Very well," said Hamilton. "You are the master."

◆ 20 ◆

Hamilton entered the cave, a log on her left shoulder.

William was sitting in the cave, leaning against his pack, his back to the wall. He was stripped to the waist. Against him, curled, her head on his thigh, lay Flower, stripped save for the collar of strands of leather and shells knotted about her throat. William had his hand on the side of her head.

"I shall want you later," said William to Hamilton.

"Yes, Master," said Hamilton, in English.

Hamilton knelt beside the fire and thrust the log in place. With a stick she thrust small, burning branches about it. The firelight was reflected in her face, redly. She was stripped save for the brief skirt of deerskin, knotted at the left hip, and the collar, that proclaiming her a female of the Men. She did her work well. Fire was precious. One of the first things she had been taught among the Men was the keeping of fires. A girl who let a fire go out, whose responsibility it was, would be mercilessly beaten. This had happened once to Hamilton. Tree had beaten her. Never again had the girl let a fire which she was tending go out, until it was no longer needed. Although it was cold outside, and snowy, the white flakes falling through the winter moon's light, she had not donned her skins, nor wrapped the hide about her feet. She had gone only to the wood shelter, and returned.

"I shall want you later," had said William to Hamilton.

"Yes, Master," she had responded.

Beside William, on his left, lay his rifle. Hamilton sat beside the fire, her feet toward it, rubbing them with her hands. They were cold from the snow.

She looked up and saw Gunther, sitting on a large rock, his rifle across his knees.

"Fetch me water," he said.

"Yes, Master," she said. She went to a crevice in the cave, in which was fitted a sewn, leather bucket in a wooden frame. With a gourd she dipped water. She carried it to the male. "Give it to me," he said. She held the gourd while he drank. Then he said, "Return the gourd." She did so. When she had returned the gourd, she returned to stand before him. "Remove your garment," said he, "Slave." She tugged it loose and dropped it to one side. "Kneel," he said, "and put your head to my feet." She did so.

"It is pleasant to have you as a slave, Brenda," said Gunther.

"Yes, Master," she said.

William chuckled, fondling Flower. "These savages are most hospitable," he said. "They even give us women." Flower began to kiss him.

Hamilton did not dare lift her head. She had not been given permission.

"Perhaps," said William, lightly, "we shall elect to remain in this place."

"Your needs here," said Gunther, "for the first time, have been satisfied."

William thrust Flower away, holding her from him by the arms. Her eyes were startled, suddenly bright with tearing. He thrust her down to the stone beside him, his hand in her hair. She waited there, held. He looked at Gunther. "—Perhaps," he said.

"Surely." said Gunther. "Never before this have you truly had a female. You have only participated in what are, biologically, distortions of, and perversions of, the instinctual, psychosexual conquest. Nature knows not equality in conjugation but only dominance and submission, conqueror and conquered, owner and owned."

"But what of love?" asked William.

"There are a variety of emotions which are indiscriminately designated by that vague expression," said Gunther. "But love and sex are not identical. One may have sex without love, as your little savage has taught you, and you may have love without sex, as you well know, as this slut kneeling before me taught you so painfully in Rhodesia."

Hamilton, her head down, was startled. Had William loved

her? Was that why, now, remembering his frustrations, he had used her with such ruthlessness? Surely he did not love her now. Now that she lay open to him as a mere slave he no longer respected her. He used her often, and insolently, and with power. Contemptuously he made her scream with pleasure, scorning her in her helplessness. If she had frustrated him in Rhodesia, he had now taken his vengeance on her, many times. She, as a slave, her use given to him and Gunther by the men, had repaid him many fold for Rhodesia. When she had been inaccessible, frigid, a lady, he had stood in awe of her, and had perhaps loved her. She smiled to herself. Now that she was fully alive, arousable, impassioned, and his at a word, a glance, a snapping of his fingers, his as a helpless, yielding slave, he no longer loved her, no longer respected her. And it was not that he was content to use her as a mere instrument of his pleasure; he was not so kind; when he ravished her, it was to devastate her complete person; he would call her by name, tenderly, and, she held in his arms, remind her of their experiences in Rhodesia, how she had looked, what she had said, what he had said, and then, when he was ready, he would inform her, "Now I am going to have you, Miss Hamilton, use you, use you as the slut and slave you are," and then he would do so; sometimes he would stop, cruelly, making her beg, in tears, for him to continue. "Please fuck me, William," she would whisper. "Please fuck me, William!" she would beg, crying out. Then he would laugh, and give her pleasure. It was interesting. Before she had diminished him, and he had stood in awe of her. Now that her helplessness, her humiliation, his success, exalted him, he scorned her. He was far kinder to Flower. Once, when she had not obeyed him promptly enough, he had beaten her with a switch. No one had interfered, even Tree. He, William, as a male, had had this right. She was only a woman. After the beating, she feared him, knowing him then, as she had not before, as being capable of disciplining her; moreover, she now knew he was willing to discipline her, and would, if he thought it necessary, or it pleased him to do so. After the beating she, for the first time, profoundly respected him as a male. And after the beating he no longer respected her, as anything. She was then only an imbonded wench to him. From a lady she had become only a slave. As a lady she had been admired and respected, perhaps even loved; as a slave she found herself relished with the delight of a master in his property, ravaged with the joy of a conqueror amidst the daughters of his enemies, and scorned as no more. She found herself tempted to love William, but her heart belonged to Tree.

"And, of course," said Gunther, "at times sex and love may coexist, though commonly briefly, infrequently, and sometimes incompatibly." Gunther grinned. "And, of course, one might have neither love nor sex. This, I submit, is the endemic condition of our much-vaunted civilization, constructed according to agricultural values, shaped by the fanatic, diseased brains of celibates, battening, not working, on the increase of the land, those with a vested interest in the perpetuation of superstition, misery and fear."

"These matters are rather above me," said William. "I am only a lowly physician."

"Make men miserable in this world," said Gunther, "then promise them a better one somewhere else, a promise on which you are never required to pay off. Tell them to behave themselves and roof the temples with gold. Control sex. Exploit the fear of death, invent terrors, and ring up the proceeds on the cash registers. Tell them you have secret magic. Cultivate their fears, their ignorance, carefully. It is valuable to you. Claim to hold the keys to the mystery. But the mystery mocks them. The mystery mocks us all."

"What are you speaking of?" asked William.

"Tyranny, despotism," said Gunther. "Existence, life, the world."

The fire in the cave crackled; there was silence otherwise; shadows flickered on the walls of stone.

"Let us speak of simpler things," said Gunther. He looked at Hamilton, who still knelt before him, her head and hair to the stone floor of the cave. He regarded her for some time, as did William. She did not move.

"Every male, from time to time," said Gunther, "desires absolute power over a female."

"Yes," said William.

"One who admits to this desire," said Gunther, "in our familiar world, is characterized as peculiar or perverted, or weak, or timid or sick, and usually characterized as such with a belying hysterical intensity, for here some obscure nerve is touched. On the other hand, since this desire, from time to time, is universal in males, it seems that an entire sex, literally billions of human beings, must be then characterized as we have suggested. In a different reality, the tiger, wanting meat, in a world of antelope, would be characterized similarly. It is a way the antelope have of trying to protect themselves from tigers. Program the tiger's brain in such a way as to conflict with its instincts. Let the tigers die in misery, starving. But when the tiger has taken meat, he no longer starves; he is then determined to feed. You, William, for the first time, have fed."

William turned Flower's head to face him. His hand was still in her hair. Then he turned her about again, holding her face to the stone.

"How do you feel, William?" asked Gunther.

William released Flower, who rolled against his leg, her lips to his thigh. "I feel strong, and powerful," said William.

"Are you happy here?" asked Gunther.

"I have been more than happy here," said William. "I have been joyful."

"That is interesting, is it not?" asked Gunther.

"Perhaps," said William.

Flower had lifted her eyes timidly to those of William. "Look into the eyes of your pretty little blond sow," said Gunther. "She adores you."

William smiled.

"That pleases your vanity, does it not?" asked Gunther.

"It does not displease me," said William, grinning.

"The important point," said Gunther, "is to note that it does please you."

"Certain weaknesses, I suppose," said William, "are natural."

"That it is a weakness is a value judgment, automatically generated from your conditioning program," said Gunther. "All we know is that it is natural. What if feelings of power, of pleasure, of dominance, were not weaknesses, but strengths? The tiger's ability to tear flesh, to break a heifer's back with one blow, is not weakness." Gunther grinned. "One need not claim the natures of men are either weaknesses or strengths. One need only recognize them as realities, which, thwarted, produce miseries, diseases, deaths."

"Nothing natural can be evil," said William.

"But what of your desire to dominate, to own, a desirable female?"

"In a male," said William, "speaking as a physician, that is a natural disposition."

"Can it then be evil, or strange, or peculiar, or perverted, or timid, or a symptom of illness?"

"No," said William. "No more than breathing or the circulation of the blood within the musculature."

"But to say that it is not evil, is not to say that it is good?"

"No more than to say that breathing or the circulation of the blood is good. In themselves, they simply exist."

"True," said Gunther. "Here we speak not of goods and evils, but of realities. We are here, so to speak, beyond good and evil."

"But," said William, "surely, relative to a species, one might speak of good and evil."

"Perhaps," said Gunther. "But what is to be the criterion of such appraisals. Shall we say that that which is good creates misery, produces illnesses and shortens life?"

"I suppose we could," said William.

"But we need not do so," said Gunther. "We might, alternatively, say that is good which makes men strong, which makes them healthy, which prolongs life, which enhances their power and exalts them, which lifts them to vitality and kingship, which makes them great."

"Do you dare," asked William, "speak of alternative moralities?"

"I speak," said Gunther, "of a morality to which there is no alternative, save disease and misery."

"I do not understand," said William.

"Moralities, in their own times," said Gunther, "seem, in the optical illusion of the present, manifestations of eternal necessities. The moral revolutionary is as convinced of the justice of his position, its moral necessity, as is the defender of the threatened tradition of his. They join arms in the naivety of their dogmatisms. But in the trek of history these moralities, with their martyrs and their victims, appear as fashions, as transient expediencies, usually enlisted in the service of either defending an establishment or altering one, that a new establishment, that in which the moral revolutionaries will stand high, take its place."

"You speak as a cynic," said William.

"I think of myself as a realist," said Gunther. "But consider, some morality is a necessary condition for the existence of social orders, as essential as access to drinking water or a supply of food. Moralities, to some extent, are selected for, as are visual sensors and prehensile appendages. Groups the members of which cannot rely on one another, groups without conviction, discipline and courage, perish as groups, though their women are commonly spared to bear sons to the conquerors. Have you ever wondered why women, after some tears, yield themselves so readily to masters? It is because women desire, innately, to belong not to their equals but to their superiors, to the strongest, to the mighty, to the conquerors. Woman desires to submit; one cannot submit to an equal. The conqueror is not an equal; the woman is property to him; she submits; as a humiliated, submitted property she knows sensations that can never be experienced by her free sister, who, in her own frustrations, must be content to denounce her for her ecstasies. Women, too, wish to place their children in the future. The future belongs to the conquerors. Her own group lies already in the rubbish of the past; but the life stirring in her much-ravished body belongs to the tomorrow of the new conquerors; she, thus, chained at the heels of her new masters, turns gladly to the future."

"If evolution selects for moralities," said William, "that would tend to explain a considerable amount of the resemblance among moralities, similarities and continuities among them."

"Surely," said Gunther. "For example, a group would not be likely to survive which permitted broadcast intragroup perfidy, disloyalty or slaughter. It is no surprise that these tenets are not recommended by historically tested moralities. Groups which might have adopted such tenets, if any groups had had so little sense, presumably left their bones in the jungles of history."

"Yet," said William, "apparently diverse moralities have escaped the filters of history."

"Of course," said Gunther. "There are many ways to survive. The sponge does so in one way, the crab in another, the antelope in another, the tiger in another." He smiled. "That there is a morality is essential, not that there be a particular morality."

"Is there any way to adjudicate between moralities?" asked William.

"Assuredly," said Gunther. "Ruling classes have always managed this quite well. For them, the correct morality is the one which consolidates and enhances their own position and power."

"Do you mean to suggest that adjudication can be only by means of armament?"

"No," said Gunther. "One could draw straws or throw dice."

"Can there not be a more rational decision procedure?" asked William.

"Rationality," said Gunther, "is the instrument of the passions. Rationality, in itself, does not prescribe ends, only how they might be sought."

"Surely it is rational to wish to survive," said William.

"It is a fact that man wishes to survive. Rationality can help him attempt to do so. But man's desire to survive does not logically imply that he should survive. 'I wish to live' does not logically imply 'I should live'. Only the passions can give you that premise. No decision follows from logic alone. Logic is empty."

"The British empiricist, David Hume, once said as much," remarked William. " 'According to reason alone I may as well prefer the destruction of the world to the pricking of my little finger.' "

"The passions, of course," said Gunther, "fortunately for us, are more clearly partisan. And I thought David Hume was a Scotsman."

"He was," said William.

"You referred to him as a British empiricist," said Gunther.

"We always so refer to him," said William.

"You are incurable imperialists at heart," said Gunther. "Next you will be after Mach and Goethe."

"We have already claimed Wittgenstein," laughed William.

Hamilton understood little of this. It was the talk of men. She was a woman. And only a slave. She knelt; her head was to the stone; she wore a collar of shells, and claws, and strands of leather.

"There must be, however," said William, "some intelligent way to adjudicate among competitive moralities."

"One may choose criteria," said Gunther, "and evaluate them in virtue of these criteria."

"But is there any way to adjudicate among criteria?" asked William.

"In virtue of other criteria," smiled Gunther.

"But ultimately?" asked William.

"No," said Gunther.

"Then there is no morality?" asked William.

"No," said Gunther. "There must be a morality. It is a necessary condition of social order."

"But there is no ultimate, rational vindication of a morality, and there can always be, at least logically, competitive moralities?"

"Yes," said Gunther. "You see, William, a choice must be made. There must be a commitment. There must be a decision. You must choose your morality. And, if you are wise, you will choose, or pretend to choose, the morality of your time and place, or an approximation to it."

"If one were wise," said William, "one would not have looked into these issues."

"The earth shakes beneath your feet?" asked Gunther.

"Yes," said William.

"I shall tell you what my criteria are," said Gunther, "though they are only one set among a possibly infinite number of alternative sets of criteria. I ask two questions of a morality. First, is it natural, truly natural, compatible with and answering to the full needs of human animals, an animal genetically coded for the hunt, and, second, does it produce excitement, meaning, greatness, the swiftness of the blood, the brightest and fiercest fires of the glands and the intellect?"

"Your morality," said William, "is dangerous; it is not one of pretense and leveling; it is a recipe for human greatness, an incitement to triumphs."

"No other will lead to the stars," said Gunther.

"What do you think of this, Hamilton?" asked William.

She trembled, her head down. A slave fears to enter into the conversation of free men. "Perhaps men are not meant for the stars," whispered Hamilton.

Gunther seized her hair, jerked her forward and turned her body, exposing it to William. "Here is the enemy," he said. "The female. If she can, she will defeat you; if she can she will reduce and destroy your dreams; when the mountains call it is she who will remind you of pressing duties; it is she who will keep you in the field with your hoe; should you stand on the beach, and be seen looking to sea, it is she who will recall you to your hearth; security and comfort to her exceed adventure, the chance of touching grandeur; she is ignorant of adventure, the meaning of man; her ears cannot hear the cry of a man's heart!"

Hamilton twisted. Gunther's hand was cruel in her hair. "Here, William," said Gunther, "is the fair enemy. Behold her, your beautiful foe. Should she conquer, the adventure is done, grandeur lost, man fallen, not risen, the arrow of promise broken, the ships left rotting on the beach."

"Please, Gunther," wept Hamilton.

"And Herjellsen told her to turn their eyes to the stars!" scoffed William.

"Herjellsen was insane," said Gunther.

"But she need not conquer," said William.

Gunther's hand tightened in her hair, and Hamilton winced. "No, my dear," said Gunther, "you will not conquer. You will be ruthlessly dominated. You will not keep us, and others, from the stars. We will take you to them, following us, carrying our burdens. No, my dear, you will come with us to the stars, if necessary in chains."

"Yes, Gunther," wept Hamilton.

He threw her back, and she wept. Flower, lying on her stomach, William's hand on her neck, was frightened.

"Kneel as you were before," said Gunther. Hamilton did so, head to the stone.

Gunther regarded her.

"It is natural, and wise," said Gunther, "for a man to control such desirable creatures. They are by nature his enemy, he by nature their master. Freed they are petty and dangerous; enslaved they are delicious and useful."

Flower whimpered. William silenced her, by tightening his fingers on the back of her neck.

"You see, William," said Gunther, "you need not be ashamed of your desire to dominate a woman. It is an expression of your manhood. She who tells you otherwise lies. Regard the hunters. Listen to the song of your blood. Furthermore, if you do not dominate her, she will own and rule you, inch by inch, until, like a bled, drugged, tethered lion, you lie at her mercy, helpless. One or the other must be master. The right by nature is yours. Will you take it or will you ask the advice of the slave?"

"But what of her?" asked William. "What of the woman?"

"What of her?" asked Gunther.

"I see," said William.

Hamilton trembled.

"Slave," said Gunther.

"Yes, Master," said Hamilton.

"Are you the enemy of your precious hunter?"

"No," said Hamilton. "I am his slave. I love him!"

"But he can buy and sell you as he pleases," said Gunther.

"Of course," said Hamilton.

"And yet you love him?" asked Gunther.

"Yes," said Hamilton.

"How do you feel about your slavery?" asked Gunther.

Hamilton's shoulders shook. She dared not raise her head. For a long time she did not answer. Then she spoke softly. "It is indescribably thrilling," she said.

"Do you love your slavery?" asked Gunther.

"Please, Gunther," she wept.

"Do you love your slavery?" asked Gunther.

"Yes," she whispered.

"Slut," said Gunther. Then he turned to William. "You

scc, William," said hc, "in thc dcpth of thc brain of thc female, as old as the genes selected for in the time of the hunters, lies a desire to submit, to belong. These are complementary natures, formed in man's dawn by laws more harsh and terrible than we can conjecture, laws that formed the flank of the antelope, the teeth of the tiger. Just as it is your nature to hold, it is hers to be held; just as it is your nature to own, it is hers to be owned; just as it is yours to be master so it is hers to be slave."

Gunther regarded Hamilton again. "Do you love slavery?" he asked.

"Yes!" she cried.

"Serve me, Slave," he said.

"Yes, Master," she whispered.

Hamilton heard Flower cry out as William drew her to him. Then she felt her own shoulder blades forced back against the stone of the floor of the cave. Her left shoulder lay in warm ashes. She thought of Tree. Then helplessly, a slave, she began, unable to help herself, to respond to Gunther's touch. She knew he would force her to yield fully to him.

◇ 21 ◇

"I will cut meat first," said Knife.

He stared across the roast carcass of deer, hot and glistening. The group fell silent. Even William and Gunther, who knew little of the language of the men, sensed the sudden stillness. Hamilton, kneeling behind Gunther, held her breath.

It had come.

Spear did not seem surprised. He had expected this for more than a year.

"I will cut meat first," said Spear. Hamilton watched them, crouching across from one another, over the meat.

Stone puzzled as to why Spear, in the last years, had not killed Knife. There were none in the group who did not know that Knife wished to be first. Tree thought he knew why Spear had not done this thing. Had Tree been Spear, he, too, would not have wanted to do this thing. The two men, Knife and Spear, stared at one another over the carcass of the deer. Short Leg, behind Spear, wondered why Spear did not strike. The two men, in many ways, seemed not unlike. There was a heaviness about the jaw of each, like rock, the same narrow eyes. Yet there seemed in Spear a heaviness, a weightiness, that was not in the younger man, Knife. Spear's eyes, too, were quicker. Tree knew that he himself would not have wished to fight Spear. He knew that Spear, the leader, would have had little compunction in killing him. But with Knife, it was different. Knife had walked before Spear once in the last month, entering the camp first; he had said once, in the men's hut, that Spear was old, that he could not hunt as well as Knife; then, ten days ago, he had taken meat from one of Spear's women and given it to Flower. But Spear had not killed him for these things. Tree had little doubt that Spear would have killed any other in the group who had done these things. But he did not kill Knife. He did not seem to notice.

"No," said Knife.

Seeming to pay Knife no attention, Spear thrust the flint blade into the cooked meat.

With a cry Knife, his own flint blade in his fist, leaped across the meat.

With one arm Spear struck him to the side and stood up. The women screamed. William and Gunther leaped to their feet. The men remained sitting, watching. Knife rolled twice and seized up his flint ax. Spear, standing by the fire, over the meat, did not move. His eyes, strange for Spear, who had often killed with equanimity, seemed agonized. "Kill him," said Stone to Spear. Spear did not move.

Many times, subtly, then brazenly, had Knife challenged Spear, and sought to undermine his authority. He had interpreted Spear's patience, his unwillingness to take action, as weakness.

There were few in the group who understood Spear's unwillingness to slay Knife. Tree thought he understood, and perhaps Arrow Maker knew, and Old Woman.

Tree wondered if Spear were too old to be first. Perhaps, after all, that was why he had not killed Knife. Perhaps Spear was, after all, afraid of Knife.

Knife raised the ax. Spear stood there, like rock.

"I am first," said Knife.

"No," said Spear.

"Take your ax," said Knife.

"I do not want to fight you," said Spear.

"I am first," said Knife.

"No," said Spear.

Brenda screamed as the ax struck down. It hit Spear on the upper left shoulder. Spear's body shook with the impact but he remained standing. Almost immediately the shoulder was covered with blood. "That is not how one kills with an ax," said Spear.

"Show him," said Stone. He thrust an ax into Spear's hands.

Again Knife struck, his two hands on the handle of the ax, but this time Spear, with the ax handed to him by Stone, blocked the blow.

"That is better," said Spear. "Strike always for the head, above the eyes, or at the back of the neck."

Knife drew back two paces, breathing heavily, holding the ax.

"I do not want to fight you," said Spear.

"I am first," said Knife.

"No," said Spear. Then he turned away. He dropped the ax to one side and crouched again beside the meat. He gripped the flint knife to again begin the cutting. His head was down.

Brenda screamed.

Again the ax fell, without warning. Spear looked up only in time to move his head to one side. The blow of the stone tore downward at the side of his head, stopped in the shoulder; Brenda saw, sickeningly, in that instant, skin sheared to the bone at the side of Spear's head, bone at the side of his jaw; then there was only blood at the side of his face, and his eyes, suddenly like those of the maddened cave bear, burned and prodded, and he cried out, leaping across the meat and seized Knife, throwing him a dozen feet away against the stone, wrenching away the ax; four times he struck the dazed, reeling Knife, twice in the back, once on the left arm, once on the leg, until Knife screamed and tore at the dirt, unable to run or lift himself. The men sat impassive, watching. William and Gunther stood to one side. The women, crouching, some standing, alert, frightened, too, watched.

Spear stood over the fallen Knife. His eyes were red with the madness of beasts. He was covered with his own blood, and the ax he lifted was stained with both that of himself and Knife. The handle of the ax was as thick as a girl's ankle; its head was as large as the doubled fists of a large man; it was fastened to the haft by strips of rawhide more than an inch in width; the ax was more than a yard in length; it was a hunting and killing ax; not a simple tool.

Knife looked up. His left arm and leg were broken. He tried to shield himself with his right arm.

"Kill him," said Short Leg.

But then Spear lowered his ax, and dropped it to one side. "I am first," he said to Knife.

"Yes," said Knife. "You are first."

"I do not want to fight you," said Spear. He went then to the meat and, with his own blood running down his shoulder and arm, cut the meat, throwing the first pieces to the children. There was no word in the language of the men for a man's son, though there was a word for the child of a woman. If there had been such a word, Spear would have said to Knife, "You are my son."

Spear was still cutting meat when Brenda saw Gunther lift his rifle and point it at him.

"Do not shoot," cried Brenda.

Spear looked up, his face bloody and terrible. He regarded the weapon with equanimity. But he knew its power. Gunther had seen to that. It had been Gunther who had, yesterday, felled a deer on which the Men had made feast, a clean shot, dropping the animal to its knees and side, from more than three hundred yards.

"Tell him," said Gunther, "that I am now leader here."

Brenda turned white. "No," she said. Then she translated his words into the language of the Men.

The Men did not seem surprised.

"Tell them there is no meat for them," said Spear.

Brenda translated.

Annoyance crossed Gunther's features. "He does not understand," said he to Hamilton. "Make it clear to him that I, and William, are now leaders here." His gun was leveled at Spear.

"He has much power," said Brenda to Spear. "We know his bow is very powerful. He claims leadership. If you resist, he may kill." Then she said to Gunther. "You are a fool. These men could kill you. You need them. You cannot watch all the time. Do not repay their hospitality with treachery. You cannot be successful."

"This is obviously the time for us to assume leadership," said Gunther. "I gather a struggle for dominance has just occurred. This savage at the meat is clearly leader. It now remains only to depose him. I have no wish to kill him. He might be useful. Tell him that if he cooperates no one will come to harm." Gunther smiled. "It is all very simple."

"Beware, Spear," said Brenda. "His weapon is powerful. He does not wish to kill, only to rule. He is dangerous. He says that if we do as he says, no one will come to harm."

"I cut meat first," said Spear.

"He says it is he who is leader here," said Brenda.

"I am leader," said Gunther.

"He says," said Hamilton, "it is he who cuts meat first."

"Go," said Spear to William and Gunther. Hamilton translated.

Gunther, furious, stood up, the rifle leveled at Spear. He moved the hammer back.

"Yield to him!" cried out Hamilton to Spear. She looked from face to face. The Men did not seem perturbed. "Do you not understand?" asked Hamilton. "He can kill. His bow can kill! Yield, or he will kill you!"

"Tell them to leave our camp," said Spear.

Hamilton, in tears, translated. "I gather," said Gunther, "it will be necessary to kill one man. It is unfortunate, but these are harsh times. I had thought his intelligence greater than it apparently is. He saw the gun kill yesterday. Surely he understands it can kill today as well. He is either stupid, or deficient in his fondness for life."

Suddenly Hamilton was startled. Suddenly she understood. It had been Gunther's mistake to show the Men the power of his weapon. The men were not fools. Slowly she said, "Gunther, this man who cuts meat first is neither stupid nor is he deficient in his fondness for life."

"Go," said Spear to Gunther and William.

Gunther looked puzzled. Then his face turned white. Swiftly he jerked the weapon open. "Wilhelm!" he said.

William examined his weapon.

"Go," said Spear, in the language of the Men. "There is no meat for you."

Hamilton translated. Then she added, "Take your lives and go!"

Gunther examined the Luger swiftly. Angrily he thrust it back in his holster. He looked at William. William dropped his own pistol back in its holster. He shook his head. He seemed numb. Gunther's eyes were terrible upon Hamilton.

"I know nothing!" wept Hamilton. "I know nothing!"

"Traitress!" cried Gunther.

"We will die without ammunition," said William, numbly.

"I know nothing of it!" wept Hamilton.

The Men rose to their feet. Gunther and William backed away. "We will die without ammunition," said William.

"Go back to your own time!" said Hamilton. "Go back!"

William looked at her. "We can't," he said. "It is not an experiment! Retrieval is impossible! Herjellsen forced us into the chamber, at gunpoint! It was a misunderstanding! He overheard Gunther speaking to me of political and military applications of the translation device. It was only speculative, theoretical. We had no intention of exploiting the device! Herjellsen didn't understand. He has exiled us, Brenda, as much as you! He transmitted our gear and weapons after us! We are prisoners here as much as you, marooned, banished, as you are!"

Hamilton was stunned.

"Herjellsen is insane!" moaned William.

"There are clear political and military applications of the technique," said Gunther. "Herjellsen is not insane. He is only a fool. With the device he could command the world."

Cloud brought forth the gear of William and Gunther, and threw it to their feet. They looked down at it.

"You must go," said Brenda:

They did not omit to notice that it was a female who had brought their things, and threw them to their feet.

"Tell him," said Gunther, nodding at Spear, "that we will take two females with us." He gestured at Flower and herself.

"He says," said Hamilton to Spear, "that he will take Flower and Turtle with him when he goes."

Spear responded. Hamilton, shoulders back, faced Gunther. Her head was high. "Flower and I," she said, "belong to the Men. We are their's, not yours."

"Give us our bullets," said Gunther. "We will go."

Hamilton said, "He said, give us our arrows. We will go." She then translated Spear's reply. "You will be put in skirts and made the slaves of women," she said.

Angrily Gunther slipped into the pack straps. He glared at Hamilton. "I shall not forget this," said he, "Traitress."

"I did nothing," said Hamilton.

His eyes burned upon her.

"I would not have had the courage to steal from you," she said.

"Who then?" asked he. "Who?

Brenda saw Spear, for the first time, throw a piece of meat to Ugly Girl.

"Ugly Girl," whispered Hamilton, stunned. "Ugly Girl."

Knife was lying in the darkness, in the cold, away from the fire.

As William lifted his pack, he looked at Spear, and then at Hamilton. His eyes were troubled. He gestured with his head back to Knife. "I can set his bones," he said.

"He can make Knife heal straight," said Brenda.

Spear squinted at the fallen Knife. "Do so," he said to William, in the language of the Men.

Brenda nodded. William put down his pack.

Cloud prodded Gunther with a switch. He turned about, fiercely. But he saw, with her, Stone and Wolf.

"Go," said Spear to him.

"I shall wait for you beyond the camp," said Gunther to William.

Cloud struck him with the switch and, angrily, he turned away. Butterfly, the girl, too, followed him, striking him with a switch. And then the other women, and the children, leaped about him, pushing and jeering. He was conducted from the camp. Men, too, followed him. Among the children only the boy to whom Butterfly had been cruel did not follow. He watched.

Hamilton knelt before the bloody Spear. She put her head to the ground in submission. "Do not let them kill him beyond the firelight," she begged.

"Are you his woman?" asked Spear.

"No!" cried Hamilton. "I belong only to you, and the Men! I am yours!"

"Then be silent," he said.

Agonized, Hamilton withdrew. She looked at Tree. He got up, lightly. "I will not let them kill him," he said. Then he disappeared in the darkness. In a short time Cloud, followed by Wolf, returned. About her upper left arm she wore Gunther's wrist watch, as an armlet. Then the others returned. Lastly, Tree came back.

"They did not kill him?" she asked.

He looked at her, angrily. She was suddenly terrified. She realized how much she feared this magnificent man.

William rose from the side of Knife, whose leg and arm he had set and bound, using spear wood and leather. Arrow Maker, intently, had observed.

Flower came to William. He took her briefly in his arms and kissed her. Then, not speaking further, he walked from the camp, beyond the perimeter of firelight, following the direction in which Gunther had been conducted. She looked after him. "Flower," called Knife. "Flower." But Flower went and knelt behind Spear.

Brenda went to the edge of the firelight, looking out into the darkness. She became aware of Ugly Girl, standing near her. She turned, shuddering, and looked down into the wide, simple eyes. Ugly Girl put out her hand, very gently, touching her arm. "Go away," said Hamilton. "You are a monster."

When Hamilton returned to the side of the fire, Tree looked up at her.

"Did they kill him?" asked Hamilton. "Is he still alive?"

Tree looked at her as she had never seen him look before. It frightened her. Then he stood up and seized her by the left arm, dragging her along beside him, and, angrily, threw her ahead of him into the darkness of a small cave. There, brutally, he beat her and raped her. When he had done with her, he said to her, angrily in the darkness, "He is still alive." Then she felt him binding her wrists behind her back. Then she felt her ankles being crossed and being tied tightly together. She then lay at his side, bound. Suddenly she laughed with pleasure. "You are jealous!" she cried. She squirmed, but could not free herself. She laughed, deliciously, delighted to the quick with this evidence of the depth, the intensity, of his wanting of her. He would give her no chance to follow Gunther and William. She would not be able to run away and pursue them. She knew she would spend the night bound, and, doubtless, the next day would wear leather ankle shackles. She was pleased that Tree knew her limitations as a tracker. If she were natively of the Men's women, she might have been kept a week in such confinements. She snuggled up to Tree. "No, Master," she said, "I shall not run off to follow Gunther. You will see to that." She smiled to herself. A man of her own times might have asked her to choose between himself and another, and freed her to follow her own wishes. The Hunter, wanting her, kept her. It was he who would choose, not her. It was she who would obey. Then in the language of the Men she spoke to Tree, softly, breathlessly, in the darkness. "It is only you whose slave I am," she whispered. "It is only you whom I love. I love you, my Master. I love you. I love you!"

She heard, to her indescribable pleasure, Tree's great laugh in the darkness, and then she felt him untying her ankles, and then, as she suffused with warmth, he thrust them apart, widely. "I love you," she whispered, and then threw back her head, and cried out with pleasure.

Toward morning, Brenda in his arms, her wrists tied behind her back, her ankles still untied, Tree said, "I gave them back their arrows. Ugly Girl gave them to me, for them. She did not wish them to die. Do not be afraid for them."

Brenda then understood the meaning of Ugly Girl's touch that preceding evening, that she was trying to tell her that she had had returned to Gunther and William the means of their survival.

"Thank you," said Hamilton.

"Whose slave are you?" asked Tree.

"Only yours," said Hamilton, "—Master."

He then used his slave again, quickly, without much thought. He then tied together her ankles. Before going to sleep, he wrapped a robe of fur about them, that of a giant cave bear he had slain the preceding spring. Hamilton pressed her bound body against his, and kissed him, but he did not know this, for he was asleep.

◈ 22 ◈

"Hurry, Butterfly! Sew more swiftly!" scolded Hamilton.

Butterfly looked up, angrily, and then bent again to the deerskin, thrusting the awl through the doubled skin, one layer at a time, and then pushing the wet sinew, lubricated with her spittle, through the small hole. With her small fingers she drew it tight, but too tight, wrinkling the skin. She looked up, in misery.

"It is too tight," said Hamilton. "You will bunch the skin."

"I will not have enough sinew left to finish," wailed Butterfly.

"You did not measure it correctly," said Hamilton.

Butterfly looked at Hamilton. About Butterfly's throat, tied, was a necklace of shells, and claws, and loops of leather, and, threaded on the loops, with the shells and

claws, were small squares of leather, five of them, bearing
the sign of the Men. The young man, Hawk, had tied it
there.

"Old Woman will beat me again," wailed Butterfly, "with
her switch!"

"You must learn, Butterfly," said Hamilton.

Hamilton stood up. She was happy. She stretched. The
spring air was delicious. She threw her hair back over her
shoulders with her hands, and a luxurious movement of her
head. She wore her brief wrap-around skirt, exposing the
left thigh. Besides this she wore only her own necklace, proclaiming her, like Butterfly, as a woman of the Men. She
smiled. It had been the hunter, Tree, she recalled, long ago,
who had tied the necklace on her throat, in a high prison
cave. She closed her eyes deliciously. She gritted her teeth
against the surgency of her desire. How she, his helpless
slave, loved him! How delicious it was to belong, to literally *belong,* will-lessly, helplessly, to a strong man, to such a
magnificent brute, to a true master of women, whose needs
and pleasures, and smallest whims, she must gratify and
serve with the full perfection of the slave girl, his to command *as he pleases.* She opened her eyes, happily. Brenda
Hamilton, the slave girl, was happy.

Life was different than it had been among the Men.
Changes had come about.

"Just hope, Butterfly," said Hamilton, "that it will not be
Hawk who will beat you."

"Is she not old enough to kneel with the women?" had
asked Hawk of Spear.

Spear had looked at Butterfly. "Kneel with the women,"
he had said.

"No," she had cried, "Please!"

But Old Woman had hobbled to her and, seizing her by
the arm, drawn her among the women. They had laughed
at her. She had knelt miserably among them.

Even before the snow had melted, it was clear that the
boy, to whom Butterfly had been often cruel, was ready to
run with the hunters. In the winter he had gained many
pounds, and some five inches of height, and, even since the
melting of the snow, it seemed he had grown the width of
another hand. The voracity of his appetite, even among
hunters, was a joke in the camp. He was large-boned. Some
thought he might grow as large as Spear or Tree. The
preceding summer and early fall Butterfly had still been
taller and heavier than he, but, now, in the spring, to her

dismay, she must lift her head, even to look into his eyes. She was angry and jealous, for he had grown larger and stronger than she, until now there was no comparison between them, and for, soon she knew, he would run with the hunters; he would be a Man. Sometimes she was frightened, because of the way in which he now regarded her; often she caught him watching her body, and how it moved; sometimes she felt naked before him.

One day, even before the last snows had melted, Spear, and the Men, had met below the base of the cliffs. Among the Men, too, was Knife, who, in the winter, had challenged Spear to be first in the group. Spear had not killed him. Knife's limbs, set by William, had healed straight. He now said little. He seldom, now, used one of the women, even Flower.

Spear, the left side of his face terrible with its scarring, from the ax of Knife, with the Men, had stood at the base of the cliffs. The women, and children, too, had stood with him.

"Lift this stone," had said Spear to the boy. He had lifted it. No woman or child in the camp could have lifted it. "Throw this spear," had said Spear. The boy had thrown it. It was a fine cast. No woman or child in the camp could have thrown it one third so far. Hamilton, and the other women, thrilled to see it thrown. Soon, they knew, there would be a new hunter among them. There would be more meat. And he seemed a fine lad. He might make a great hunter. But Hamilton, too, was uneasy. She fingered her necklace. She was a woman of the Men. Should the boy become a hunter she, as much as the other camp females, would belong to him, as they did to the others. "Fetch the spear," had said Spear. The boy had retrieved the spear. "Do not return to camp," said Spear, "until it is bloodied." The boy left the camp. Late that afternoon he had returned. Rolled on his shoulder, tied with hide rope, was a fresh skin, wet and dark. The bluish, chipped stone blade of the spear was stained with reddish brown. He had slain a young, male bear, vicious, irritable, come not more than a handful of days ago from its hibernation. He looked at Hamilton, and Cloud, and Antelope, and another woman, Feather. "There is meat at the rock," he said, "by the stream." Swiftly the women, Hamilton, and the three others designated, had left the camp, to fetch back the meat. They took a pole, and rawhide thongs, with them. In half an hour the women, stumbling, two on each end of the pole, the animal tied by its paws to it, returned to the camp. The kill was tied to the rack at the foot of the cliffs and Spear, with his stone dagger, at the animal's throat, into a leather sack, drew blood. Then the men, with the blood, took the boy into the Men's cave, back, deep in the cliffs, where the women were not permitted to follow. What they did in the Men's cave the women did not learn, and would never be told. But when they had emerged, Spear had said, "A hunter is born." The young man had stood among the men, tall and straight. "This is a hunter," had said Spear, pointing to the young man "His name is Hawk. He is of the Men!" The men had cheered him. Spear pointed to the earth before the young man's feet. Short Leg first, and then Nurse, and even Old Woman, and then the other adult females of the camp, knelt before the young man, their heads to his feet. He regarded them. Then he said, "Prepare a feast."

"Up, lazy women," scolded Old Woman, getting up, even hitting Cloud and Antelope with her switch. "Prepare a feast!" The women sprang to their feet to prepare a feast. The children, with the exception of Butterfly, who were standing nearby, leaped up and down and clapped their hands. Butterfly did nothing but, apprehensively, regard the new hunter. But Hawk was now sitting with the men, talking with them. Later he did notice her, with the children. It was then that he had said to Spear, "Is she not old enough to kneel with the women?" And Butterfly had been made to kneel with the women. None of the men had fed her. It was to the new, young hunter that she went last.

"Feed me," she asked.

He cut a large, hot piece of meat. She eyed it. Then he began to eat it. "Feed me," she begged.

He looked at her, and she dropped her eyes. When she again regarded him, he said, "We will see if you please me."

He then rose to his feet, taking the meat and taking, too, the rolled skin of the bear he had slain in the afternoon. He left the fire and she slipped to her feet and followed him. Beyond the edge of the fire, when he had untied the skin and thrown it, spreading it, across the damp turf and snow, she had suddenly, with a cry of misery, fled. In a few steps he had caught her and, carrying her, returned her to the fur, on which he threw her, at his feet.

Tooth called two children away from them, who had wished to watch.

"Feed me!" she wept.

"We shall see if you please me," he said. Then he dropped to his knees beside her.

In an hour he returned to the fire. She, now naked, her head down, blond hair disheveled, followed him, and knelt behind him. About her throat, visible under her hair, knotted there by the hunter, was the necklace of loops of leather, and claws, and threaded shells; Butterfly was now of the women. Her cheeks were stained with tears. Hamilton regarded her. She thought that, in another year or two, Butterfly would be the equal of Flower. Butterfly reached her hand forth, gently, to touch the hunter. He paid her no attention. Hamilton then saw her lie on her back, eyes moist, reproachful, and lift her body to him. He threw her a piece of meat. She ate it eagerly, kneeling quite closely behind him.

To one side Hamilton saw Ugly Girl lift her body to Tooth. He fed her.

This made Hamilton happy. Then she went to Tree and, on her back before him, lifted her beauty before him, arching her back. He threw her meat, it striking her body, and she scrambled up and ate it happily, kneeling behind him. Wolf fed Antelope, and Runner fed Cloud.

No more had been heard of William and Gunther. Tree had, knowing Hamilton would have wished it so, returned their bullets to them. They had gone. There had been no meat for them in the camp of the Men. For more than two weeks following their departure, Tree, in his jealousy, had made her serve him exquisitely well, scarcely permitting her out of his sight. The first two nights, when not using her, he had kept her bound, hand and foot. During the first two days, he had kept her in close ankle shackles, as had been done with her when she had first been only a captive stranger in the camp, not even necklaced.

She glanced at Tooth and Ugly Girl. He held her in his left arm and fed her with his right hand, bits of meat. Huge, homely Tooth, with the prognathous jaw, the extended canine, the lover and teacher of children, cared for the simple, doglike thing in his arm. She held him, and put her head against him. Then she looked up at him, the large eyes wide, soft, moist. She licked him softly with her tongue, and lifted her head again to him, to see if he would rebuff her. He gave her another tiny piece of meat. She could not aspire, of course, to wear the necklace, for she was only of the Ugly People. Hamilton supposed Tooth was fond of her body. It was short, and squat, and round-shouldered, but, from the point of view of Tooth, Hamilton supposed, it cuddled well, and the breasts were not displeasing. Even Tree, Hamilton recalled, occasionally ordered her to cuddle to him, drawing up her legs; it pleased her, too, when commanded, to do so, feeling his strength, his protection, making herself a small, helpless love kitten in his mighty arms. But the face of Ugly Girl seemed so repulsive to Hamilton. How could Tooth stand to gaze upon it? It was broad; the neck was short; the hair was stringy; the eyes were so large, so wide, so simple, so empty. Hamilton wondered how Tooth saw Ugly Girl. Did he see her as she did? Or did he see, or sense, something else in her? How could he stand to look upon her? Hamilton chewed on the meat which Tree had given her. Tooth looked down into the eyes of Ugly Girl. They were soft, wide, moist. He kissed her. Her face, to Hamilton, startled, in that moment, had seemed somehow different than before. She did not understand what it was that she had seen. Ugly Girl now had her head against Tooth's shoulder. When she lifted her head from his shoulder there were tears in her eyes. Hamilton shrugged; the Ugly People were animals; yet Hamilton was pleased that Tooth should be kind to Ugly Girl. It was she whom the Men had used to steal bullets from Gunther and William.

"Feed me, Master," wheedled Hamilton, putting her chin on Tree's right shoulder.

He passed her back a piece of meat, with his right hand, over his right shoulder, not looking at her.

"Here is a piece of sinew," said Hamilton to the miserable Butterfly, "which I have been saving. It is long enough. Now sew well. Next time measure more carefully."

"Thank you, Turtle," said Butterfly, gratefully. She knelt, bending over her sewing.

The brief skin which Butterfly wore about her hips was tanned from a hide, that of a deer, which Hawk had slain. Her first task, after pleasing Hawk, had been the preparation of the bearskin which he had brought back to camp with him. Turtle and Cloud had helped her with it.

It had been evident, from the first, that Hawk had a special interest in slender Butterfly. It was almost always she whom he called upon to serve him. He insisted on exact and total obedience from her, as Tree did from Hamilton. Hamilton could see that the girl, to uphold her self-respect, pretended to resent this, and hotly, but was secretly, as could be seen from her smiles and expressions, much pleased. Hamilton supposed that Butterfly, an intelligent, arrogant, spoiled, vital girl, could only respect a man who was her total master. Hamilton, in living among the Men, had, for the first time, begun to understand the ratios of dominance and submission, endemic in the animal kingdom. She saw it in wildlife about her, and among the Men. Had Hawk been crippled by a subsequent psychological conditioning or caught in the meshes of social restraints, Butterfly would have constantly, protected by his imprinted conflicts, his self-alienation, and reinforced by a world invented to exclude hunters, fought him for dominance and, instinctually yearning for his authority to be imposed upon her, she genetically a hunter's woman, challenged him continually, both to his misery and hers. But Hawk was not weak. He could not have been weak, unless there had been a defect in his brain. His world had not been built to make him weak. Weakness is not a useful property of hunters. It reduces their effectiveness. Weakness and gullibility are virtues only in an agricultural world, or a technological one, where, in a complicated network of interrelationships, it is important to keep men bound to the soil, or to their machines or desks. Weakness in a hunter would work against the survival of the group. But this did not mean that Butterfly would not, from time to time, if only to call herself to his attention, or to reassure herself of his mastery and strength, challenge him. It only meant that her subordination, on such occasions, to her pleasure and satisfaction, would be again taught to her, promptly and effectively. Yesterday, Hamilton recalled, when Butterfly had spoken back to Hawk, he had, laughing, taken her by the hair into the woods. There he had switched her a few times and, finishing her discipline, thrown her over a log. She had followed him back to camp, red-faced, but pleased.

"Since I gave you the sinew," said Hamilton to Butterfly, "you must, when the men return tonight, give me your share of the dried sugar berries, if Old Woman lets us have them." These were almost the last of the berries, dried and hard, but sweet when chewed, left over from the preceding fall.

"No!" said Butterfly.

"Give me back the sinew!" laughed Hamilton.

"No!" said Butterfly. "I will give you the sugar berries! I will, Turtle!"

"Very well," said Hamilton. She looked down at Butterfly. "For whom are you making that garment?" she asked.

"For Hawk," said Butterfly, angrily. "He makes me work so hard!"

"Men are all beasts," said Hamilton.

"Yes," said Butterfly. "They are! They are!"

Hamilton looked away from Butterfly, happy. She breathed in the delicious spring air.

The men were hunting. They would return by nightfall. There was now no man in the camp, with the exception of Hyena, who seldom ran with the hunters. He was in his cave, arranging stones in patterns, about the skull of an aurochs. He spent much time doing this, and such things. Hamilton hoped that the men's hunt would be successful. She was hungry. They had been gone now for two days. She had missed Tree last night. She saw Antelope returning to camp with water. Cloud was with her. Cloud no longer wore Gunther's watch, taken from him when he had been driven from the camp. She kept it among her belongings.

Hamilton made her way up the face of the cliff. She made the ascent less circuitously than she would have the preceding fall. She did not take the sloping path used by Old Woman, that used, too, by those who carried burdens, but scrambled upward, foot by foot, toward the second tier of caves, to the first broad ledges. Some forty feet from the ground, on a broad ledge, she looked out across the woods. The sky was very blue, with white clouds. The first leafage, delicate, very green, was on the trees and bushes. This past winter there had been only one visitor other than Gunther and William, a trader from the Bear People. He had brought shells from the Coast People, for which he had traded skins, and, for them, received salt from the Men. He had stayed for ten days. He had been known. Gunther and William had arrived some four weeks later. Hamilton was looking forward to the summer camp, in which the Men moved sometimes marches away, for new hunting, in which huts were built. It had been to a summer camp that Tree had first brought Hamilton. And from the camp they had gone to fetch flint and salt before returning to the shelters. The women did not know the location of the salt. Hamilton recalled how hard she had worked at the flint lode. But she was anxious to see it again. Flint, and salt, were necessary. She recalled how Spear had scratched out the sign of the Weasel People at the flint lode and drawn over it the sign of the Men, the arm and the spear. She wore that same sign on the five leather squares of her necklace, among the leather, the claws, the threaded shells. The flint belonged to the Men, and so, too, she thought, smiling, did the women of the Men, no less claimed, no less owned. She saw Flower below, at the foot of the cliffs. Flower, too, of course, wore the necklace of the Men. It was a pleasant day, shortly past noon. From where she knelt she could see the children playing.

"Lazy Girl," said Old Woman, emerging from the cave behind her. "Chew this hide for Runner." She threw a hide, scraped, beside Hamilton. What flesh and dryness remained in it would be chewed away, bitten and licked by the mouth of a woman; the acid in her saliva, moistening the hide, Hamilton knew, too, was important. "Let Cloud do it!" protested Hamilton.

"I will switch you," said Old Woman.

"No," said Hamilton. "I will do it!" Quickly Hamilton picked up the hide and began to chew it, beginning at one edge.

"You are a lazy girl," said Old Woman. "You should be traded to the Coast People. Their girls are good for nothing."

Old Woman cackled with satisfaction, and left.

Hamilton chewed on the hide.

She saw Flower below. Why had Flower not been given the hide? Flower did not work well when the men were not present and Old Woman could not see her.

"Flower," thought Hamilton, "is a lazy girl. If anyone should be traded to the Coast People, it should be Flower." If Flower were traded, Hamilton thought to herself, she, Hamilton, would be the most beautiful woman in the camp, except perhaps in a year or two, when Butterfly was older. Hamilton thought of herself as being the camp beauty. The thought did not displease her. Then she laughed at herself. How strange it all was. She recalled her own time, her own world, her former identity and self, her education, her degree, her proficiencies, former friends, former surroundings. Now she smiled. Now she was only Turtle, a slave of primeval hunters, and of one in particular, a primeval woman kneeling on a stone ledge before a cave, chewing hide for a master, waiting for the return of hunters.

"I am happy," said Brenda Hamilton to herself. "I am truly happy!"

It was then that, from the ledge, she saw him, at first only a shaggy pelt of hair, the tip of a stone-bladed spear in the brush, more than fifty yards away, across the clearing at the foot of the cliff.

She knelt on the ledge, speechless, frightened, confused. Then she saw others.

She leaped to her feet, screaming.

At the same time, moving swiftly, crouched over, carrying spears and clubs, they emerged from the brush about the clearing.

They wore headbands.

She saw Flower stand as though frozen. In an instant one of them was upon her, striking her with a club to his feet.

She heard Antelope scream. Old Woman came running from the cave. The children, crying out, shrieking, scattered. Men struck at them with spears. Hamilton saw one of the men kneeling over Flower, jerking her hands behind her back and tying them. She saw Antelope in the arms of another man, squirming. Then she was thrown to her belly, to be bound. Other men swept around the clearing. Some began to climb. Numb, half in shock, not comprehending, Hamilton stood watching. "Run!" cried Old Woman. Hamilton saw the face of a man appear suddenly above the ledge to her left. Then his arm was over, and half his body. "Run!" screamed Old Woman. Hamilton suddenly felt the stinging cut of the old woman's switch. Frantically Hamilton began to scramble up the cliff. Gasping, fingernails scratching in the crevices, miserable, Hamilton climbed. She heard Old Woman's switch below strike the man. He cried out with rage. She turned, looking over her shoulder, hearing Old Woman's scream, then seeing her dropping, hitting, rolling and dropping, turning, down the steep slope, sprawling to the clearing below, and the face of the man below.

She climbed another foot. She heard his cry to her, ordering her to return to the ledge. Desperately she sought a new handhold. He cried out again. She found it, and moved higher on the cliff. She had seen Tree climb the cliff here, and others, even some of the boys. A rock struck her, hard, on the left side, above the small of her back. She slipped, but caught herself. Then she heard the man begin to follow her. Then there was another, too, with him. She reached a small ledge, and, breathing wildly, with two hands, grasped a heavy stone. With difficulty she raised it over her head and, moaning, flung it downward. It struck the first climber a glancing blow on the side of his head. He lost his hold, scrambling and scratching against the side of the cliff, and, skidding, and then dropping, fell back to the broad ledge, twenty feet below. The second climber reached over the ledge on which she stood and grasped her ankle. She shook free and began again to climb. He ordered her back. He was swift behind her. He leaped for her but she was too high for him. For minutes Hamilton climbed. At first he did not climb after her but stood on the ledge, shouting at her. Twice he threw rocks. One struck her on the left leg, behind the knee, hurting her. The other struck near her face on the left side, nearly causing her to lose her hold, but, again, she did not fall. She heard men shouting below. She sensed that some were looking for a new ascent, an easier one, to head her off. Then she heard the man below, not wanting to risk losing her, perhaps wanting to be the one to take her, begin to climb. On a tiny ledge she turned. He was still following her. Far below she could see men in the clearing. At the feet of one, bound hand and foot, lay Flower. Between the feet of another, similarly secured, lying on her side, lay Antelope. The butt of his great spear, upright in the dirt, in his imperious grasp, that of her taker, lay near her face. She saw Old Woman lying at the foot of the cliff. Another man was dragging Butterfly by the hair, bent over, down the sloping path leading up to the first level of caves. In his free hand he held a bag of salt. She saw one child, bleeding, lying in the clearing. From the brush one man emerged, pulling a young, pregnant female by the wrist. He tied her hands behind her back and made her kneel. With a rope he tied her by the neck to Flower's bound ankles. She saw two more women of the Men being prodded to the center of the clearing, shoved stumbling before the spear butts of captors.

Hamilton was miserable. She did not see how she could climb further.

She heard the man below her, now making his way upward. He shouted angrily at her. He gestured that she should come down.

Again, moaning, Hamilton climbed. She slipped, cried out, and again climbed. She now clung to the cliff a yard below its summit, but could not reach the summit. She was more than eighty feet above the nearest outjutting ledge below her at this point, the height of an eight-story building. She did not dare to turn and look back to the valley, which lay some two hundred feet, the equivalent of some twenty stories, below. She wept, and put her cheek against the granite of the cliff. Never before had she tried to scale the cliff on this face. She realized, sickeningly, she had not chosen an ascent which was proper for her. She had seen Tree climb the cliff at this point, but he was powerful and long of limb. The boys, she now remembered, had been to her left. She could not retrace her steps without falling into the hands of her pursuer. He laughed below her, seeing her predicament. She cried out with misery and, suddenly, as she felt the wind moving against her on the cliff, was frightened of falling. She heard the man moving closer to her. She looked down. He had taken a thong from his waist and put it in his teeth. In a moment she knew he would reach up and tie it on her ankle, and she would be caught. There was a sound above her. She heard a clicking noise, a tongue click, and a smacking of lips and hiss. Ugly Girl reached over the cliff, extending her arm and hand down to Hamilton. "No!" cried Hamilton, frightened. Then she reached for Ugly Girl's hand and, seizing her on the wrist with her other hand, swung out over the cliff. Hamilton screamed with misery. The man below cried out with rage. Then, inch by inch, Ugly Girl, with her squat, powerful body, the strong arm, drew Hamilton to the summit of the cliff. Gratefully Hamilton scrambled over it. She looked about herself. She saw Nurse and another woman of the Men two hundred yards away. They had made the ascent by the side, and were now, running and scrambling, making their way down a side path to the brush and trees far below. She saw the woman with Nurse abruptly, suddenly, change her direction, and take a new descent path. Ugly Girl pulled on Hamilton's arm, hurrying her. Hamilton shook free of her touch, shuddering, but ran beside her. Nurse and the other woman of the Men had disappeared. Hamilton and Ugly Girl sped across the roof of the mountain of stone in which were the shelters. There was some brush and twisted plants on its summit, where, over years, dust had gathered and seeds had fallen. She heard a cry behind her, the man pursuing her having gained the height of the cliff. Suddenly they saw two men appear before them, some two hundred yards away, emerging over the rocks. Hamilton moaned. She turned back, and then back again. They were approaching swiftly. She did not know which way to run. Then, crying out, she felt the hand of the man behind her in her hair. She was painfully thrown to her knees on the stone. She tried to reach his hand in her hair. Ugly Girl darted away. The other men neared. She tried to struggle. He, his hand tight in her hair, wrenched her head viciously back and forth and she, screaming, half blinded with pain, knelt with absolute quiet, a captive female; she now feared only, his hand so tight in her hair, that she might move in the slightest, thus again causing herself that excruciating pain. She had been taken. She saw Ugly Girl stop, and look about herself, wildly. Hamilton lifted her hand to Ugly Girl, tears in her eyes. The two other men were now within fifty yards. Ugly Girl suddenly turned back and, to the astonishment of the man who held her, threw herself upon him like an animal, stratching at his eyes, biting at his throat. He fended her away from himself with his right arm, releasing Hamilton, who, crying out, scrambled away. She heard Ugly Girl cry out with misery. Turning back Hamilton saw that the man had thrown Ugly Girl to his feet by her hair. He kicked her. Ugly Girl whimpered and reached out to Hamilton. Hamilton turned away, fleeing. She heard the other two men behind her; she heard the cry of another man from somewhere; she fled. Now she was on the side path, which she knew well, each hold and step; she darted, leaping and scrambling, from one ledge to another, and then she was out of sight of the men above her; she darted into one of the caves on the second level, slipping into its darkness. "Turtle?" said a voice. It was Cloud, huddling in the darkness, trembling. "Yes," whispered Hamilton. Then, on her hands and knees, she, from this cave, crawled down a crooked, sloping passage into an adjoining cave. "That is the way to the Men's cave," wept Cloud. "You may not go there!" Scarcely had Hamilton entered the small, crooked, sloping passage then she heard men, three of them, entering the cave she had left. She heard, behind her, Cloud's scream, and the sound of blows. Hamilton emerged into the next cave. She screamed. A monster, it seemed, reared up before her, something with a twisted human body and the head of an aurochs' skull. It shook a rattle at her wildly. It was Hyena. She fled past him into the darkness. She heard men entering the cave from the ledge outside, from the sunlight, and another, calling out angrily, emerging from the small passage, who had followed her into it. She heard Hyena's rattle. Then she heard men brush past him. She fled deeper into the passage, feeling the sides of the passage.

Then she was alone in the absolute darkness.

She moaned. She ran. She struck her left thigh on a projection of rock. She fell on the stone. She struggled to her feet. She heard pursuit. She fled deeper into the passage.

Then she stopped. No longer did she hear sounds from behind her.

She crouched down. She waited, frightened. She crouched in the pitch blackness, breathing heavily, terrified.

There was no sound behind her.

She went further in the tunnel, slowly, carefully, silently. Then again she stopped, crouched down, waited.

Again there was no sound from behind her. The pounding of her heart seemed loud. She did not move.

Perhaps the men were searching elsewhere. There were many caves in the cliffs. There were other females to thong. There were bags of salt to find. There was fur to locate, and flint to be sacked and carried off. Surely not all the women would be caught. There was no pursuit. She waited, scarcely breathing now. Perhaps the intruders had gone. Perhaps they wished only to strike with swiftness and, swiftly, be gone. Perhaps they had taken enough fur, and flint and salt, and women, to satisfy them. Perhaps even now they were on their way back to their own camp.

She gradually became sure of this as the minutes passed. I am safe, she thought.

Then, from far down the passage behind her, she heard a sound, and, to her misery, saw the flicker of torches.

She, moaning, leaped to her feet and ran deeper in the passage. Then suddenly she stopped, terrified. She knew that there was, at a place in this passage, a drop to the left of some fifty feet. She recalled it when Old Woman, with her torch, had shown her the passage months ago. Occasionally in the shelters there were such crevices and pits. One pit, in another shelter, was used for refuse. It was more than twenty feet deep, and had sheer sides. She hugged the right side of the passage. Her foot dislodged a small pebble and she heard it drop away from her to the left. It made a clear sound as it struck the stone, in two places below. She almost cried out with anguish. She heard a shout from behind her, reverberating in the twisting passage. Looking over her shoulder she saw the flicker of torches, four of them. She moved, back against the stone, past the crevice. She then sped on. Her thigh felt wet and she knew it was bleeding, from where she had struck it on the projection of stone.

Suddenly her left foot splashed in cold water. She cried out in misery, startled. She stopped, and felt about herself in the darkness. She heard the dripping of water. She scraped her right forearm on the stone. There were other passages, she knew, some hundred yards beyond the crevice, passages other than that leading to the cave of the hands, the animal paintings, which had once been shown to her by Old Woman. She sank to her knees, moaning, disoriented. She shuddered. She realized she did not know where she was. She was lost.

From somewhere behind her, seemingly from far away, she heard shouts.

She crouched very still, hoping that her pursuers would choose other tunnels, would give up the chase.

But the noises came closer. Then, again, as though from afar this time, she saw the dim flicker of torches.

She struggled to her feet. Gasping, weeping, she put forth her hands, her fingers, and felt the stone sides of the tunnel. Irrationally, heedlessly, she sped forward. The torches, the noises, were behind her. Then suddenly, crying out, she plunged forward; she seized at nothingness; sprawling, knees and hands scraped, she struck stone some two feet below; she lay there sobbing; then, crawling, weeping, holding her hand before her, she moved deeper into the tunnel; she crawled for some four to five minutes; she could hear the sound of pursuit from behind, louder now; then to her misery she felt solid stone before her. In the darkness, groping, frantically, she tried to discover an opening. Wildly she stood up. She felt about the sides, and before her, and over her head, and at her feet. There was no opening. She had fled into a blind tunnel. She sank to her knees in the darkness at the wall of stone; she leaned against it, putting the side of her face against the cool, granular surface which prevented her further advance.

She rose to her feet and put her back against the wall of stone, putting her hands back, feeling it with the palms of her hands.

She watched the torches growing closer, heard the sounds of the men. She saw them then, far down the tunnel, stepping down from the ledge from which she had fallen, then approaching. There were four torches, six men, primitive hunters. She pressed back against the wall, in terror, watching them approach. They came closer. Then the first of them lifted his torch, and she was illuminated. Her hair was wild; her eyes were deep, frantic, filled with fear; she wore the brief, wrap-around skirt of deerskin, exposing the left thigh; about her neck was knotted the several loops of the necklace of shells, of claws and leather. She faced them, a bare-breasted, cornered, primitive woman. But, too, she was Brenda Hamilton, a woman of our time, at the mercy of primitive hunters. Inwardly she moaned. Had she hoped to elude them? They could follow her even in the twisting darkness of the caves; had she been calm they could have followed her, by the simple woman smell she could not help but leave; but she had been running, terrified, broken out in the sweat, the unmistakable secretions, of driven feminine quarry; she had been game to them; the chase was now ended; the snare was readied; they had followed their girl quarry, their woman fugitive, easily; the outcome had never been in doubt; behind her, marking her trail, belying her passage, like a traitor's signal, perfidious, treacherous, had hung the perfume, stimulatory to hunters, excitatory to predatory males, of her terror; the female fear-smell. She, caught, had had no chance. The others, too, lifted their torches. They regarded her, she could see, with pleasure, with anticipation. Their leader, a heavily bearded fellow, lifted his hand. In it, coiled, were several narrow loops of leather thongs. He grinned. Then he handed his torch to another man and approached her. In his hand were the thongs. She could not take her eyes from them. He held them up before her. She felt almost hypnotized. She could not take her eyes from them. In his hand were the thongs with which to bind her. She felt her shoulder blades, the deliciousness of her ass, press back against the stone.

Then there was another torch, from behind the men.

"Gunther!" cried Hamilton.

"Where are the hunters?" asked Gunther.

"They are gone," said Hamilton.

"These are the Weasel People," said Gunther, indicating with his head the men about.

"Oh, no," whispered Hamilton.

"Blood enemies of the Men," said Gunther. He smiled. "And you are a woman of the Men."

"Protect me, Gunther," whispered Hamilton.

Gunther stood there, the men of the Weasel People parting to admit him. His torch was in his left hand. Across his back was strapped his rifle. In his right hand, reddish in the light of the torch, was the drawn Luger. She saw, on his left wrist, the watch which, months before, Cloud had brought back from the darkness, when he and William had been driven from the camp.

"Save me, Gunther!" cried Hamilton.

He regarded her. Then he turned away, carrying the torch, and made his way back down the passage.

"Gunther!" screamed Hamilton. "Don't leave me!"

Then she saw again only the thongs in the hand of the primitive leader, the savage. These were the thongs of the Weasel People. The Weasel People were the blood enemies of the Men, and she was a woman of the Men. She pressed back. At her back was the wall of stone. The leader reached for her. She screamed. The others crowded about.

◊ 23 ◊

Hamilton opened her eyes. Every bone and muscle in her body seemed sore. She tried, weakly, to separate her hands. They were thonged tightly behind her back. Butterfly lay near her, her small body similarly secured. "Turtle," said Butterfly, tears in her eyes. Hamilton looked about herself, at the other women, crowded together, bound, at the close, rounded walls of roughly fitted stone. She sat up, putting her back against the stone. She looked up, toward the top of the circular, stone-lined pit, some ten feet above, some eight feet in diameter, to the grille of heavy branches, weighted down with stones, closing it. She was puzzled that the stone had been roughly shaped. The blocks were large, some as much as a yard in width. Their prison reminded her of a well, save that it was too wide, and too shallow. In the pit the prisoners were naked. They had been stripped days ago at the shelters, and not permitted clothing afterwards. In the clearing before the shelters, the necklaces, proclaiming them of the Men, had been cut from their necks with stone knives and thrown aside. They had then been switched and put in throat coffle, thonged by the neck with rawhide, and given their burdens, the spoils of the camp of the Men, flint, fur, salt, weapons, tools, dried roots, dried meat. The journey had been a nightmare for them, hurried, switched, exhausted, driven beasts of burden. They had been forced to move under the switch even after dark. The Weasel People had no wish to encounter the Men.

"Turtle," said Butterfly.

Hamilton smiled at the girl. She crept near to Hamilton, and put her head against her arm. "Do not cry," whispered Hamilton. Butterfly put her head down, and lay close to Hamilton.

Hamilton's attention was caught by a scattering of small objects on the floor of the pit. They were tiny, and seemed to be of some vegetable matter. She did not understand what they could be.

She moved her abused body, then closed her eyes in pain and remained still.

"I am afraid of him," she heard Cloud whisper to Antelope.

Hamilton opened her eyes and regarded Cloud, who was kneeling. Cloud was bound as the others. "What will he do with me?" asked Cloud.

Hamilton did not envy Cloud, for it had been she who had, with the strength of the Men behind her, thrown Gunther's and William's belongings to their feet when they had been driven from the camp, who had struck Gunther with a switch, herding him into the darkness, who had taken his watch. In the cave, when Hamilton had been captured, she had seen that Gunther had already recovered the watch. Cloud had been captured shortly before Hamilton had. She looked at Cloud. Cloud was trembling. "What will he do with me?" asked Cloud of Hamilton.

"I do not know," said Hamilton. She did not envy Cloud. Antelope kissed Cloud on the shoulder, and Cloud put her head, eyes wide, against Antelope's shoulder.

Hamilton looked up, through the grille. The pit was not open to the sky. Some five feet above the grille, on poles, was a roof of branches and thatch. Rain could not fall into the pit.

Hamilton could not understand the meaning of such a construction. She did not think it was to shelter female slaves. No solicitation had been shown to them in the journey from the caves of the Men. She looked about herself. They were the females of hated enemies, and the Weasel People, with primitive arrogance, with primitive brutality, had treated them precisely as what they were.

Flower looked at her. The right side of Flower's head bore a deep bruise. She had been the first female of the Men taken. From a ledge at the shelters, Hamilton had seen her assailant brutally club her senseless to his feet, then jerk her hands behind her back and tie her. Flower looked away from Hamilton, miserable.

Ugly Girl was sitting, like Hamilton, with her back against the stone. Her eyes were open, and she was staring across the stone floor to the wall opposite her, seeing nothing. Hamilton looked at her broad head, the simplicity of the eyes, the almost chinless face, the heavy, lank hair, the squat, breasted torso, the short, thick legs. Hamilton shivered. Ugly Girl's wrists, like those of the others, were crossed and tied tightly behind her back. It is almost as if she were human, thought Hamilton. Why should they tie her like the rest of us? She is not even human. Why did they take her? What would they want her for? The thought crossed Hamilton's mind that they might have taken her for food. Perhaps the Weasel People were cannibals? She shuddered at the thought that they might all be being kept for food. But she had not heard that the Weasel People ate human flesh. Perhaps they only ate those women who did not sufficiently please them? Hamilton shuddered. She knew she would do what was necessary to survive. She was a primitive woman. She closed her eyes. Pride was not a luxury a primitive woman could afford. To avoid being eaten she knew she would do anything, and eagerly. She opened her eyes and glared across the flooring to Ugly Girl, feeling a sudden hostility for the simple, doglike creature. When Hamilton had first been caught, held by the hair, on the roof of the cliffs, Ugly Girl, wickedly, with ferocity, biting, scratching, had thrown herself on her captor, and he had released her, and she had fled. Turning back, she had seen that Ugly Girl, in turn, had been caught. Ugly Girl had held out her hand to her, but she had not returned to help, but had turned away, continuing her flight. Surely it was irrational that both of them should be apprehended. But later, in a blind tunnel, trapped, cornered, she, too, clever, modern woman, had felt the relentless snare thongs of captors. Ugly Girl, after this, had not looked at her. She would look past her, not seeing her. This infuriated Hamilton. "Sow!" said Hamilton to Ugly Girl, in the language of the Men. Ugly Girl did not look at her, nor seem to listen. What would they want with her, Hamilton asked herself. She was angry that they even kept Ugly Girl with them, as though she might be human. She was bound as might have been a human female! Did the Weasel People intend this as a humiliation, an insult, to the women of the Men, their new slaves? Hamilton was furious.

Nine females of the men had been caught, Cloud and Antelope; Butterfly and Flower; Ugly Girl; Turtle; a pregnant female, whose name was Feather; and two others, who had been slow of foot, Squirrel and Awl. Several others had escaped. Some had not been at the shelters at the time of the attack. Some had scattered and fled successfully. Nurse, and one other, Hamilton knew, had fled over the roof of the cliffs and escaped down the other side. Short Leg had not been caught. Old Woman had been thrown down the side of the cliff. Hamilton did not know if she had lived or not. The children had broken and run and the men, intent on adult females, had not pursued them. She had seen one child struck at and bloodied before the shelters. She did not know if he had survived or not.

For a time Hamilton had hoped that they would be trailed by the men, and recaptured. But, day by day, her hopes had diminished. The first night there had been a heavy rain, after which Gunther, who seemed to lead these men, turned his trail to the side. If the Men followed the trail to the rain, they would have no way of knowing, after the rain, that it had been diverted. They would follow a line which, in effect, would, after a time, have been erased. It would be rational to suppose that the line, even though erased, would have continued in the same direction. Gunther's cunning had foreseen this reasoning, and he had diverted their trek. The Weasel People had been thorough. The hands of the female prisoners, who were herded in throat coffle, were thonged, usually to the burdens they bore. Hamilton's hands had been tied at the sides of the squarish bundle of furs which she had been forced to carry in the common manner of primitive women, balanced on her head. Ugly Girl's hands, differently, had been tied together before her body and fastened, by two loops, at her belly. On her back was tied a heavy sack of flint, loot from the shelters. She had walked almost bent over, her thighs red from switching. One of the men of the Weasel People, other than those who were the rear guard of the march, followed the coffle line, to see that no girl attempted to leave a trail. Another, following him, with a branch, with leaves, had obliterated footprints. On the second night of the march it had again rained, and Gunther had, again, altered the course of the march. The minds of primitives, even those of the Men, Hamilton knew, could not follow the trail, concealed by one of great experience, a master. Hamilton hated Gunther, but she could not but respect him. William had not been with the attacking party. Even at the shelters of the Men he had seemed to exert little influence over Gunther. Gunther was in his element, leading men. With his rifle he was a captain, a hero, king in this savage world. Hamilton had seen Cloud, bound, groveling at his feet in terror. Gunther had scarcely looked at her. He would make her wait. He was, she knew, saving her for later, for his leisure. At night the women of the Men, alternately, the head of one to the feet of the next, had been, thrown from their feet, and bound, wrists behind their backs, and the neck and ankles of each tied to the ankles and neck of the next, each girl, thus, besides her wrists, being twice secured, once by ankles, once by throat. Hamilton had hoped, the first night, to attack with her teeth the bonds of the girl next to her. Then she, and the others, as they were on the following nights as well, had been gagged. Escape was impossible. Primitive thongs, tightly knotted, did not slip. In the morning the girls had been released, jerked to their feet, their spoor covered with dirt, and put again in coffle. On the fourth morning, the men of the Weasel People, herding the coffle, came to a river. Here, to the dismay of the females, there were four rafts, already built and concealed, waiting. The captives, bound hand and foot, and the loot, were placed on the rough, vine-thonged logs. With long poles these rafts were then thrust out into the current. Before she had been thonged hand and foot, and thrown to the rafts, Ugly Girl, doubtless in misery and fear, had soiled herself. Hamilton had been disgusted. Ever since Ugly Girl had attempted to rescue her on the cliffs, and she had not reciprocated, but fled, Hamilton had hated Ugly Girl. See, had thought Hamilton to herself, how simple, how stupid, how repulsive she is! She has even soiled herself! She shuddered in repulsion. To be coffled with such an animal, as though she might, too, have been human, as though she might have been of the same sort as she, was found by Hamilton to be degrading, humiliating. It insulted all the women of the Men, perhaps Hamilton most of all, for she retained something of the refined sensibilities of a modern woman.

Hamilton sat with her back against the stone, bound, imprisoned with the others. She looked up, through the grille of branches, to the roof of thatch some feet above it. Hamilton was less fastidious now than she had been.

She looked across to Ugly Girl. Ugly Girl had again, to Hamilton's contempt, when the rafts had landed, on the other side of the river, perhaps two hundred miles from where they had entered upon the river, soiled herself. She recalled how irritated, how scornful, she had been.

But now she thought less of such matters. She tried again to free the wrists bound behind her back, weakly. The women of the Men, bound, had now been long in the cell. Even she, Hamilton, had been unable to help herself. She looked up again at the grille. She hated the men of the Weasel People!

"How long will you keep us here?" she cried out in anger, looking to the grille.

The other women looked at her in puzzlement. Hamilton heard a girl's laugh from above. Since they had been placed in the cell, they had seen, once, only two girls, looking down upon them: one had been fair complexioned with long, bright red hair, the other had been dark-eyed, dark-haired, short. Both had worn hide tunics, concealing their breasts. It was now these two again who, hearing Hamilton's cry, looked again down on them. They did so furtively, and Hamilton knew that it must be that they were forbidden to do so. The red-haired girl looked down, contemptuously. She hissed something in anger down at them, and, with a switch, sharply, struck twice one of the branches of the grille. Hamilton winced, as though she might have been struck.

"You will have us all beaten," whispered Flower to her. "Be silent!"

Hamilton heard a man's voice warn the girls above away from the grille and, giggling, they quickly fled away.

"Will they beat me?" asked Butterfly of Hamilton.

"If the men permit it," said Hamilton. She could well remember how it had been when she had been only a stranger, a mere captured female brought to the camp of the Men by Tree. Could not Butterfly remember? She, Butterfly, though then fed with the children, had been cruel to her. Did she now expect to be treated differently?

"Lift your body to the men," said Hamilton to Butterfly. "If you please them enough they may protect you sometimes from the women."

Butterfly looked in anguish at Flower.

"Turtle is right," said Flower. "We have no choice," said Flower. "We are only females." Then she looked at Hamilton. "I will please them most," she said.

"Perhaps," said Hamilton. "Perhaps not."

Hamilton then closed her eyes again and leaned back against the stone. She wondered if Old Woman was dead. She had seen her thrown, tumbling and sprawling, down the slope of the cliff to the clearing below. Tears came to Hamilton's eyes. In her own attempt to escape, Hamilton, instinctively, had fled to the cave entrance which led, by various passages, to the cave of the Men, the cave of the drawings. It was the deepest, most hidden cave in the cliffs, and she had wished to hide there. In the darkness she had taken a wrong turning. She had stumbled into another tunnel, one of several side tunnels, one in which she had soon been trapped. But Hamilton, a quarter of an hour after her capture, bruised and aching, half in shock, scarcely able to walk, wrists bound, on a leather neck tether, had been dragged into the cave of the Men, behind captors. They had found it. She watched while, with rocks, and spear points, reaching high places, they systematically defaced the walls, scraping away the glories which Drawer, years before had placed there. Then she was dragged after them. Perhaps they wished to injure or impair the magic of the Men. Perhaps, in their hatred, they wished only to destroy what was beautiful. But when they left the antelope, the bison, the lions, were gone. Even the hands, reaching for what Hamilton did not know, nor even Old Woman, were scraped away.

In the cell, Hamilton wept. Had she not led the men into the cave they might not have found the drawings. Hamilton wondered if it would be better if Old Woman were dead, that she never learn what had been done in the cave of the Men, what had befallen the work of Drawer, one for whom she had once cared, one whose works, remaining behind him, she had treasured. The antelope, the bison, the wolves, the lions, were gone. Drawer was dead. And there was left only the rock.

The grille was thrust back. Hamilton, startled, looked up. The bearded fellow, he who seemed to be a leader, stood above. He shouted down, pointing. In his hand he held loops of rawhide rope. Hamilton shrank back, but he was not pointing to her.

Flower, unsteadily, frightened, rose to her feet. She looked up. A loop of the rope was dropped about her body. It tightened. She was drawn, easily, hand over hand, from the pit. When she was on her feet, standing near the top edge of the pit, the rope was removed from her body. Hamilton saw another man take her by the hair, bending her over, and pull her away. Then the bearded man was again scrutinizing them. He looked from one to another, intent, apparently, on recognizing one among them. He looked at Hamilton. Then he pointed. Hamilton almost fainted. But it was not she at whom he pointed. Cloud, terrified, trembling, stood up, half crouching down. Then the rope dropped about her and tightened, and she, like Flower, was drawn upward. At the top of the pit, when she was standing on the surface, the rope was removed from her body and she, too, like Flower, bent over, her hair in the hand of a captor, was

dragged away. The bearded man then again regarded the
women in the pit. They shrank back. Then the grille was
replaced.

An hour later a leather bucket, on a rope, was lowered
through the grille. It contained water. The women looked at
one another. Then they fought, on their knees, hands tied
behind them, biting, shouldering, to thrust their face into
the water. Hamilton drank first. Water spilled. She heard the
laughter of girls above, and saw the red-haired girl, and
the dark-haired one, watching. They called out to the prisoners, laughing, and jeering them in the speech of the Weasel
People. Only Ugly Girl, who was not even of the women of
the Men, did not participate in the struggle for the water.
She waited and, after the others had satisfied themselves,
after Butterfly, drank. The bucket, emptied, its hide collapsed, to the laughter of the two girls, was jerked upward.
The women of the Men, angrily, regarded one another.
Then two handfuls of roots and apples were flung to them.
Again the women fought. Antelope cried out shrilly. Hamilton kicked at her viciously, then fell, and, squirming, tried
to get her teeth on an apple. She had pinned it against the
side of the cell when, from behind her, Squirrel bit her in
the left calf and she cried out with pain, jerking, losing the
fruit. Squirrel was on it, scrambling, in an instant, trying to
hold it. Hamilton bit at her shoulder, shrieking. Then Antelope kicked at Hamilton and Hamilton, unable to protect herself, caught Antelope's heel in her stomach. Hamilton reeled,
unable to breathe, against the wall, and slid down its side to
the floor. She lay there in misery. The thought struck her
that had there been a man present there would have been
no fighting. He would have eaten first, and then he would
have set them the order in which they would feed. Why are
we doing this, Hamilton asked herself. We are females, she
thought. There is no man to impose order on us. When she
could, she crawled to a piece of root and bit it, eating it.
She saw that Ugly Girl, crouching, teeth bared, was protecting the pregnant girl behind her. She had found her an apple
and two roots, and stood between her and the others.
Hamilton eyed the food. Ugly Girl snarled at her. Hamilton
clenched her fists, bound behind her back. If one of the girls
had had the use of her hands, she would have been undis-
puted queen in the cell. Ugly Girl snarled again. "I do not
want her food," said Hamilton, backing away. Hamilton sat
back against the wall again. Strange, she thought, that Ugly
Girl, not even of the women of the Men, keeps the law of

Spear, that pregnant women are to be protected and fed. Hamilton did not know, of course, but that, too, was a law of the Ugly People. Ugly Girl, perhaps in her simplicity, did not distinguish in the matter of this law whether one was of the Ugly People, or of the Men, or perhaps even of the Weasel People. The pregnant woman must be protected and fed. It did not matter to Ugly Girl, in her simplicity, of what people the woman might be. That the woman was vulnerable, that she needed help, that there stirred in her belly the beauty of life meant all that needed to be meant to Ugly Girl. Ugly Girl could not speak the language of the Men; she could not even form its sounds; but she stood between the pregnant girl, one of the women of the Men, and the others, her teeth bared.

"We will not take her food," said Antelope.

"No," said Hamilton.

The next day the grille was again thrust back. Again the bearded man loomed at the top of the pit, looking into it, again the rawhide rope looped in his right hand.

He looked from face to face. Then he pointed to one of the women.

"Stand up," said Antelope.

"No!" cried Hamilton, shrinking back.

"Get up, you fool!" said Antelope.

Hamilton looked up. The man gestured to her, roughly. Terrified, scarcely able to stand, she rose to her feet.

She had wanted desperately to be free of the pit, its filth, its stone, its confinement, its crowding, the struggles, bound, humiliating and vicious, for a mouthful of water, a scrap of food. But now she wanted only to shrink back, to stay in its protection, to remain with the other women, even Ugly Girl. Why did they not take Antelope? She looked up, agonized. It was she, Hamilton, only Hamilton, who had been singled out.

She felt the rope drop about her.

"Perhaps they will eat her?" said Butterfly. "Perhaps Flower and Cloud have already been eaten!"

Hamilton tried to jerk away, but she only tightened the rope. It was now about her waist. Terrified she turned and tried to run but the rope, tight in her flesh, stopped her. She pulled against it; it burned in her belly. She turned and, looking up, faced the man. The man was not pleased. The rope was taut. She tried to back away. But his eyes stopped her. Then, angrily, he jerked her toward him. She spun, stumbled, and then, her feet off the ground, swung, striking, hard, with her shoulder, the wall of stone. Swiftly, her burden nothing to his strength, he drew her from the pit. At the surface he threw her to his feet and, removing the rope from about her body, knotted it about her neck, making of it a tether. The two girls of the Weasel People, whom she had seen before, were standing near, apparently waiting to take charge of her. The shorter one took up the free end of the tether. The girl with the bright red hair held a switch. She struck Hamilton once with it. Hamilton scrambled to her feet. She felt a jerk on the tether and, stumbling, followed the shorter girl. The red-haired girl, following them, struck her twice more, to hurry her. Hamilton heard the bearded man replacing the grille. He was apparently no longer concerned with her. She was only a slave. The free women could handle her.

Hamilton found that the cylindrical pit, covered with the roof of thatch, on poles, was at the edge of a clearing, which lay before some caves.

Some of the Weasel People were about. Some of the men, who had not been in the raiding party, as she was dragged past them, looked up, swiftly considering her body, their eyes speculating on the pleasure that it, leaping to their touch, helpless in its slavery, might yield them. Women glared at her, their eyes stern and dour. One of them spit at her as she was dragged past. The red-haired girl struck her twice more with the switch.

Hamilton was dragged up a sloping stone ramp. On a ledge at its height, before the most imposing of the cave entrances, more than ten feet in height and width, was a block of stone, a throne. On this throne, a fur cape, from a cave bear, tied about his neck, grinning, his rifle across his knees, sat Gunther.

"Good afternoon, Doctor Hamilton," said Gunther.

"Gunther," she wept.

"Kneel, Slave," said he.

She knelt before him. "Yes, Master," she said. They spoke in English. The short girl stood near her, the tether gripped in her right hand, its free length looped, coiled several times, in the same hand.

At Gunther's feet, naked, lay Cloud. Loops of rawhide, knotted, were fastened on her neck, as a collar. Behind Gunther and to his left, on another block of stone, sat William. Flower knelt beside him, on his left. She had been given a hide tunic, of the sort worn by the women of the

Weasel People. It was brief; but it concealed her breasts. About her neck, too, were loops of rawhide, knotted, forming on her, as on Cloud, a collar. But, too, with them, about her neck, was a necklace of shells, and, too, about her left ankle was an anklet, it, too, of shells. Gunther and William had taken Cloud and Flower as their personal slaves.

"Where were your hunters?" asked Gunther.

"My hands," said Hamilton. "I cannot feel them. Please, Gunther. I beg of you to untie me."

"We did not meet your hunters," said Gunther.

Hamilton put her head down.

Gunther slapped the rifle which lay across his knees. "It is fortunate for them," said he, "we did not meet them, else they would have fallen swiftly to my bullets."

Hamilton lifted her head. "Had you seen them," she said.

"The Weasel People," said Gunther, "eat human flesh. If you do not please me, I will feed you to them."

"I will try to please you, Gunther," said Hamilton. "I will! I will!"

Gunther laughed. "But I have other plans for you," he said.

Hamilton regarded him, puzzled.

"Do you not notice," asked Gunther, "that the rock upon which I sit is of shaped stone, and, so, too, is that on which William has his place?"

Hamilton said nothing.

"Did you not notice," asked Gunther, "that the pit in which you were confined was formed of shaped stone?"

"Yes," she whispered.

"And what then did you infer?" he asked.

"I did not understand it," she whispered.

"Did you not see in its bottom tiny grains?" he asked.

"Yes," she said.

"And what did you make of them?" he grinned.

"Nothing," she whispered.

"Females, even bright ones like yourself," said Gunther, "are fools, fit only to be slaves."

Hamilton was suddenly conscious of the tether on her neck, that she knelt, that she was stripped, that her wrists were confined helplessly.

"But it is impossible," she whispered.

"Believe the evidence of your senses, little fool," said he. "The pit in which you were confined is a storage pit, used for the keeping of barley. The stones were shaped with saws and axes of bronze."

"It cannot be," she said. She had seen no tools or weapons of metal among the Weasel People, no evidence of agriculture. "Are we not exiled in the early Aurignacian Period," she asked, "sometime during the late Pleistocene?"

"Herjellsen's assertions, and the cultural and geological evidence," said Gunther, "confirm that hypothesis."

"Then, how?" breathed Hamilton.

"The discovery of metal, its utility, the discovery of food grains, their cultivation," said Gunther, "I conjecture took place many times, perhaps hundreds of times, independently, perhaps centuries ago, perhaps again millenia in the future, given our current spatio-temporal coordinates. Such discoveries, by rational creatures, given an order of social organization, a tradition, would presumably be made many times."

"But there is no evidence of such developments in this period," said Hamilton. "Not even polished rock is known to the Men, nor, it seems, to the Weasel People."

"Human groups are isolated," said Gunther.

"But why would there be no evidence of such developments in this period?"

"The groups," said Gunther, unpleasantly, "are small." He grinned. "We may surmise they will not survive."

Hamilton shuddered.

She supposed that it might be true that such developments as agriculture, before they became broadspread and irreversible, might have had tiny beginnings, perhaps over and over again failing, or being obliterated by fiercer peoples. Perhaps it would be only with the cultivation of the broader, lengthy river valleys, the Yangtze, the Tigris and Euphrates, the Nile, with their capacity for supporting gigantic populations, that agriculture, and agricultural peoples, would have the numbers and power to become the dominant mode of humanity. For long millenia they might have remained the prey of hungry hunters, raiding from the hills and forests.

"I know of only one such group within trekking distance," said Gunther. "In the language of the Weasel People, they are called the Dirt People. From them, from time to time, a bronze tool is purchased with fur, or supplies of barley. The Dirt People, incidentally, you will be interested to learn, herd sheep, though you are not familiar with the variety. They weave. They clothe themselves in wool."

"They are quite advanced," said Hamilton.

Gunther laughed unpleasantly.

Hamilton looked at Flower. She knelt beside William,

smug. Cloud, lying at Gunther's feet, would not meet her eyes.

"I am King here," said Gunther.

"How many bullets do you have left?" asked Hamilton.

"Enough to keep me King," said Gunther.

"And I," asked Hamilton, gazing evenly at Gunther, "am I to be your queen?"

Gunther spoke abruptly. The girl with the bright red hair, behind Hamilton, suddenly began to strike her, viciously, with the supple switch. Hamilton cried out and fell, twisting, turning, struck across the belly, the legs, the back, by the switch, held by the short tether in the hand of the short, dark-haired girl. "Forgive the insolence of a slave, Master!" wept Hamilton. Gunther made a swift motion, and the beating stopped. Half choking, Hamilton was dragged again to her knees. She could scarcely see Gunther for the tears; she gasped for breath; her slave body, stung and ravaged by the switch, held in its tether, burning, shook with the misery of the sharp discipline which had been inflicted upon it.

"Perhaps," said Gunther, "I should have so proud a girl as you eaten."

"I am not proud, Gunther," whe whispered, "my master. I will do whatever you wish."

"Eagerly?" asked Gunther.

"Yes, Master," she whispered, "—eagerly!"

"Cut her hands free," said Gunther to William. William rose and went to Hamilton, cutting the thongs which confined her wrists.

Her hands were white; in the wrists were deep, circular marks, the imprint of her former constraints.

"Stand up," said Gunther.

Hamilton did so. Gunther then spoke to the red-haired girl. He then turned to Hamilton. "Tonight," he said, "you will eat well. Tomorrow you will be washed and combed, and again fed well."

"What are you going to do with me?" she asked.

"Tomorrow, Brenda," said he, grinning, "you must look your best."

"What are you going to do with me?" she asked.

"I am going to use you in my plans," he said.

"What are you going to do with me!" she cried.

He looked at her for a time. Then he said, "I am going to sell you, Brenda."

She looked at him with horror, and then she felt the pull of the neck tether.

◈ 24 ◈

The hands of the man in the woolen tunic were on her breasts, roughly. He was pleased.

"Be docile, pretty little beast," said Gunther.

Hamilton felt another man feeling her legs, from behind. He grunted affirmatively.

"Suck in your belly," said Gunther. "Stand straight."

Hamilton did so. She felt a hand slap her belly, twice. She felt the man behind her testing the sweetness, the firmness of her buttocks.

"Stand straight," said Gunther. Tears in her eyes, Hamilton did so. She felt her upper arms held and released, and again held and released. Another man held out her hair, which was now quite long, in his two hands, to the light, examining it for condition and sheen. She felt, from behind, her legs, one after the other, bent up and backward, as the arch of her instep was noted.

Hamilton wore no clothing, but there was a tether on her throat. She stood on a large, flat, wooden platform. Other men, in woolen tunics, stood about, watching the appraisal of the slave girl. Four men of the Weasel People, too, were about. The large, bearded fellow was he who held her tether. She had worn, in the march, and upon the platform, at first, one of the hide tunics of the women of the Weasel People, concealing her breasts. Gunther had first torn it to her waist, before stripping it totally away from her. Ugly Girl, naked, a leather tether on her neck, in the hands of one of the men of the Weasel People, crouched to one side on the platform. She had not been clothed from the beginning.

"It is my intention," Gunther had told Hamilton, "to sell the monster, too, with you. Her presence on the platform will dramatically accentuate your beauty, my dear. It will make you seem twice as desirable, twice as beautiful."

The man who had felt Hamilton's breasts now thrust back her head and, roughly, with his fingers, pried her mouth widely open, inspecting her teeth. To one side, below the platform, Hamilton heard the bleating of a sheep. It was a large animal, long-haired, with soft wool beneath; its horns were spiraled, and yellowish in color. The platform was within a palisaded wall; there were several huts, too, some of them open, within the wall. Some children, too, idly, watched the men appraise her; in the background, before two looms, four women, too, in woolen tunics, had turned about to watch. One girl, a saucy, impudent, bright-eyed girl, perhaps seventeen years of age, with bare arms, and a copper armlet on her left arm, came to the edge of the platform. One of the women called angrily to her, and she, angrily, turned about and went back to stand with them, by the looms. Before she left, she made a face at Hamilton.

The man who had forced open the female animal's mouth, to check its teeth, now stood back from her, sizing her up. Then he walked about her. Then he stood close to her, before her, and put his heavy hands on the sides of her waist, holding her. His eyes met hers. She looked quickly down. His eyes were those of a free man. Hers were those only of a female slave. "Look into his eyes quickly, deferentially," said Gunther. "Then smile, and look down."

"Gunther," wept Hamilton.

"Do so," said Gunther.

Hamilton looked up, into the eyes of the man in the woolen tunic. Indeed she did so deferentially, frightened, for she was slave, and he free.

"Smile, Animal," said Gunther.

Hamilton smiled, then sobbed and thrust her head down.

She felt the power of his hands, gripping her waist. He laughed mightily, and shook her, then released her.

Gunther was grinning. "Kneel," he said to her, casually, as an aside.

She knelt on the wooden platform, sick, her head down. The tether was still on her neck. The man who had held it, at the indication of one of the men in woolen tunics, thrust its free end through a small circular hole in the platform; beneath the surface of the platform a child tied it about a piece of wood, not large, but too large to be drawn upward through the hole in the platform. The men, and the child, withdrew. No one looked at her. She had been assessed; she would now be bargained for. She recalled Gunther's words, "I am going to sell you, Brenda." How far away then seemed her world, her time, her friends, her education, her degrees, her aptitudes, her former experiences; she recalled, idly, her

apartment, buying a newspaper in Pasadena, noting the
mountains, the low, earth-colored, Spanish-style buildings of
the California Institute of Technology, her classes and semi-
nars, the oral examination on her dissertation for the Ph.D.
degree, the men coming up to her, shaking her hand, congratulating her. She had worn a light, white pantsuit, with
Oxford shirt, buttoned, with tie. "I am being sold," she
thought. "I am being sold!"

She looked wildly about. It seemed impossible, unreal,
but it was as real as the leather on her neck. The gate to the
palisade was shut. Ugly Girl, tethered, too, hands bound,
crouched at the corner of the platform; the line about her
neck fell to the boards, lay across them, and then disappeared
over the edge; beneath the boards, ascending again, it was
tied, high, about one of the legs of the structure; both girls,
Ugly Girl at the edge of the platform, Hamilton near its center, were alone. Hamilton closed her eyes. "I must wake up,"
thought Hamilton, wildly. "I must wake up!" The heat and
light of the clearing in the camp of the Dirt People was re-
fulgent, red and warm, through her gritted eyelids. She could
feel sweat beneath her armpits and between her thighs. The
sun was hot, beating down, burning on her back. Beneath
her knees and the tops of her toes, as she knelt, she felt the
rough, splintery surface of the heavy boards of the platform.
The tether, tight, which could not be slipped, close on her,
making her neck feel hot, broken out, she tried to reject.
She tried, too, to reject that she was naked, that the deliciousness of her beauty, so curved, so soft and delicate, so
vulnerable and helpless, which for no reason she clearly understood, but frightened her, so excited men, that drove
them to lust for her and desire her, and wish to own her, was
now, so against her will, so publicly exposed for their gaze
and pleasure. She tried, by sheer force of will, to thrust herself into another reality. She smiled to herself. She laughed.
"I must wake up," she thought. A warm wind, slow-moving,
carrying dust, stirred by the feet of those in the clearing,
moved across the platform. She felt it, fully, on the surfaces
of her body, warm, moving, granular. It was a not unpleasant sensation. She recalled that at one time she would
have been scandalized to have been naked out of doors. She
now had little choice. She was slave. Then she breathed in
some of the dust. It was not pleasant. Her mouth felt dry.
She did not open her eyes; she felt the particles against her
eyelids. "This is impossible," she whispered. "I must wake up!
I must wake up!" She tried to thrust herself into an alterna-

tive reality. The men were coming up to her. Her defense of her dissertation had been professional, and crisp. They would shake her hand, congratulating her. She wore a light, white pantsuit, with blue-pastel Oxford shirt, buttoned, with a yellow tie. The slave was jerked to her feet on the platform. A hand, hot, swift, heavy, exploded at the side of her mouth; she tasted blood, felt it running about her tongue and between her teeth; she looked into Gunther's face; he was grinning; "Wake up," said he, "pretty little bitch."

"Tell me it's not real, Gunther!" she wept.

"You have been sold," he said.

"Gunther!" she wept.

"Sold," he said.

The end of the tether was freed from the wood beneath the platform and the free end drawn through the small circular hole in the floor of the platform, and taken in the hand of one of the men in a woolen tunic. She felt the tether jerk her toward the edge of the platform. She stopped, the tether taut, and turned to regard Gunther. "Please, Gunther," she wept.

"You brought eight sacks of barley," he said, "and a bronze ax."

She looked at him, aghast. She now knew the measure of her value in the rude economy of the Dirt People. Eight sacks of barley and a bronze ax was the barter equivalent of Dr. Brenda Hamilton, stripped. She now knew that women, though they might be urgently sought, and desperately desired, when the needs of men were upon them, were not, on the whole, considered particularly valuable. She was not worth much. She was a female. She doubted that she would have brought two bronze axes.

"The monster," said Gunther, nodding toward Ugly Girl, "brought far less."

She saw Ugly Girl being jerked from the platform, and being dragged away. She felt a jerk on her own neck tether. There were tears in Hamilton's eyes. "Don't leave me here in this place, Gunther," wept Hamilton. "I beg you!" She flung herself to her knees wildly, weeping, and pressed her lips to his boots. She held his ankle, her small fingers about the dusty leather of his boots. "You have been sold," he told her. Then she was dragged away, hauled stumbling to her feet by the neck tether and, choking, pulled from the platform and conducted between the huts.

"I have been sold!" she cried out, in misery. Then she screamed when she saw where they were going to put her.

◈ 25 ◈

For eleven days Brenda Hamilton had been owned by the Dirt People.

It was now late at night, almost toward morning, after a night of a full moon. The insects were quiet. The birds, which began to cry at dawn were not yet active. The wooden plug, which had been forced into her, and secured by thongs, irritated her. Ugly Girl, who slept near her, had been similarly humiliated. In the darkness Hamilton put forth her hand, and felt, some six inches from her face, the logs of the kennel. It was a yard high and a yard wide, and some twenty feet long. The floor was also of logs, smoothed at the top, but separated by some four inches, giving access to the dirt. The logs were fastened in place by mortise and tenon joints, fitting over stakes first driven into the ground. The mortise was not open to the inside of the kennel. Hamilton and Ugly Girl could not lift the logs from the tenons, as the logs, in addition to their weight, projecting, were anchored under the front and rear of the kennel. The floor of the kennel was, thus, formed of bars of wood, in between which lay dirt. Over the dirt was thrown a straw of barley stalks. Ugly Girl and Hamilton shared the kennel with four ewes, the other sheep being penned outside. The ewes were pregnant and were penned at night. The kennel, when not secured, opened into the general sheep pen.

Hamilton was curious that the insects were now quiet. She could tell by Ugly Girl's breathing, that the simple creature was not asleep. She did not, however, speak to her. One could not, even though Ugly Girl understood some of the language of the Men, easily communicate with her. She could not even form the sounds of the language of the men. She was stupid.

Hamilton turned on her back, dry eyed. The wooden plug hurt her. She clenched her fists in the darkness.

On the first night, after she had been, in the afternoon,

locked with Ugly Girl in the kennel, she had heard the heavy door of the kennel being unfastened. She had crouched within. Then she had been ordered out. She had crawled out on her hands and knees, to be seized by the hair by a reeling farmer and dragged after him to the drinking hut. The Dirt People, from barley, half crushed and germinated, made a simple bread. This they cut into small pieces, and soaked in water. The process of fermentation was initiated by air-borne yeasts. It took only twenty-four hours to make a brew. Sometimes they strained it through cloth; at other times they drank the fermented mash, thick with barley hulls soaked loose from the crude bread. Hamilton was startled. She had not realized the immediacy, the simplicity, the naturalness of the relation between grain and beer; yet they were almost as naturally consanguine as the stone hammer and the flint knife, and as expectable; bread and beer lay at the foundation of the agricultural revolution; perhaps it was only beer, Hamilton thought, that tempted men to give up the hunt, that lured them to the slavery of the soil; or, more likely, it, the alcohol, was the drug which kept them in their fields, which broke them and tamed them, in the deliriums of which they could, in sorrow and mock hilarity, drown the dreams of freedom and the pursuit of game. He who worked bent in the dirt, poking at the soil, under the sun, his body aching, might, at night, lose himself in drunken stupor, forgetting the heritage of the hunt, keeping him in the village another night, to waken again to the dirt, the stones and seed, the beating sun, and the sticks with which he scratched at the earth. She wondered if it were not for the alcohol men might have gone mad or fled. It gave them the narcotic wherewith to endure their lot.

Hamilton well remembered, and bitterly, the night in the drinking hut.

The Dirt People were not hunters, she soon learned, though they might be but a few generations separated from the game trails. They did not look at her as did Hunters, even those of the Weasel People. Their looks frightened her, but not as did the looks of hunters. They seemed small, avaricious, venal. They even seemed, leering at her beauty, furtive. It seemed they might be afraid of something. When a hunter had looked upon her as a mere female, it had terrified and excited her. Even when she had drawn back, trembling, from a hunter she had felt the tension, the delicate erecting, the lifting, of her tiny clitoris, against her will offering itself, and herself, to his mastery. But here she did not feel the tension, or the sudden, frightened suffusion of warmth throughout her belly, the smaller body's spontaneous readying of itself for penetration, for submission to a dominant animal. She only felt cold and miserable. She looked at them, from face to face. She suddenly understood, sick, that they were about to do something secretive, something sly. She understood, suddenly, that her beauty was something which, for some reason, was forbidden them. She tried to run for the entrance of the hut, but was caught and thrown back to the center of the men. Some of them laughed. Their eyes glistened. Before a hunter she had felt a helpless doe before a lion, who in his innocent might, his innocent cruelty, ferocity and joy, would wreak devastation upon her, overwhelming her, devouring her, until, helpless, she begged for mercy, crying herself his. But before these men, somehow so different, her fear was not that with which she might have faced a hunter, even one of the Weasel People. It was the fear with which she might, naked, kneeling back against a wall in a dungeon, hands apart, chained to it, have observed the timid, then bolder, approach of rodents. One of the men seized her. Then, as they drank and watched, she was handed from man to man. They made jokes about her as she was penetrated. They hurt her, for she did not desire them. They were quick, and brutal. She was a receptacle only, unwilling, miserable, into which they swiftly emptied the pleasure of their bodies. When she lay, looking into his eyes, her arms held, in the hands of the leader, he only then finished with her, there was, suddenly, a great shout. She was thrown to one side. He scrambled to his feet, frightened, trying to pull his garment about him.

In the entrance to the hut there stood a terrible figure. Hamilton, her hand flung before her mouth, screamed. In the figure's right fist was a handful of sprigs, with red berries. The metal face, horned, feathered, painted, striped, with yellow and purple, regarded her. In the figure's left hand was a yellow stick, surmounted by a skull. He was very tall, and naked, gaunt and bony, save for a cord and strip of cloth. Through the slits in the bronze face, of hammered metal, the eyes looked upon her, in fury. On the cheeks of the horned bronze, engraved in the metal, were mystic signs. The figure's body, too, was covered with such signs, tokens heavy with magic, yellow and purple, tatooed into the skin in patient, agonizing rites, the results of deliberately inflicted wounds, kept open, methodically contaminated over a period of weeks with colored earths. About his neck was a string from which

hung small bags of herbs; to the same string, pendant, some
four inches in width, hung a round disk of hammered
bronze; on this disk was the representation of a personage,
one bearded and of dreadful mien, many times the size of
life, sitting on a great seat, handing a stalk of barley to a
tiny man, reaching upward to take it. At the cord at his
waist, too, on strings of woven grass, hung the bones of two
hands. These were painted yellow. He uttered a great cry of
wrath. He lifted the yellow stick with the skull high in the
hut. The men, miserable, moaning, unable to look up, fell
back before him. He thrust the handful of sprigs, with red
berries, at Hamilton, and shook it. She was crouching down.
She shrank back, shuddering. The figure turned away from
her and regarded the men. They cringed before him, shrinking small. None met his eyes. Hamilton, the attention of the
figure no longer focused on her, on her hands and knees,
crawled to the side of the hut, and knelt there, leaning sick,
frightened, against the mud and poles. The gaunt figure in
the bronzed mask turned on the men, berating them. They
looked down. The voice of the man in the bronzed mask was
mighty in its denunciation, in its indignation, its outrage, in
its condemnation. Suddenly the leader of the men in the hut,
furtively looking up, blurted out words, and pointed at Hamilton. She looked up to see him pointing at her. The other
men, supporting their leader, blurted their assent to whatever he had said. Hamilton, who did not even understand
the language of the Dirt People, shook her head, negatively.
"No," she said in English, and in the language of the Men.
"No, No!" The tall, gaunt figure turned on her and looked
down upon her. She shrank back against the mud and poles.
"No," she said. "No!" The impassive mask, the eyes cold
behind it, looked down upon her. "No," whispered Hamilton,
and then looked down. The tall figure turned away from her.
He said something, decisive, to the men in the hut, and then
left the structure. None of the men left the hut. The men
looked to one another. They seemed more confident now.
And, too, they looked upon her, angrily. She looked down,
and away. After a short time the tall, gaunt figure returned. No longer did he carry the handful of sprigs or the
stick, surmounted with a skull. He carried, this time, a
wizard stick, yellow, wrapped with cord, with feathers dangling from it. The men formed a circle in the hut, one point
on the circumference of which was occupied by Hamilton,
now ordered to stand, while, within the circle, stood the tall,
gaunt figure. He began to chant, a monotonous, repetitive

chant, which was taken up by the men. Sometimes he closed his eyes; he began to turn and sway; the men, too, in their bodies, reflected the rhythm of the chant; then, within the circle, the gaunt figure, swaying, chanting, began to watch the stick which he held in his hand; so, too, did the men; Hamilton, too, in spite of herself, watched the stick. Then, to her horror, the stick, though it was moved by the tall, gaunt figure, seemed to hesitate and lift itself; obviously he controlled the stick, but, in the manner in which his attention was focused on it, and that of the men, there was almost an illusion that the stick, like a snake, moved of its own accord; the gaunt man, and the others, chanting, watched the stick; it lifted its tufted, feathered end, as though quizzically, and, as though it might have had eyes, or nostrils with which to smell, it seemed to peer at them, or to take their scent; it quivered, alert; it regarded the men, turning slowly about the circle; sometimes it lingered on one; meanwhile the chant continued, sometimes growing more intense, more frenzied, louder, sometimes less intense, more subdued, softer. The stick prowled the circle, like an animal, trying to smell out something; the men, chanting, watched it with apprehension; Hamilton was terrified; twice the stick prowled the circle; twice it passed her; the second time it lingered longer; as the stick neared her the chant became more intense, louder; "No!" she said; then the stick passed her again, and she almost fainted, fearing only that it would, in its circle, return again, pausing before her, marking her out. The stick paused then before the leader of the men in the hut; he could not chant; sweat broke out on his forehead; he was terrified; then, as his knees almost buckled, the stick, as though it had not yet found what it wanted, left him, continuing its circuit; as the stick approached Hamilton this time, the chanting became ever more frenzied, louder; it rang in the hut; "No!" she cried; the stick paused before her, quivering; "No!" she cried; then it passed her, but only a yard or so; the chanting had become less, more subdued; the stick turned back, to again look upon her; "No!" she wept. "No!" The stick stopped before her, quivering. "No!" she cried. The chanting was, now wild, insistent, powerful, overwhelming, irresistible. No longer did the stick quiver. Hamilton looked upon it with horror. It pointed to her.

The tall, gaunt man cried out a single word; the chant stopped; the stick was again only a stick.

Two men seized Hamilton by the arms and, as she wept, head down, dragged her from the hut.

They thrust her into her kennel, with the ewes, the straw and Ugly Girl, and locked her within.

The next morning Hamilton was not permitted to leave the kennel with Ugly Girl for work. She was kept locked within. Throughout the morning, crouching inside, through a crack at the door, she looked out, into the compound. At noon the women came for her; the men were not with them; even the young, dark-haired girl, the beauty of the village, was with them; the younger women, under the direction of the older women, dour, and in cold fury, bound Hamilton's wrists, crossed, above her head to a post; then the women of the village, with bundles of switches, lashed her; then they loosened her from the post and knelt her down; they then shaved her head with a bronze knife; the older women then fitted her with the wooden device, thrusting it deep in her and thonging it tightly in place, tying the knots behind the small of her back; when it was fixed in place one of the older women pointed to it and then, lifting a handful of switches, threatened her; Hamilton was not, under threat of punishment, to remove the device; it was hers to wear; she was then clothed in a long, straight dress of wool; it was sleeveless, but came to her ankles; she was then sent to the fields, under supervision, to dig in the sun; the dress was hers when out of the kennel; she would not wear it within the kennel, lest it be soiled; that evening, as a matter of precaution, on the decision of the older women, one of the wooden devices was also fastened within Ugly Girl; one of the men had been observed looking upon her; Ugly Girl, too, was fitted with one of the long, woolen garments, for use out of the kennel; her head was not shaved, however, nor was she beaten; Ugly Girl did not care for the long garment; it discomfited her muchly, more so than it did Hamilton; Ugly Girl had worn hitherto next to her skin only the soft freedoms of tanned hides and furs; the inhibiting, scratchy, hobbling skirt of the Dirt People, thought fit to conceal the bodies of females, their shames, disgusted her. Hamilton looked at her bloodied, cut head in a bowl of water, and wept; how ugly she was; one of the older women then poked her; that she be up and about her work, that she take her digging stick and go to the fields; the young, saucy girl, with her flow of dark hair, waited to conduct her; Hamilton followed her guide to the fields; she walked with difficulty in the long, tight dress, with small steps, her body sore about the wooden device within her; the men did not look at her as she walked among them; once she passed the tall, gaunt man, now without the bronzed, horned mask; she did not lift her eyes to him; shamed, carrying her digging stick, she went to the fields.

It was now late at night.

Hamilton lay in the kennel, stripped, the wooden device within her.

This morning her head had been again shaved. So, too, had been that of Ugly Girl. But this time the older women had not hurt her. They had only shaved her head.

Hamilton could tell by Ugly Girl's breathing that she was awake, but she did not speak to her. She seldom spoke to Ugly Girl. Ugly Girl was stupid. Hamilton wondered why Ugly Girl was awake. She wondered why the insects had become quiet.

There had been a full moon.

Hamilton, with Ugly Girl, had participated, in their way, in the ceremony. They had stood far back, with the children, holding, like them, two bars of bronze, which, repeatedly, they struck together. The moon had bathed the fields in white light. There had been incantations and chants. In the fields, turning, twisting, leaping, holding up barley shoots to the sky, to the moon, had been the tall, gaunt man. The gaunt man had then cried out a command, his arms lifted. To Hamilton's amazement the villagers had then put aside their clothing and, openly, lying in the furrows of their fields, engaged in sexual congress. While this was occurring, the tall, gaunt man, with great solemnity, had cast barley seed about. Something similar, four days ago, had been done with her. In the sheep pen, before the rams and ewes, under the supervision of the tall, gaunt man, the leader of the Dirt People had stripped her, placed her on her hands and knees, removed the wooden device and used her; it had caused her only pain as she was sore from the wood which had been within her; after he had been finished with her, two of the older women had again reinserted the device, thrusting it in and thonging it more tightly than ever, again knotting it behind the small of her back; they had then made her hold her arms up and had pulled the long, tight garment again over her body; she had then been set to work carrying water. In the ceremony of this night, however, neither she nor Ugly Girl were involved, other than, as the children, in striking the bars together. Only one suitable female of the village, strangely, was not put to her back in the dirt, her face to the moon. That was the young village beauty, the saucy, dark-haired girl. She, white-faced, sat alone on a wooden stool in the fields. No one touched her. She wore white wool. Her hair was combed. A white flower was put in her hair. She seemed frightened.

When the couples rose from the furrows, Hamilton regarded them closely. She saw nothing of the shame, or furtiveness, which she might have expected in them. One older woman suddenly ran to the girl on the stool but, before she could touch her, the tall, gaunt man, with a wave of his arm, warned her away. The older woman began to weep, but a man took her by the arms and pulled her away. The young girl on the stool, so beautiful in the white wool, the flower in her hair, said nothing to the older woman. White-faced, she stared across the barley fields.

When most of the villagers had returned to the compound, Hamilton, Ugly Girl, and the children, had accompanied them. The tall, gaunt man, and certain of the other men of the village, had remained behind in the fields, with the girl in white wool.

Hamilton could not sleep. Ugly Girl, too, for some reason, was not asleep.

Only one of the villagers had been kind to Hamilton, a young man, gangling, little more than an adolescent, with long hair; he was tall, but not powerfully built. While she had worked in the fields he had once brought her water. Another time he had given her a small flower. She smiled. Had he been a hunter, he would have torn the wood from her body and forced her to serve his pleasure. He had given her a flower. He had wanted her to like him. He had tried to please her. He had put himself at her mercy, and she only a shaven-headed, forbidden, shamed slave girl. How naive he had been, so sweet, so foolish. Did he not know that he was a man, and she only a woman? Why did he put himself at her mercy, not her at his? The males of the Dirt People, she conjectured, had forgotten their manhood. It had been mislaid in the ceremonies. The tall, gaunt man, perhaps, had taken it. But she had not wished to hurt the young man. Moreover, she was touched by the sweetness of the gesture. But how could she tell him that she was a woman, and, truly, could love only a man, not a boy in a man's body? She had taken the flower, and had thanked him as she could, nodding her head, and smiling. Too, she had said thank you in English, and expressed gratitude, as well, in the language of the Men, that words might be uttered. He had smiled, reddened, and turned away. She had watched him go. She fixed the flower at the neck of her garment. An older woman, working near her in the field, took the flower from the garment and threw it away.

Ugly Girl made a sudden, soft noise, of warning.

Hamilton tensed. But she heard nothing. Ugly Girl took the scent of the air. Hamilton could imagine her, crouching in the kennel, the nostrils in that wide, flat nose distended, the eyes half shut, concentrating every fiber of her awareness on the still, night air.

Then, after a moment, she heard the sounds of footsteps, soft, furtive, outside.

Then there was the sound of fumbling with the leather that bound the door bolt in place. The door of the kennel swung open. Hamilton could see the poles of the sheep pen, the stars, framed in the small square opening, and, too, silhouetted in the opening, dark, the horns of the painted bronze mask.

She shrank back on the straw. One of the sheep bleated, softly. The man was then quiet, motionless, as though listening. But there was no other sound.

He whispered to her. She did not respond. Then, again, more insistently, more harshly, he repeated himself. She had learned in her days with the Dirt People certain words of their language, simple commands, expressions for common objects, the name by which she was addressed, which expression was also used for a ewe. "Come forth, Ewe," said he. She crept back on the straw. She felt Ugly Girl behind her. The man, his frame filling the doorway, crept forward. She felt his hand close about her ankle. His grip was unusually tight. "Make no sound," he said. He dragged her on her belly from the kennel. Outside the kennel, holding her by the arm, he dragged her to her feet. Holding her, he dragged her to the door of the pen, which he opened, and then closed. She was helpless. Over her shoulder, with a sudden start, she noticed Ugly Girl slipping from the kennel, swiftly, silently. The man thrust her along, stumbling, with him. "Make no sound," he said again to her. His grip, above her elbow, on her left arm, was tight. He took her from the compound, slipping through the gate. The fingers of her left hand began to feel numb. He pulled her toward the barley fields, away from the compound. Soon she knew her screams would not carry to the compound. "Make no sound, Ewe," he told her. Silently, dragged, sometimes losing her footing, she accompanied him. He took his way across the fields. In the center of the fields was a large, rectangular stone. Hamilton had seen it before but had thought little of it. They took their way near this stone. Before it, he stopped. Near the stone was a small wooden stool. On the stone, on her back, arched over it, her arms over her head, bent back, elbows bent, a wrist fastened on each side of the stone, lay the young girl. She was stripped naked. Her ankles were tied widely apart, knees bent, an ankle fastened on each side of the stone. Between her legs, its point facing her, lay a long, bronze knife. The white moonlight streamed down upon her. She struggled, and whimpered. The gaunt man regarded her for a moment, holding Hamilton. Suddenly Hamilton felt sick. The girl, she understood now, for the first time, was being raped by the moon. She was intended as a virgin sacrifice. The girl struggled, and regarded the gaunt man wildly. The bonds held her, easily. Hamilton looked at the knife, and trembled. Doubtless, after the moon's rape, or that of a god, it would not do to return the girl to the village; she would then be different; doubtless she would not then be simply another village woman, to be profaned by the touch of a common digger. In the morning, the moon or god finished with her, Hamilton sensed, the girl, perhaps drugged with beer, would be slain. The knife lay ready. She saw the girl's wild eyes; surely she was not reconciled to her fate; if she had, earlier, had a belief in the moon, or the god, clearly she no longer held that belief; but that did not matter; in the morning all that would matter would be that others held the belief, or pretended to hold it; she might have lost her faith, repudiating it as her heart detected the falsity of its tenets, but it mattered little if others kept theirs, or pretended to; in the morning it would not be the truth that would matter but the bronze knife; truth, Hamilton surmised, was a feeble weapon, compared even to a knife of bronze. What would the truth matter when the gaunt man, with bloody hands, lifted the heart from her body?

The gaunt man, in the mask, turned away from the girl bound in the moonlight, tied over the altar, and pulled Hamilton behind him, making his way across the furrows, to the grass on the other side of the fields.

The girl on the altar was not a despised person, or a lowly one, saving that she was female, and thus fit for sacrifice. She was the prize of the village. Only the most beautiful, the highest born, would be dared to be offered to the moon or the gods.

Hamilton knew, with mixed feelings, that she was safe

from such a fate. She, a despised slave, would not be deemed
fit for such sacrifice.

On the other side of the fields, the gaunt man thrust Hamilton down to her belly in the grass, and then knelt across her
legs. Even if she cried out she was too far from the village
to be heard. She felt the man's fingers fumbling at the
small of her back, in the moonlight undoing the knots. He
did not cut the thongs. She realized then that he would, when
finished, replace the wooden device. It would be as though
nothing had happened. She wondered how often he would
come for her, ordering her from the kennel, in the darkness.
She lay on her belly, her cheek on the grass; she clutched at
the stalks of grass with her small hands; she felt the knots
undone; with his fingers he pulled at the device; she felt it
slip free. He rolled her on her back; she, opened, breasts,
belly, face bared, an exposed slave, looked up at him; he
crouched over her; the moonlight streamed down upon her
slave nudity; the bronze mask, horned, hideously painted,
leaned toward her. She screamed; the body fell forward,
struck with great force, the mask lost in the grass.

Hamilton scrambled to a position half crouching, half
kneeling, her hands on the grass. Then she knelt, aghast,
covering her body as best she could with her hands.

The young man was half crouched down, his hands still
on the handle of the bronze ax, the head of the ax buried in
the skull and brain of the tall, gaunt man.

Then, with his foot, pressing, and pulling upward, he
freed the ax. He stood there, looking at Hamilton.

He was white-faced.

He turned the body on its back. The sightless eyes stared
like glass at the moon. The face, Hamilton saw, was mediocre, but ugly; there was something sly about it; without the
mask, it seemed not so much forbidding and powerful, as
sly and weak, mediocre and vicious. It was the face of a man
who had found a way to live, but not by hunting, not by digging.

Hamilton cried out. Two figures emerged from the darkness. Even in the darkness she knew with what sort of men
they dealt. They had appeared as if from nowhere, lithe,
silent, swift, powerful, menacingly purposive, armed. "Run!"
she cried to the young man. "Run!" The strangers had appeared from downwind. They did not speak. The young man,
so foolish, lifted the ax. "They are men!" she wept. "You are
a boy! Run! Run!" But he was determined to defend her.
"Run!" she cried. "Run!" She watched him struck to his

knees, and then to his belly. He lay, his head broken, in the grass. "No," she wept. She was scarcely conscious of the leather strap being tied about her throat. She saw the head of a weasel tied at the belt of the man who secured her. By the strap, his fist six inches from her neck, half choking, she was jerked to her feet. In the distance, across the barley fields, she saw the sky glowing; the compound was being fired. She could see, here and there, a tiny figure, dark against the flames, running. The two men made their way across the barley fields; Hamilton, given some two feet of leash, was pulled behind them. On the other side of the field, they saw some two or three villagers running, but none successfully fled their pursuers; two, older women, were struck down before they reached the fields; the other, a man, reached the edge of the fields; it was there where, from behind, the ax, with its head of stone, lashed to the yard-long handle, caught him. Another hunter, carrying a torch, came behind them. Another appeared to Hamilton's left, he, too, with a torch. They dipped the torch to the young barley. Hamilton's captors made directly for the stone altar in the center of the field. They had well reconnoitered the area. Their strike had been well planned. The barley now, at two edges of the field, was blazing. Hamilton had little doubt that the Dirt People were encircled, and that the circle, like the strings on a trap, was now, the first strike made, to scatter the villagers and destroy the center of their strength, drawing shut. Hamilton's captors stopped beside the stone altar. They looked down on the girl, on her back, arched across the stone, stripped, tied, on the helpless, virginal delicacies of her body, with the relish of hunters. About them the barley blazed. The girl, bound, looked at them wildly, piteously. Then, to Hamilton's amazement the virgin, the prize of the village, the intended sacrifice, bound on the altar, her eyes imploring, lifted her hips to Hamilton's captors. They regarded her eyes, desperate, the sweet, delicate, supplicatory arch of her body. Her eyes, her body, begged piteously to be freed of the stone; her eyes, her body, begged piteously to be permitted to serve them on any terms which they might please. One of them lifted his stone ax, as though to crush her face against the stone. She writhed, screaming, in the light of the flaming barley; he held the ax poised, and grinned, then lowered it; she almost fainted; then, again, desperately, eyes piteous, whimpering, she lifted her hips, begging, to them. They laughed. Each, in turn, swiftly, brutally, took her. She threw her head back, screaming with agony and elation; she was

jolted viciously, mercilessly, in the bonds; when they had
taken their sport, and blood lay on her thighs and the stone,
her head, and her shoulders, were back, hanging over the
edge of the stone. Flames leapt about the altar. The girl, in
her bonds, looked at them, turning her head piteously;
were they pleased enough with her? To her joy a thong was
knotted about her neck and, with the sacrificial knife, she
was cut free of the altar. She was dragged through the
flaming barley on her tether, beside Hamilton; she laughed
with pleasure; she was alive; she, naked, leather on her
throat, regarded Hamilton, unashamed, her face transfused
with a brazen joy; she again laughed, putting her head back,
screaming with pleasure; she was alive, alive!

The two captors, with their captives, left the flaming
fields, approaching the compound.

A man, in torn woolen tunic, fled toward them. A hunter
seemed to rise from the ground before him. He, with a
sweeping, horizontal blow of his ax, caught the running figure
in the gut; the man stopped, bent over, retching, unable to
move; then the ax fell again, striking him down. A woman's
scream came from the compound. The man who had struck
the running figure walked over to greet the captors. They
spoke, while more screaming came from the burning compound. A sheep, bleating, ran past. The leashes of Hamilton
and the girl cut from the altar were tied together, forming
a single leash with double collar. This the man who had
struck the running figure took in his fist, he subordinate to
the two others, holding it in the center. The three men then
approached the compound, the two captors in the lead, he
who had struck the running man a step behind, holding the
leash of the two female captives, naked.

The stockade, and the huts within, were burning. Almost at
the gate, two more of the Dirt People fled outward. One
was a woman, who was struck down from behind by a
hunter within. She reeled against the palings, the back of her
head bloodied, and stumbled into the darkness and fell. The
second was a man. The first captor tripped him, and he
rolled sprawling in the dirt; as he tried to climb to his feet
the ax of the second captor struck him frontally, and he fell
heavily, forward, into the dirt. Four sheep, bleating in terror,
one with flaming fleece, hurried out of the compound.

Hamilton and the girl, her leash-mate, were dragged within
the compound.

On a stake in the compound was the head of he who had
been the leader of the Dirt People.

The gate was opened, widely. The work of the men of the Weasel People had been easier than they had anticipated for the tall, gaunt man, in taking Hamilton from the compound, had left it open, that he might return silently. Yet this would, Hamilton knew, have made little difference. The men of the Weasel People would have, without great difficulty, scaled the palisade. A loop hurled over a pointed log and a swift climb, feet against the logs, would have brought them to the top, whence they might have leaped down to the dirt within. The palisade was effective against animals; it was not effective against men.

Hamilton turned her head away as she saw an older woman struck to the dirt.

From a hut, half burning, two men of the Weasel People dragged forth a man, throwing him to the dirt before them, then striking him six times with their axes. The flint of the axes of the men of the Weasel People, and their faces, sweaty, exhilarated, glowed in the reflection of the flames. Inside the compound it was almost as light as day, reminding Hamilton of the electric lights of the compound in Rhodesia, where she had been held captive. About the compound. in the dirt, lay several bodies, bloodied, their heads broken open. Before one wall four of the younger women of the Dirt People stood, huddled together; they were separated and thrust back against the wall; their clothing was cut from them; shuddering, they were inspected, closely, and felt; the leader of the Weasel People, the heavily built, bearded man, pointed to two of the women; immediately they were turned about, their hands tied behind their backs, and a rope put on their necks; they were dragged across the compound, to the post at which Hamilton, several days before, had been tied and whipped with switches; they were tied by their necks to this post; the leader turned his back on the other two women, who were not comely; Hamilton and the girl with her screamed with horror; then they turned away. From a storage pit, where she had hidden herself in the barley, another girl, caught in the grain, was forced to climb the ladder to the surface of the compound. She was stripped and bloody; there was grain on her body, stuck to the blood and caught in her hair. The hunter who had found her followed her up the ladder. When she stood on the surface of the compound, she stood before the leader of the Weasel People. Proudly she threw back her head, shaking her hair, unafraid. He said a word and, as she stared angrily ahead, her hands were tied behind her back and then she was thrust, stumbling, to the post, where she, too, was fastened to it by the neck.

Suddenly Hamilton remembered Gunther, in the camp of the Weasel People, remarking to her that he surmised that such groups, so small, so isolated, which had initiated at this early date a form of herding, of agriculture, of metalwork, would not survive. His words, for the first time, now seemed weighty to her, rich with an insidious import she had not at first understood. Why had he brought her here? Why had he sold her to the Dirt People? It had puzzled her, for she had suspected, given the contempt in which he held her, his irritation with her intelligence, his scorn for her vulnerabilities, the profound, desperate needs of her female sexuality, which could turn her into a helpless slave in a man's arms, that he would have kept her for himself, a despised love captive it might have pleased him, from time to time, to abuse and use for his pleasure; surely he would not have soon relinquished his title to the helpless, delicious slave who had once been the prim, reserved, formal, proud Dr. Brenda Hamilton? No, it was his intention to have her back, and he had never intended for the Dirt People to keep her. She had been brought here for another reason, to give him an opportunity to take reconnaissance of the compound of the Dirt People; under the pretext of selling two females he had studied the compound, its men, their numbers, the weapons, the land; oh, it had amused him, doubtless, to sell her as a nude slave, the once proud Dr. Hamilton, but that, pleasing though it might have been to him, had not satisfied the full intention of his plan; her sale had been a pretext, a diversion, to permit himself access to the compound and conduct the inquiries of his espionage. Hamilton knew then that she had been a dupe in the plans of the brilliant Gunther; she wondered if, in the stresses of the temporal translation, in his accession to power among the men of the Weasel People, in his finding himself, with his rifle, almost a god in this wild country, he had gone insane. She recalled the throne on which he had seated himself, the robe of bearskin he had worn about his shoulders. In Rhodesia Gunther had been hard, brilliant, efficient, and, even then his genuis had bordered on the fine line that separates incomparable intellect from madness, but he had been, clearly, sane; here, in this ancient, primitive time and country, she feared he had crossed the border into madness; what had the Dirt People done to him; had he seen fit to ventilate on them his hatred of diggers, his esteem of hunters; she recalled the violence, the force, with which, in Rhodesia

he had once spoken to her of such things; the hunters are
dead, he had said; but perhaps they are not dead, but only
sleeping, he had suggested; perhaps they will come again;
perhaps they will hunt again, he had seemed to feel, building
ships and voyaging to stars, taking up again the hunt, that
which gave meaning to man. But how, wondered Hamilton,
could the hunters waken if they had not slept; one cannot attack the stars with ships of stone, and poles and logs; the
world must change a thousand times before the fleets of steel
ships could be built, before they could be launched for the
systems of distant suns. It would be a contest between the
hearth and the mountains, between barley and the call of
Tau Ceti and Epsilon Eridani, Arcturus and the clouds of
Andromeda. Turn their eyes to the stars, had said Herjellsen,
who was mad, mad. Hamilton could do nothing. And Gunther, she feared, had gone mad, too. It was wrong to kill
the Dirt People. They had not harmed him. The Men would
not have injured them, though they would, in all likelihood,
have avoided them, or, if they wished, taken their stock, or
one or two of their women. The Weasel People, she recalled,
fed on human flesh. She wondered if Gunther, in his hatred
for diggers, had gone insane.

   She looked up, startled. The leader of the Weasel People
was looking upon her and the other girl. Her leash-mate
stood very straight, frightened; she arched her tiny, virginal
breasts toward the bearded beast who looked upon her; she
sucked in her belly, and put her head back; she trembled; he
looked upon her face and figure; she was white and small
before him; he was large and hairy, and darkened by the
sun; would he find her pleasing; if he did not she knew she
would be killed, struck down by the heavy axes; he turned
from her, stopping before Hamilton; he looked closely at her
face, squinting, seeing that it was truly her; he took her by
the head and pulled it down, looking at it, running his hand
over the head; it was still cut and scraped, from the first time
it had been shaved; only this morning had the older women
shaved it again; it had not been their intention to let Hamilton soon forget her shame; furthermore, a vital girl, with
long hair and bared legs, might trouble their men; much less
would they be troubled, or should they be troubled, by a girl
with shaved head, heavily and grossly clad, and kept busy
constantly, kept exhausted and bent with labor, with digging
and the carrying of water. She had had, since the first day,
very little to do with the men. Women had been, constantly,
her merciless supervisors. Often, indeed, even the young girl,

now her leash-mate, had been in charge of her labors. How proud the young girl had been. Now she was stripped and tied by the neck, only a slave girl, naked, trying desperately to stand and display herself in a way that would please the brute who had led the attack on her village. Hamilton's head was released; she straightened; she was sure that, even in spite of her shaved head, she would not be killed; she looked into the leader's eyes. Gunther, she was sure, would have told him to bring her back. The leader, with a grunt, gestured to the man who held the common leash. Hamilton's leash-mate uttered a tiny, joyful cry. They were pulled stumbling to the post. There were three other girls there, each with her hands tied behind her back, each tied by the neck to the post. The man who held Hamilton's leash, that shared by the raped, virginal beauty, did not tie their hands behind them. He forced Hamilton, rather, to walk once completely about the post, stepping over the ropes of the other tethered women; the leash was thus looped about the post; then, pulling the loop out from the post, he forced Hamilton to duck beneath it and then step over it, and draw it tight; then, having used Hamilton's body to tie the loop about the post, he bade them kneel; they did so.

The roof of one of the huts tumbled in, burning. The men of the Weasel People busied themselves gathering the loot of their raid; they sacked barley, gathered bowls, fetched axes and implements of bronze; one of them overturned a vat of sourish beer; another fell to his knees and sniffed at it; Hamilton's heart leaped; there was another vat; but the leader, striking it with his ax, puzzled, broke it open, and it, too, spilled onto the earth, mixing with blood; Hamilton saw the knotted thong on the young girl's throat; she could not see the knot on her own; "Make no sound," said Hamilton, in the language of the Dirt People. The girl looked at her with horror. She shook her head negatively. Hamilton crept to her and began to pick at the knot on her throat. "No," whispered the girl, fearfully, and struck Hamilton away. Hamilton tore at her own knot, but could not see to undo it. The men, with bowls, were now dipping into the broken vat, toward its bottom, below its rupture, from the leader's ax. The leader did not stop them. One of the men spit out the fluid in disgust. The others laughed. Hamilton, desperate, looked at the open gate, and then at the young girl. Then she seized her by the throat, choking her, putting her to her back; the young girl's eyes were wild; "Make no sound," said Hamilton. Then she took her hands from the frightened girl's throat and untied the knot; she then, with the free end, slipped the knot about the post free. The men at the beer laughed. Another had tried it, and swallowed it. He looked puzzled, then smiled. The leader then, gruffly, commanding a bowl, partook. He drank it down, all of it, and grinned. Hamilton slipped from the compound.

◆ 26 ◆

By the Dirt People Hamilton had not been fed well. Too, she had been worked hard and long, ordered from the kennel shortly before dawn, thrust back within it, and locked within it, after dusk. She, and Ugly Girl, who had escaped when the gaunt man had secretly come for her, before the attack of the Weasel People, had been fed on barley cakes and water, and roots pushed through an opening in the kennel gate, after dark, which they had found on the straw and eaten. She had also, when she could, stolen apples. Once, detected, the young, dark-haired girl, now the slave-by-capture of the Weasel People, had, ordering her to remove her long, woolen garment in the brush, beaten her unmercifully with a supple switch. She had not dared to resist, not wanting to die. She had not stolen apples thereafter. She had done her work with the digging stick, and carrying water to the fields, well. But her diet, actually, had not been much different from, or too inferior to, that of the Dirt People themselves. They were less well nourished, at this early stage of agriculture, than the surrounding hunters, whose diet included the fats and concentrated proteins of fresh meat; and were inferior in physical stature to the hunters; and were less self-reliant and were mentally slower than the hunters, and more prone to superstition and fear, the latter properties perhaps functions, in part, of their inferior nourishment, with its attendant psychological consequences, and their greater dependence upon factors beyond their control for their livelihood, in particular the weather and temperatures of the seasons. Thus it was perhaps not surprising that the shamans, wizards and priests exercised more power among the Dirt People, and their kind, than among hunters. Yet, if their men were physically smaller, more bent by labor and inferior diet, than hunters, their women were not always, to hunters, without interest. It was not unknown for hunters to come down upon such communities to kill their animals and strip and lead away, tethered, the more interesting of their daughters. Hamilton knew that her own people, the Men, might well have raided the Dirt People, slaughtering sheep, and carrying off, for their slaves, the best of their women; surely they would have at least taken the dark-haired girl and the wench, proud, raped, who had attempted to conceal herself in the barley; but Hamilton did not believe they would have slaughtered the Dirt People, as had the men of the Weasel People; the Men, she did not believe, would not have indiscriminately slaughtered, certainly not the weak, the old, the children, the less desirable females; the Men would simply have left the less comely of the females free; they would not have wanted them; only the wrists of the most beautiful would have been bound behind their backs for the return trek to the shelters; only they would have been coffled; only they would have been taken for slaves; only on the necks of the most beautiful would the Men have deigned to tie the leather collar that marked its lovely wearer as their slave. The men of the Dirt People would not have been injured, unless, perhaps, they had dared to resist. There was little honor in a Hunter slaying a man of the Dirt People, or of that type. Such an act would not entitle a boy, for example, to enter the Men's Cave, any more than the slaughter of a sheep or the killing of a female. Accordingly, the Men would, presumably, had they known of the Dirt People, and been interested in them, raided them in darkness, taking what animals and women they pleased, leaving the rest. The Dirt People might have awakened to find sheep killed and carried away, and some of the village girls missing; that would have been all. This was not because the Men would have feared the Dirt People, but because they did not wish to bother overly much with them. Later, Hunters would impose tribute on the small agricultural communities, letting them survive, taking from them a levy of produce, animals and, annually, a female or two; but, unmolested, permitted to survive and thrive, in time the agricultural peoples would accumulate the numbers to withstand the hunters, and, eventually, to resist them. Then, over the period of millenia, patiently, felled tree by felled tree, acre by spreading acre, the defeat of the hunters would be wrought. The hunters would be gone; the priest and the wizard would triumph; the bow and the spear would be exchanged for the hoe, and the horizon for barley.

But this would not come about for thousands of years. This was, and would remain for hundreds of generations, the time of the hunters. They were not yet dead. Gunther, Hamilton recalled, had conjectured, in a bare room in Rhodesia, under a dim light bulb, that perhaps the hunters were not dead; that perhaps they only slept, and might awake; Herjellsen had told her, Turn their eyes to the stars; but Herjellsen was mad; and she had not understood him. How could she turn their eyes to the stars; what could she do in such matters; she could do nothing; and why should man turn his eyes to the stars; the stars were far away; the journey was long and cold; Earth was the home of man; let him stay at home; let him be happy; there was much to do on Earth; one might always, sometime, look to the stars; do not think of the stars, for now. The hoe waits; the barley must be planted.

Hamilton recalled that the men of the Weasel People ate human flesh. She wondered if that was why the men of the Weasel People had killed so indiscriminately, to obtain food. It was a law of the Men that this not be done. This was one of the laws, Old Woman had told Hamilton, which had been made by Spear. He had made many laws. He was a giver of laws. Spear is a great man, had said Old Woman, though he had killed Drawer, whom Old Woman had loved, when he could no longer hunt, when he had grown blind and was old. But Hamilton did not think that the men of the Weasel People had killed so indiscriminately because they wished food. She had seen them. They had enjoyed themselves. It had given them pleasure. Hamilton supposed then that perhaps the men, her masters, though the thought made her shudder, were not too different. She supposed they, too, had their blood been aroused, in a similar situation, might have enjoyed killing, the ugly carnival of it, the sport; in all humans, she knew, there was a terribleness, the ecstasy of carnage, the joy of ferocity, the joy of the biting lion; but even then she did not think they, the Men, would have killed so indiscriminately, not the weak, the old, the females, for they were the Men; had they chosen to raid in the light, in a game of war, of intraspecific aggression, they might, she conjectured, have slain the males of the Dirt People had it pleased them to do so, had they offered resistance; but she thought rather they would prefer simply to make them

grovel and while they knelt trembling, to tie their best wom-
en and take them away from them; it was not the killing that
the Men would have wanted, for there was little honor in
killing so miserable a foe, but the victory, the demonstration
of their will, their dominance; "We are taking your women,
and tying them and leading them away," might have said
Spear; "We want them and thus we are taking them."; they
would not have wanted the blood of the Dirt People, for they
would have despised them, only their humiliation, and their
best women; they would hate the Dirt People and would
have, thus, enjoyed making their females their total slaves;
and, too, Hamilton smiled to herself, and knew in the secret
heart of her, the ancient heart, the heart in the blood of her,
which had never been irradicated, not even by her studies or
the civilization in which she had been raised, that the captive
females, bound, led away, would have then, in spite of
their superficial crying out, weeping, have experienced a
strange, wild, surgent elation, knowing by the thongs that
bound them that they were now the slave-brides of men
mightier than those of their kind, that they were now, helpless, doomed to feel mighty arms about them, from which
they could not escape, strong, rough hands on their pitching
bodies, arrogantly forcing them to climax after climax; and
that they would be forced to serve as rightless wenches; and
would be forced, too, in time, to bear the children of their
mighty masters, that the Men, that group, might increase
and wax great. How eagerly, soon, in their thongs, being led
to servitude and ravishment, they would have followed their
masters, the hunters. Hamilton threw back her head and
laughed. She knew herself, she, too, Hamilton, was a slave of
the men. Her veneers of culture, the eroding crusts of her
conditioning, the slimes, the sick varnishes, the cosmetics, the
concealing, confining garments of an antigenetic, diseased
civilization had been stripped from her. They had been
stripped from her by a man called Tree, leaving her naked,
and a female.

She closed her eyes, and felt the forest breeze on her
body. She imagined returning to Tree, and the joy of being
taken in his arms, and carried to the recesses of his cave,
and being hurled to the furs in its shadows and him bending
over her, and, first, swiftly, knotting about her neck the
necklace of the Men, the thongs, claws and shells and then,
that done, unhesitantly and ruthlessly inflicting the might, the
power, of his will on her beauty; she smiled to herself,
thinking, if only to prolong her pleasure, of trying to resist

him; how amusing he would find that; then, when he tired of her game, he would force her to yield herself, regardless of her will, totally to him; he would rip from her what control he had, until then, permitted her to retain, and, in torrents of sensation, she would find herself then his shrieking prize, and nothing more. Hamilton stumbled. She was weak. She felt fevered. The diet and the exhaustion of the village of the Dirt People told upon her. Her eyes suddenly failed to focus. A strange smell came to her nostrils. She turned about, suddenly, startled. On the trail, behind her, some ten yards away, was a short, broad, squat, thick-legged shape. The eyes were large, the chin receding, the hair like greased string, black. It was a woman, a mature female, of the Ugly People. She carried a bone, a femur.

Hamilton backed away from her, her hand out. The woman did not approach her.

A large hand, immensely strong, closed on the back of Hamilton's neck. It was like a vise. She felt the thumb and fingertips, like blunt gouges, deep in her neck; she could not move her head, or turn; the woman approached her; then she felt herself, a captive, turned about; she looked into the broad, heavy face of a male of the Ugly People; it was the first of the males of the species she had seen; the face was incredibly broad and swarthy, the eyes, black, large, set back, beneath heavy brows, the chin receding; the face, powerful, seemed, at once to her, simian and intelligent; it frightened her; he was short legged, round-shouldered, long armed; he was only five and a half feet in height but his body, not fat, was heavy and thick, heavy boned and deep chested; it weighed nearly three hundred pounds; he was not human; he was of the Ugly People; she whimpered; she felt herself, by the back of her neck, lifted from her feet, as a small, sleek animal might be lifted; the arm which lifted her was long, longer than that of a human, and much heavier; the bones within she knew could be as large as twice the width of the comparable human bone; a gorilla might have lifted her as did the male of the Ugly People; then he put her to her feet, bent partly over; he regarded her head, which had been shaved by the Dirt People, with interest. He turned to the woman and together they spoke. Hamilton would have found it difficult to repeat the sounds. It was swift, their speech, and it was not human. "Please," wept Hamilton. Then he took her, by the back of the neck, to the side of the trail. He put her head down across a rock, holding it there. Her left cheek pressed hard against the rock; his left hand, by the

back of the neck, held her in place. She saw the woman
regarding her; too, she saw the face of the man regarding
her. In their faces she saw disgust. "Please!" she wept. She
understood, trembling, that they found her repulsive. In the
right hand of the male was a stone ax, its head bound with
leather, hafted in a stout shaft, a foot in length. "I will do
anything," she cried. "Don't hurt me!" But she saw only
disgust in their faces. "No!" she cried. "Please, no!" She
wept. "I will serve your pleasure," she cried. "I will lay for
you! Turtle will kick for you!" She slipped from English to
the language of the Men, both unintelligible to her captors.
Sick, she realized that the one shield, her sex, her beauty,
which might protect her from death at the hands of human
males was now of no avail. The leopard had its claws, the
hawk its wings, the deer its fleetness, the human male his
strength, the human female her beauty; but the beauty of
the human female was useless save against the masculine
predators of her own species; it might disarm a human male,
he being moved to keep her as his slave, should she beg
piteously enough, and perform instinctual servile submission
behaviors, tears, smiles, grovelings, mouth and hand caresses,
rather than slaying her, but against a male of the Ugly People the very lineaments of her beauty, her slender, lovely
legged, subtle voluptuousness, so different from that of his
own females, she could see, produced only repulsion. "No!"
she cried. "Please!" The ax lifted. Her head was pressed
down on the rock; the huge hand held her by the neck; she
could not move. "Please, no!" she cried. The head of the ax,
in falling, with the strength of the male of the Ugly People,
she knew, would dash through her skull, like a hammer
through an egg, the stone striking even against the stone on
which her head was held. "Please, no!" she wept. The ax, she
knew, was at the height of its arc. "No!" she cried. "No!"
    Suddenly, piercing, shrill, she heard, fierce, imperative, a
cry. And a head thrust itself between her and the ax. She
felt a girl's arms about her. The ax lowered, slowly. The
fingers of the great hand removed themselves from her neck.
Hamilton felt Ugly Girl kiss her. "Ugly Girl," she wept, then
lost consciousness.

◆ 27 ◆

Hamilton opened her eyes. Her body stiffened, but she was held. She half lay, and was half sitting; Ugly Girl's arm was about her shoulders, holding her up. She felt a gourd, broken, brimmed with water, held to her lips. She drank. She tried to pull away from Ugly Girl but could not do so. Ugly Girl, with the strength of her people, was much stronger than she. Then she drank again. Hamilton half lay, half sat, held by Ugly Girl, on a shelf of rock, on boughs. Hamilton moved her legs. She looked upon her ankles. They were free of leather capture shackles. Her hand went to her throat, half expecting to find a tether upon it. But she was not secured in any way. "Thank you," she whispered to Ugly Girl, in the language of the Men. Ugly Girl grimaced, trying to imitate the smile of the Men. Ugly Girl withdrew the gourd, and withdrew her arm from about Hamilton. Hamilton drew her legs beneath her, on the shelf of rock. She was clothed. She wore a rough garment of crudely scraped skin, chewed and beaten. It covered her breasts, and body. The garment was too large for her, for the bodies of the women of the Ugly People are broader than those of the women of the Men; it was belted at the waist with a hide rope. On one of the short women of the Ugly People it would have fallen below the knees; on Hamilton, who was taller, it did not reach her knees.

Hamilton must have looked frightened, for Ugly Girl made soft, clucking noises to her, to pacify her.

Hamilton looked out the wide mouth of the shallow cave. She could see brush, trees.

She could escape!

She reached out again for the gourd of water. Ugly Girl handed it to her, and, again Hamilton drank.

On the other side of the cave, squatting down, was the woman of the Ugly People. She was moving hide string through two pieces of leather, sewing. The large, widely set

319

eyes looked up at Hamilton, curiously. Near her, standing
against the other side of the cave, was a small boy, his head
almost a fifth the size of his broad body; he was round-
shouldered, long-armed; his jaw was receded; his hair had
been cut with stone from his face; he might have been eight
years of age.

He pointed at Hamilton, and said a word. Ugly Girl
laughed. Hamilton felt uneasy.

The mother seemed to assent to what the boy had said.
She, too, repeated the word, and looked down, smiling, to return to her sewing.

Hamilton tried to say the word. It was hard for her to
pronounce.

Ugly Girl laughed at her miserable effort. It made Hamilton angry that Ugly Girl, in her stupidity, should laugh at
one who was human.

Hamilton looked again to the wide mouth of the cave.

Her body, subtly, tensed. She was, concealing the intent,
readying herself to dart for the opening. Ugly Girl, smiling,
put her hand gently on Hamilton's knee. She shook her head.
Hamilton angrily brushed aside Ugly Girl's hand. Then
Hamilton looked away, as though to consider other parts of
the cave. Ugly Girl stepped back. Hamilton swung her legs
over the side of the shelf. Then, suddenly, Hamilton sprang
to her feet and darted toward the opening. She stopped
suddenly, almost losing her balance, some feet before the
opening, for, at that moment, in the opening, appeared the
short, broad frame of the male of the Ugly People. Hamilton, terrified, stepped back, retreating from him. In his hand
he held the short ax, so mighty, yet more shortly handled
than the axes of the Men. On his left shoulder, steadied
there, by his left hand, was the body of a deer. He did not
raise the ax against Hamilton, but regarded her, puzzled.
Hamilton backed from him. Then, against her back, she felt
the shelf of rock. But yesterday this brute, without a thought,
save for the intercession of Ugly Girl, would have crushed
her head between a rock and the blade of his ax. He looked
at her. Hamilton approached him, submissively, looking
down, and knelt before him, the monster, putting her head
to the stone, desperate to pacify him, in her femaleness to
make obeisance to the male in him, to be pleasing to him,
to plead with him for her life. She, a human female, kissed
the stone before the feet of the short, mighty male of the
Ugly People. Then, timidly, trying to smile, she looked up.
She was startled. He was regarding her, stupidly. The males

of the Men, she knew, expected and demanded, thereby triggering and releasing, complete subservience behavior in their females; they produced stimulus situations in which her blood instincts had no choice but to bare themselves, detonating the fantastic psychophysiological reflex, or response, of female submission to the aggressive, mightier animal, the male. Cringing and smiling in a female, she knew, warded off male wrath; it indicated with her body that, if she should be spared, she would be his work object and his sexual pleasure-object. But the male of the Ugly People looked at her, puzzled. Then she realized that the males of the Ugly People did not relate to their females as did the males of the Men. They were of a different species. She rose to her feet, and backed away from him. He did not approach her. He looked to his own woman. Suddenly Hamilton felt contempt for him. He was a male. Yet he did not make her his slave. He could do so, if he wanted, but he did not do so. Hamilton felt emotions of both relief, for she did not wish to be the slave of the monster, and irritation, and frustration, for, triggered by fear, her slave reflex had not been satisfied. Too, suddenly, almost unaccountably in her mind, she despised the male of the Ugly People. He was strong, stronger even than most of the human males doubtless, but yet, too, so weak, so stupid. She saw, in his broad back, as he squatted near his woman, and threw the deer down to the floor of the cave, both weakness and strength. His woman rubbed her nose along the side of his neck, and he grunted and thrust his head to her shoulder. Hamilton stood back, her arms folded, her feet widely spread. She held the male of the Ugly People in contempt. She did not feel then he was a true male. He is weak, she thought. This kind will not survive. They are too weak to survive. The male, she thought, irritably, who does not make his female his slave, either cannot do so, and is a weakling, or is a fool. If I were a male, she thought, I would make my females slaves, the pretty, weak, lovely little things! Since when, in nature, does the strong not dominate the weak? Since the weak have crippled the strong, she told herself, thereby denying the strong their birthright, and, inadvertently, in the same act, to their own frustration, depriving themselves of theirs as well, the opportunity to join in that contest in which, in any normal situation, she will meet her defeat, that contest which, if truly carried out, must terminate with her conquest, her joyful, abject surrender to the will, the absolute domination, of the mightier animal, the male. She realized then that male dominance has little to do, directly, with physical strength, though it is customarily linked with it. An extremely strong man, physically, she recognized, could be, and sometimes was, a psychological weakling, emasculated and petty, unable to satisfy complete dimensions of a female's nature; sometimes such men even prided themselves on this form of impotence; sometimes, Hamilton suspected, such men, out of hostility and spite, and self-hatred, and hatred for women, refused to recognize the desperate wants of their lovers, scorning them for the realities of their genetic nature; refusing to respond to the most obvious, most desperate and profound unspoken pleas; and should the woman repudiate her conditionings, cast aside her guilts, and, humiliating herself, shamelessly beg, "Dominate me!" such men, frightened, knowing themselves unable to fulfill her needs, might laugh at her, thus ventilating hysterical anxiety, or pretend not to understand, or look upon her strangely, and deny her, thus making her miserable, making her suffer, in a culturally approved form of sadism; the female is not, Hamilton conjectured, simply a physical organism, but a psychophysical organism, and her blood needs for submission to a male express themselves beautifully in the totality of her response, not only in the weakening of her body, its secretions, its heightened sensitivity, its helplessness, its readiness, but in her psychic vulnerability, helplessly willing, waiting for him to impress his will upon her, to command her; she is eager to be made a mere instrument of his pleasure, eager to be subjected to his will, eager to be ruthlessly, uncompromisingly, dominated, eager to be, should he have the courage, literally the slave girl of a master; and should she be fortunate, it is just that which, perhaps to a thrill of horror, she finds herself to be. Once Hamilton had attempted to make aggressive love to Tree. He had struck her, bringing blood to her mouth. "Lie still, and endure," he had told her. "I will tell you when to touch and caress." "Yes, Master," she had whispered. Few men, Hamilton thought, are strong enough to satisfy the slave in a woman. Few women, she thought, though all wish to be stripped and subdued, are fortunate enough to find a Master. Across thousands of years, remote from her own time, in an age of peril and barbarism, she had found hers, a hunter called Tree.

Hamilton then looked at the broad-backed male of the Ugly People, squatting near his female, cutting the hide from the deer with the ax, and then ripping it with his teeth and fingers. He took a bit of meat from a rib and gave it to the woman, and then to the boy, and then to Ugly Girl, who joined them. They were not human, Hamilton knew. Then, no longer did she scorn the male of the Ugly People. Perhaps, to him, she was no more than a female monkey might have appeared to Tree, different, small, ungainly, of no interest sexually. This annoyed her to some extent, for she was vain of her beauty, but, too, she was relieved that he had not wanted her. He gave another piece of meat to the child. It was growing dark outside. Hamilton edged toward the mouth of the cave. They were of a different species. The innocence and cruelty with which a human hunter treated his human females was, apparently, not that of the Ugly People; too, she suspected, the deep needs in her own body, and in those of the other human females, to seek out and respond to sexual domination, were apparently much less pronounced in the Ugly People; they were less sexually driven, Hamilton conjectured, than humans; doubtless, they, too, had their dominance and submission behaviors, but such behavior seemed less clear cut, less evident, than in humans; their sexual drives were less she conjectured than those of humans; the sexes in the Ugly People, she recognized, shuddering, were much less clearly differentiated than in humans; she suspected they would not breed as well. They were an experiment in evolution quite different from that of humans, Hamilton recognized, an interesting alternative, one which humans would survive, but one which, in its long millenia, when all was said and done, should man destroy himself, might prove to have endured the longer span on the calendars of time. They seemed very gentle with one another.

Hamilton again eyed the large open mouth of the cave. It would be difficult to defend, she thought. They are fools, stupid. The shelters of the Men were more rational, more defensible. Hamilton did not realize that the best shelters were indeed those of the Men, and various other human groups. The Ugly People were peaceful. They were not as aggressive as men, nor as swift, nor as intelligent, nor as cruel. Accordingly they would take what little, if anything, was left. They would compete unsuccessfully with fiercer groups. As would Pygmies and Eskimos they would be driven farther and farther from desirable land, good hunting and adequate shelter; unlike Pygmies and Eskimos, clearly distinguishable as human types, the Ugly People were not human; human beings, loathing them, would not tolerate them as competitors; they, in a peculiarly intense fashion, with their mockery of human shape, would trigger the instinctual

fear of the stranger, the different; they would be hunted
down and exterminated. The man thrust a tiny piece of meat
into the mouth of the boy, and then rubbed his bearded chin
on the boy's shoulder.

Hamilton suddenly bolted from the cave, running into the
night.

In an instant Ugly Girl was up and after her.

Hamilton plunged through the night, cutting her feet,
branches striking her body. She ran. Behind her, always,
sometimes closer, sometimes farther, she heard Ugly Girl.
Sometimes Hamilton stopped, to hide, to elude Ugly Girl,
but each time, to her misery, Ugly Girl turned toward her,
approaching. Then Hamilton realized that Ugly Girl, like a
hunter, could follow her trail by smell; that, like a hunter,
she might hear her breathing, even from yards away. Miserable, Hamilton would leap up and run again. Her hope was to
outdistance Ugly Girl. But Ugly Girl seemed tireless. More
than once, Ugly Girl called out to her, in the strange tongue
of the Ugly People. Then, gasping, Hamilton turned and
picked up a rock. Ugly Girl stopped, a shadow among the
branches. "Go back! Go away!" said Hamilton. Ugly Girl
spoke to her in the language of the Ugly People. "Stay
away!" cried Hamilton, lifting the rock. Ugly Girl stepped
toward her. Hamilton, with a cry of misery, flung the heavy
rock. It hurtled past Ugly Girl. Hamilton struck at her.
Briefly the girls grappled. Hamilton wildly bit and clawed,
and scratched, weeping, screaming, at Ugly Girl, but Ugly
Girl handled her with ease, with much the same ease with
which a man might have handled her; the women of the
Ugly People, Hamilton realized to her misery, were much
stronger than human females; she was no match for her, no
more than she would have been for a strong boy; Hamilton
was thrown to her belly; Ugly Girl knelt across her body; the
women of human beings had not been bred and sexually
selected by males for sturdiness and strength, and indepen-
dence, but for beauty, obedience, submissiveness, responsive-
ness to masculine domination; Hamilton wept as she felt the
hide belt on her garment removed, and felt Ugly Girl pull
her wrists behind her back, and, as though she might be a
man, fasten them together. Ugly Girl then removed the belt
from her own garment and tied its ends together and then,
slipping one end of the loop behind Hamilton's neck, passed
the other end of the loop through the first, pulling it tight,
putting Hamilton in a choke collar and short leash. She then
dragged Hamilton to her feet. Since the leash was short

Hamilton had to walk bent over, at her side. Pulling Hamilton, half choking, beside her, Ugly Girl then returned to the mouth of the cave of the Ugly People. There was a fire there now, rather near the mouth, and various branches and rocks had been brought and put before the opening, to close it somewhat. But the opening had not been yet completely closed. Ugly Girl had not yet returned.

The male of the Ugly People, and his woman, and the child, emerged from the cave.

Hamilton stood next to Ugly Girl, bent over, her hands bound behind her back, in her simple choke collar and leash, helpless, a prisoner of Ugly Girl.

The child looked at her, and laughed.

He said the word she had heard before, and he laughed again, as did the male and the female.

"Please don't eat me, or kill me," she whispered.

The male and the woman, and the child returned to the cave. Then, to Hamilton's astonishment, Ugly Girl removed the leash from her throat, and untying its ends, refastened it as her own belt. Then, to her greater astonishment, Ugly Girl untied her hands. Hamilton dared not run. Ugly Girl tied the belt about Hamilton, as it had been before. Then she stepped toward the mouth of the cave. Hamilton turned to face her. She was free. Ugly Girl gestured that she should enter the cave. She made a clucking noise.

Behind Hamilton, in the forest, she heard the roar of a leopard. She shuddered. Well did she recall the leopard which, long ago, had stalked her, which, to her good fortune, had been slain by Tree.

Again Ugly Girl gestured that she should enter the cave. Again, from the forest, closer this time, she heard the roar of the leopard. Swiftly, gratefully, she entered the cave.

Ugly Girl gestured that she should kneel beside the fire, where some of the meat from the slain deer was roasting on a stick. Hamilton would have knelt behind the male, but Ugly Girl shook her head and placed Hamilton by the fire. She knelt to the left of the woman; the child was on the woman's right; the male squatted diagonally across from Hamilton; when Ugly Girl had closed the entrance to the cave with thick branches, she came and knelt between the child and the male. The male, with a sharp piece of flint, and a stick separated pieces of meat from the roast. He gave a piece first to the child; he then gave a piece to the woman; then he gave a piece to Ugly Girl. Then he handed Hamilton a piece of meat. "Thank you," she whispered. He then cut himself a piece of meat, a large one, and, holding it in two hands, squatting, grease running between his fingers, began to eat it.

That night Hamilton lay down beside Ugly Girl, in the cave of the Ugly People. She looked at the glowing redness of the embers of the fire.

"Can you understand me?" asked Hamilton of Ugly Girl, in the language of the Men.

Ugly Girl, her head illuminated by the redness, signified her assent, nodding her head. Ugly Girl, as Hamilton had suspected, understood much of the speech of the Men, but it was difficult for her to repeat the sounds. Hamilton, too, of course, would have found it difficult to imitate, with adequate exactness, the phonemes of the Ugly People. There was, she suspected, subtle differences in the anatomy of the throat, a thicker, less nimble tongue, a different oral cavity, and, too, of course, a somewhat differently formed brain, with a speech center wrought through an evolution divergent for generations from that of the human.

"What is the word by which they address me?" asked Hamilton. "What is it they call me?"

Ugly Girl repeated the word.

"Yes," said Hamilton. "What does it mean?"

Ugly Girl crawled over to the fire. She knelt by it. Hamilton joined her there.

Ugly Girl repeated the word. She made, in the sign language common to many of the groups of humans, the name sign, pointing to Hamilton. Tooth, and Fox, at the behest of Tooth, had taught her several signs.

"That is the name they have given me?" asked Hamilton. "It is my name here?"

Ugly Girl nodded.

"What does it mean?" asked Hamilton. She remembered how they had laughed at her, even the child.

Ugly Girl, with a twig, beside the fire, scratched an animal. Hamilton could not make it out. Then Ugly Girl made the sign in the hand talk of the human groups. Hamilton then looked down. She then understood the drawing.

It was a drawing, primitive, simple, an outline drawing, but one now unmistakable. It was the drawing of a small, female bush pig. Hamilton leaned back on her heels, and smiled. "You are so ugly," signed Ugly Girl to her, and then, smiling, kissed her. Hamilton, among the people of Ugly Girl, was no longer the beauty, a casual, inadvertent movement of whose body might lead one of the hunters, to whom she and the other women belonged, to throw her on her back and, without ceremony or courtesy, rape her. Here, among the people of Ugly Girl, it was she, not Ugly Girl, who was the ugly girl. Ugly Girl, of course, among the men, had been used. They were fierce, sometimes indiscriminatory breeders. Hamilton did not feel the male of the Ugly People would bother her. To her he seemed large, kind, and sexually sluggish. If he did wish to use her, of course, she would have to serve him, for she was a female. As a primitive woman she would have no choice but to obey the male, and do what he wished. Hamilton smiled to herself. Among the Ugly People, her name was "Sow."

"What is your name?" asked Hamilton.

Ugly Girl laughed, an almost human laugh. She made the sign for "Flower." Hamilton smiled.

"What is the name of your people?" asked Hamilton. She had thought only of them, in the habitual manner of the Men, as the Ugly People. She knew, of course, of the Horse People, who hunted horse on the prairies; she knew of the Bear People, with whom the Men sometimes exchanged women; of the Shell People, who traded shells; and of the Weasel People, enemies of the men; and of the Dirt People, vanished now, save for some of their females in the thongs of the Weasel People. "What is the name of your people?" asked Hamilton again of Ugly Girl.

Ugly Girl grinned, not responding.

Her people, this family, had taken her in, she, Hamilton, a female of an enemy kind, different even biologically from them, one displeasing to their senses. They had protected her, fed her, sheltered her.

"What is the name of your people?" asked Hamilton.

Swiftly Ugly Girl made the signs. "The Love People," she said, in the hand talk of certain of the human groups.

◈ 28 ◈

"Oh!" cried Hamilton, angrily, stung on the thigh. Bees swarmed about her. "Hurry!" she cried. She looked up the height of the blasted, desiccated tree. On a branch, a smoking torch in one hand, stood Ugly Girl. She thrust her other hand, and arm, into an aperture in the tree. Bees, in a cloud, swarmed about her. She scooped out combs of honey, pounds, mixed with bees, smearing them on the branch next to her, on a large, flat leaf. Then she thrust the torch, as she had done before, into the hole in the tree, trying to overcome the bees inside the nest. Her left eyelid was swollen. Hamilton could see welts on her body. Another bee stung Hamilton, on the side of the left ankle. Beside Hamilton, about her feet, were several leaves, laden with honey. Ugly Girl rolled the leaf and dropped it to Hamilton, who caught it, put it with the others, and then, as Ugly Girl bent down, squatting, handed her another leaf. Hamilton put her finger into the sweet, whitish mash. There were dead bees in it. Hamilton licked her finger. She could taste the smoke from Ugly Girl's torch. "Oh!" cried Hamilton, as another bee stung her, on the left side of the neck. "We have enough!" she cried. "Please come down! Please, Flower!" Ugly Girl, with the last leaf in one hand, the torch in the other, had, too, had enough. Bees hot and black about her head and shoulders, she leapt down. Hamilton and Ugly Girl bent down, picking up the leaves. Another bee stung Hamilton on the back of the left leg, some seven inches above the knee. Then another stung her on the back of the neck. Weeping, laughing, she and Ugly Girl scooped up the honey and, torch smoking, fled.

When they were free of the lingering avengers of the nest, the two girls sat down in the grass, beside a large rock. Ugly Girl extinguished the torch. She knelt by Hamilton. Ugly Girl picked a flower, and fixed it in her hair. Hamilton could not do the same, for her own hair had been almost cut from her head, leaving her scalp cut and scraped, by the Dirt People. Hamilton, looking at Ugly Girl, did not feel any longer that she was ugly, though she was much different from a human female. The large eyes of Ugly Girl, dark, deep, Hamilton found to be beautiful. Ugly Girl dipped her finger in the honey, and tasted it.

"I wish to return to the Men," said Hamilton. She thought of Tree. "Will you help me?"

It seemed not strange now to Hamilton that she wished to return to the Men, that she wished to return to a group where she would be no more than a rightless slave, where her neck would be given no choice but to bend beneath the yoke of a complete masculine domination. She could not, in her new knowledges, envy the frustrated, denied females of her own artificial times, cheated of their absolute sexual subjugation to a male, thereby denied the attainment of the totality, the fullness, of their sexuality.

"I will help you," said Ugly Girl, in hand talk.

Hamilton hugged her with joy.

"You need not come near their camp," said Hamilton. "Just show me the way. Then I can go into the camp alone. You will not then be recaptured."

Hamilton wondered if Tree would tie her and beat her, for not having returned sooner. She hoped he would not do so. She had done her best to return to his collar.

"I will go with you," signed Ugly Girl. Then she looked at Hamilton. "Tooth," she said, making the sound, saying the word in the language of the Men, as nearly as she could. Her face seemed strained with the effort.

"You like Tooth?" asked Hamilton. She recalled the prognathous-jawed giant, with the extended canine, so fearsome seeming, so much loving children, he who had been kind to Ugly Girl, of all the Men. "I care for him," said Ugly Girl. "I love him."

"But you are of another people," said Hamilton.

"I love him," she said, speaking the words in the language of the Men. It required effort. Sweat stood on her forehead. Then she reverted to hand sign. "Do you not want to be owned?" she signed, asking Hamilton a question which, in Hamilton's time, would have been a forbidden question, one which one woman would scarcely dare to ask another, but which, in this honest time, was natural, a straightforward, civil inquiry.

"Yes," said Hamilton, smiling. "I want to be owned."

The two girls hugged and kissed one another, and Ugly

Girl touched Hamilton with her nose, in the manner of the Ugly People, drinking in her scent. Then, laughing, the two girls gathered up their honey, and made their way toward the shelter of the Ugly People. In the morning, they had decided, they would begin the journey back to the shelters of the Men.

Hamilton preceded Ugly Girl to the shelter of the family of the Ugly People, carrying the honey. Ugly Girl delayed, stopping to gather sticks for the fire that night. Inside the shelter, its mouth now open, as it was during the day, Hamilton saw the male of the Ugly People, and his mate. She called out to them. The child did not come forth to greet her. Hamilton, tired, sweating, carried the honey to the cave, putting it down, in its rolled leaves, to one side. She turned to face the male and his mate, and froze with horror. He sat cross-legged, two pieces of flint in his hand, his head bent over. She, too, sat cross-legged, to one side, leather, with a rawhide thread and awl, in her hands. She was staring straight ahead, not seeing. Hamilton threw her hand before her mouth with horror. Blood was about the head of both. Both were dead. They had been propped in position and each tied to a short stake thrust into the dirt behind them. Hamilton screamed. She turned. In the mouth of the cave, behind her, blocking her exit, was a bearded man, the leader of the Weasel People.

◆ 29 ◆

"My power here is precarious," said Gunther. "I can do nothing to save you."

"Please, Gunther!" wept Hamilton. "I beg you, Gunther! As a helpless human female, I beg you!"

"I can do nothing," said Gunther.

"You are mad," said William, behind him.

The drums began to beat more madly. The chants became more wild.

Hamilton struggled on the pole, lying on the ground, to which she was tied. It was some two inches in thickness, supple, green, some ten feet in length. Her wrists, over her head, were crossed and tied to the pole; she was stretched at full length; her ankles, drawn down, crossed, were tied, too, to the pole; rawhide ropes about her body, at the knees, at her thighs, her waist, her shoulders, her neck, held her tightly to the pole; she could scarcely squirm; she was stripped; honey had been smeared on her body; to one side, in a ditch a yard wide, and some eight feet in length, the red-haired girl prodded the fire.

"Please, Gunther," wept Hamilton.

"No," said Gunther. "It is beyond my power now to interfere. Did I oppose them now, did I interfere in this thing, my power here would be at an end."

Hamilton heard the moving back of the hammer of a pistol. "It is not beyond my power to interfere," said William. "You have gone too far, Gunther. If we die, we must stop this."

"If we stop it," said Gunther, "we shall die. Do you not understand this? Do not be a fool."

One of the men of the Weasel People, standing nearby, regarded them, puzzled.

The red-haired girl, followed by the shorter, dark-haired one, who had been cruel, weeks before, to Hamilton, now brought sticks, throwing them on the fire.

Two of the men of the Weasel People bent to the hide drums, stretched over hollowed wood. Others, slapping their knees, sitting cross-legged, chanted.

Gunther looked up, into the muzzle of the pistol leveled at his head by William. "I cannot permit this," said William. "I have followed you, too far. You have taught me much of what it is to be a man, but this I conjecture, can be no part of that instruction. I, simply, do not find this acceptable. It isn't to be done."

"This," said Gunther, "has nothing to do with manhood. It is neither of a man nor not of a man. My action now is simply that of a rational organism. Better one lost, and that only a female, than three. How much do you value your life?"

."Not this much," said William. "Untie her." Gunther looked up at him. "You are not the Gunther I once knew, once admired, once saluted," said William. "He is gone, left now is only a monster, corrupted by greed for a pittance of power. You were the mightiest of the men I ever knew, Gunther, but you have fallen. Gunther is gone. You pretend

to his name, but you are not him. The Gunther I once knew
would have led in this action. He would have been too proud
to have valued his life in this situation; you have betrayed the
Gunther I once knew, who was a great man, one who could
dream in steel and theorems, and envisage a world bold
enough to lift its hands to stars."

"Untie her yourself," said Gunther, standing.

William holstered his pistol and knelt to Hamilton's bonds.
Hamilton wept with relief. She screamed. From behind William, Gunther struck down with the butt of his Luger.

Gunther spoke to two of the men of the Weasel People,
who dragged William to one side.

Hamilton wept as two other men lifted the pole and set it
across the two tripods, one at each end of the fire. She
screamed. She felt the honey melt from her body and heard
it fall, hissing, into the fire.

The leader of the Weasel People squatted nearby, watching her body, tied on the spit.

Hamilton cried out, a long, piteous scream. Nearby, kneeling, her head down, her neck tied on a short strap, some six
inches long, to a short stake, her wrists tied behind her back,
Ugly Girl whimpered with misery. Her back was covered
with switch welts.

The women of the Weasel People, at a command from the
men, threw aside their garments and, legs flexed, hands lifted
over their heads, stood before their men. They stood perfectly still. The drums stopped. Then, when the drums, with a
sudden sound began again, the females, as one, danced,
turning, stamping, about the fire, crying out, their hair wild.
The eyes of the men glistened; they slapped their knees
and thighs; Hamilton's ears rang with the chant; about her,
blurred, whirled the nude women, pleasing their men; she
heard the honey fall from her body, crackling, in the fire;
she screamed in pain, her body a sheet of heat, bound on the
thick, greenwood spit.

The screams of the women startled her. The dark shape,
which seemed to fall from nowhere, stood beside her. The
men shouted, springing to their feet. The man stood with his
feet spread, in the fire itself, and then, slowly, angrily, lifted
the spit from the tripods, kicking apart the burning wood. He
carried Hamilton, on the spit, easily, well over his head, his
eyes terrible. Then he thrust the spit a foot into the ground at
the side of the fire.

"Tree!" she cried. "Master!"

But he had turned from her and was facing the leader of

the Weasel People, who, warily, looking about, was backing away from him.

She became aware of consternation in the camp. A man of the Weasel People lifted a spear in his hand, but the arrow, loosed from the branches at the side of the camp, already was piercing his throat. He tried to speak, turned and fell, breaking the arrow with his hands, then sprawling into the dirt.

Men fought, hand to hand, with stone knives, with stone axes. The women of the Weasel People screamed. Hamilton saw Hawk strike the red-haired girl in the back, felling her, and leaping upon her. She saw Fox with the shorter, dark-haired girl, nude, her arm in his grip, thrust his prize to the side of the red-haired girl. They were thrust back to back; the wrists of each were tied behind her back with the hair of the other; they were then thrown from their feet and Hawk, with a bit of rawhide rope, lashed together their right ankles hobbling them.

The leader of the Weasel People struck down at Tree with his ax but Tree caught the ax, and they grappled; then Tree, like an animal, insane with fury, was behind the leader of the Weasel People; one hand was on his upper jaw, the other on his lower; he broke the lower jaw away from the face; then, methodically, he broke the arms and legs of the man, leaving him in the dirt.

Stone and Knife stepped away from bodies. Knife cut the head from his man.

Arrow Maker strode into the camp, his quiver empty. Runner withdrew his spear from the back of one of the Weasel People.

Flower ran to Knife, Cloud to Runner.

One of the men of the Weasel People fled toward the brush. He met the ax of Wolf, who stepped over his body.

The men of the Weasel People lay about the camp, fallen. Only one lived, their leader, helpless in the dirt near the fire, jaw and limbs broken.

Tooth, his ax bloody, knelt to free Ugly Girl. She whimpered, and he took her in his arms.

Hamilton put her head back, helpless on the pole thrust in the dirt. Her body was blistered. It stung.

She saw Gunther backed against a rock. He had been disarmed. She saw Spear take the rifle by the barrel, and break it over a rock, then the other rifle, which had been William's. William lay to one side, unconscious.

Fox returned to the clearing. Preceding him was the girl

of the Dirt People, who had once hidden in the granary bin during the raid of the Weasel People. Her wrists were tied behind her back. In the camp, Fox threw her from her feet and, with an end of the rope tying her wrists, pulled her right ankle up behind her, tying it tightly to her wrists, that she might not run. In a few moments, from another direction, came Hawk. His prisoner was the virginally bodied girl of the Dirt People, who had been saved from the sacrificial altar by the strike of the Weasel People. She had exchanged slaveries. She would find that of the Men even more complete than that of the Weasel People. The Men demanded more, as was the right of masters, from their females. Hawk put her to her belly and tied her wrists together behind her back, and then, with the same lash of rawhide rope, crossed, pulled up, and tied her ankles. He then turned her on her side, and left her helpless. She lay in the dirt. She looked after him, his by capture. Hamilton saw that his ax was bloodied, and knew then that, in the brush, he had killed for his lovely prize. Hamilton saw her eyes, as she, lying on her side, a secured slave, wrists bound to ankles, watched the hunter walk away from her, paying her no more attention. She was forgotten, until wanted. She knew then that she would have to strive desperately to please a hunter such as he. Hamilton smiled to herself. She did not doubt that the new slave, his by victory and seizure, would serve him well, like Butterfly, who now, freed of the female-holding pit, like the others of the Men, followed him, trying to touch him, to hold his arm, to press her lips to his shoulder. Good-naturedly, he shook her off, but she continued to follow him, closely, as closely as she dared.

Hamilton saw Runner and Arrow Maker turning Gunther about, pushing him against the rock, and tying his hands behind his back.

Tied on the pole, upright in the dirt, hands lashed to it, crossed, over her head, ankles crossed and tied, body tied tightly against it, Hamilton was helpless.

She saw Tree turn and now, that the work of men, the killing, the victory, the vengeance, was done, face her. He motioned Hawk to cut her loose, and turned away. Hamilton, bond by bond, was freed of the pole. She fell to the ground, crouching, scarcely able to stand. Her hands, and feet, from the lashings, were white. Her body was blistered, wet with hot honey.

"Tree," she called. "Master!"

She held out her hand to him. He looked at her. He did

not seem pleased. Tears formed in her eyes. She knew how frightful she must look to him, her hair muchly gone, cut away from her head by the women of the Dirt People, her scalp cut and scraped.

"I love you," she said.

He frowned. Then he laughed, mightily, for he had been teasing her, with the cruel humor of the hunter. He grinned at her. Then he held open his arms to her, and she fled to him, weeping, putting her head against his chest.

◆ 30 ◆

Hamilton turned her head to one side. Her eyes were frightened. She bit her lip. "Old Woman!" she cried. "Old Woman!"

"Antelope will fetch her," said Cloud. "Do not cry out."

Hamilton struggled to her feet, bent over. "Lie down," said Cloud.

She felt wet. The interior of her right thigh, her right leg, her right shin, were soaked with water. There seemed so much. She had awakened. "Tree," she had cried. "Tree!" Then she had cried with pain. He had taken the scent, and, getting to his feet, had left her. He would sleep elsewhere. She had cried for a woman. "Please, Cloud! Old Woman! Flower! Antelope!"

"Lie down," said Antelope.

Hamilton's fists turned white with pain. She cried out. "Do not make noise," said Antelope. "You will disturb the men."

Antelope lowered Hamilton to a sitting position. Her head was up. She could feel the water about her. She tore away, grimacing with the movement, the brief skirt and threw it from her.

"Old Woman!" screamed Hamilton.

Old Woman had not been killed in the raid of the Weasel People. When she had been led away, Hamilton had not known if she were alive or dead. Struck unconscious in the fall, Old Woman had lain at the foot of the shelters. She now hobbled about with a heavy stick, favoring the leg which had been broken, the pain of which had cost her her consciousness for hours, and had, inadvertently, saved her life from the Weasel People. They, like many predators, found inert objects of little interest. Left for dead, she had been found, several hours later, when the Men had returned.

"Old Woman!" screamed Hamilton.

"Antelope will fetch her," said Cloud. "Lie down."

Hamilton, suddenly in the grip of the reflex, screamed.

"Be quiet," scolded Cloud. "Do not awaken the men!"

Hamilton eased herself to her left thigh, lying on the stone. There was no pain now. Her eyes were wide in the darkness. She felt the stone, granular, against her body. She felt the dampness on her left thigh, where she lay in the wetness.

With her own hair, which was now fully grown again, Cloud wiped her forehead.

"Your hair is very beautiful," said Cloud. It was seldom that Cloud paid compliments. Hamilton did not respond to her. But Hamilton was grateful.

Hamilton lay in silence. She must try not to arouse the men. "Old Woman will come soon," said Cloud.

Hamilton, lying in the darkness, legs drawn up, frightened, waited.

Four months ago, when the men had fought a cave bear, contesting a deep shelter with it, with torches and spears, hunting it deep in its own lair, Knife had, suddenly, withdrawn. The bear, freed of the prodding spear, had leaped forward, striking Spear. The great claws had raked, like hooks of steel across the face of Spear, taking his left eye from his head, and blinding, with a long, hot furrow of red, his right eye. Spear, his face and head covered with blood, had fallen backward, the bear biting at him. Tree, from the side, on the bear's exposed flank, had driven his stone-headed spear to the heart and the great animal, a thousand pounds of fury, thrashing, snapping the shaft of the spear, had rolled to the side of the shelter, biting at the rock, and died. "Why did you fall back?" demanded Tree of Knife. If the Men did not stand together, they would die. Each must depend on the other. He who saves himself slays his brother. But Knife had not been afraid. Knife was not a coward. He looked at the bloodied head of Spear, pulling the large man's hands away from his face. Knife had grinned. "Spear is blind," said Knife. "I am first among the Men."

Hamilton screamed, her head back. It was like nothing she had felt or imagined.

When, at the end of the preceding summer, Hamilton and the others had been retaken by their men, Gunther and William, stripped and bound, had been brought back, too, to the shelters. Their clothing, weapons and other accouterments had been destroyed, cast in a river. Spear, and the others, not knowing the power of them, such strange artifacts, would take no chances. Even Gunther's wrist watch, which Cloud had liked, was destroyed. Perhaps such objects had some strange affinity with their owners; perhaps they were loyal to them; perhaps they would betray or injure others, or strangers? They would be destroyed. Gunther and William, thus, hands tied behind their backs, ropes on their necks, herded by women, came naked to the camp of the men. They did not know what would be done with them. The leader of the Weasel People, his jaw torn from his face by Tree, his legs and arms broken, had been left behind for the leopards.

"I want Old Woman!" wept Hamilton. "Please! Please! I want Old Woman!"

"She will come," said Cloud.

With the men to the camp had come, too, the captive females, taken from the Weasel People, some of whom had been girls of the Dirt People. Hamilton, herself, with pleasure, had tied the wrists of the nude red-haired girl behind her back. She had knotted the coffle rope, too, tightly, about her throat; she had similarly secured the nude virginally bodied girl of the Dirt People. "You will learn what it is to be the girls of the Men," Hamilton told them in triumph. She turned away. Already Fox had his hands on the waist of the red-haired girl; already Spear, grinning, stood before the virginally bodied girl; she shrank back, bound; she pulled back against the coffle rope; it stopped her; she, by her right arm, above the elbow, and her left ankle, was lowered to the ground. Before even the Men quitted the destroyed camp of the Weasel People, the newly captured women, tied in coffle, in the dirt, were well taught the domination of their new masters; but Tree did not busy himself with the new slave flesh; rather, four times, pounding, scarcely moments between them, he struck Hamilton with his force; it had been long since he had held a female body and he was not kind with her; the slave Brenda Hamilton, clung to her master, her head back, her eyes closed, beaten by his body and will; so swiftly, so ruthlessly did he satisfy himself with her, that no common pleasure was permitted her; she held to him, as though for her life; struck again and again she gasped, and knew no simple pleasure, but that she was helpless again in his arms, that she again was held by him and that she belonged to him; she looked at him, adoringly; his will and might had again been impressed upon her; she pitied women who· had never known such men; then, when Tree had again looked upon her as Turtle, and not simply a thing to beat and abuse for his pleasure, he alerted himself to her responses, it pleasing him to pleasure her, and, subtly and at length, reduced her to submissive splendor. She was, at the last, carried from the camp of the Weasel People in Tree's arms, on the trail of the Men and their loot and captives. Behind them the camp lay shattered; behind them lay the fires, broken, sticks about, weapons snapped, dying ashes; behind them lay the coming of darkness, and the wailing of a man, broken jawed, broken limbed, who would wait for the leopards.

She had not felt the pain now for more than five minutes. She recalled gentler times with Tree, among flowers.

"Tree!" she cried out.

"Be quiet," said Cloud. "Do not disturb the men." Tree had left her, to go sleep elsewhere when it had begun.

William and Gunther had been brought, bound, and naked, to the camp of the Men. The women had thrown Gunther on his back over a rock, several of them holding him. Cloud, with a shell, had bent to cut his manhood from him.

"Please," had wept Hamilton. "Do not hurt him!"

Spear had looked at Tree, who had nodded. "Stop," had said Spear.

Half in shock Gunther and William had then been put in the brief skirts of the women of the Men, necklaces tied about their throats.

The women had much laughed. The children had struck them with sticks.

Then the Men had hurled them into a pit in the shelters, roughly circular, more than twenty feet in depth, filled with refuse, infested with the brown rat. They had been left there to die.

One night, the second night of the return to the shelters, Hamilton, with a torch, had crept to the edge of the pit.

"Gunther! William!" she called softly.

In the light, she saw William's face, raised to her. In his left hand he held, by the left hind foot, a dead rat, more than a foot in length. It was partially eaten.

He stood ankle deep in the bones, the filth. She saw there were pools of water in the pit.

"You're alive," she whispered.

He had taken the necklace from his neck. It was looped in the waist of the garment he wore.

"Gunther?" she asked.

"He is alive," said William, blinking against the light of the torch.

Hamilton fought nausea, the impulse to vomit from the stink of the pit.

Hamilton lifted the torch. At one side of the pit, not sleeping, staring into the darkness, sitting, his back against the stone, was Gunther.

"He's dead," whispered Hamilton, sick.

"No," said William.

Hamilton looked down, tears in her eyes.

"I make snares with this," said William, lifting the leather strands of the necklace of the Men. "Sometimes," said William, "I catch them with my bare hands, by feel. Sometimes I pretend to be asleep. Sometimes I let them crawl over my arm and then, like this," he making a sudden grasping motion, "seize them."

"You will die in here," said Hamilton.

"What the rats eat we can eat," said William. "But I must feed Gunther."

"He's dead," whispered Hamilton.

"No," said William. "He is alive." Then he added, "His body is alive."

"What is wrong with him?" she asked.

William shrugged. "He has met defeat. He has met hunters. He has met men greater than he himself. Inside his body, this has killed him."

Hamilton looked upon the body that had been Gunther, so mighty, so proud and fine. It now stared into the darkness. She suspected he did not even hear them speak.

"Do not worry for him," said William. "I shall keep him alive as well as I can."

The minds of men greater than Gunther, Hamilton suspected, might have broken under the dislocations of the last months.

"Is he insane?" asked Hamilton.

"I do not think so," said William. "It is more like the will to live is gone."

"Gunther was so much alive, so strong," said Hamilton.

"He was not a hunter," said William. "He thought himself such, but he was only a man of our own times, my dear Hamilton, a small man, greater than most, but frail, crippled, far from the mightinesses he envisioned. It is a tragedy. For such a man it would be best that he never met what he conceived himself to be, one worthy of the spear, the hunt and knife."

"You are a kindly man, William," said Hamilton.

William shrugged. "I respect Gunther," he said. "I admire him. He is, for all his faults, and mine, my friend."

"What can you do?"

"It is my intention," said William, smiling, "to continue to live."

"I must free you somehow," said Hamilton.

"Do not be foolish," said William. "They would kill you."

"Do you care for these men?" asked Tree.

Hamilton cried out. She almost lost the torch. Tree crouched in the darkness behind her. He had followed her. He took the torch from her. He held it up. William, in the pit below, stepped back. Tree looked down at Hamilton. "Do you care for these men?" he asked.

"They are my friends," said Hamilton.

Tree looked at her. It was strange for a man to be a friend of a woman.

Yet he did not think the concept could not be understood. Once on the height of the shelters, on the rocks, under the stars, they had lain together, looking up.

"There are fires in the sky," had said Tree.

"Someday, perhaps," had said Hamilton, "men will seek the fires in the sky."

"They are far away," said Tree. "Once, when I was little, I climbed a high mountain, to light a torch from them. I could not reach them. They are very high. They are higher, I think, than the tallest trees."

"I think so, too," she said, "but someday, perhaps, men will touch them."

"Do you think so?" asked Tree, turning to look at her.

"Perhaps," said Hamilton.

"But we would have to build a ship," said Tree.

"Yes," said Hamilton.

"There are seas in the sky," said Tree, suddenly, "for rain falls from them to the land. If we took a ship to a high mountain, overlooking the sea in the sky, we could sail to the stars!"

Hamilton kissed him.

"Let us build such a ship!" cried Tree.

"About these fires," said Hamilton, "about some of them, there are, warmed by them, lit by them, new worlds, new forests, new fields, game, places where the Men have never gone."

"I will make a ship!" cried Tree.

"And for every fire there is another fire, and another world, and for every fire a fire beyond that, and a world beyond that."

"I want to go there," said Tree.

"You cannot go there, my love," said Hamilton. "It is a long journey, my love, with many lands and skies to cross, more than you could know, and many lifetimes would it take to build even the ship, and who knows how many to complete even the first step, to place the first foot upon an island other than our own."

"An island?" asked Tree.

"We live upon an island in a vast and endless sea," said Hamilton gently.

"I want to see what is on the other islands," said Tree. "I will see what is on them!"

"Not you," said Hamilton, "not I, but others, perhaps the sons of your sons."

"The seed of the Men?" asked Tree, slowly.

"Yes," said Hamilton. "The sons of the Men." Then the life had stirred within her. She felt it, a heel or knee, tiny, vital.

"I want to go," said Tree, angrily.

"The sons," she said. "The sons of the Men." Then she had rested back, looking upward, looking on the stars. And Tree, too, puzzled, restless, biting his lip, watched the stars.

At the brink of the pit, holding her torch high, Tree looked down on the woman who had come, though it was forbidden her, to see the prisoners.

"I am your friend, not them," said Tree.

"Yes, Tree," had said Hamilton. "You are my friend. I am your friend."

"It is Tree who is your friend," he said, belligerently.

"They, too, are my friends," said Hamilton, boldly. Because of the life in her she knew Tree would not strike her. Women within whom the mystery of life waxed might not be beaten.

"I will kill them," said Tree, simply.

"No," said Hamilton. "One does not kill the friends of one's friend."

"You are mine, none other's," said Tree. It was rare of him to speak so possessively of her. Was she not, after all, a woman of the Men, belonging, like the other females, to all with equal justice?

"Yes, Tree," she whispered. "Though they are my friends, and you are my friend, it is to you, and you alone, that I belong." Hamilton spoke truly.

"Do you want me to help them?" asked Tree.

"Yes," said Hamilton.

Tree regarded Hamilton's swollen body. "I will speak with Spear," said Tree.

Hamilton screamed again, her head back. She felt Cloud's hand on her arm. Then another body was beside them. She saw the head of Ugly Girl. Ugly Girl whimpered. Then Ugly Girl began to lick at the fluid on her body, cleaning her. "I want Old Woman," whispered Hamilton. Two other women entered the shelter, blond Flower, and the virginally bodied girl, who had been taken from the Weasel People. They knelt near her. The virginally bodied girl was frightened. Then Antelope was beside her, touching her arm. "Old Woman!" said Hamilton. "I want Old Woman!" "Old Woman says there is time," said Antelope. "She will come later." The girls knelt about Hamilton. Hamilton was silent. The pain was gone now. There were tears on her face. She began to sweat. "Old Woman says there is time," repeated Antelope. "She will come later." Hamilton felt Flower kiss her. Hamilton's fists clenched.

William and Gunther, bound, had been herded far from the shelters. The Men had traveled easily. William had indicated to them the way.

The judge, Spear, had made his decision.

"If Herjellsen has mastered the retrieval problem, we will live," said William.

On the way the Men did not cover their movements, for they trekked lands of people with whom they shared sign talk, with whom they traded. With them they brought their women, their children. They did not come to raid, or war.

On the plains, across the great forded river, they were joined by men of the Horse People, the hunters of the small horses, scarcely more than brush-maned ponies, many of them striped with brown and black. Sometimes these animals were hunted on foot, pursued, encircled, surprised, killed; at other times they were driven toward pits or between lines of bowmen, who leaped from the ground to fire their small, stout bows at them as they raced past. The Horse People wore the skins of horses and, some of the males, in their hair, crests, of leather and horsehair, resembling the manes of the animals they hunted, which headdresses terminated with a swirl of horsehair, which fell behind the back, formed from the tails of their prey.

On the sixth day they came to the place, the gate, the corridor. Gunther and William had marked it with a ring of stones.

"They may return to their own country," had said Spear, "but if they do not do so, then we will kill them."

These conditions had been agreed to by William. Gunther had not spoken.

William, unbound, stepped within the ring of stones. He stood there, in the circle, on the grass.

At a sign from Spear the men lifted their axes.

"I sense it," said William. "I sense it!"

The Men stood about the ring, their axes lifted.

"Good-bye, Brenda," said William. "Good-bye!"

The men of the Horse People cried out with amazement. They drew back, eyes wide. They jabbered. Fox looked pale. Hyena began a dance, shaking a stick. Hawk reached out, to touch a stone. Spear lifted his ax. Hawk drew back his hand.

Gunther was unbound. It was Tree himself who freed his wrists. Gunther looked at Tree, once, outside the circle of stones; then he looked down; he looked to Hamilton, then turned his eyes aside; he entered the ring of stones.

Tree regarded him calmly.

"Good-bye, Gunther," whispered Hamilton.

Gunther said nothing.

Again a cry went up from the Horse People, who fell back, then crowded about. Their leader thrust among them, with his bow, driving them back. The Men regarded the stones curiously. There were many things they did not understand. They did not know why the sun rose, or water flowed downward, or how a child was born.

Hyena began to chant and dance, making strange signs with his yellow-tufted stick.

Then Spear, and Tree, and the others, had turned away. Hamilton remained looking at the stones for a time. Then he, too, turned away, and followed the Men. Behind them they left the Horse People, regarding the ring of stones. Lastly came Hyena, shaking the yellow-tufted stick, dancing, uttering sounds in no language, but which seemed to him mighty in meaning, dream-sounds, of the sort which came to him in the night, when he, in his dreams, communed with the night hyenas.

"It hurts!" screamed Hamilton. "I'm dying! I will die!" It

JOHN NORMAN

was impossible suddenly it seemed to her, that it should occur. It could not happen! "It will kill me!" she wept. She reared up, screaming, half sitting, then fell back, arching her back. "I will die!" she wept. "I will die!" Then she cried, "Kill me! Kill me!" Then the spasm abated, and she wept and sweated. Ugly Girl put her head to the side of her waist, to comfort her. The other women of the Men, one by one, came to the shelter. Only Old Woman and Nurse did not come. "Go for Old Woman!" cried Hamilton. "There is time," said Antelope. Then the pain came again, and Hamilton, crying out, felt blood in her mouth, where she had, with her teeth, torn open her own lip. She gritted her teeth, eyes closed, swallowed the blood.

It had been some months ago, toward the beginning of the fall, several weeks after Gunther and William had taken their leave of the Men, that the men, in one of the shelters, had come upon the bear, when Knife had fallen back, exposing Spear who had then been blinded. "Spear is blind," had said Knife. "I am first among the Men." None had gainsaid him.

For more than a week Spear, in one of the large shelters, had sat silent. Short Leg would not feed him. Some of the younger women came to him, remembering him, giving him food. Hamilton, too, had fed him. Sometimes Old Woman had come and looked upon him, staring out, one eye gone, missing from the head, the other without pupil, only scar tissue beneath the upper lid. He did not move. He did not speak. One day Knife had come upon him and, seeing Old Woman standing nearby, had said to her. "Take Spear hunting." Knife had given Old Woman a spear, Spear's own. Then he had gone to Spear and, by the arm, dragged him to his feet. "It is time to go hunting," he said to Spear. Then he turned to face Old Woman. "Take Spear hunting," said Knife. "Take him hunting on the high cliffs." Old Woman nodded and took Spear by the arm. He permitted himself to be led away. As they had left the shelter, Knife said to Old Woman. "Spear killed Drawer."

That afternoon Knife had been in a good mood. But in the evening, Old Woman had returned with Spear. Knife leaped to his feet, in fury. Old Woman led Spear to a place by the fire, and sat him down. "The hunting was not good," she said to Knife, who looked upon her with rage.

Hamilton, and Flower, gave Spear meat from the fire. He chewed on it.

The Men, and the women, too, gathered about. "Old Woman," asked Tree, "who is first among the Men?"

She looked from face to face and then, after a silence, said, "Spear—Spear is first."

"No!" cried Knife. "I am first!"

"Spear is first," had said Old Woman.

"Spear is blind," said Short Leg, touching Tree. Hamilton had thrust her from Tree.

"Spear is blind!" cried Knife. "I am first!"

Old Woman said, "Spear—he is first."

"Who is first!" demanded Knife. He looked at Tree.

Tree did not meet his eyes, but bent to the meat in the firelight, cutting it. He looked down, but he was smiling. "Spear," he said, "is first."

Knife cried out with rage. "Spear is first," said Arrow Maker. "Spear is first," said Runner. Knife looked about the fire. Stone stood up, who had hunted with Spear since their childhood. "Spear is first," he said, without emotion. Knife glowered at Fox. Fox looked about from face to face. Then he said, "Spear—Spear is first." "Spear is first," said Wolf. Knife looked at Tooth. He sat cross-legged, chewing on meat. Behind him, in a collar of the men, knelt Ugly Girl, frightened. Tooth threw a bone into the fire. "Spear is first," he said. Hawk, the youngest stood. "The first among the Men," he said, "is Spear."

"Give me meat," said Spear. It was given him. Knife, looking about himself, left the shelter.

Hamilton, on her back, put her hands on her belly. Then she threw back her head and screamed again. It was large and alive and moving and wild and had begun its descent. She arched her back, shrieking, and pulled up her legs and threw them apart, her whole body caught up in the wildness of the contraction, the pain, even to the fingertips, the skin of the forehead and it would fight loose of her and the spasms more tight, more frequent, the impossible pain, the rocking, the violence, the escaping living thing unimaginable pressing from her and she saw the torch and Old Woman's face and she reached her hand to her and Old Woman said "Be quiet," to her and then, to the other women, "Gag her," and Hamilton, fur thrust in her mouth, tied in place with leather, was, as Old Woman had ordered, gagged and her arms were held and the thing, alive, coming, pressing, moving, the agony, the contraction and Old Woman's hands, sure, at her body, reaching and there was a tearing and Hamilton, arms held, gagged, back arched, silently, screamed to the silent, torchlit roof of the shelter her pain and the women pressed about and there was Ugly Girl and Flower

and Antelope and the others and another pain, more terrible, and then less and from her distended body foul with
stink and slime and life Old Woman lifted the thing from her
body, cackling, the cord and tissue bloody, dangling from it,
and, laughing, struck it, and Hamilton reached for it, tears
in her eyes, and heard the tiny sound, the choking sound,
and was terrified, and then, after a moment, the coughing,
the intake of breath and the cry, the first cry, the lusty wail,
the shriek of the offended life torn from her, lifted in torchlight among the primitive women, its lungs, tiny, widening,
startled, contracting, instinctually drawing painfully within
themselves the first shrieking, invisible draught of oxygen.

"It is alive," said Old Woman. "And it is beautiful."

Hamilton, weeping, reached for the child, and, as the
women fumbled to take from her the gag of fur and leather,
held its bloodied, dirty body to her own between her breasts.
"I love you," she wept to it. "I love you. I love you."

"Give it to Nurse," said Old Woman. "We must clean it,
and cut the cord."

Old Woman bent to the cord with a sharpened shell and
bit of string. Ugly Girl and Nurse, with their tongues, licked
the infant, cleaning it.

"You must not cry," said Old Woman to the bawling life.
"You will disturb the men."

Then she put back her head and laughed.

"He may cry if he wishes," said Antelope, laughing.

"Yes," said Cloud.

They held up the child before Hamilton. She smiled. "He
is of the Men," she said.

Then she took him, and, in the torchlight, noted that on
his neck, beneath the left ear, there was a tiny mark. It was
not unlike a tree.

She held the child to her. "I love you," she said to it. "I
love you." The pain was gone. She held the child to her,
loving it. "I love you," she wept. "I love you. I love you. I
love you!"

◆ 31 ◆

"Cricket! Cricket!" called Hamilton.

She returned to the camp at the foot of the shelters. With Antelope and Ugly Girl she had gone to the river bank. She had gathered berries. Ugly Girl, climbing the sloping dirt bank, in places almost sheer, over the river, had thrust her hand into hollowed, tunnel nests, taking eggs, from the brownish, sharp-billed birds who nested there. Antelope, over her shoulder, like Hamilton, carried a sack, filled with berries and tiny fruit.

The children of the camp ran to them, putting their hands into the sacks. "No, No!" scolded Antelope, but not stopping them. They leaped about Antelope and Hamilton.

"Cricket!" called Hamilton. "Cricket!" She had selected some large, juicy berries, which she had hidden in a corner of the sack, at the bottom, for Cricket.

The child, Cricket, truly, had as yet no name among the Men. He had not yet gone to the Men's cave. They called him, sometimes, Turtle's son, and sometimes, Cricket, for that was the name that Tooth had called him by when he had taken his first steps. "Cricket!" called Hamilton.

"That is enough!" laughed Antelope. Ugly Girl had already taken the eggs to Old Woman. On the way, she had, turning her head, bit one open and, spitting out the end of the shell, sucked out the white and yolk. Antelope bent down to give one of the berries to Pod, a small child, reaching up, Short Leg's son, no more than two years of age, a few months younger, no more, than Hamilton's son.

"Cricket!" called Hamilton. Then she asked Cloud, "Have you seen Cricket?"

Shortly after Spear had been blinded, he had been abandoned by Short Leg. Refusing to care for him, she had left him in the shelters, until one of the men would kill him. But none of the men had killed him. She had tried to attach herself to Knife, but Knife wanted none of her, for she was

347

older than he wanted, and his choice was the girl, Flower, who had then been high woman in the camp. But Spear had again become first among the Men. None of the men had killed him. And Old Woman, when ordered to take him hunting on the cliffs, had merely done so. Spear had killed Drawer. But Old Woman did not leave him to die, or fall, among the cliffs. She had brought him back to the fire. Tree had asked her who was first among the men. "Spear—Spear is first," had said Old Woman. "Spear is first," had said the other men. Knife had turned away.

"Why did you not leave Spear on the cliffs?" asked Cloud. "Why did you not kill him?"

"Because among the Men," said Old Woman, "he is first."

Cloud, nor Antelope, nor the others, had questioned her further.

"Give me meat," had said the blind, scarred Spear, huge and terrible, at the fire, and it had been done. Spear was again first.

"Spear," said Old Woman to Hamilton, when they were alone, though Hamilton had not spoken to her, "is a great man. Spear is a wise and great man."

Hamilton had looked at her.

"The Men," she said, "need Spear."

"He killed Drawer," said Hamilton.

Old Woman nodded. Then she said, "Spear is needed by the men."

When Spear had again become first, Short Leg had returned to kneel beside him, but he, terrible, one eye torn away, the other blinded, staring out, his face ridged and white with rivers of scarring, with one hand, gestured her from the fire behind which he sat. "I will die," she had whimpered. Then she cried, "Feel my belly. I carry life!"

"I will not feed you," said Spear.

Then she cried, "It is your law, that I be fed!"

"I will not feed you," said Spear.

"I will feed her," had said Stone. Short Leg had once been Spear's woman. Since Spear and Stone had been children they had known one another. Stone had been with Spear many years ago, when Spear, for pelts, had purchased Short Leg from the Bear People. In Short Leg's body was life. Law was to be kept. Stone remembered Spear, from long ago. He remembered Short Leg. She had had flowers in her hair. "I will feed you," he said, his voice without emotion.

And so Short Leg was fed by Stone, but he did not make her kick, nor use her.

Hamilton's son was born some months before that of Short Leg. When Hamilton's son was born Spear had had the infant brought to him. He had lifted it up, over the fire. "A child is born to the Men," he had said. Then he had given it back to the women. Little attention would be paid to it from that time on by men, except for gentle, loving Tooth, the ugly giant, with the extended canine. When the child could run with the men, when it could throw, when it could kill and take meat, then the men would take it unto themselves, removing it from the children and the women, and by training and counsel, make it wise in lore and skills, make it one of themselves, one of the Men.

But when the child of Short Leg was born, though it was doubtless Spear's own, he would not take it in his arms, nor lift it in his arms, warming it at the fire, sharing its light against the cold and darkness with the child.

But Stone did this, for the child was not to be cast out. 'A child is born to the Men," said Stone, lifting the child by the fire. Then he handed it to Short Leg. Her son was called Pod by Tooth, and the children.

"Have you seen Cricket?" asked Hamilton of Flower.

"No," said Flower.

Hamilton gave the berries, except for those she had hidden for Cricket, to Old Woman, and began to look about the camp. "Cricket!" she called. "I have something for you!"

Tree had not been too pleased at what had come between him and his woman, Turtle.

The devotion, the love, which had been fully his, he must now share. It was clear he resented the child, for it came between him and the female.

"It is your son!" had laughed Hamilton.

"I am not a woman," he had said angrily.

Among the men the mothers were clearly known, and children were spoken of as the sons of the women, or the daughters of the women. Beyond this they might be spoken of as the children, or the young, of the Men. The Men understood the relationship of seed to young, but the possessive concept of a specific, individual paternity, laying a unique claim to a given offspring, was not cultural for them. For the women it was biological. Generally, for the men, such a concept would not become significant until the victory of agriculture, with claims to specific possessions and lands, when inheritance would become crucial. Then, too, of course, with the coming of agriculture, and the need to guarantee specific paternity, because of inheritance rights, accordant cultural provisions would be established. Women would be consigned in impressive ceremonies to individual males. Chastity would become a virtue. Private ownership contracts would become universal. Fear and hatred of sex, and frigidity, and other economic desiderata, conditioned by agricultural priesthoods, would become the hallmarks of the exemplary female. The stirrings of a girl's glands, for the first time, frightening her, terrifying her, instead of being an occasion for rejoicing, would become evil, and rationally so in the twisted net of economically essential perversions, soon to be invested with all the sanctimonious cant of ignorant pieties. In the trek of civilization, the hunt and the horizon, predictably, for at least a time, must yield to the soil and the hobble. The chains, once climbed upon, if to be lost, must be burned away, melted, in the heat of the stars.

"Look!" had laughed Hamilton, pointing to the tiny birthmark, the small, bluish black treelike stain on the child's neck, beneath the left ear. It was as though it had been Tree's own.

"From your seed I have made this child," said Hamilton, in the language of the Men. "He is my son. He is your son." It seemed strange to Tree to think of a man as having a son, though doubtless there was a sense in which it might be meaningful to say it.

"Hold him," smiled Hamilton.

She held out the infant to Tree. Timidly, fearing to drop it, fearing that it might squirm, or cry out, Tree took the infant. He held it in his two hands, and lifted it, looking at it. He looked at the mark under the ear. Then he had held the baby again before his face. He knew that Knife was Spear's son, though he did not think Knife knew this. Some of the other children he thought he could identify with certain of the men. But with others he was not sure. With this child, however, there seemed no doubt but what it had been his seed that Turtle had tended and nourished.

He looked at Turtle and smiled.

Turtle, radiant, touched him. "I love you, Tree," she said. "It is your son. You have given me a son."

Tree looked at the child. He hoped the boy would grow to be a good hunter. He thought perhaps, when the others were not near, he might talk to him, or show him things. He would want him to do well in the Men's cave. Once, years ago, he had seen Spear teaching Knife. He never told Spear he had seen this. It was an unusual emotion which Tree, briefly, felt for the tiny animal in his arms, so weak, so help-

less. "You have given me a son," said Tree, slowly, thinking
about it. He held the tiny thing in his arms. It weighed so
little. Its hands were so tiny. He looked at Turtle. Never before had he seen her just as he saw her then. He knew she
was beautiful. He knew she was his woman. "I do not think,"
he said, "I will ever beat you again." "Beat me when I de-
serve it, or you will spoil me," smiled Hamilton. Tree looked
at her. "I will," he said. "I love you, Tree," said Hamilton.

Then Fox had ventured by. He saw the child in Tree's
arms. "Tree," he asked, poking Wolf, who was with him, in
the ribs, "do you have a son?" In the language of the Men
this joke was rich, for only women had sons and daughters.
"When did you have this son?" asked Fox. "Was it last
night," added Wolf, grinning.

Tree looked angry, and turned red. He thrust the child to
Hamilton's arms.

"A child is born to the Men," he said.

"We are going hunting," said Fox.

"I will come with you," said Tree, quickly.

"Had you not better tend your son?" asked Fox.

Tree leaped to his feet and, laughing, as they fled away,
slapped both on the back of the head. "Let us hunt," he said.

Hamilton, smiling, secure, had held the child to her. She
felt its hunger, its eagerness.

"Cricket!" called Hamilton, wandering about the camp. "I
have something for you!" She held a handful of the largest,
juiciest berries, taken from the sack, in her right hand. "Butterfly," said Hamilton, "where is Cricket?" "I do not know,
Turtle," said Butterfly.

Short Leg, for more than two years, had been fed by
Stone. But Stone was not a leader. He was strong. He was
hard. He could follow like a bear or horse, but he was not a
leader. And she was not close with him. He fed her, little
more. Short Leg, who was an intelligent woman, considered
the Men with care. Who, she asked herself, after Spear, will
be first among the Men. She did not think it would be Knife.
Stone, for some reason, did not like Knife. The others had
not accepted Knife. Who, among the Men, she asked herself,
was it who first proclaimed Spear again the leader. It had
been one of them only, at first. It had been Tree. It had been
he who had asked Old Woman who was first. It had been he
who had, following her words, unemotionally declared for
Spear. The others had followed. Tree, too, was strongest, and
tallest, and the finest hunter. It had been he who, among the
men, had first again declared for Spear. The others had fol-

lowed. Short Leg had smiled to herself. After Spear, she told herself, it will be Tree who will be first among the Men. He did not want to be first, but it would be he, she did not doubt, whom the others would have as first among them. She could not see them, among the Men, following any other. It would be Tree, after Spear, who would be first. Short Leg was no longer young, but she could bear young; she could work; she knew what transpired in the camp; other women feared her; and she was wise; she could be a great asset to a leader. Short Leg was not the only one who could read the signs of the future. Flower, too, after Knife's repudiation as leader, and the restoration of Spear, calculated that Tree would be the successor. Accordingly, when she could, she slipped away, usually to meet Tree on his return from the hunt, to lie beside the trail, on the grass, and, as he returned, to hold her arms out to him, and lift her body. "Feed Flower," she would beg. "Flower will do anything for you." Tree would look upon her, her uplifted hands, her eyes, her lifted body, begging for even his casual rape. Tree, a hunter, throwing his kill from his shoulders to the grass, and one angry with Hamilton of late, for she no longer gave him the totality of her undivided attention, but spent much time suckling and loving her child, was not one to refuse this free gift of beauty. Sometimes, furious with Hamilton, Tree would throw the startled Flower on her side and using one of her lovely legs as a fulcrum for his body, freeing it of the ground, release the full spasms of his irritation upon her, pounding her, she gasping, clinging to him, mercilessly, and then, leaving her, standing over her, she half shattered at his feet, her eyes looking up at him, her legs now drawn up, he would look down upon her. "Knife will feed you," he would say.

Once Tree let Flower carry the antelope he had killed to the camp. She did so, proudly. Hamilton was angry. Knife beat Flower. Flower did not care. But that night Short Leg, with a chipped knife, crept to Flower. She held her hand over Flower's mouth. When Flower opened her eyes, she was terrified. She could not move. She felt the chipped blade of the flint weapon pressing across her throat. "Stay away from Tree," whispered Short Leg. Then she added, "Tree will be mine."

"Did you see Cricket, Pod?" asked Hamilton, the berries in her hand.

"No," said Pod.

She gave the toddler a berry.

"I will help you look for Cricket," said Butterfly. "I will help, too," said Antelope.

"Cricket!" called Hamilton. "I have something for you!" She clutched the berries more closely.

"Tooth," asked Butterfly, "have you seen Cricket?"

"No," said Tooth.

"Arrow Maker, have you seen Cricket?" asked Butterfly.

"No," said Arrow Maker.

"I will help you look," said Tooth. "Ugly Girl!" he called. "Let us find Cricket."

She came, nostrils distended, filtering the scents of the camp. Her sense of smell was superior to that of most of the Men. She stood still in the camp. Then she began to walk about its edge.

"Short Leg," said Antelope. "Have you seen Cricket?"

"No," said Short Leg, looking down, scraping a skin. She smiled.

"Where is Cricket?" asked Tree of Hamilton.

"I am looking for him," said Hamilton.

"Oh," said Tree. He did not look up. Hamilton turned away, the berries in her hand. When she was not looking, Tree rose to his feet. Perhaps Cricket was by the river. He liked to throw stones in the water. Tree was thirsty. He would look. He would see, on the way, if he could pick up a trail. It would not be out of his way.

Tree did not much care for Short Leg. She had been Spear's woman. She was not beautiful. She was now fed by Stone. She was a cunning woman, and hard and sharp. Her mind was quick, her tongue cruel. Many times she had knelt behind Tree, but he would not throw her meat. He threw it to Turtle. Then Short Leg would hobble to Stone, and take her place behind him, and he would give her meat. Sometimes Hamilton, herself, thrust her away from Tree. "Tree is mine!" Hamilton said to her, though she would not have dared to say this within the hearing of Tree. "Stay away from him! He is mine!" Once she threatened Short Leg with a heavy stick. "You will be fed by Stone," she said. "Go away!"

Although Tree did not want Short Leg, he was not displeased that this powerful woman wished to be fed by him. He was more pleased that Flower had begged for food. But Flower, for some weeks now, had not pressed herself upon him. She no longer met him on the return trails. This puzzled Tree. Once, in the camp, he took her, making her cry out, moaning, with unwilling miseries of pleasure, but she had seemed frightened; he had had, literally, to rape her;

then she had fled away from him, terrified. He supposed that
Knife had threatened her. "I can please you more than
Flower," had said Turtle, begging him for his touch, taking
his hand, putting it on her body. "Tend your son," had said
Tree to her, angrily. She had wept.

Although Tree was careful to show little attention, and
certainly no favoritism, to the boy, Cricket, it was clear to the
women in the camp, and to many of the men, that he was
much pleased with the boy, and that, somehow, his relationship to the boy was not simply that of one of the Men to one
of the children of the Men. Tree had been present when the
boy had taken his first steps. It was with pride and pleasure
that Tree had laughed. It seemed strange to several of the
men that Tree should be thus pleased. Did not all the children
of the Men walk? Did he think that Cricket would not be able
to walk?

"Old Woman, Nurse," asked Hamilton, "where is Cricket?"

"I do not know," said Old Woman. "I do not know," said
Nurse.

About the edge of the camp, followed by Tooth, Ugly Girl
had dropped almost to all fours. She bent over, nostrils
wide. The knuckles of her long arms, on the thick, short
body, brushed the ground. She took scent deeply.

At the river Tree, angrily, examined the near bank. None
of the camp were there.

Short Leg had seen that not all was well between Turtle
and Tree. Tree was angry with her, many times. This pleased
Short Leg, but, to her puzzlement, he continued to feed her.
Sometimes, when Turtle suckled the child, or fondled it, and
played with it, paying Tree no attention, he was clearly
angry. At other times, he seemed fond of the child, inordi-
nately and inappropriately so for so powerful a hunter. Why
should he so care about the child of Turtle? Even if it was
his seed, it was not important; it was the son of the mother,
and the mother's alone, until the men should want it and
take it from her, to make it a hunter. Turtle's son, Short Leg
understood, was, for all his irritation, important to Tree. It
made Turtle, to him, somehow different from all the other
females of the camp. If it were not for the boy, Short Leg
reasoned, Turtle would be to him no more than Cloud, or
Flower or Antelope. If Tree would feed Short Leg, Short Leg
would not object if he took Flower or Cloud, only that she,
Short Leg, would be first woman. Flower would be behind
her. She would not be first. It would be then as it had been
with Spear. Short Leg would be the woman of Tree, but he

would have others, too, which he might feed, and use for his pleasure. Stone could have Turtle, or Runner or Fox. Or, she could be traded to the Bear People, or the Horse People, for another girl, a new girl, not knowing the group, who would do as Short Leg told her. Short Leg had seen Tree's anger with Turtle. Why did he continue to feed her? It had to do, somehow, with Turtle's son.

Hamilton, with Cloud and Butterfly, struggled through brush about the camp.

"Cricket!" Hamilton called.

The berries were only stains and pulp in her clenched fist. She could hear others, too, the women, and Tooth, calling out, elsewhere in the brush.

Then she heard Tooth call out to her. "Turtle!" he cried. She, with the others, struggled through the brush, towards him. Ugly Girl, on her hands and knees, looked up at them. She looked frightened, sick.

"What is wrong?" whispered Hamilton.

"She has found the trail," said Tooth.

Ugly Girl could not tell in the language of the Men the mingled scents she had detected, for her mouth and tongue could not make the words. But she did not sign the scents either, in hand talk. Tooth could not look Hamilton in the face.

"What is it!" cried Hamilton.

She saw a broken branch, a crushed leaf. "Cricket!" she cried. "Cricket!"

Ugly Girl, the others, and Tooth, did not follow her.

Hamilton made her way through the brush, pushing aside branches.

◆ 32 ◆

"He liked berries," said Hamilton.

She placed, in the tiny trough, a dozen berries. They were large, juicy, red. She put in the tiny trough five tiny, pretty shells, and a toy, of stuffed leather, in the shape of a small,

four-footed animal. Pod, who was the son of Short Leg, put a
shiny pebble in the trough. Tree crouched nearby, but back
with the others. He put a tiny bow, with tiny arrows in the
trough. The Men put stones over the trough.

Hamilton stood up.

Short Leg, seeing her return, seeing her eyes, and that she
knew, had leaped, eyes wild, terrified, to her feet and fled.
"Turtle will kill me!" she cried to Stone. "Cricket is dead,"
had said Stone. Short Leg fled to the cave where Spear
sat, on a rug of fur. "Turtle will kill me!" she cried. "A child
of the Men is dead," said Spear. "Protect me!" cried
Short Leg. "Are you here, Stone?" asked Spear. From the entrance to the shelter Stone had said, "I am here." "With
stones cut off her fingers," said Spear. "With sticks punch out
her eyes. Then take her into the forests. Leave her far from
the shelters. Leave her far from the shelters at night." "No,"
cried Short Leg. She scrambled past Stone. On the ledge outside Spear's shelter she saw Hamilton below. Hamilton began
to climb toward her. "Turtle will kill me!" cried Short Leg.
She picked up a rock and hurled it down toward Hamilton.
Hamilton continued to climb toward her. Below, at the foot
of the shelters, Short Leg saw Ugly Girl, Tooth, Cloud, the
others. They were looking up, watching. "Protect me!"
screamed Short Leg. "I am Short Leg!" she cried. "Protect
me!"

Then Hamilton was on the ledge.

Short Leg turned to the cliff and, scrambling, hand by hand,
feet scraping for holds, began to climb.

Hamilton followed her.

Some seventy or eighty feet from the stones below, clinging to the cliff, Short Leg turned her head, looked back, and,
fingers scratching, sliding, lost her grip, and, screaming,
plunged backward, falling, twisting, until she struck the
stones.

At the foot of the cliffs Hamilton saw Pod, the infant of
Short Leg. Suddenly screaming with hatred she seized the
child and lifted it over her head, to dash its skull open
against the cliffs, and then, sobbing, wild, Hamilton stumbled
to Nurse, and thrust the child in her arms.

Hamilton rolled on the stones, striking at them, howling,
shrieking at the sky in misery. She cut her body with the
stones, and her tears and her blood marked the granite. In
her right hand were the stains of the berries. Old Woman
went alone into the forest and cut her face with rocks. With
a flint knife she cut from her left hand two fingers.

Hamilton stood up. She looked down at the stones, covering the trough. All night Hamilton had sat with the child in her arms. By force Old Woman and Nurse had taken it from her arms, and placed it in the trough. Some articles, too, had been placed in the trough, some berries, some shells and a toy of stuffed leather. A child, too, had placed a pebble in the trough and one of the hunters had added a bow, a tiny one, with tiny arrows. Then the men had put stones over the trough.

Then Stone had said, "The meat must be roasted. There are skins to clean."

The Men, followed by the women, and the children, turned away.

Hamilton, and Tree, remained behind.

"He liked berries," Hamilton said.

Tree did not respond to her.

Hamilton took from her throat the necklace of the Men, unknotting it. She handed it to Tree. "I am going away," she told him.

The hunter did not detain her.

◆ 33 ◆

"You are my daughter," said Herjellsen.

"Do not excite him," said William. "He is dying."

"It has finally caught up with me," said Herjellsen. "My own body. I am to be killed by my own body."

"The child died," said Hamilton. "It died. There is no child."

"We have all failed," said Herjellsen. "All of us have failed."

Gunther, sitting on a wooden chair in the corner of the room, regarded him, not speaking. William sat near the bed, a stethoscope about his neck. In the background stood Herjellsen's two blacks, the large fellow, who was called Chaka, though it was not his true name, but the name of a black king, and the smaller man, his friend. They wore khaki shorts and open shirts.

"Your scheme was a mad one," said Gunther, slowly. "You are insane."

Herjellsen looked at them, peering through the thick lenses of his glasses. He rested his head back. He sat in bed, propped by pillows. He was far thinner now, and whiter than Hamilton remembered him. His body seemed small beneath the sheets. He wore a ragged pair of red-striped pajamas. The neck was open. The first two buttons were opened. His face suddenly tensed, and his body was tight, clenched on a saw's edge of pain.

"You should rest now," said William.

"No," said Herjellsen. Then he looked at Hamilton. "I had hoped," he said, "there would have been a child."

"It died," said Hamilton.

"I am sorry," said Herjellsen. Then he looked at her. "I chose you," he said, "because you are my only daughter, my only child."

Hamilton had not known her parents.

"It was essential to my hopes," he said. "But now we have all failed."

"What was it," demanded Gunther, suddenly, angrily, "that you hoped to accomplish in your madness?"

"To inaugurate the renaissance of man," said Herjellsen. "To touch the stars." He lay back against the pillow, but his eyes were open. "Man," he said, "has within him beasts and gods, and he is only truly man when each may thrive and both are fed."

"On what," asked Gunther, "can gods and beasts feed?"

"On meats and horizons," said Herjellsen.

"The two natures of man?" asked William, smiling.

"No," said Herjellsen, "that is the odd thing, for there is truly only one nature, though there is no name for it in any language I know. If there were to be a word, I suppose it would be the nature of the god-beast or beast-god. The important thing to understand is that it is the beast brain which thinks, which perceives, which acts. There is only one nature, that of the beast which can lift its head and catch the scent of the fires of stars."

"Surely one nature or the other must die," said William.

"No," said Herjellsen, "that is the teaching only of those who have little of either nature." He thrust his head forward. "If the god dies, so, too, does the beast, and if the beast dies, with it expires the god. The heart may not be removed to succor the brain, nor the brain removed from the skull to pacify the heart. It is one system, one glory, one splendor, called Man."

No one spoke. And Herjellsen again rested his head back on the pillows. He seemed scrawny, almost, now, and futile, and silly in the red and white pajamas. He was only a primate with delusions, one who could not understand evident realities. To whom could such a man speak? To the world he despised he could count only as a madman. It could only kill such men, or ridicule them, for he was like a knife to the belly of complacency. "The enemies," said Herjellsen, "lie about us, outside us and within us. They are the little men, the small men, the insects who can dream only the dreams of insects. They cannot know the greatness of man. It cannot register on the compound eye; it eludes the antennae, his strides cannot be understood by the tiny feet to whom a leaf is a country, a weed a continent. Their measurements and scales are not those of men. Comfort, security, softness, too, lie about us, and within us, more deadly than the aging heart, the wretched, brittle valves, the withered tissues." The old man's eyes blazed, and it seemed his weakness, his tortured frailness vanished, and there was only, for the moment, burning within him, flaming, the intellect, the heart, the indomitable will. "Civilization," said he, "is not the end, not the termination, the destiny. It is the vehicle, the path, the instrument. Without it we cannot achieve Man, nor discover him."

"And where," asked Gunther, "shall we achieve man? Where shall we discover him?"

"Among the stars," said Herjellsen. "We will not achieve Man until we, his precursors, stand among the stars. It is then, and then only, that we will discover him. He may be found there, and there only! It will be only in the landscapes of infinity, you see, that he shall rise to his full height, for in what other country could a man stand as high as a man can stand? He will not be fully man until he can see the stars as pebbles at his feet."

"The child died," said Hamilton.

"We have all failed," said Herjellsen, turning ashen, falling back to the pillows.

"What is so important," asked Gunther, "about the child?"

"And how," asked Hamilton, "could you seriously have expected me to turn the eyes of men to the stars?"

"By the child," whispered Herjellsen. "By the child!" He looked at her, sadly, through the thick lenses. "Words will not turn men to the stars, though they may open the eyes of men who have eyes with which to see the stars. Words are little, and futile, a bit of noise, briefly heard, swiftly forgotten, and fatuous, and not enough. I did not expect you to argue with hunters, nor to explain physics to them, nor to instill in them dreams."

"What did you expect me to do?" asked Hamilton.

"Whether a man can see the stars, in his heart as well as in his eyes, like cattle or birds, is a little understood factor locked in his genetic codes. It is much like the factor that permits one man to detect the beauty of music and forever precludes another from its raptures; it is like the factor that permits one man to be strong and denies strength to another; it is like the factor that makes it possible for one man to be touched by love, and forever makes this splendor an enigma, a fiction, to one who might otherwise be his brother."

"The hunters are dead," said Gunther. "They died, and many thousands of years ago."

"What did you expect me to do?" asked Hamilton.

"Bear the child," said Herjellsen. He looked at her. "Civilization totters," said Herjellsen. "It is dying. It is choking on its own filth. Ever more toxic grows the atmosphere. Ever more abundant grow the multitudes, crowding and pressing, hating and sweating and squirming for room to love, to breathe and live, and dying, denied and crushed, gasping in the jungles and sewers of their own garbage. And looming on the brink of this poisoned tank we note, poised, the ultimate purificatory instrument. Insects will survive, and, it is likely, certain forms of reptiles. Little else. Surely not man."

"How would the child make such a difference?" asked Hamilton, puzzled.

"It would be, in its way," said Herjellsen, "not only my ancestor, but my grandson. It would have borne within it my seed, my genetic coding, a part of me, a particle of a protoplasmic, carnal chain which might reach high enough to explode in its fragments of significance among the stars."

"How can it be before you, and after you?" asked William.

"Time," said Herjellsen, "is not understood. It is perhaps a condition of our representations, constituting for us a reality, but not in itself the ultimate reality. The concept of time, as we think of it, is filled with conflicts, and it cannot, as we think of it, correspond to a reality. Our minds are perhaps not equipped to understand the true nature of time. What we experience as time may be something in itself quite different, a color we cannot see, a sound we cannot hear, a reality we can know only under our own consecutive forms of perception."

"Surely, for us," said William, "time is quite real."

"Surely," said Herjellsen. "That is not at issue. What is dubious or problematic is the nature in itself of that which we experience as time. Doubtless time is a real mode in which that reality expresses itself, and in this sense is not unreal, but only is not understood. Color and sound, too, are real, but they are not, surely, identical with vibrations, gross and tenuous, in an atmosphere. Similarly the vibrations themselves may not be ultimate, for in one of their dimensions, they are temporal, and time, as we have suggested, cannot be as we conceive it. Could there be a first moment of time? Or, could there not be a first moment of time? The dilemma, my beloved friends, makes manifest the limitations of our concepts, points clearly to their inadequacy, and hints timidly at what must lie beyond, the different, the mystery, the reality."

"How," asked Hamilton, "could one child make a difference?"

"It could," said Herjellsen, "make all the difference in this world, and in others, because of the hundred geometries of biology. The child begets its children, and each of these begets others in turn, and others." Herjellsen smiled. "All of you," he said, "you, Gunther, you, William, as well as you, my beloved daughter, may be my children."

"I look about the world," said Gunther. "I do not think so. These are not Herjellsen's children."

"The child, Herjellsen," said Hamilton, "died."

"Consider the world," said Gunther. "It is not populated with the children of Herjellsen."

"The hunters are dead," said William.

It was only the Dirt People who, in the long run, survived, thought Hamilton. Victors in the long course had not been the hunters, so vain, so proud, so arrogant, so vital, so cruel, so strong, but the Dirt People, with their seeds, and their sacrifices and their sticks. Horizons and stars had not been victorious; but barley and beer.

"I am sorry, Father," said Hamilton.

"Let him rest now," said William.

Herjellsen laid back against the pillows. He pretended to be asleep. When they had left, he wept.

◇ 34 ◇

It was in the neighborhood of ten in the morning, in late June. It was a light, brightly sunny day, cool. The short night preceding had been pleasant, even chilly.

Hamilton sipped her coffee, black, sitting at the small table in the open-air restaurant on the Vester Farimagasade.

From the harbor, more than a kilometer away, there was a breeze, carrying over the city. She could smell fish, and salt.

She liked the city. It was clean, as cities went, and the people calm, industrious. She liked the Danes. She liked the sky over the city, the wind.

Hamilton thought of Herjellsen. Herjellsen had been Finnish. He had had something of their appetites, their stubbornness.

"Have you been long in Copenhagen?" asked the man of the couple, sitting near her, in English.

"No," she responded. She smiled, but she did not want to talk. They returned to their conversation. Hamilton looked again into the small cup of coffee, and then lifted it to her lips and drank. She buttoned the top button on her sweater.

There was no particular reason, as far as she knew, why she had come to Copenhagen. She was now well fixed. Herjellsen, before she had left the compound, had seen to that. William and Gunther, not speaking, had driven her more than two hundred and fifty miles to Salisbury.

"Good-bye," they had said to her.

"Good-bye," she had said, and boarded the plane. They had returned to the compound.

Her eyes had been dry, but inside her body there had been only emptiness and ashes. Herjellsen was dying. He had failed, and William and Gunther had failed and she, too, had failed. She had boarded the plane, and fastened her safety belt, and the runway had slipped away beneath her and in a few moments she saw Rhodesia, whitish and dry in the sun, vanish under the metallic wing.

The adventure, the experiment had ended. Tree was gone. And the child had died.

William and Gunther returned to the compound. William did not wish to leave Herjellsen. Both, in that lonely, fenced compound in the bush, with the blacks, would keep the vigil, waiting for the old man to die.

Then there would be nothing to keep them there.

The compound, deserted, would fall into disrepair and ruin, and the dry wind would blow across a simple grave.

The adventure was ended. The experiment had failed. Herjellsen had lived in vain.

It was then that Hamilton saw them, the young couple. They were entering. They were seeking a table.

She felt faint, and held to the edge of her own table.

They sat not far from her, arguing. The girl looked not unlike Flower. There was something subtle, about the eyes, the mouth, that reminded her of Flower, but her eyes, stunned, could see little of the woman, for the body, the face, of the young man, half blurred, seem to swim in the center of her vision, and all else about, ringing his shoulders and head, and face, seemed dark, vague, meaningless, peripheral to the central reality dominating her focus; slowly the image formed itself, sure, precise, bright, startling. Hamilton caught her breath. The world seemed to swirl about her, turning about that face and shoulders, and then stopped. There could be no mistake. She sobbed. She wanted to reach out, to touch him. But she knew she must not.

Slowly, in snatches, she caught the conversation, between them. She did not understand all of it, for her Danish was poor, but she understood its purport, its themes.

There was silver to be bought, for table settings. There was a shop where furniture might be purchased. Already she had located an apartment. She must show it to him. His studies were completed. He wished to spend a year at sea. He was not ready. That was foolish. In her father's company a place was waiting for him. His position was secure. She loved him. He would rise in the business. In time they would be wealthy.

Hamilton paid little attention to what they said. Mostly she could not take her eyes from the boy. She wanted to go to him with her fingers to lightly brush the blond hair from the side of his neck. He had taken off his student's cap, and put it on the table. He was saying, he did not wish now to do something. He did not know how to speak to her.

She was impatient. Did he not love her? He must make his decision. He spoke of further studies. There was no money in such things. He wished to do advanced work. He wished to think. He wanted to go to sea. Later perhaps he would return to the university. He spoke of astronomy, physics.

If you do not do what I wish, she was saying, I will leave you. You must decide, she said. If you love me, you will please me. If you do not do what I wish, she was saying, I will leave. I will leave you. She was adamant.

Hamilton saw the boy's eyes become agonized.

He looked up.

"Forgive me," said Hamilton, softly, in English, "I do not mean to intrude."

The girl looked angrily at her. What did she want, this strange woman? Indeed she was intruding!

The young man stood. He seemed startled.

"No," said Hamilton, softly, "you do not know me. But I know you."

"Tell her to go away," said the girl.

The young man, puzzled, somehow shaken, regarded Hamilton. He did not tell her to go away.

"Forgive me," said Hamilton. Then, very slowly, with incredible tenderness, she lifted the hair away from the side of his neck. "Forgive me," she whispered, and kissed the mark which lay below his left ear.

"I do not understand," he said, slowly, in English.

"I love you," said Hamilton. "That is all."

"Come away!" said the girl to him, in Danish. Then she repeated the imperative, insistently, in English, that Hamilton would clearly understand. She took him by the hand. He shook loose her hand, angrily. He looked down at Hamilton.

"I love you," said Hamilton.

"I do not know you," he said, very slowly.

"No," smiled Hamilton. "You do not know me."

"Who are you?" he asked.

She smiled. "Your mother," she said.

The blond girl cried out with irritation.

"No," smiled the young man. "You are not my mother."

"I am, and I am not," said Hamilton. "I am the mother of the mothers, the mother of the sons." The blond girl snorted with irritation. Hamilton smiled. "No," she said, "I am not insane, though you cannot understand how I should speak like this, and that not be so. I do not mind. Regard me as you will. It does not matter. What matters is you, and the stars. Be true unto your mightiness, and do not forget the stars."

He looked at her strangely.

"But," said Hamilton, "I speak foolishly. You can never forget them, for the call of the stars, their heat, their light, lies within your blood. Into your blood and bones, though you do not understand how this can be, the seeking of the stars is bred. It was the intention of a man you do not know, called Herjellsen. You will not relinquish infinity, my love, my son. It is your destiny. Seek the stars."

Then Hamilton stood back from the young man, proudly. She drew herself up and pointed to him. When she spoke, it was in the language of the Men. "Here, Tree," she said, "is my son." "Here, Tree," she said, "is your son. Do not laugh, Tree. He is your son and mine. And you would, as I, find him pleasing." Then she addressed herself to the young man. She looked upon him fiercely. Again she spoke in the language of the Men. "Make the hunters proud of you!" she said.

He stood, startled.

"Come away from this madwoman!" said the blond girl, seizing him by the hand.

Again he, angrily, shook away her hand. She was furious.

"I will tell you of your heritage," said Hamilton to the young man. She spoke in English. "I will speak briefly. It is simple, and it is deep. It is this. In your veins lies the blood of hunters, and masters."

He looked at her.

"Come away!" cried the blond girl.

"This female," said Hamilton, pointing to the girl, "belongs in a collar at your feet."

The girl's fingers inadvertently touched her own throat.

"If she pleases you," said Hamilton, "keep her. If she does not please you, discard her. If you keep her, keep her on your terms, not hers. Enslaved, she will adore you; freed, she will kill you."

"Be quiet, madwoman!" screamed the girl. She turned to the boy. "Nils!" she said.

"In your veins," said Hamilton to the boy, "flows the blood of hunters and masters. Make them proud of you."

He regarded her.

"Seek the stars," she said to him.

"I will," he said. He turned about to leave, and then turned back, to look again at Hamilton. "Good-bye," he said.

"Good-bye," whispered Hamilton.

"Nils!" cried the girl.

He had turned away and was walking away, crossing the wide pavement. He moved rapidly. There were tears in Hamilton's eyes. The walk was not unlike that of Tree.

"Nils!" cried the girl. Then she turned, furiously, to Hamilton. "What have you done?" she cried.

"I have met my son," said Hamilton, "one who is of the Men, a son of sons of sons. And I am the mother, and I have seen him. The hunters are not dead."

"Nils!" cried the girl. He did not turn.

"My father," said the girl, "will not understand. What of the business? He is holding a position for him!"

"Your father," said Hamilton, "is not your master." She looked after the young man. "He is," said Hamilton.

"How will we live!" wailed the girl.

"As he wishes," said Hamilton, indicating the young man, small now in the distance.

"I love him," cried the girl. "I will not lose him! I love him!"

"He is sovereign," said Hamilton. "If you would be his, you will be his on his terms, and his alone."

The young woman fled from Hamilton's side, pursuing the young man.

Far away, she saw her, stumbling, reach him. He turned to regard her. Hamilton saw the girl, it seemed as natural as the falling of rain or the turning and opening of a flower, kneel before him, placing herself, and her pride, at his feet. She saw the young man lift her gently to her feet, and, holding her, regard her. Then he removed his belt and looped it about her throat, more than once, and then, tightly, under her chin, buckled it. She wore about her throat his belt, as a collar marking her his, as a symbol of his authority over her. Then their lips met.

"Good-bye," whispered Hamilton, "my son."

◇ 35 ◇

Hamilton stood beside the dusty grave in the bush country. It was not more than four hundred yards from the compound. There was grit in the air, carried by the wind. There was a quite simple marker, a white board some two feet in length, some one by six inches, driven into the dry earth at the head of the grave. Some stones were set about the board, reinforcing it in the ground. Gunther had, in German script, small, precise, written on the board the name 'Herjellsen'. William, below it, in Roman script, once the language of gladiatiors and Caesars, had added an inscription.

Hamilton threw her head back and stood beside the grave, fists clenched. "Herjellsen! Herjellsen!" she cried. "There was another child! There was another child!"

"I think he knew," said William.

Hamilton looked at him.

"Before he died," said William, Gunther standing silently behind him, "he opened the chamber."

"It had to be open," said Hamilton. There had been no doubt in her mind that it would be open. She had seen, in Denmark, that there had been another child.

"Herjellsen," said the large black, Chaka, "gave me this for you." From his shirt he drew forth a yellow envelope. Beside the grave Hamilton opened it. She read it, and gave it to William and Gunther, that they, too, might read it.

"Gunther," said Hamilton.

He looked down at her.

"Find a woman, Gunther," said Hamilton.

Gunther shook his head.

"The hunters are not dead, Gunther," said Hamilton. "In your veins, as in those of others, flows the blood of hunters."

"No," said Gunther. "Not in mine." He shook his head, sadly.

"You are wrong, Gunther," she said.

"I died," said Gunther, "thousands of years ago."

"You are not dead, Gunther," said Hamilton. "It is only that you, like many others, do not know you are alive."

He looked at her strangely.

"There is work to be done," said Hamilton. "Herjellsen would have expected it."

"I can no longer think, no longer work," he said.

"Find a woman," said Hamilton. "Find the strongest, the most intelligent, the finest, the most beautiful, the noblest, the most proud, and then, in your arms, make her your slave, and breed great children on her."

Hamilton looked up into the eyes of Gunther.

"Your seed," said she, "and that of William, and Chaka, and mine, and the others, that of us all, will meet a thousand years from now among the stars."

"It was the intention of Herjellsen," said William.

"There are possibilities," said Gunther. "Some are practical with modest technological developments. Others are interesting also."

"We do not know, as of today," said William, "if the light barrier may be broken."

"We know," said Gunther, "that velocities beyond the speed of light have been obtained by certain particles under laboratory conditions. This is a small beginning, and perhaps will have few practical consequences. It does, however, demonstrate that velocities greater than those of light are feasible."

"Dimensions, too," said William, "exist other than those in which we commonly think."

"We may not find the answer," said Gunther, "but if we do not find it, or this century does not find it, someday, somewhere, somehow, if only men continue to search, and care, it will be found." He looked at Hamilton. "I will be one of those who searches," said he to Hamilton.

"You see, Gunther," she said, "the hunters live."

"I have some interesting ideas on extensions of temporal topologies," said William. "Doubtless little will come of it, but it might be worth exploring."

"There will never be another brain like Herjellsen's," said Gunther, "the brilliance, the madness, the capacity, incomprehensible, to touch the shores of foreign realities."

"Herjellsen did not expect to be always with us," said Hamilton.

"We are alone now," said Gunther.

"We have ourselves," said William.

"Herjellsen," said Gunther, "would have liked to see the stars." He looked down at the grave.

Then the party turned about, and returned, slowly, to the compound.

Behind them they left the grave, with its simple marker. It bore the name Herjellsen. It bore, too, a brief inscription, which William had added, 'Ad Astra.'

At the gate to the compound, Hamilton turned to William. "What is the meaning of 'Ad Astra,' " she asked him.

William smiled. "To the stars," he said.

◊ 36 ◊

Hamilton lifted her head. She rose to her feet, and stood in the high grass, among the stones in a circle.

The Horse People had, in the months intervening, added other stones. Some they had placed on others. Many of these stones were large, and had, apparently, been brought, doubtless on rollers, from long distances. Many of the stones, now, were higher than Hamilton's head.

Then she walked from the place. Two men of the Horse People saw her. They cried out. She paid them no attention. They did not touch her, though, for a time, they followed her. Then they returned to the circle of stones. Looking back, Hamilton saw them dancing about its edges.

She continued on, not again looking back. About her thighs she had wrapped the brief deerskin skirt of the women of the Men, which she had worn when she had returned to Rhodesia and the compound. She had not brought supplies with her, nor a compass. She knew her way. She knew she could live off the land. She was a woman of the Men.

Tree turned her roughly about, her back to him. Hamilton stood very straight. She felt the collar, of thongs, and teeth, and leather, and shells looped several times about her neck and then, behind her neck, knotted tightly. He turned her about, to face him.

"You have been long from my collar," he said.

"Beat me," she said.

"If you run away again," he said, "I will kill you."

"I will not run away again," she said, "—Master."

Her body, abruptly, was half turned about, as he tore the deerskin skirt from her.

"Lie down," he said. "Lift your body."

Swiftly Hamilton, half frightened, obeyed him. He did not take her immediately, but looked upon her.

She looked at him, and saw his anger. She knew he would take his vengeance on her, deep and incredible vengeance, a ruthless hunter's vengeance, for the months in which she had denied him her body. She trembled, but yet with eagerness to feel his wrath. She waited for him, her body trembling; she waited, a slave, for the master to ventilate, fully, on her helpless beauty, the extreme, pent-up fury of his mighty displeasure; she, a slave, awaited her discipline; she knew she would be sharply disciplined; she, a slave, awaited her punishment; she looked at Tree; she knew she would be well punished; "I love you," she said; he looked at her with fury, with desire, with lust, such as she had not seen since he, long ago, had tied her in the high prison cave; "I lie before you, as you have ordered me," said Hamilton; "I lift my body to you, as you have commanded. I am yours. Do with me what you will, Master"; she smiled, tears in her eyes; she arched her back, lifting her body more vulnerably to him; but she saw that he would not be so easily placated; she did not know how long it would take to placate such an anger; it might, she suspected, take weeks, or months; perhaps for more than a year she might be forced to eat from his hand; she looked up again at him, tears loving and sweet in her eyes; "I love you," she whispered; then she said, "I await my punishment"; then she said, "Punish me, Master."

Hamilton, turning her head, with her teeth, took the bit of meat from Tree's hand. He held it. She looked at him. Then he permitted her to have it. She chewed it, and put her head delicately against the hair on his wrist.

"Punish me, Master," she had said, lying before him, his naked slave, in his collar.

With a cry, almost animal, of rage, of joy, of lust, Tree, a hunter, brutal and cruel, had thrown himself mercilessly upon her.

Well had he punished her. Never again would she so much as dare to think of leaving his side.

"I have come back!" she had cried. "I love you!" she had cried. "I love you!"

Antelope came to Hamilton and, as a joke, put her hand on Hamilton's back. Hamilton cried out, and winced, but then, as she saw Tree's frown, was silent, and put down her head, smiling. He did not wish her to cry out. Her back was laced with welts, deep, from the switching she had been given. It hurt her to move, but she was pleased. He had used her five times, almost consecutively, before dragging her to a sapling and lashing her wrists about it; then he had beaten her; when he had done this, he untied her and again, by the hair, threw her to the grass, where he raped her until he could rape her no more, and then told her to run to Old Woman, to help with the food. Stinging, laughing, pulling her skirt about her bruised, aching thighs, she had stumbled to Old Woman. "Hurry, Girl," had laughed Old Woman, cackling with pleasure, "turn the meat on the spit. Be busy, lazy, good-for-nothing girl!"

"Yes, Old Woman!" had cried Hamilton. "Yes, Old Woman!"

Ugly Girl had come to her, to lick the wounds on her back. "I love you, Ugly Girl," said Hamilton, kissing her.

About the camp she saw the small boy of the Ugly People, whose parents had been killed by the Weasel People. He had fled to the woods. Ugly Girl, months ago, had found him, and brought him to the camp. He played with the other children, as one of the Men. Tooth was to him as a father. Ugly Girl's own belly was swollen with young, perhaps, it was possible, with the child of Tooth. Hamilton knew the relationship in evolution of the bands of Ugly People to the bands of the Men was obscure. It was not known if the Men themselves had sprung from a form of Ugly People, or if there had been only, in the remote past of these peoples, a common animal. That seemed most likely. But there was little doubt, in gross matters, as to the similarity of the species. The Ugly People and the Men, in the great patterns of life, were brothers. And the belly of Ugly Girl, even if it were only from the gentle, shambling male of the Ugly People, was heavy with life. Hamilton looked into the wide, deep, simple eyes of Ugly Girl. They are called, among themselves, she thought, the Love People. "I love you, Ugly Girl," said Hamilton again, kissing her.

Hamilton looked up.

Stone, huge, dour, stood near her. He reached out his large hand. He, gently, touched her head.

"I am pleased to be back," said Hamilton.

Stone had been long with the Men. He, as a boy, had hunted with Spear. He knew the trails, the weather, the land, the animals. He was powerful. He was hard.

"I am pleased, too," said Stone. Then he turned away from her. Hamilton smiled. It was about as much emotion as she had ever seen the dour Stone evince.

As she turned the spit, various of the Men, on one pretense or another, welcomed her. "I will need sinew, fine sinew, to bind the points of arrows," said Arrow Maker. "I will get it for you," said Hamilton. "I will need hide softened," said Runner. "Bring me the skin," said Hamilton. "I will soften it for you." "Where have you been, and what lands did you see?" asked Fox, Wolf behind him. "Many far places," said Hamilton. "I went as far, even, as the land of the Horse People," she said. Hyena, from a ledge, crouching, watched her. He carried a yellow-tufted stick. Then he went back into his cave. He would draw signs on the floor. It had not been important. It had been only the return of a female. Hamilton felt a hand on her buttocks. "Turtle," said Hawk. For an instant she felt irritation. She felt like telling him to go away, that he was only a boy, but when she turned to face him, to scold him, she was forced to put her head back, that she, a female, and suddenly aware that she was only such, might look him in the eyes. She was startled. He was much taller. Confronting her, looming over her, was a hunter. "Turn the spit," he said. He was, she recalled, of the Men, and she was only a woman of the Men, a mere female. He grinned down at her. "Yes, Master," she said, lowering her eyes. Behind Hawk, on wobbly legs, following him, was a wolf cub. It was the survivor of a litter which the Men had found.

When Tree indicated that the women, other than Ugly Girl, might approach her, they flocked about her, holding her and kissing her. There was Cloud, and Antelope, and Feather, and Flower, and Butterfly, and the others. Among them, even, were the red-haired girl, pregnant, radiant, who had been with the Weasel People, and the girl of the Dirt People, who had been she who was to have been sacrificed, who had once been so exquisitely virginally bodied; but no longer was her body the slip that it had been, for now it had known the will and pleasure of hunters; her breasts were larger now, filling with milk, and, beneath the tiny skirt of the hunters, her belly, like that of the red-haired girl, was big with child; she was Hawk's second woman, fed behind Butterfly.

Nurse, too, and Old Woman, when the others were not looking, kissed her.

When it had been time for the meat to be distributed, Hamilton had taken Flower by the hair, and, baring her teeth, threw her from Tree's side.

Tree did not interfere, but busied himself with the cutting of meat.

Flower looked furious, tears in her eyes. "You will bear daughters," said Hamilton, derisively, "who will serve my sons."

Flower shook with fury, and then went and knelt behind Fox. He threw her a piece of meat. She picked it up, and, angrily, ate it.

Then Hamilton, extending her neck, took the piece of hot, juicy meat which Tree thrust between her teeth.

Chewing it, she smiled at Flower, who looked angrily away.

Hamilton wondered why she, a runaway girl, had not been dragged before Spear, to see if she would be permitted to live.

She had not seen Spear, nor Knife, since she had come to the camp. She had not seen, either, the small, dark-haired girl who had been taken from the Weasel People.

Butterfly had gathered apples. She gave Hamilton one. Hamilton handed the apple to Tree, who ate it.

Late that night, after Hamilton had been much used by the hunter, Tree, she crept to Old Woman.

"Where is Spear?" she asked.

"He is dead," said Old Woman, who sat by a fire, poking it with a stick.

Hamilton did not speak.

"Knife," she said, "killed him. He had tried before, twice. Then he was successful. He wished to be first. He went to his side in the night and, with the ax of Tree, broke open his head. He left the ax beside Tree, that the Men might think this had been done by Tree." Old Woman jabbed the fire, and sparks flew up. "But Spear," she said, "was not dead. He is hard to kill. Some say Spear is not dead yet. He had not been asleep. He knew, sometime, Knife would kill him. He waited. He did not cry out. But in the morning, before he died, he told the Men it was not Tree, but Knife, who had done the thing. But the Men knew Tree would not do it. Only Knife would do it. Knife was foolish. He was not wise, not cunning, like Spear. He did not have Spear's intelligence. He was not Spear."

"Was Knife killed?" asked Hamilton.

"Do not kill Knife, said Spear," said Old Woman. "I care for him. I love him, said Spear. He is of my body. I love him, said Spear." Old Woman stirred the ashes. The reflection, red, was on her chin and upper lip, glowing in the wrinkles. "He is not bad, said Spear. He only wants to be first."

"What happened?" asked Hamilton.

"Tree sent Knife away," said Old Woman. "He gave him a woman, too, to take with him, the brown-haired girl, from the Weasel People."

"Why did he do that?" asked Hamilton.

"So that Knife would have a woman," said Old Woman. "Spear would have wanted Knife to have a woman."

Hamilton said nothing.

Old Woman looked up, to one of the ledges, where there was a dark hole in the face of the cliff. No fire burned there. It had been the shelter of Spear. None lived there now. "Some say," said Old Woman, "that Spear did not die, that he could not be killed. Some say he sits, even now, in the cave, in the darkness." Old Woman turned to Hamilton. "Mothers," said she, "frighten their children with Spear. They say, be good, or Spear will get you. Some think Spear is not dead."

"But that is foolish," said Hamilton.

Old Woman shrugged. "Hyena," she said, "says Spear is not dead."

"That is foolish," said Hamilton.

"He says he has seen him," said Old Woman.

"In dreams," said Hamilton.

"And once by the river," said Old Woman.

Old Woman thrust a brand in the fire. "Come," she said. "We will look."

Hamilton glanced at her, frightened.

"Are you afraid of Spear?" asked Old Woman.

"Aren't you?" asked Hamilton.

"I am too old to be afraid," she said. "Come with me."

"But what if Spear is not dead?" asked Hamilton.

But Hamilton followed Old Woman, who, stiffly, climbing, limping, made her way to Spear's ledge.

She entered the cave, the brand high. The cave was empty. "Spear is dead," said Old Woman.

Then she turned about, and left the cave. "We must not fear Spear," she said. "Spear was a great man. We must remember Spear and love him."

"I thought you hated Spear," said Hamilton. "He killed Drawer, when he was blind and Old Man."

Old Woman looked up at Hamilton. Her eyes were moist. "Stone told me," she said, "after Spear died, wanting me to know, though he would not say this while Spear lived, because I am a woman, and because Spear did not want the Men to know."

"What?" asked Hamilton.

"When Drawer could not hunt, when he went blind, and could not draw, he could only eat and be led about, and he did not wish to be a burden on the Men." Old Woman's voice broke. "He told Spear to kill him."

Hamilton was silent.

"For a long time, Spear did not do this thing. Then, one day, he did it. For a long time only Spear, and Stone knew, and then, after Spear died, Stone told me. Spear would not tell me. He was first among the Men. I tell you." Old Woman's voice choked. "Drawer wanted me to be fed," she said. "I would have starved, or eaten scraps, or stolen," she said. "When he died, I became Old Woman. The meat was mine to cook. I would eat." Old Woman sobbed. "Spear," she said, "was a great man. Let us not fear him. Let us remember him and love him."

"The memory of Spear," said Hamilton, "will be twisted into an insanity by Hyena."

"Hyena is Hyena," said Old Woman, shrugging. "He cannot help himself." She then hobbled from the cave of Spear. She descended to the ledge of her own fire. There she lit another brand. "In the morning," she said, "the Men trek. Tree has decided it. We will leave these shelters and seek others."

Hamilton was startled. Had she so narrowly accomplished her rendezvous with the Men? Then she recalled the young man in Copenhagen, with the young, blond woman. The rendezvous had been accomplished.

"Follow me," said Old Woman, holding aloft a second brand. For the second time in her life, timidly, Hamilton followed Old Woman through the tunnels to the cave of the Men. Women were not permitted there, but Old Woman, as was her custom, gave little consideration to such strictures.

At last they stood in the lofty cave. The drawings which

had once decorated the walls, the bison, the cave lion, the bear, the antelopes, the great mammoth, had been effaced by the Weasel People.

"I am sorry, Old Woman," said Hamilton. "It was I who, fleeing, led men of the Weasel People to this place. It was I who was responsible for the destruction of the work of Drawer."

Old Woman sniffed. "We are leaving the shelters," she said. She poked about, on the floor of the cave. Then she bent down, and seized up the rock, the large, flattish pebble she had been looking for. Hamilton remembered it. On it, in overlaid marks, a complex variety, almost indecipherable, of precise, flowing lines, were the images of the animals which had roamed and fought and fled in vibrant color on the sloping walls of the cave. "They are here, the animals," cackled Old Woman, "in this rock. Drawer put them here." She held the rock, and pressed it to her thin lips. "I will take it with me," she said.

"They will know you were in the Men's cave," said Hamilton.

"Let them kill me," said Old Woman. "But they will not do it. They are only Men and they need Old Woman. And I will hide it." She looked up at Hamilton. "When I die," said Old Woman, "I will give it to you. Give it to your sons. In the new shelters, when they are hunters, let them use this rock. Let them there, on the walls of the new home of the Men, release the animals. Let them free them of the stone where Drawer put them."

"The stone was where Drawer practiced," said Hamilton.

"Do not be stupid," said Old Woman. "They are here, all the animals, and each one once, and perfectly. Do you think there was only one flat stone in the country of the Men?" She laughed. "No," she said. "Drawer made this stone for the sons of his sons. It is Drawer's stone, for his sons. The Men have always trekked. It is their nature, in the times of the fathers or the sons. And Drawer made this stone, that he might, always, with them, join in the trek. As long as this stone, or these images, survive, Drawer treks with the men. It is his work, this stone. Men will keep this memory, of Drawer, no matter how far they go, no matter how remote the lands to which they make their treks." Old Woman grinned. "As long as I live," she said, "I will keep this stone, for love of Drawer. When I die, I will give it to you. Give it to your sons. Tell them Drawer made it."

"I will," said Hamilton.

"Look!" said Old Woman. She lifted the torch. There was one drawing on the walls which had not been effaced. But it was not a work which had been put there by Drawer. When Hamilton had last been in the cave it had not been there. It had been placed there after the depredations of the Weasel People. Old Woman walked closer, and lifted her torch. She knew the sign. It was a symbolic representation. The Horse People used the sign, and the Bear People, and the Men.

It was the symbolic representation of a star.

Old Woman shrugged. She did not understand how this sign had come here.

Hamilton did not speak. The letter given to her, from Herjellsen, handed to her by the large black, Chaka, which she had read, and had given to William and Gunther to read, had read as follows:

"My beloved daughter,
    There is another child. I have seen it. The chamber
is open.

I love you,
                    Herjellsen."

Hamilton looked at the representation on the wall of the cave.

She could not tell Old Woman. Old Woman would not understand. But in this cave, at some time, Herjellsen had stood.

"Give me a stone," said Hamilton. Old Woman, with the torch, examining the floor, found a flattish stone. Then Hamilton, with a sharp pebble, drew on the stone the sign of the star. She gave it to Old Woman. "Keep them both," said Hamilton. "Carry them together. They belong together, forever, in the long treks, the animals and the star."

Old Woman nodded. She did not understand, but she would do as Hamilton had wished.

The torch was burning lower and, quickly, Old Woman and Hamilton left the Men's cave. In a few minutes they were again on the ledge before Old Woman's shelter. They heard a child crying. "I will see to the child," said Old Woman, hobbling away into the darkness. Hamilton, by the light of the moon, made her way back to the shelter which she shared with Tree. Tree met her. He was not pleased to find she had left the shelter.

"Where have you been?" said Tree.

"Walking," said Hamilton.

"In the morning," said Tree, "we are leaving the shelters."

"I know," said Hamilton. "Old Woman told me."

Tree looked up at the sky.

"Have you forgotten the fires in the sky?" asked Hamilton.

"No," said Tree, looking at her. Then he said, "Bring the furs to the ledge."

Hamilton gathered the furs from inside the cave and brought them to the ledge.

"Spread them on the ledge," said Tree.

She did so.

Hamilton stood straight as Tree approached her. He walked about her; she looked up at him. Then he walked behind her, and stood behind her. She did not turn. Casually, with a tug, he freed her of the brief skirt of the Men. She now, standing before him, her back to him, wore only her collar. He walked again before her; he pulled away the leather he wore about his hips; with his two hands, each on the thongs of her collar, he drew her to within inches of him; she felt faint, wanting to yield to him, his manhood claimant, surgent, against her belly; his hands, then, were on her arms, above the elbows; he drew her yet more closely to him; she felt, against the sweetness, the softness, of her breasts, the pressing hardness of his chest; she felt first, as he bent over her, the hair touch her nipples, and then, as she was half lifted to him, so that she could only stand on her tiptoes, she felt the grip of her beauty, held in such uncompromising arms, fully against the chest of the male who owned it. She turned her head to one side; she looked down; her body moved, inadvertently, she sobbing, against the manhood, swift and alive, which would dominate it. She knew she was only his slave. He threw her rudely to the furs at his feet. She gasped, one leg under her, head down, the weight of the upper part of her body on the palms of her hands, on the furs. By the hair he turned her on her back. She winced from the pain of the switching she had received earlier. Oblivious to her discomfort, he stood over her. She was small between his feet. "Lift your body," he told her. Brenda Hamilton obeyed her master. Then, laughing, hands strong and eager, he bent to the body of his slave.

The next morning, after a sacrifice of meat to the Power, the Men began the trek.

The hunters went first. Hawk roamed before the group. Runner and Arrow Maker flanked the march. Stone brought up the rear.

The women carried the burdens, and the children ran be-

side them. Turtle carried heavy rolls of furs and skins. Old
Woman was the last of the women and children. She did not
carry a great deal, but she did carry a small bundle, wrapped
in fur, which contained two stones.

Hyena had stayed behind at the shelters, to take up the
trail later.

There were things he did not understand, and he would
wait for a time, considering them.

He was uneasy that the woman had returned to them, for
he sensed, somehow, that the Men would now be different.
Tree held her as his own. He might not be willing to share
her, and if this were true, the men had changed. The simplicity, the innocence, of the group, the community, might
be rent. They would be other than they had been. Because
of the woman, though it seemed incredible, the men would
no longer be the same. They would have changed. They
would no longer be the same.

On the trail, Tree, though Hawk served as the point of
the advance, led the column. Close with him were Fox and
Wolf, and Tooth. Near Tooth, carrying a sack of flint across
her broad shoulders, was Ugly Girl. Her nostrils were distended. She was excited. She was with them on the trek.
Runner ranged to the left of the column, and Arrow Maker
to the right. Behind them, protecting the rear, came Stone.
He stopped once to look back at the shelters. In this country
he had hunted with Spear. Then he turned again, carrying
his ax, to bring up the rear of the column.

In the column with the children, naked and dirty, walked
Pod, who had been Short Leg's son.

There were tears in Antelope's eyes, for they were leaving
the shelters.

At the feet of Butterfly, following her, clumsily, came
Hawk's cub, ears tiny and sharp, lifted, tongue hanging out,
who had survived the destruction of the litter.

In the refuse pit at the shelters the brown rats lifted their
noses, round eyes peering. No longer did they hear the
sounds of the camp. They nibbled on the refuse, and, from
time to time, stopped to listen. Then, some of them, turning
about, scampered through cracks in the stone, squeezing
their bodies through the apertures, and emerging, quizzically,
at the foot of the cliffs.

Birds cried overhead. The rats lifted their heads, and
stared at them.

Turtle, though she would commonly be spoken of by this
name, had now another name as well. Tree had given it to

her, when he had finished with her the night before, and lay
beside her, she in his arms, looking up at the stars. There was
much about her he did not understand. She was different.
The second name he had given her, by which she would
sometimes be called was, in the language of the men, 'A-Va'
or 'Ava', which, in their tongue, means "Star Woman."

Tree, carrying a spear, his ax at his side, led the column.
The spear was mighty, and its head, of chipped stone, was
more than a foot in length, lashed to the shaft by cords of
leather. He lifted his head, surveying the greenery, the white
trunked trees, with his eyes, and with his ears, and taking,
too, the scent of the new world. He did not look back to the
shelters. He was first in the column. He did not look back,
either, at the women and the children. They would follow.
He did not look back, even, at the woman Turtle, or Ava,
who carried, rolled, furs and skins behind him. She would
follow.

Tree strode forth into the new country, not looking back.
He was pleased.

They followed him.

Tree was first among the men. The word for this in the
language of the Men was 'Adam.'

In the moonlight, on a flat rock, whitish in the light,
Hyena bent to the seeds of the apple. He shook them and
muttered, and cast them again and again on the flat rock.
Then he looked at them and, with a piece of flint, drew
lines connecting the points constituted by the seemingly ran-
domly scattered seeds of the apple. The design was unmistakable, and was a common symbolic representation, to the
Men, to the Bear People, to the Horse People. The lines
formed, unmistakably, on that flatish, whitish rock in the
moonlight, as had those of Herjellsen in the cave, a representation of a star. Hyena rose to his feet and looked at the
representation. Then, slowly, alone, unnoticed by anyone,
for the men had gone, his head down, his body turning,
shaking the yellow-tufted stick, he danced beneath the stars.

DAW=sf BOOKS

Lin Carter's bestselling series!

☐ **UNDER THE GREEN STAR.** A marvel adventure in the grand tradition of Burroughs and Merritt. Book I.
(#UY1185—$1.25)

☐ **WHEN THE GREEN STAR CALLS.** Beyond Mars shines the beacon of exotic adventure. Book II. (#UY1267—$1.25)

☐ **BY THE LIGHT OF THE GREEN STAR.** Lost amid the giant trees, nothing daunted his search for his princess and her crown. Book III. (#UY1268—$1.25)

☐ **AS THE GREEN STAR RISES.** Adrift on the uncharted sea of a nameless world, hope still burned bright. Book IV.
(#UY1156—$1.25)

☐ **IN THE GREEN STAR'S GLOW.** The grand climax of an adventure amid monsters and marvels of a far-off world. Book V. (#UY1216—$1.25)

DAW BOOKS are represented by the publishers of Signet and Mentor Books, **THE NEW AMERICAN LIBRARY, INC.**